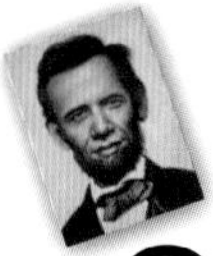

Abraham Obama

A Guerrilla Tour Through Art & Politics

Compiled and edited by Don Goede and Ron English

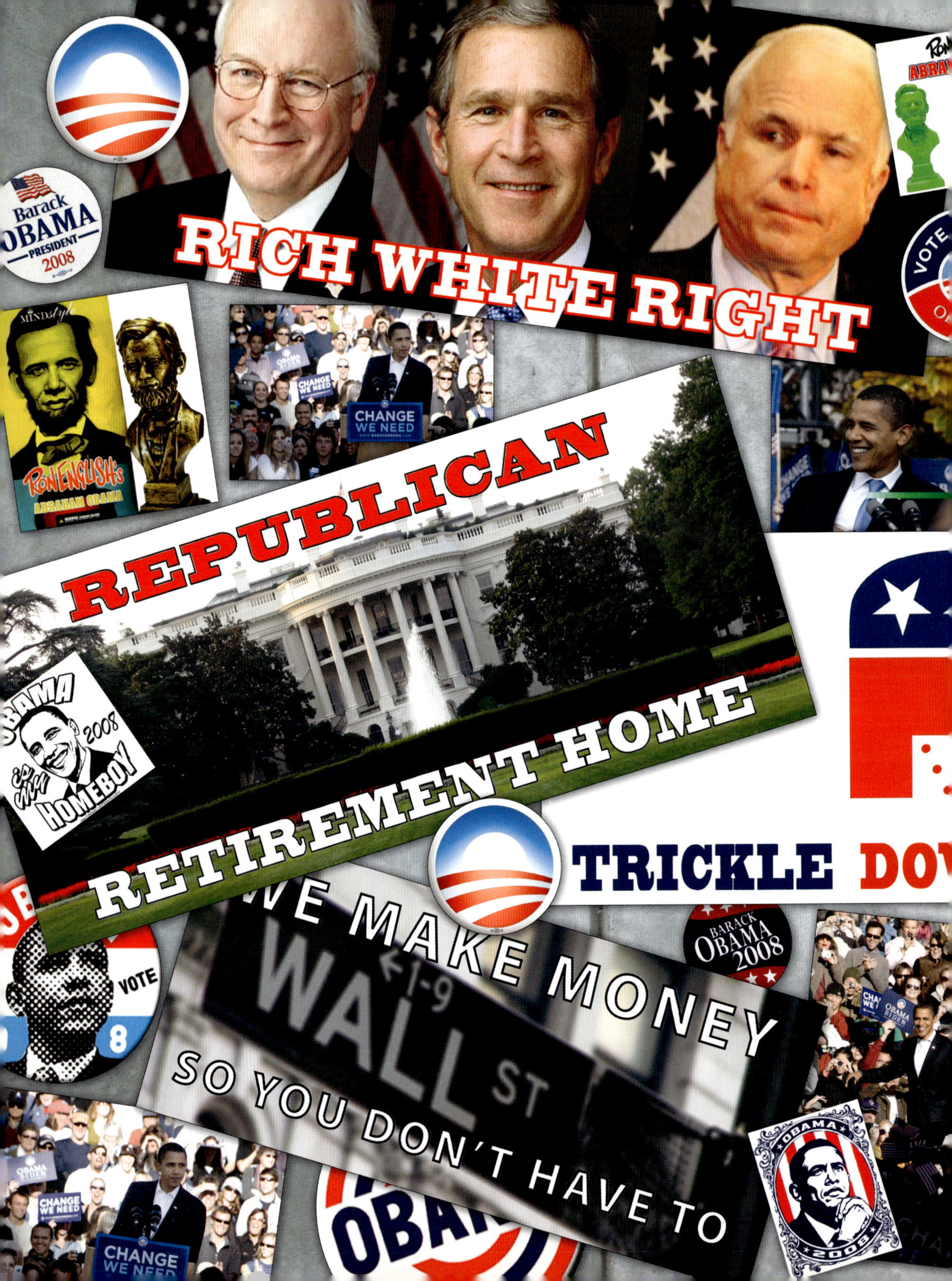
Barack
OBAMA
PRESIDENT
2008
RICH WHITE RIGHT
MINDstyle
RON ENGLISH's
ABRAHAM OBAMA
CHANGE WE NEED
REPUBLICAN
RETIREMENT HOME
OBAMA
2008
HOMEBOY
TRICKLE
WE MAKE MONEY
SO YOU DON'T HAVE TO
WALL ST
BARACK
OBAMA
2008
VOTE
OBAMA
2008

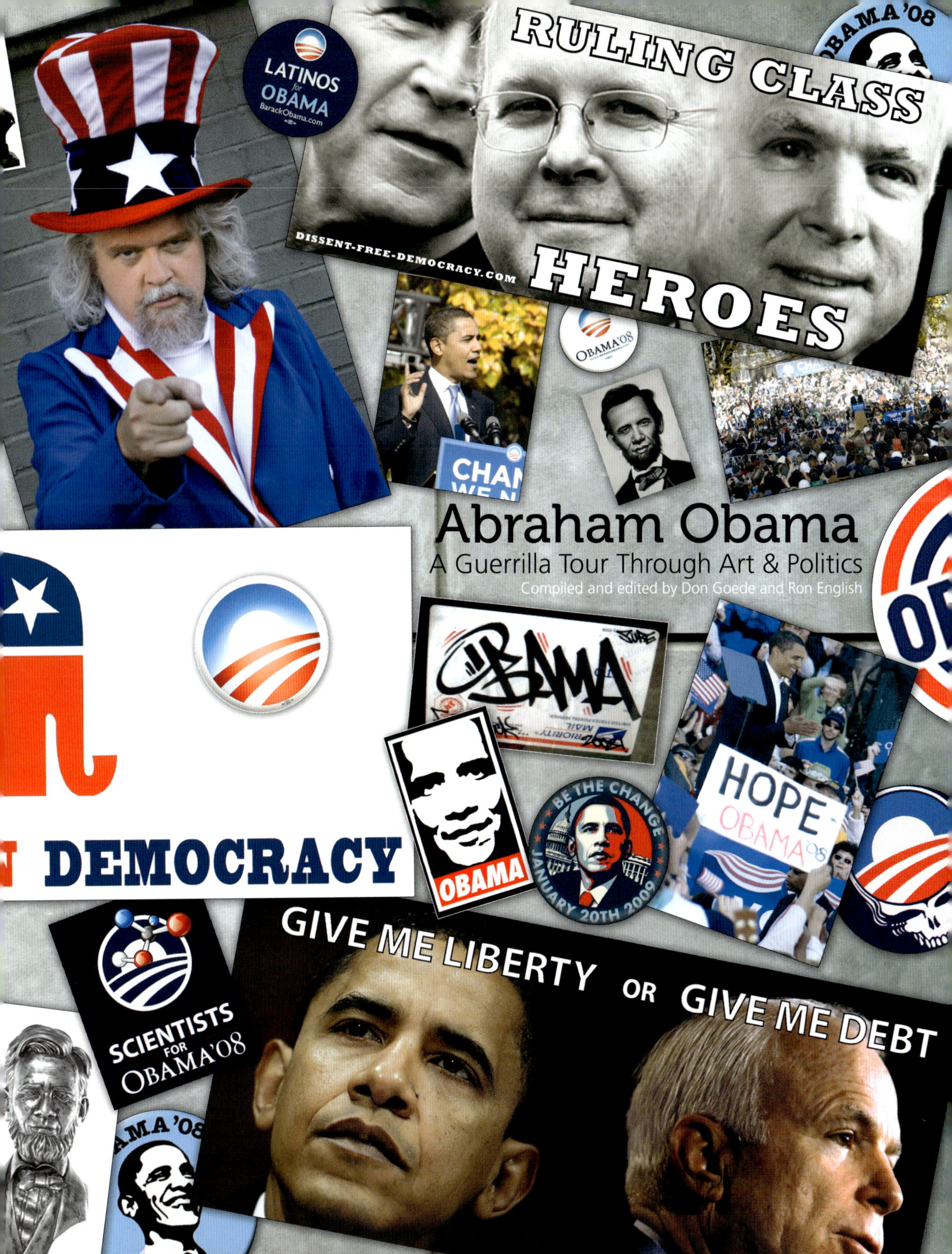

Abraham Obama

A Guerrilla Tour Through Art & Politics

Compiled and edited by Don Goede and Ron English

Barack Obama campaign photos by Bill Young

Abraham Obama

Last Gasp of San Francisco
777 Florida St.
San Francisco, CA 94110
www.lastgasp.com

Smokemuse Media
322 N. Tejon St. STE 224
Colorado Springs, CO 80903
www.smokemuse.com

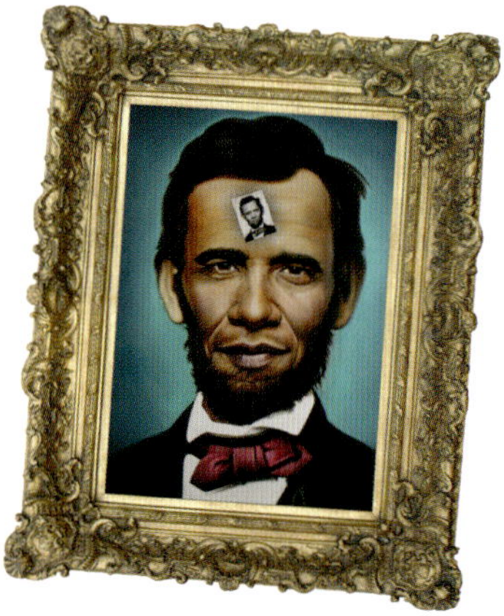

Printed in China by Prolong Press Limited

ISBN: 978-0-86719-722-8

Credits:
All photos by Don Goede or Ron English unless otherwise noted
Photo manipulations of Abraham Lincoln and Barack Obama by Don Goede
Cover and book design by Ele Annand
Layout and page design by Don Goede

Stuart Bagwell, Managing Editor

Special thanks to: Boston, Los Angeles, San Francisco,
Denver, Colorado Springs, New York City, Brooklyn, and Jersey City

This book is dedicated to
Barack Hussein Obama for
inspiring us to get off our asses.

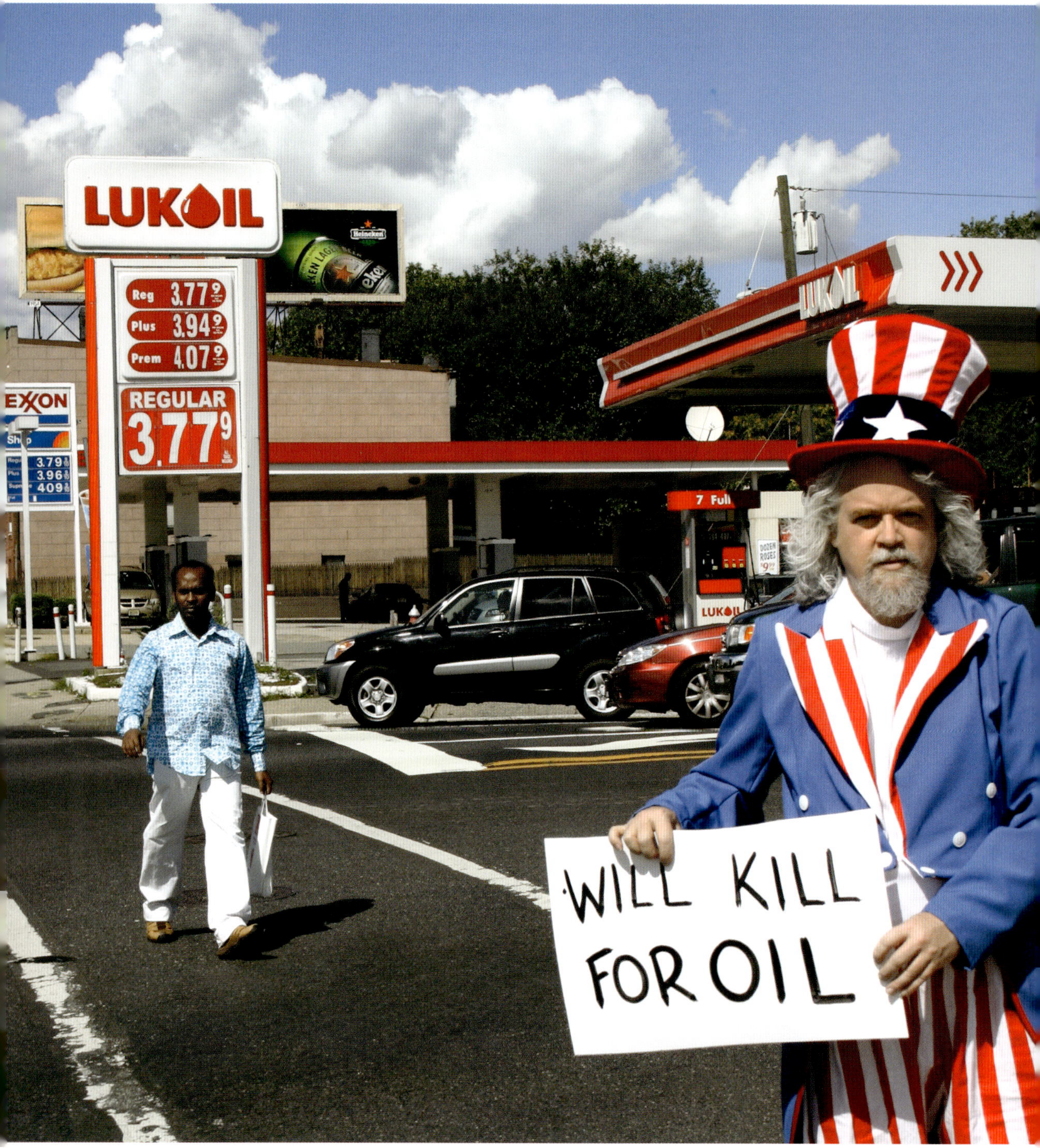
LUKOIL
Reg 3.77 9
Plus 3.94 9
Prem 4.07 9
REGULAR
3.77 9
EXXON
3.79
3.96
409
LUKOIL
7 Full
LUKOIL
WILL KILL
FOR OIL

Table of Contents

Foreword

By Morgan Spurlock, Filmmaker

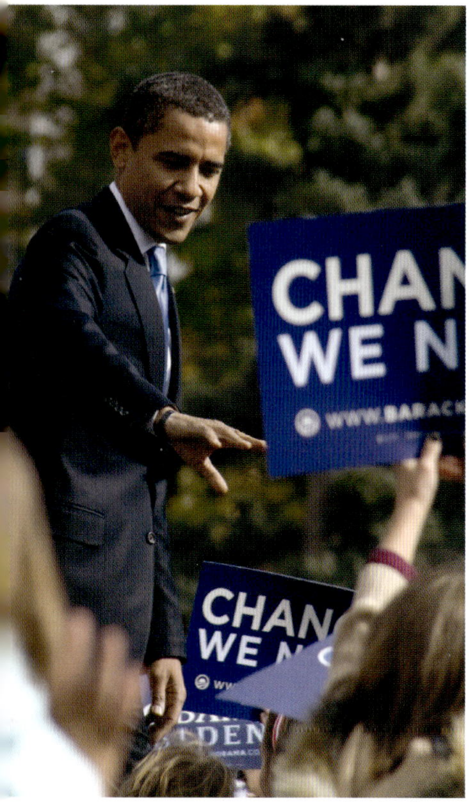

photo by Bill Young

My dream is of a place and a time
where America will once again be seen
as the last best hope of Earth.
–Abraham Lincoln

Change will not come if we wait for
some other person or some other time.
We are the ones we've been waiting for.
We are the change that we seek.
–Barack Obama

Barack Obama campaigning in Pueblo, Colorado.

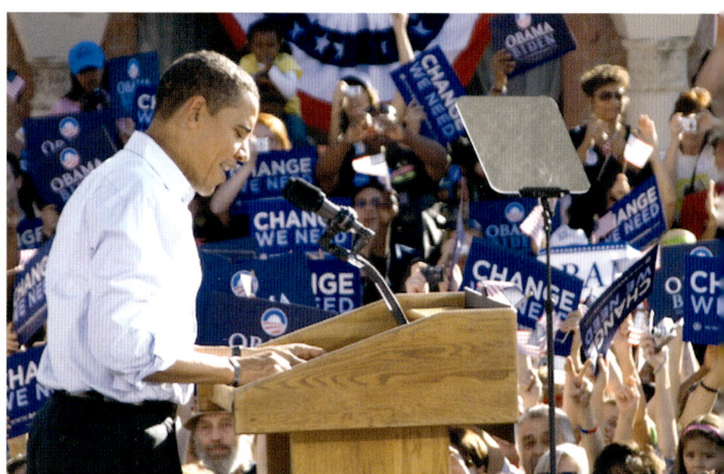

photo by Bill Young

In the spring of 2008, it felt as though we were almost out from under the heavy seven-year weight of the sitting President. After what had seemed like an endless campaign for the White House by dozens of smiling-faced used car salesmen, two frontrunners finally emerged. People around the world were placing their bets on a horse for 21st century America as the race came down to two honorable men: one, a decorated war hero from Arizona; the other, a well-spoken, lanky senator from Illinois. The first was a hard-nosed conservative who represented a path and vision cut from the cloth of the current President; the other, a lone voice seeking to inspire millions to have the faith to take a different path. As we came to this intersection of past and future, two disparate worlds collided in the present in a spectacular moment of anguish, fear, desperation and, most of all, hope...they were the worlds of art and politics.

Fueled by inspiration and self-determination, some of the most talented people working in the arts today delivered an onslaught of creative coercion to an unassuming American public. Artists from across the spectrum were compelled to take action. Singers, songwriters, musicians, actors, dancers, poets, and painters all tapped into the one thing they knew how to do better than anything else and used those God-given talents to touch an eager, listening and watching world. The inspired acts of passion and patriotism that emerged will be written about, examined and discussed for years to come. But the greatest deed that emerged from all of their selfless actions was showing the world that the acts of a few can truly move and motivate millions.

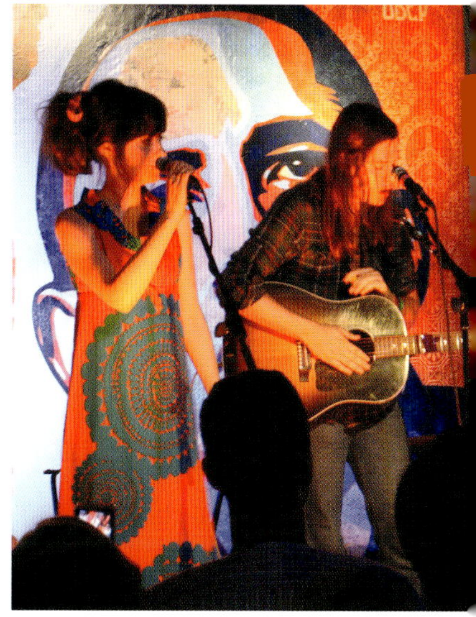

Top: Zooey Deschanel and Jonathan Rice perform at the Manifest Hope Exhibition in Denver, Colorado.
Bottom: will.i.am outside the Andenken Gallery.

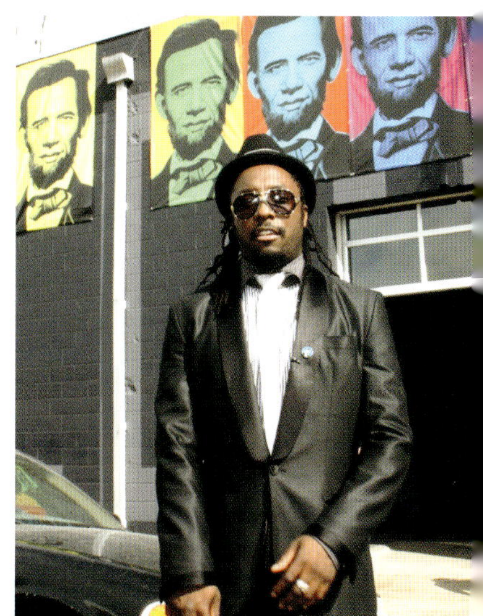

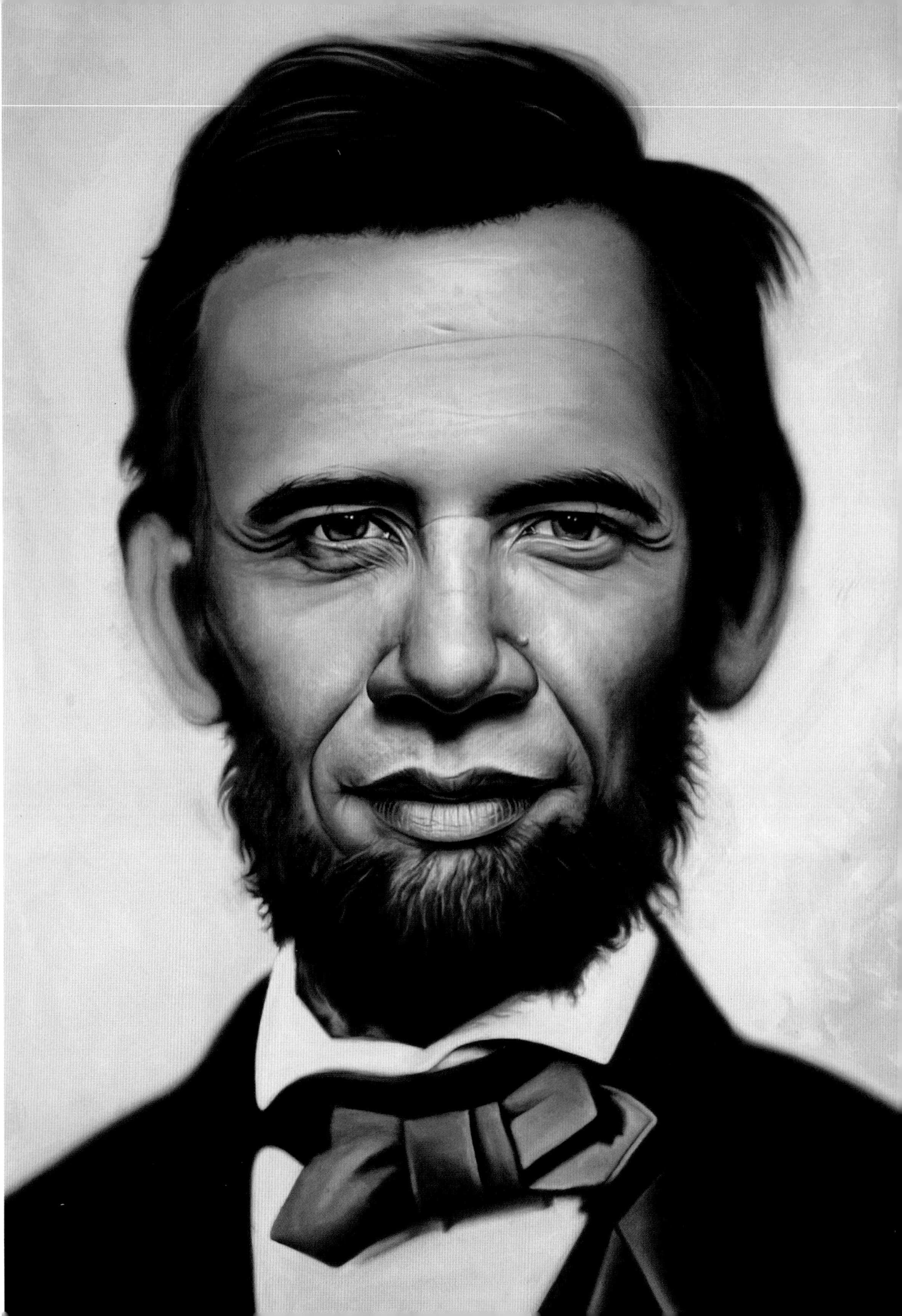

Introduction

By Ron English

It all started in February 2008, when Matt Revelli at *Upper Playground* asked me to get involved in a print series he was organizing to support the Obama candidacy. At that time I had already been working on my own typical Ron English pirate street art initiative, with billboards like *Trickle Down Democracy* and *Wall Street–We Make Money So You Don't Have To*. I had never used my art to actively campaign for a candidate. My approach is usually the opposite–to make art that opposes something. But the idea of supporting Obama through art was intriguing.

We were politely asked by the Obama campaign to keep whatever efforts we were engaged in to promote the candidate super-positive, which is typically antithetical to my approach. But I decided that they were far more knowledgeable than me, and I capitulated, dropping my *I Wanna Be Erected*–style campaign in favor of a completely legal, positive effort.

The image of Abraham Obama came to me very quickly and seemed to be relevant for obvious reasons. They were both self-made, skinny lawyers from Illinois–although for me, the point is not the similarities, but the complementary effect. Obama completes Lincoln's promise. The process of freeing the slaves culminates in a black president.

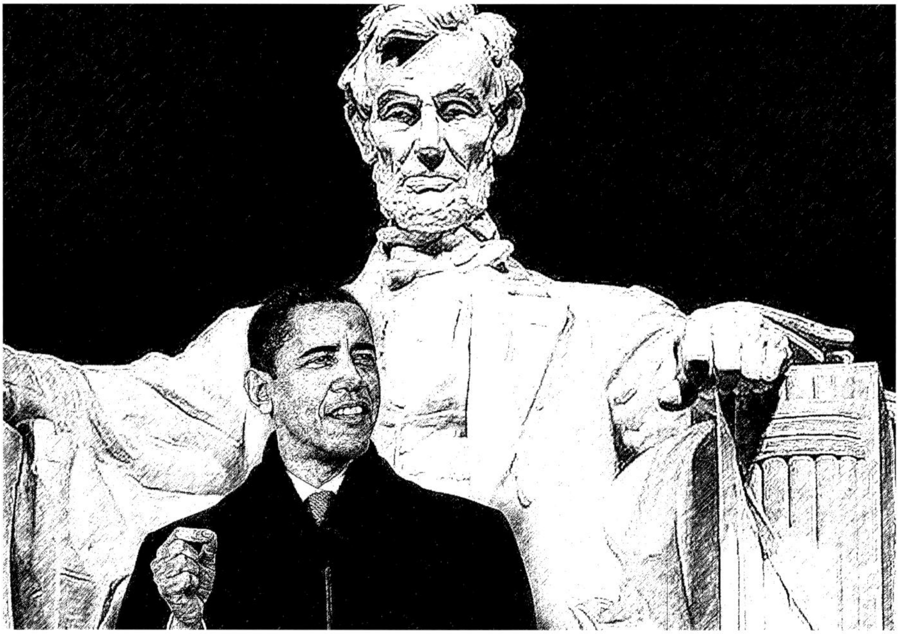

In creating the image, I found that, fortunately for me, all the proportions in their faces lined up perfectly–an extremely rare and coincidental symmetry which made the image possible. I was also glad that Lincoln was a Republican, because the intent of the image was to first promote Obama as the most desirable candidate, but also to illustrate that Republicans and Democrats in the end were all one, even after the Civil War.

I believe that although their ultimate goals might be similar, Republicans and Democrats are strikingly different in approach. Democrats engage in a fact-based philosophy, while Republicans are more in tune with their feelings. "If you believe, it doesn't have to be true" would be a good mantra for Republicans. Republicans think that Democrats' criticism of aspects of American policies are equivocal to hatred of America, whereas Democrats believe that greatness is achieved through self-criticism and reflection. But ultimately, greatness is the goal of both parties.

I felt that voting and contributing money to the campaign was the very least I could do, and I wanted to do more. So I decided to tour the image in as many cities as possible throughout the summer and fall before the election. I contracted with a billboard company to print hundreds of the Abraham Obama image in a Warholian pop style in sizes ranging from five to seven feet-tall, in various color combinations that included a double rainbow effect, in which the background colors create a rainbow in one direction as the colors on the face create a rainbow going the other direction, with yellow on yellow as the central piece: Obama's chosen color to represent hope.

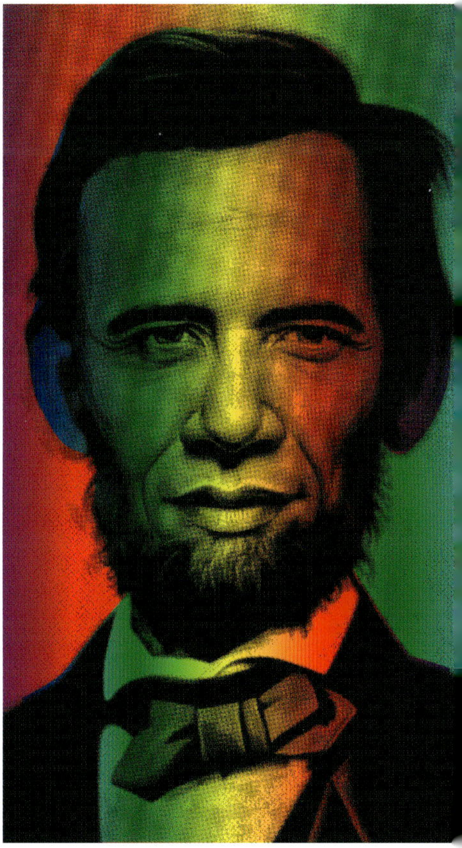

To complete the mission, I recruited a team that included musician Jack Medicine, art dealer Daniel Lahoda, and filmmakers Kevin Chapados and Chunwoo Kae. Jack and I had written a campaign song that we had posted on the Internet. In the early 1900s, people created popular songs in support of candidates, and I wanted to follow some older traditions that have been abandoned.

We called in advance to secure a legal wall in Boston. Although I'm notorious for doing outlaw billboards, I wanted to make sure that everything I did in support of the campaign was absolutely legitimate. We hit Boston on July 3.

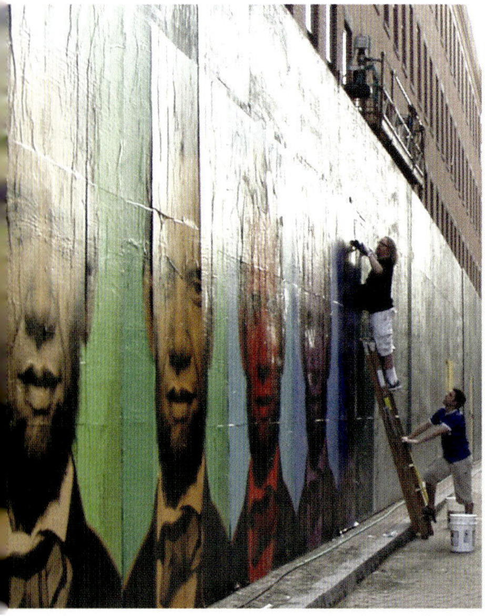

photo by Daniel Lahoda

Top: Ron English details in Boston.
Bottom: A row of Abraham Obamas adorn the side of Poor Richard's, a downtown Colorado Springs restaurant.

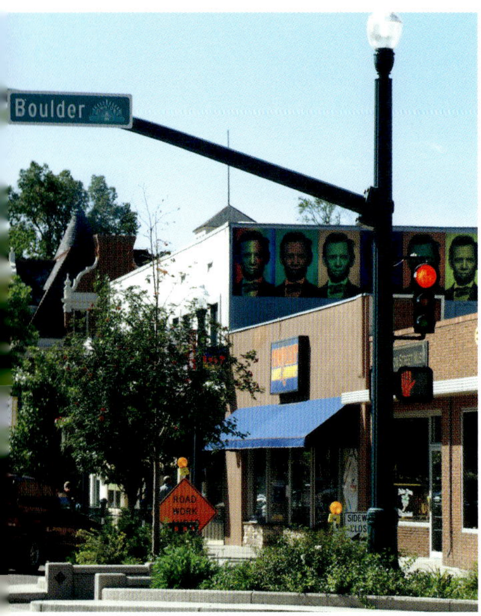

It was raining when we got there, and it looked like we might not be able to create the mural; but around 4:00 pm the rain let up and we went to work. For the next couple of hours, we posted a mural that was approximately 300 feet long by 17 feet tall along a construction wall in the arts district. After completion, a local gallery threw us a reception, where Daniel handed out free Abraham Obama posters to all the young hipsters that came to the party.

The next day on the way out of town, we stopped to shoot a video to be used in conjunction with the song as a **YouTube** post, and headed back to New York. A couple of hours into our journey, we got the first of many frantic calls from the gallery. Evidently the town was in an uproar over the mural and subsequent illegal postings of the smaller posters given away at the party. National network news had already sent in affiliates, and the gallery owner, who had secured the wall, was quite distressed. We were, of course, quite amused. Ultimately, the mayor and a few building owners threatened lawsuits, but nothing materialized.

The next stop on the Abraham Obama tour was Los Angeles. Then on to San Francisco, Seattle, and the Democratic National Convention in Denver, where we caught up with other artists on the same mission, including Shepard Fairey, David Choe, and Sam Flores. Jack Medicine, who lived in the next town over–Republican stronghold Colorado Springs–brought us over to shake up his home turf. He had secured numerous buildings for us to post on, then hosted a party where we shot a video for another English-Medicine song, *The New Fool on the Hill*, performed by our band, The Electric Illuminati. The posters in Colorado Springs created a second national uproar, resulting in a lawsuit for illegal campaigning, which was dismissed when an arts commission and the city declared the Abraham Obama images were art, not political propaganda.

After the convention, we returned to our homes in New York City, Jersey City, LA, and Brooklyn, where we all continued posting on our own, up until the night of the election. Much to my surprise, interest in the image only increased after the election. I was invited to post the images in Hong Kong, the Philippines, and Australia. The image also appeared in many publications and on television, from *Adbusters* to CNN.

In my opinion, Abraham Lincoln was the first great modern candidate, and he was not so different from Obama in that he allowed artists to depict him and disseminate the resulting photos, lithographs, and sculptures to increase his stature and recognition factor. He also presented himself as a new modern American–a Midwestern rail-splitter who lived by his own labor and not by the labor of slaves–and he allowed himself to be represented as an independent frontiersman, not as a Greek God.

Obama has also allowed a plethora of artists to interpret and distribute his image, and those of us who had any involvement with the campaign were only nudged with one mandate–please stay positive. The Obama art phenomenon was truly a self-initiated, populist movement. It's a culmination of a lot of events that happened at the same time, including the global rise and embrace of street art–with the most important street artists to the least known seizing their own power.

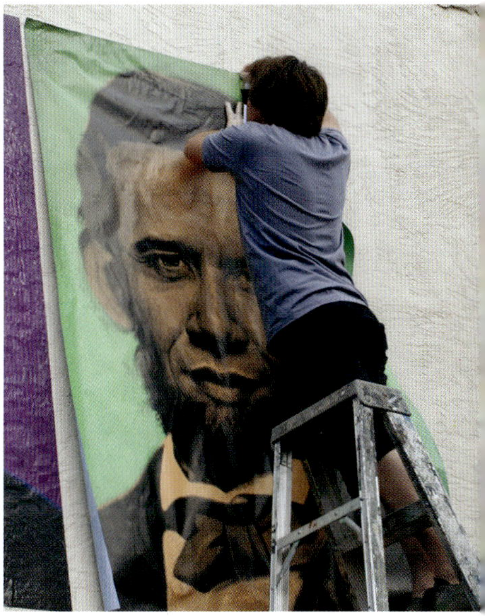

Top: Daniel Lahoda outside the Smokebrush Gallery in Colorado Springs. Bottom: Daniel Lahoda and Ron English on the rooftop of Munky King in Los Angeles, California.

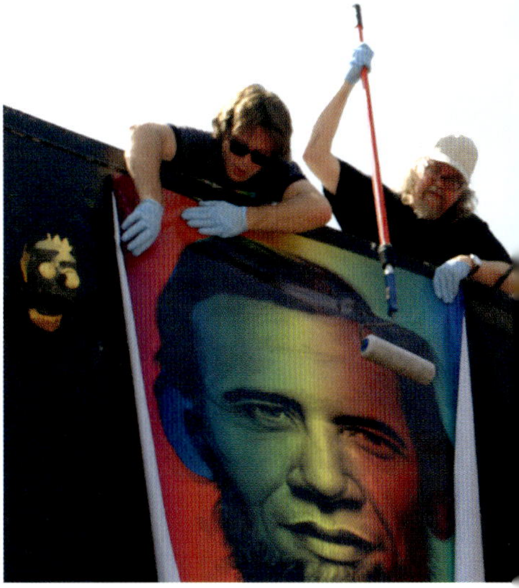

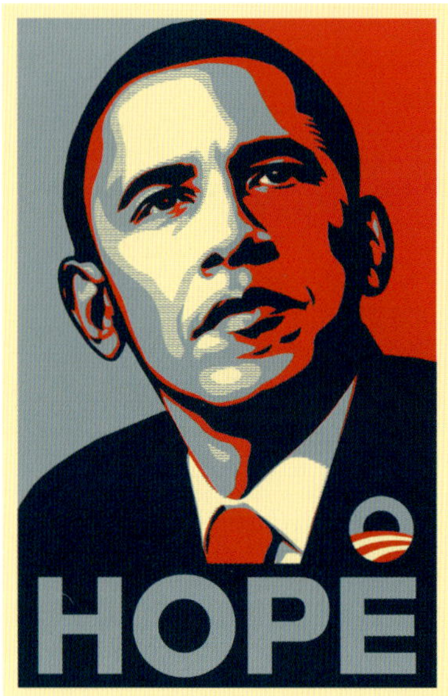

Shepard Fairey

Top: Shepard Fairey's iconic Hope image for Barack Obama's presidential campaign. Bottom: A street artist alters the Abraham Obama installation in Boston, Mass.

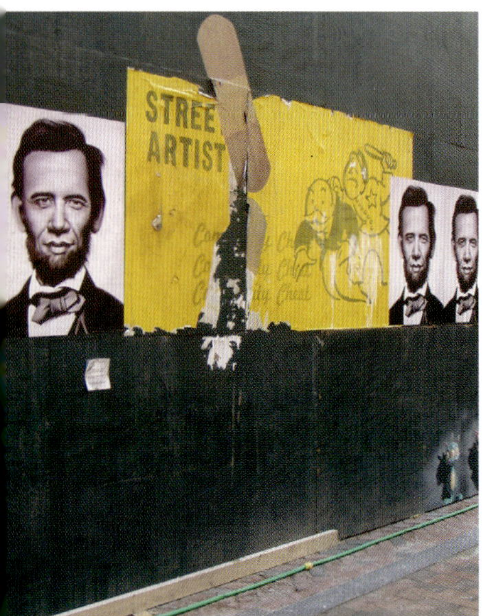

photo by Mark Favermann

Iconoclasts Take On The Icon

By Holly Parker, Artist and Curator

The ardent uprising of artists throughout our nation to create inspiring iconography about President Obama is a testament to the newfound hope and patriotism he symbolizes. Ron English's portrait Abraham Obama, a mash-up of Abraham Lincoln and Barack Obama, uses these two significant figures–of American history and American history in the making–to stimulate dialog that is at the intersection of art and politics. But the image aspires to a greater potential than this alone, as its engineered ambiguity allows it to be read in many contexts. This indeterminacy is the image's strength and interest, sure to allow its read (or meaning) to unfold over the course of years rather than representing a comment on one moment in time.

Artist Shepard Fairey's endeavors to rally artwork depicting the optimistic sentiment of President Obama's *Campaign for Hope* through his Manifest Hope exhibitions (first during the DNC in Denver, September 2008, and then during the inauguration in Washington DC, January 2009) reveal a new movement in contemporary art. This movement illustrates the energy of our nation and its intense desire for positive change. It is no coincidence that many artists involved in this effort are street artists – a genre whose defiance is typically marked by the attitude that public property is literally owned by the public, therefore the right of the artist exists to reface its surfaces. The public figure is just as susceptible to being absorbed into the vernacular of artists, resulting in a range of symbolic iconographies.

English, known in part for his subversive guerilla billboard advertisements, created a national street-postering tour with his Abraham Obama image, touring it to eight cities around the US. Both *Manifest Hope* exhibitions also featured versions of English's photorealistic and posterized Abraham Obama images. Out on the street, the image's presence confronts the average Joe and Jane in the midst of the daily hustle. At first glance it is but Honest Abe; then the eye detects a certain twist. With a more sustained gaze, one can tell it is the familiar, iconic head of Lincoln seamlessly mashed with the fresh, confident face of Obama. This is the point where the individual's personal experience collides with the art experience, rousing dogmatic fervor in some, and inspiring comparative contemplation in others. There is no single message to be determined by the viewer, though each is likely to come to their own unique conclusion.

The search for knowledge, truth, and a greater understanding of the world around us. That will be my goal as President of the United States.
–President Barack Obama

Icons often serve as reminders of values, hope, and truth. Abraham Obama is meant to create a forum for creative discussion. It initiates a comparison of the two political figures, yet it offers an open-endedness, allowing the viewer to go beyond the consideration of the combined characters, perhaps even encouraging the formation of a new idea (or ideal). This is where the image becomes most engaging in its iconology, as it is at this junction that it presents the promise of revealing what truth stands for within each person.

Abraham Obama, like the material with which many fine statues are constructed, eloquently asserts the pride and vision of a marbled nation finally accepting itself. But most importantly, it encourages people to think and decide for themselves what this image is and what it represents while providing a conversation that will continue as the new president's story and legacy unfolds.

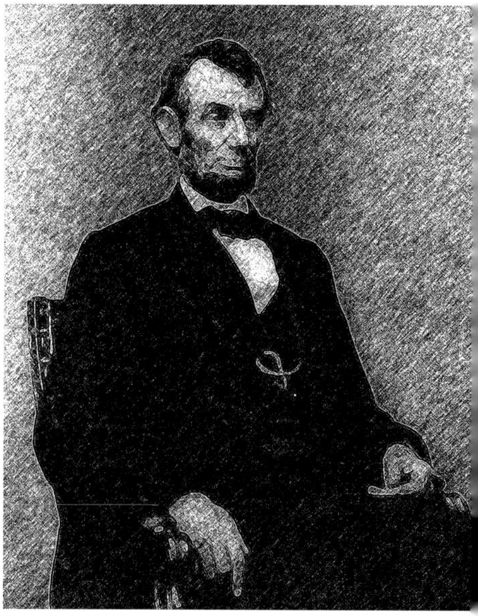

Top: Abraham Lincoln, February 9th, 1864.

Bottom: Senator Barack Obama.

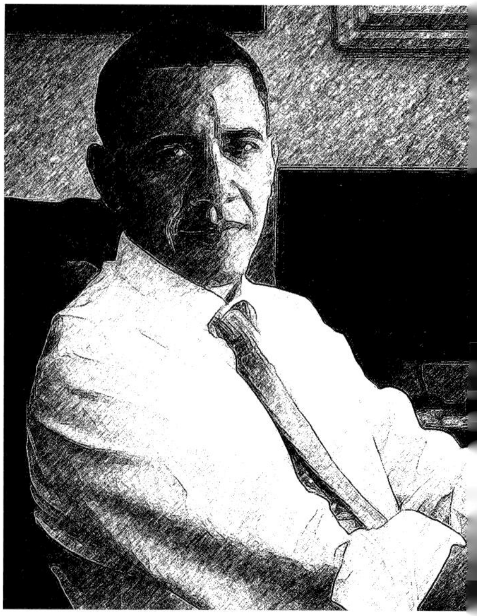

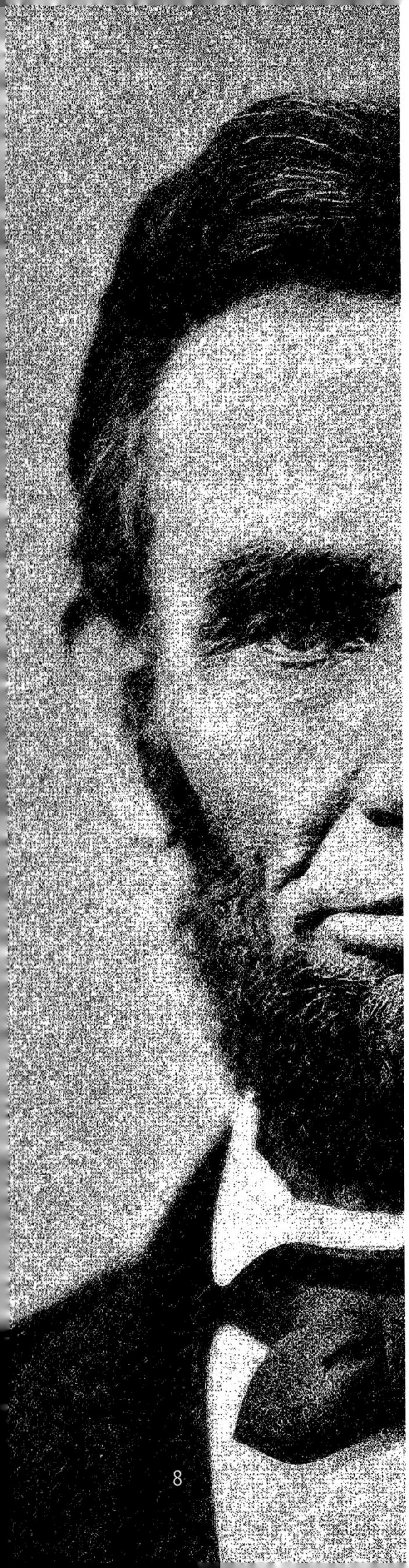

Obama's Lincoln

By Katlin Walter, Journalist

The cover of the November 24, 2008 issue of *Newsweek* is a black and white image of Barack Obama standing in Abraham Lincoln's shadow. Obama stares at the man from Illinois with admiration and for inspiration, and the story's title, "Obama's Lincoln," invites comparison of these "two thin men from rude beginnings." The article locates Lincoln's humility as a pivotal point of inspiration for Obama, a quality that he frequently refers to as a cardinal virtue. As Evan Thomas and Richard Wolffe write, "A Lincolnesque leader is confident enough to be humble–to not feel the need to bluster or dominate, but to be sufficiently aware of one's own judgment and self-worth to really listen and not be threatened by contrary advice." This statement points out a fundamental likeness between the 44th and the 16th Presidents of the United States: both men have chosen to surround themselves not only by those with whom they agree, but also by their adversaries. This particular leadership style of Abraham Lincoln, governing with a "Team of Rivals," lends an administration a bipartisan look and cast, a political exigency that has defined Barack Obama's campaign. Both Lincoln and Obama chose to appoint their rivals–incidentally both senators from New York (William H. Seward and Hillary Rodham Clinton, respectively), as Secretary of State for their administration.

The theme of Barack Obama's inauguration, "A New Birth of Freedom," comes from a line in Lincoln's Gettysburg address. And it seems appropriate, in this age of terror-justified contractions of civil liberties, "that this nation shall have a new birth of freedom; and that this government of the people, by the people, and for the people, shall not perish from the earth." These words highlight another important similarity between Obama and Lincoln: both men speak and write with supreme eloquence and are superb rhetoricians.

Barack Obama launched his presidential campaign at the Old State Capitol in Springfield, Illinois, where Abraham Lincoln gave his famous "House Divided" speech in 1858, and on January 20, 2009, Obama was sworn into office on the same Bible that Lincoln used for his first inauguration in 1861. Both tall, lanky men, (Lincoln stood at 6'4", and Obama is 6'2"), neither of them began their presidency with a large amount of political experience. Both relatively young compared to other presidents, the two men rose to political fame because of their extraordinary eloquence and their great oratorical talent. They were able to engage the the apolitical, the apathetical, and the marginalized with a message of enpowerment. Obama's inaugural journey exhibits another parallel between the 16th and the 44th Presidents. Obama's trip to Washington by train included stops with speeches and big crowds, a replication of the last leg of Lincoln's inaugural journey to the capitol in 1861. Obama's frequent Lincoln references come from a deep respect for and study of Lincoln's political temperament and decisions. Obama studies Lincoln because he inherits a country at war, a country ridden with social unrest and economic uncertainty. And in time of national crisis the presidency of Lincoln may hold the most appropriate lessons.

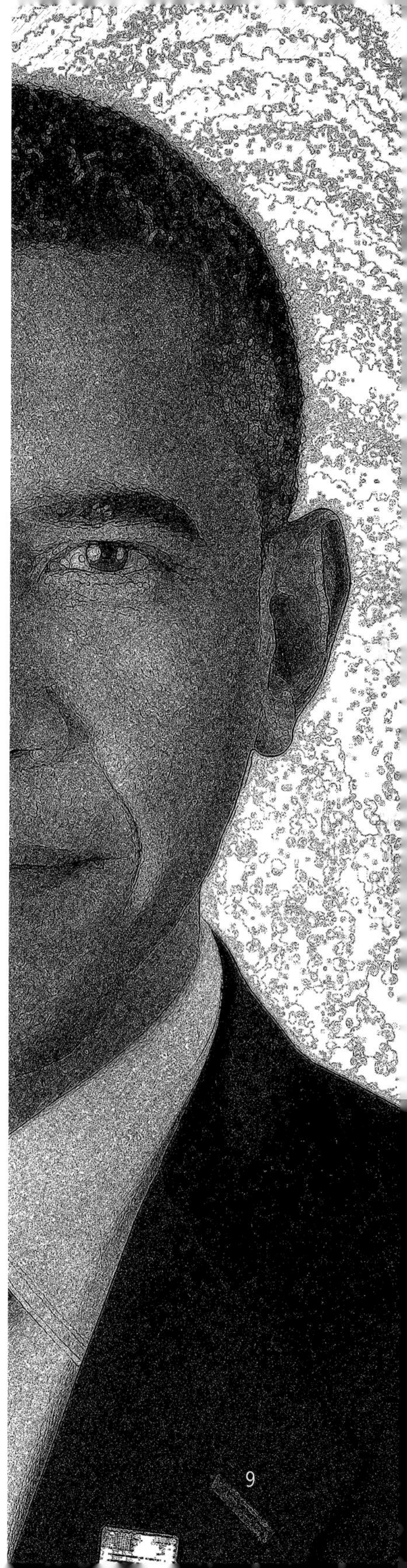

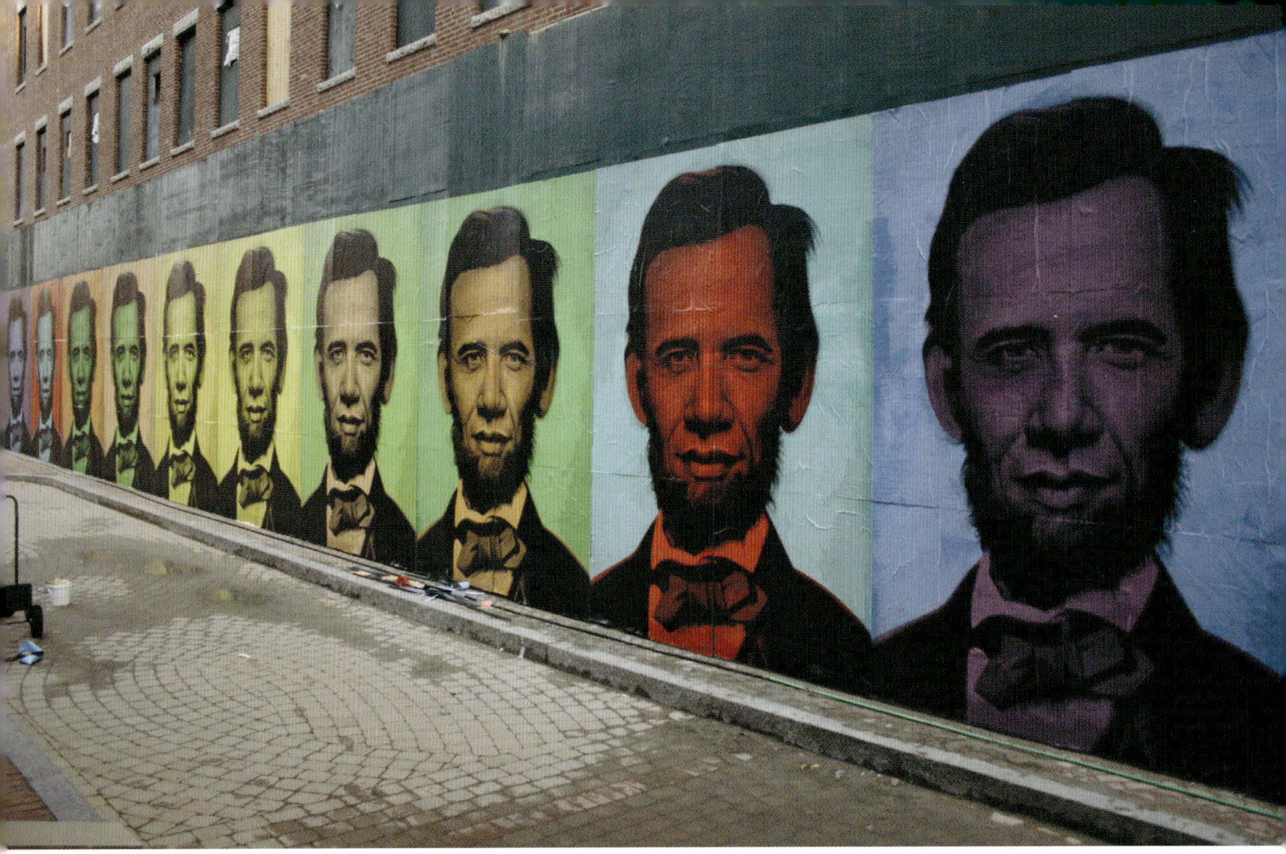

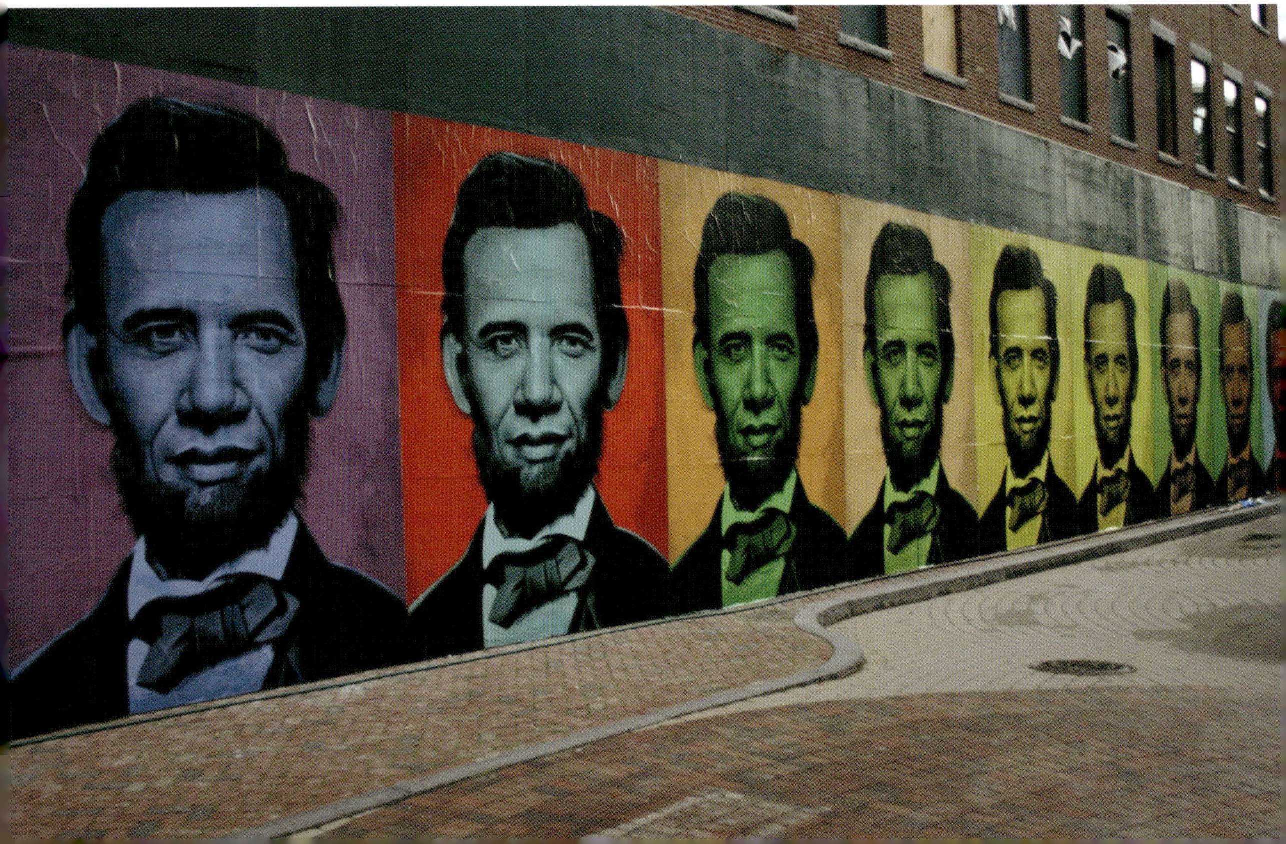

Boston

Abraham Obama Morphes Art and Politics

Ephemeral Public Art in a Time of Angst

by Mark Favermann, Critic and Urban Designer

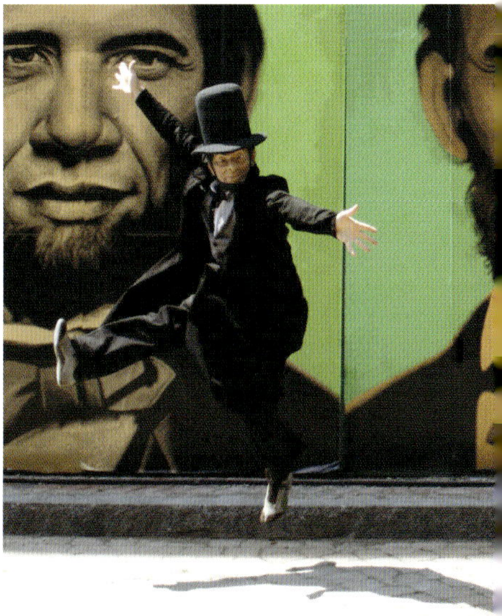

An intriguing, provocative, large scale art piece by Ron English was installed in July in Boston's South End neighborhood. The project is a series of repeated large portraits morphing Barack Obama's face with Abraham Lincoln's. It is art intertwined with politics, a transcendent postmodern visual statement.

Political art can mean a lot of things. Art that takes an ideological stand on a specific issue or addresses a public concern or just underscores viewers' sensitivity can be considered political art. Certainly, artists throughout history have been called creators of political works. This term is often quite loosely applied. An artistic piece might be called political because its subject or form causes a sensation, or it might be considered political because its subject matter pertains to a current event. The best political art has a special quality beyond the concept, the technique, or sensationalism. It has a certain universal resonance.

Major examples of this notion are Francisco Goya's passionately charged *The Third of May*, 1808 (1814; Museo del Prado, Madrid), depicting French violence against Spaniards during the Napoleonic Wars; many of Honore Daumier's French political satire images, which actually got him thrown in jail; and Pablo Picasso's *Guernica*, about the pain and agony of life during the Spanish Civil War.

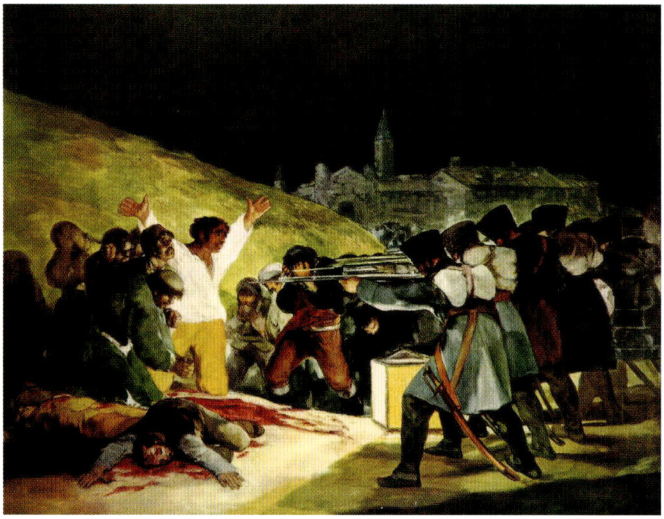

Francisco Goya's "The Third of May," 1808 (1814; Museo del Prado, Madrid)

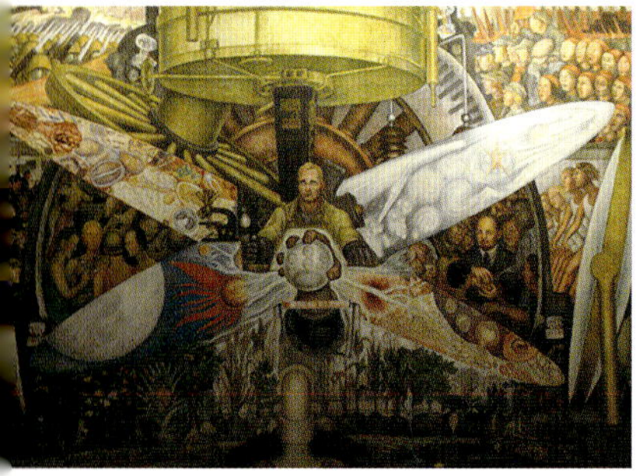

Diego Rivera's repainted "Man at the Crossroads" in a smaller scale at the Palacio in 1934 and renamed "Man, Controller of the Universe."

Another prominent creator of political art was Mexican artist Diego Rivera. Rivera was a passionate ideologue. He was a communist. His mural *Man at the Crossroads* was begun in 1933 for Rockefeller Center in New York City. He was dismissed from this commission by Nelson Rockefeller for including a portrait of Vladimir Lenin. Because of this, other United States commissions were withdrawn or denied him. Political art often invokes major reactions and consequences.

Wall murals have often been statements of neighborhood aspirations, political ideology or moral philosophy. Wall murals have been interior décor elements since the Lascaux cave paintings were created. Murals can be purely decorative, they can cause or celebrate controversy, or they can underscore ethnic or community pride. Emerging from 1960s radical poster art, in the 1970s there began a mural movement throughout the US often expressing ethnic identity or idealistic concepts.

Digitalization has allowed for temporary murals to be created the same way that billboards are made. Today, the whole idea of murals has changed due to this technology. Artists can create anything and have it blown up and printed at a gigantic scale. Photorealism is not just a painting style but an Adobe Photoshop possibility. Today, artists can still paint walls by hand the old fashioned way or produce images by digital printouts that can be supersized and attached to walls.

On July 4, 2008, the very provocative digitized print mural by artist Ron English was installed on a construction hoarding (temporary wall) at the Thayer Street complex in SOWA, the art gallery and studio district south of Washington Street in Boston's South End, as part of a 40-artist group show at Gallery XIV. The 13-foot-high by 100-foot-long mural was made up of nine portrait repeated in different Warholic colors. The piece has generated incredible amounts of Internet discussion, television pieces, and print media–not only in Boston, but nationally, as well as around the world.

The two politicians have been expertly blended, somewhat erasing the line between art and politics. The piece is about political and historical image making. The mural was commissioned by Will Kerr, the Gallery XIV director who sought to generate buzz for the gallery, stir discussion, and stimulate controversy. He was told by many not to do a political show. They said that it was the kiss of death, as no one wanted to be visually lectured to during our lean times of political discontent. Clearly, they were wrong.

Ron English is a 21st Century American Pop Art Bad Boy. He primarily explores pop culture, brand imagery and advertising as themes for his work. Technically gifted, English often installs his works in places not specifically intended for fine art, like inner-city empty lots, existing billboards, bus shelters or construction sites–sometimes illegally.

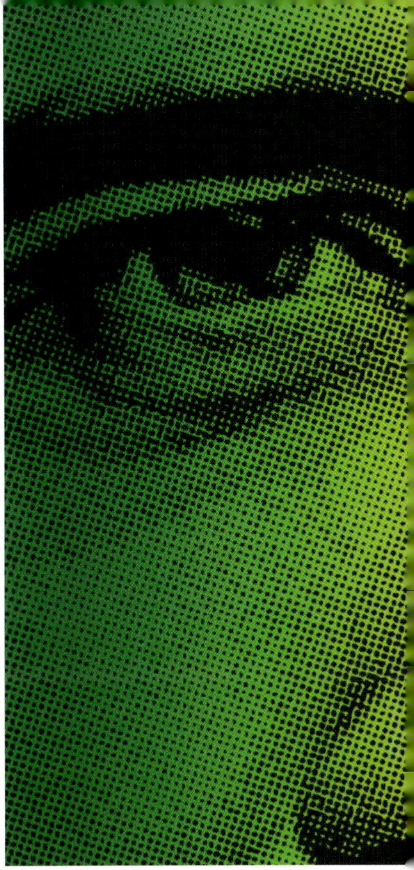

Top: Close up of digitized Abraham Obama

Bottom: Inside the now-defunct Boston Gallery XIV.

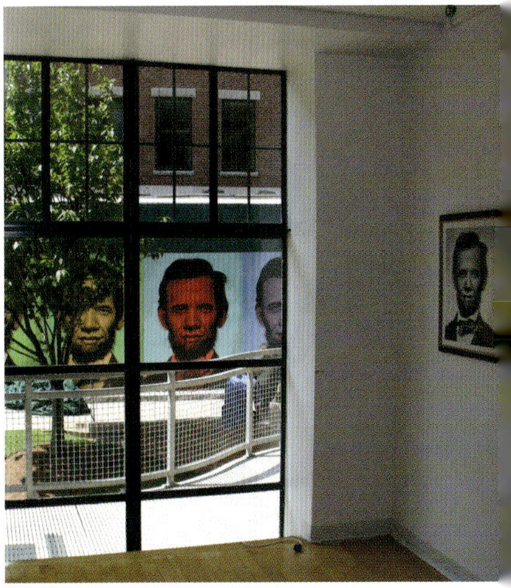

His work is frequently political, but laced with unexpected humor. Taking disparate cultural elements and mashing them together to conjugate new statements and contruct new paradigms with which to reexamine opinions and norms we have taken for granted, English is blunt, bold, and often hilarious.

One of English's most frequent references is Picasso's Guernica, an image English has used dozens of times, transforming the original evocative Spanish civilian characters into Disney figures, soccer players, and school children, among other iterations. The basic Guernica construct serves as a template, in which the artist recombines seemingly incongruous elements to drive home complicated messages about civil responsibilities.

Similarly, Abraham Obama serves as a template. Here, the great liberator and the great articulator are combined. Lincoln changed America, and Barack Obama's candidacy and election suggest great potential - national and even world change. The mural's Warholian shifts in color and value suggest racial undertones and nuances. There is a black-and-white unspoken reference in the color. Obama is of mixed race. All this is significantly and inherently stated in the mural.

English has an enthusiastic following who travel to see his new works, sort of the way the Grateful Dead had its camp followers. Overly enthusiastic English fans pasted versions of the Abraham Obama image all over Boston's South End neighborhood, angering some of the residents. Kerr received some very nasty mail about political influencing. This seems to suggest that something else is going on besides the visual clutter and perhaps vandalism of illegal bill posting. This is more about race and color than art and coloration.

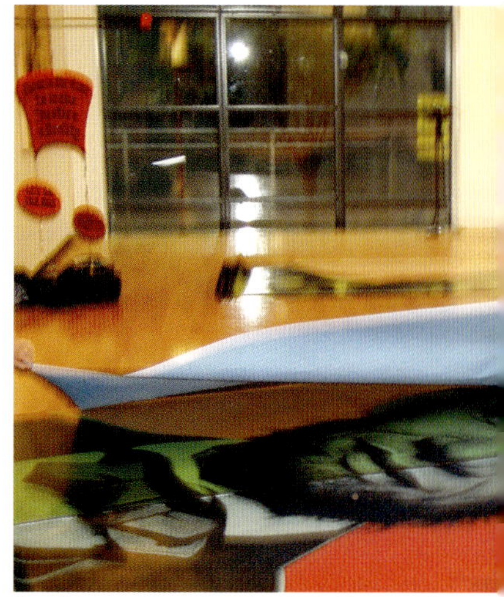

English prepares to take the AO's outside

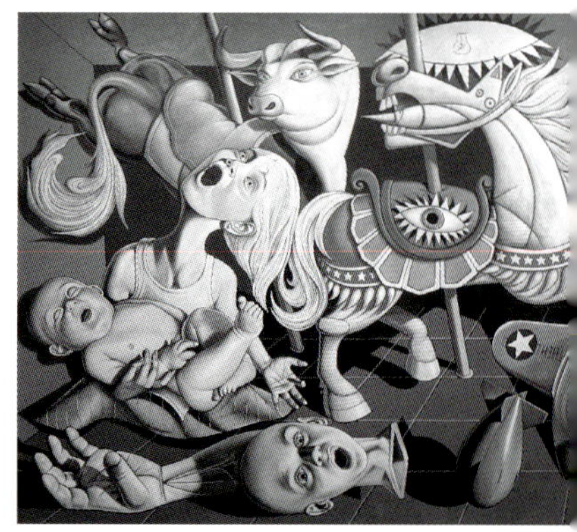

Ron English's Grade School Guernica

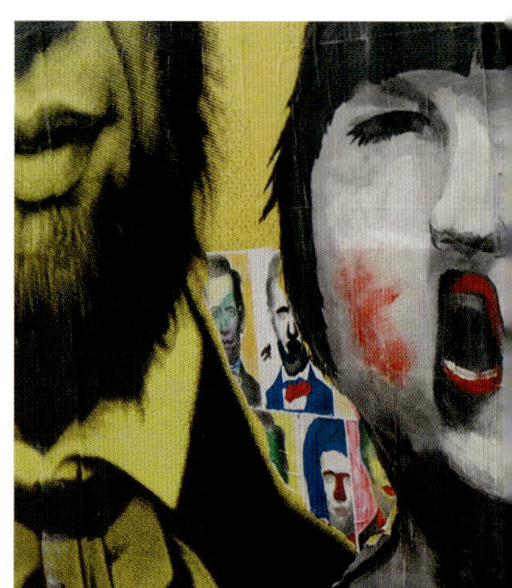

Artist additions in Boston

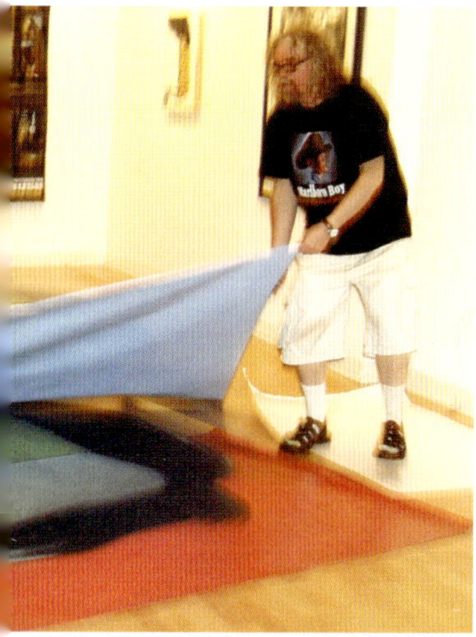

This ephemeral piece is about the layers of art and politics. Not like an onion, but more like a geological formation, the structural layers of this piece suggest how our society and body politic have been formed through inflated images, popular myths, perceived impressions, and artful manipulations. This is a counter-message to the rather buttoned-down post 9/11 lack of criticism fostered by the Bush Administration's national security mantra of no question, no protest. Too bad the conventional media has bowed to this un-American notion of noncritical involvement for eight long years.

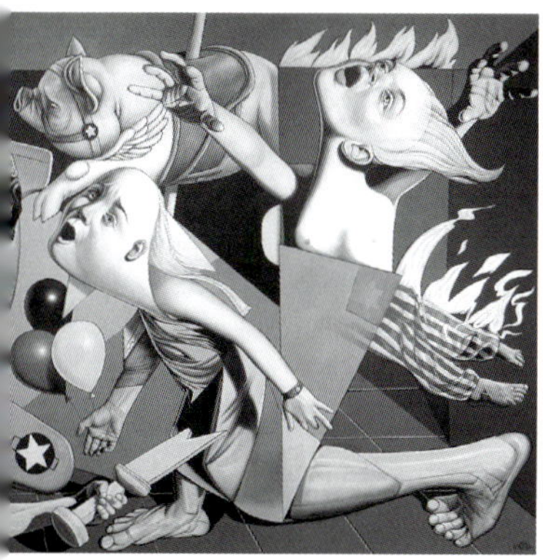

Another interesting facet of this image is the over-elevation of a popular figure. Combining Lincoln and Obama visually integrates myth and man, history and potential, as well as martyrdom and youthful vitality. Is the artist saying that the Obama supporters should beware as well?

Kerr has added additional images to the mural by having artists insert supplementary figures (including a broke Monopoly Man, aliens, and screaming or crying women) to the mural and has incorporated drawings by middle school students to form an Abraham Obama collage. This is traditional grafitti as it should be, illustrating and protesting the ills of our time while celebrating a sense of our place in society.

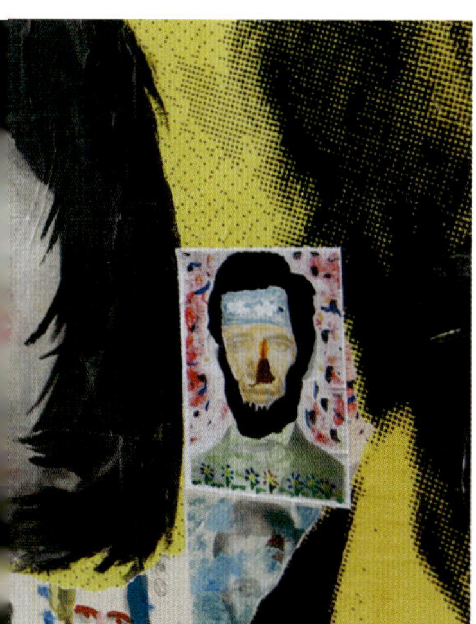

photo by Mark Favermann

After a month and a half of summer sun and intermittent monsoon-like rains, along with some slight vandalism, the Abraham Obama mural is deteriorating. It is high level temporary art that will eventually come down when Gallery XIV moves from its present quarters. The gallery has documented the life of the mural on video. To those who experienced the mural the image will be lasting. This piece is not merely temporal public art, but a civic and generational touchstone.

Reprinted with permission from berkshirefinearts.com.

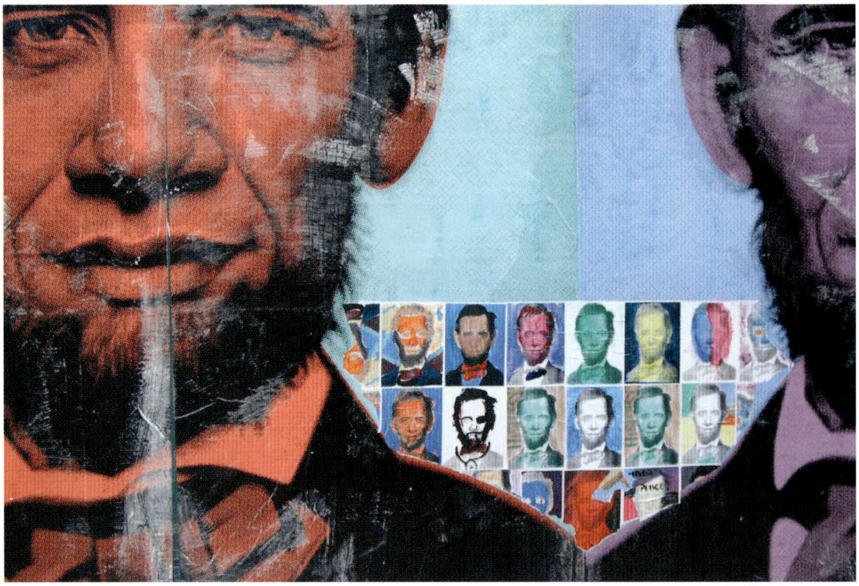

photo by Mark Favermann

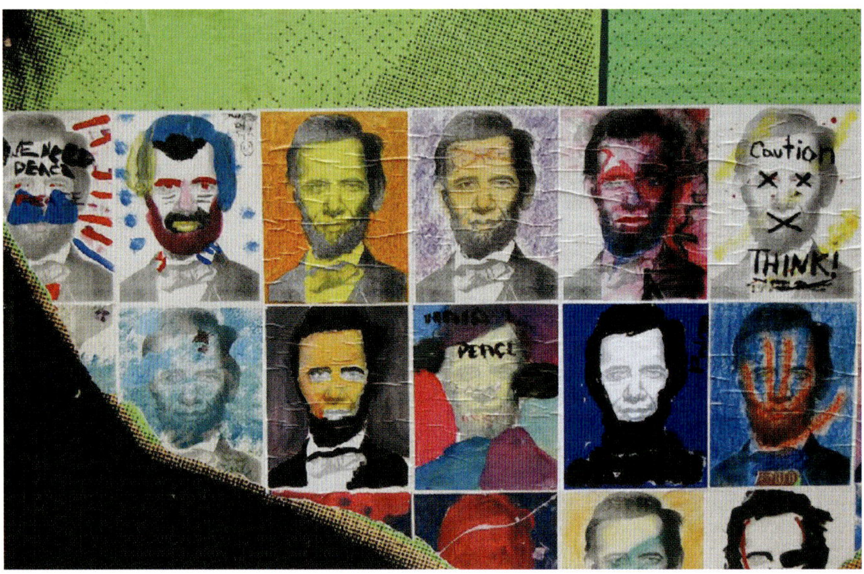

photo by Mark Favermann

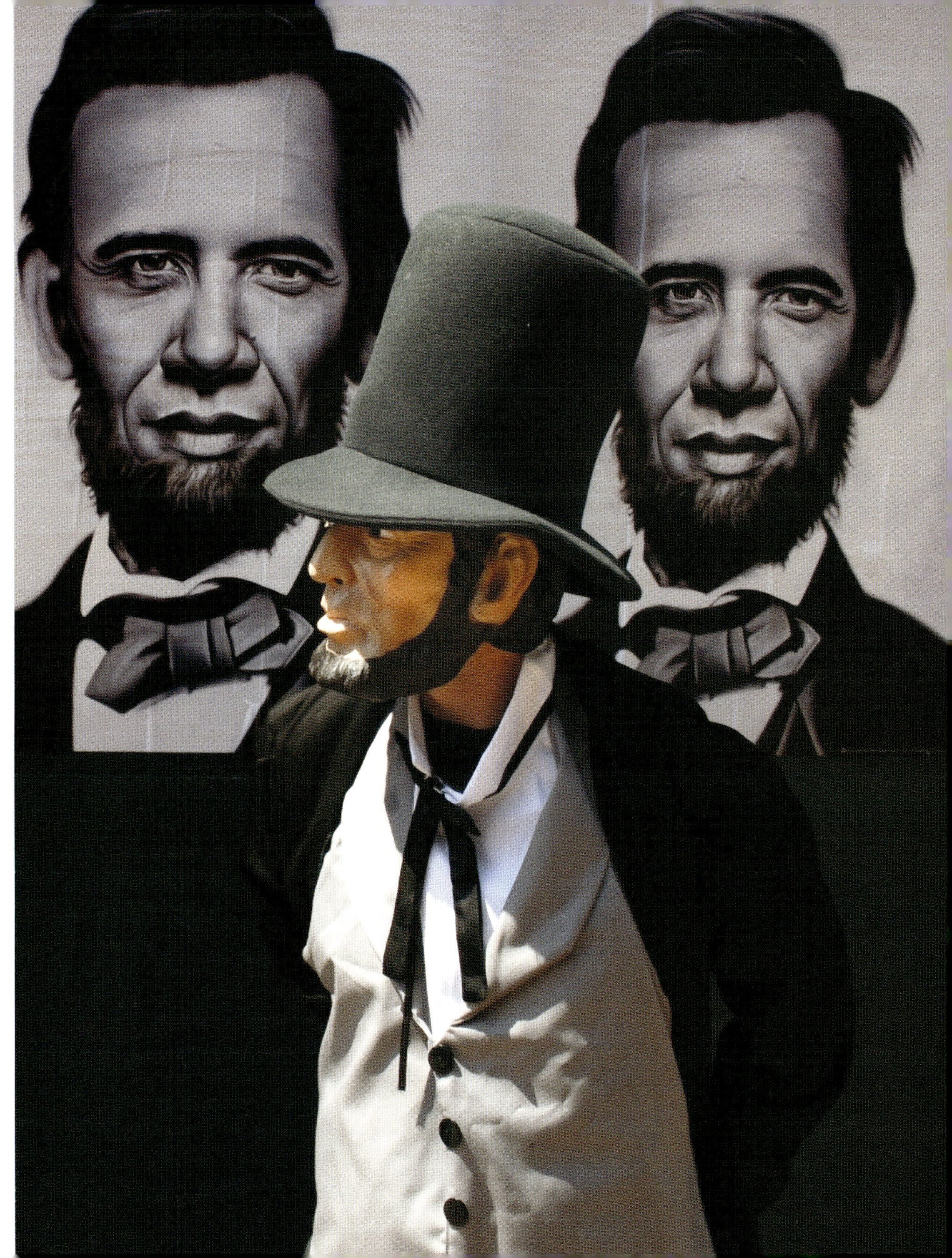

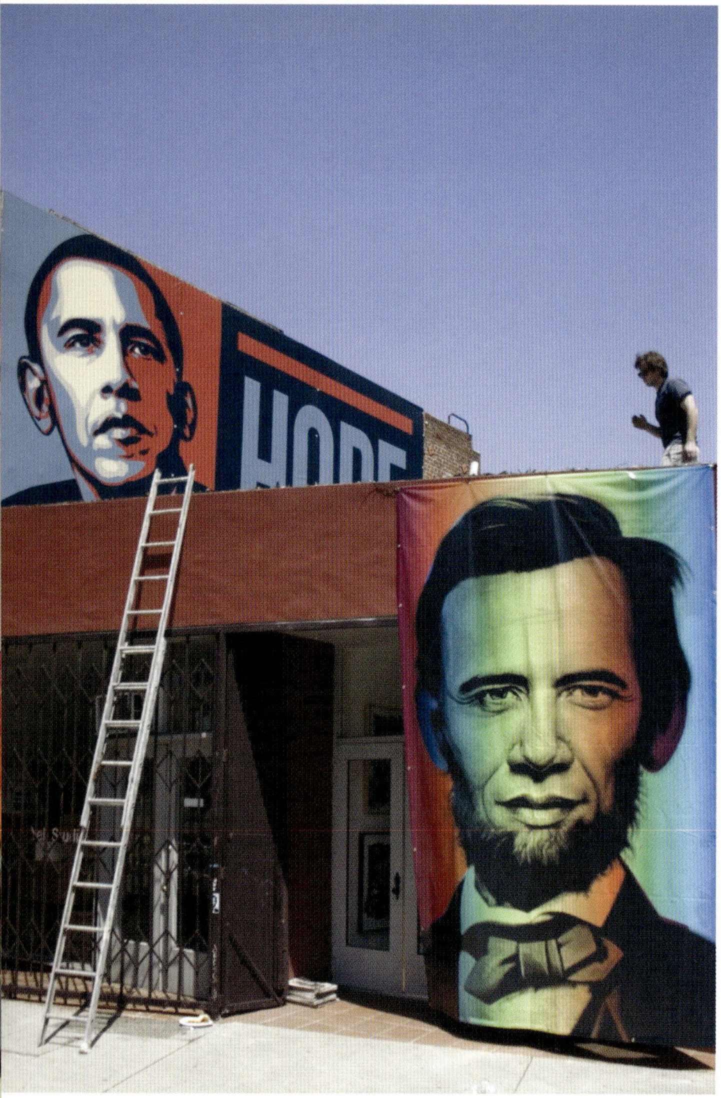

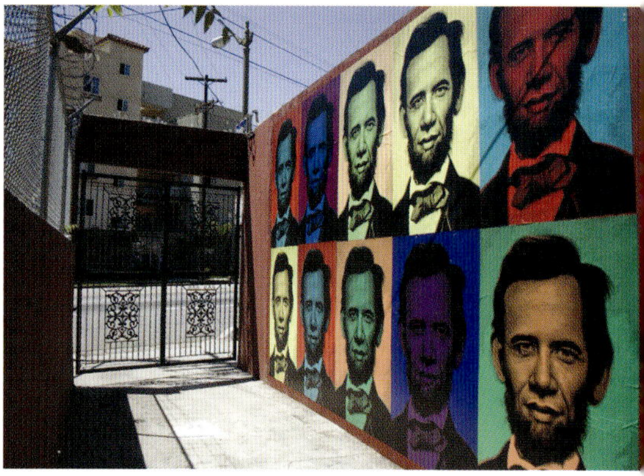

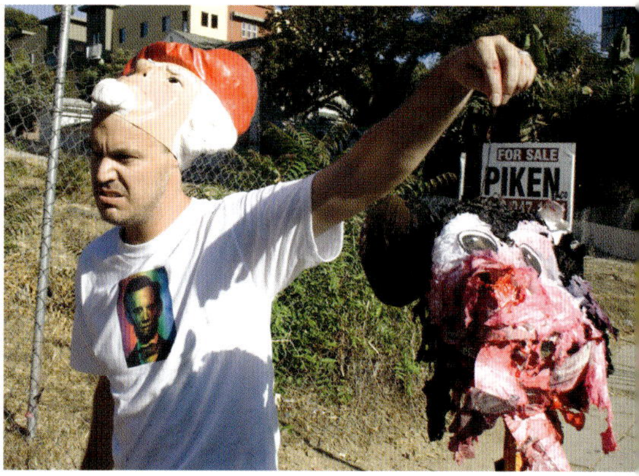

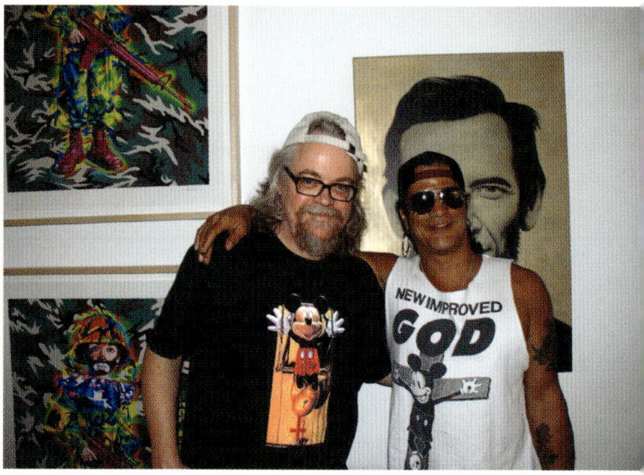

Left: Hijinx outside the Jet Set Graffiti Gallery on Sunset Boulevard in preparation of a small release party to kick off the tour. Graffiti artist Saber and musician Slash visit. Right: A visit next door at Studio Number One with Shepard Fairey and his crew, and then some warm-up pasters throughout the city.

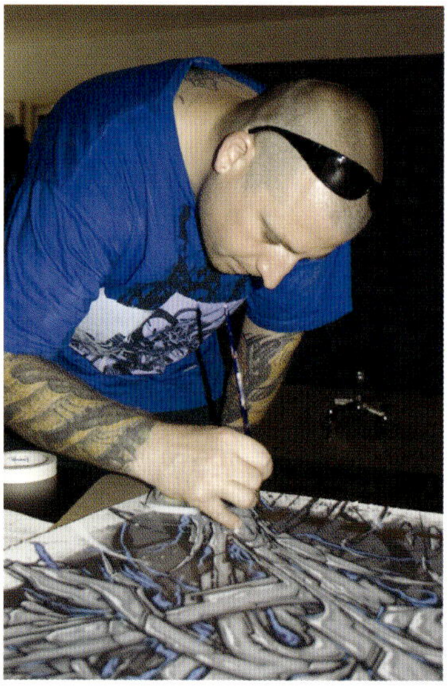

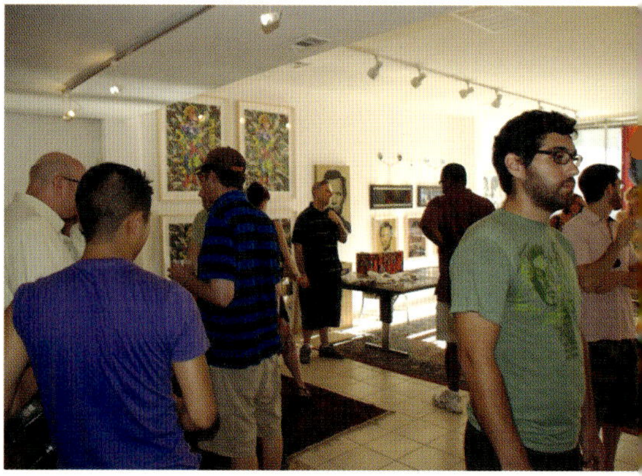

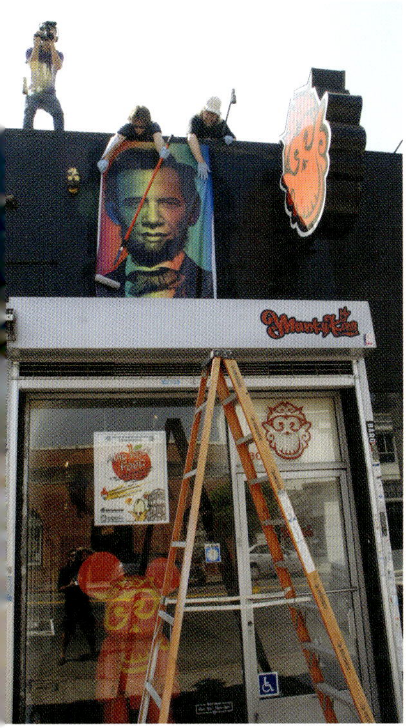

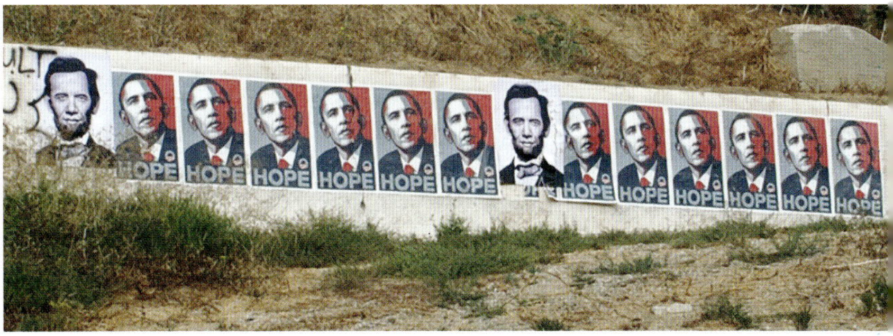
HOPE

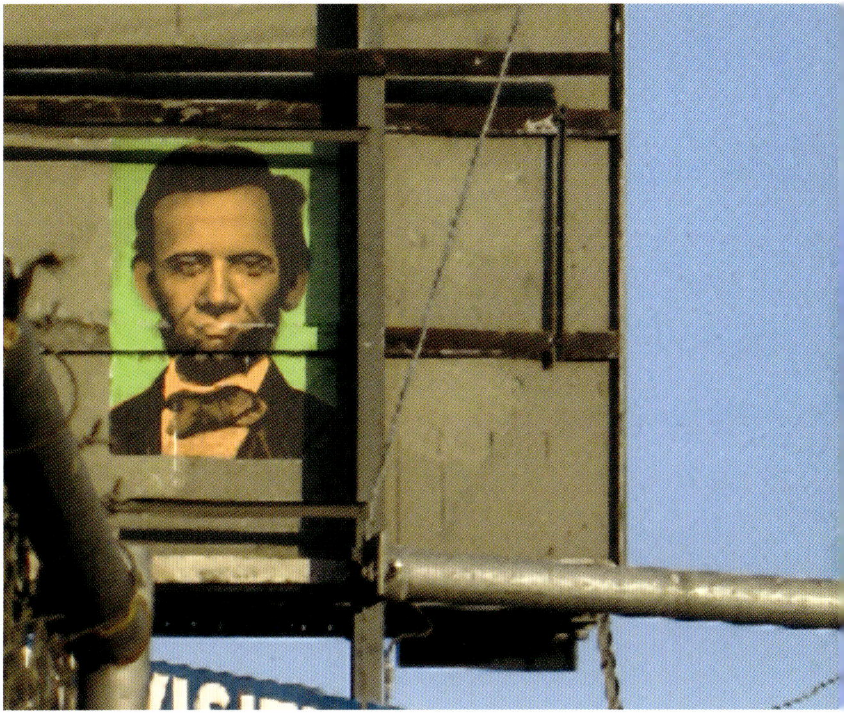

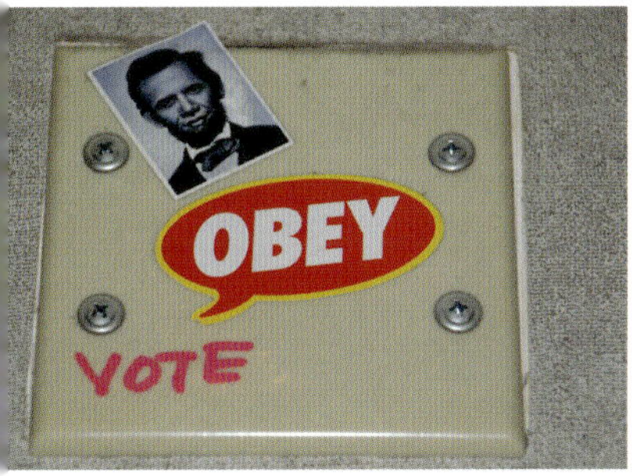
OBEY
VOTE

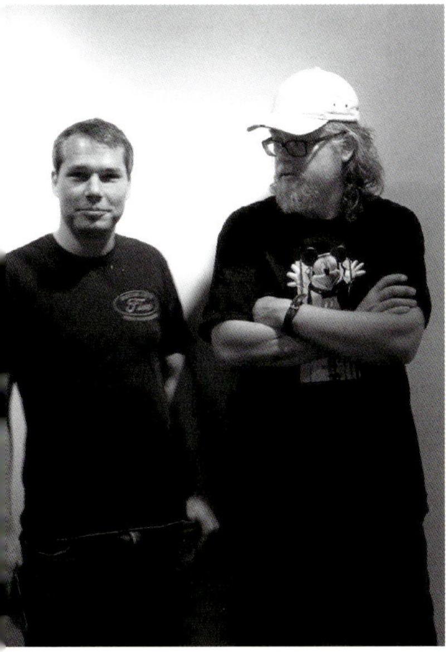

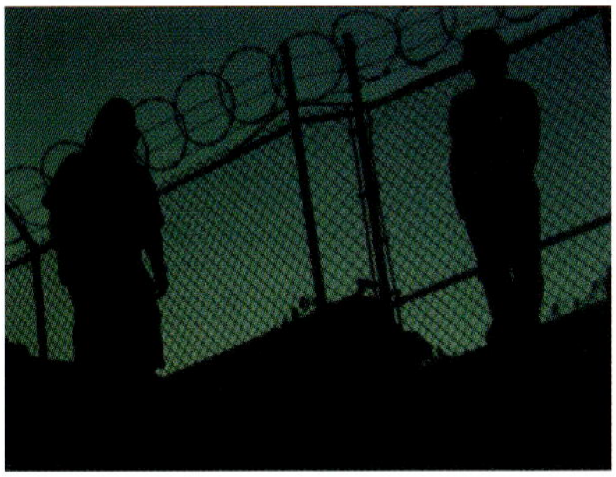

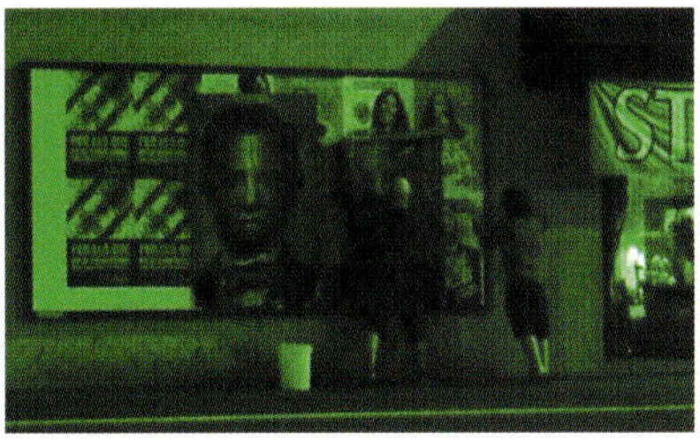

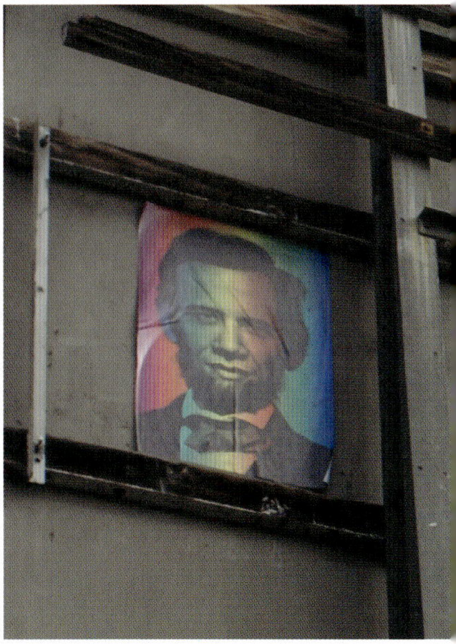

Shepard Fairey

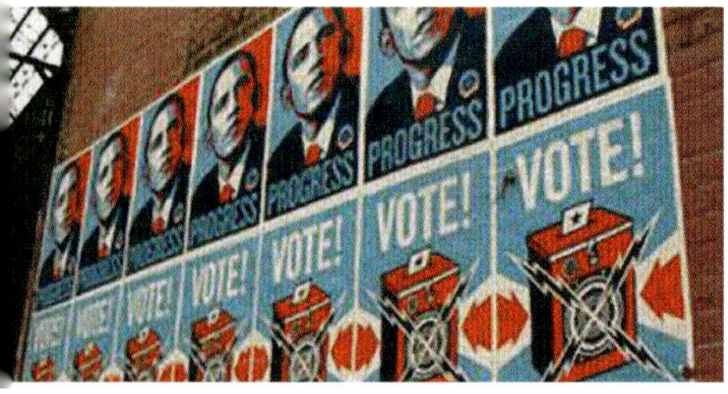

A lot has happened to Shepard since his *André the Giant Has a Posse* sticker campaign hit the streets in the late 1980s, but the one sure thing that will always remain is his desire to have his art in public places. It made perfect sense that he hooked up with the Obama campaign and the rest, as they say, is history.

It would have been hard for us to go anywhere on our tour across America without seeing Shepard's "Hope," "Progress," or "Vote" images either published, printed, or pasted. We had the pleasure of hanging out with him in his studio in Los Angeles, and at the DNC, the *Manifest Hope Exhibition* in Denver, and later in Washington D.C. for the inauguration. The amazing thing about Shepard is that he has helped citizens take back public space. Whether it be a sticker or a billboard, legal or illegal, his street work should be a reminder to all of us that corporate America can't control everything.

There is no doubt that his images of Barack Obama helped us all create a sense of calm and focus during that very nerve-racking time leading up to the election. And did I mention he is a helluva DJ?

–DG

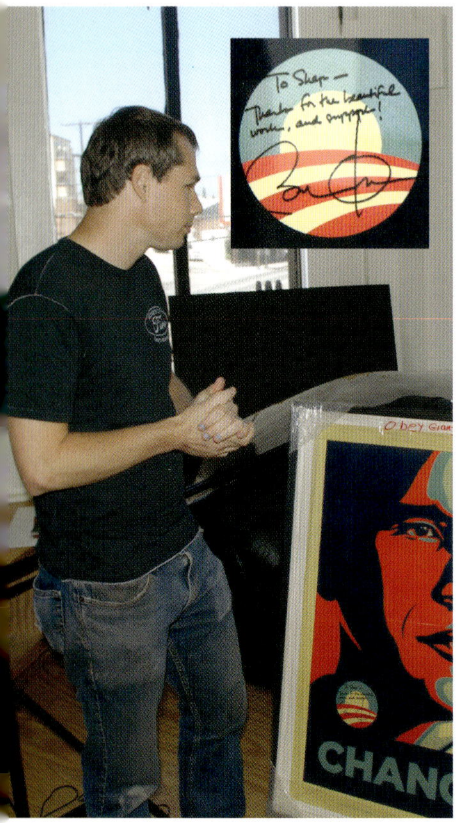

Shepard Fairey stands next to his signed Barack Obama print. It reads:

" To Shep – Thanks for the beautiful work, and support!"

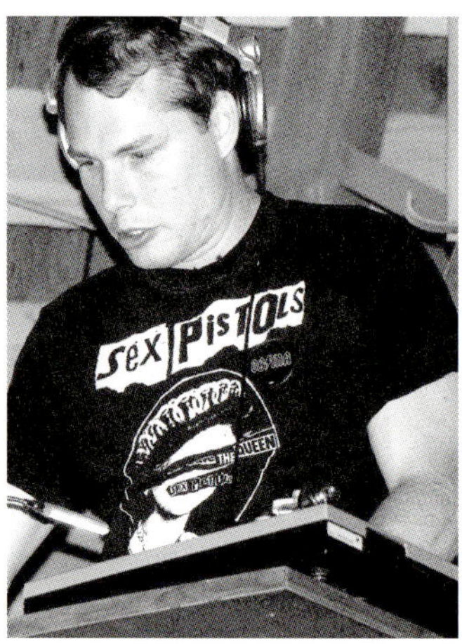

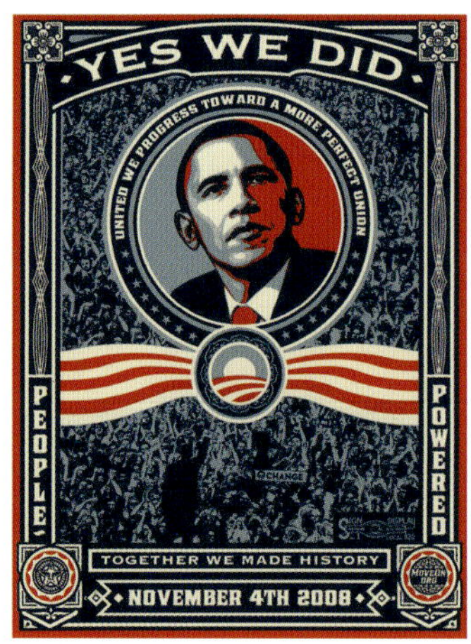

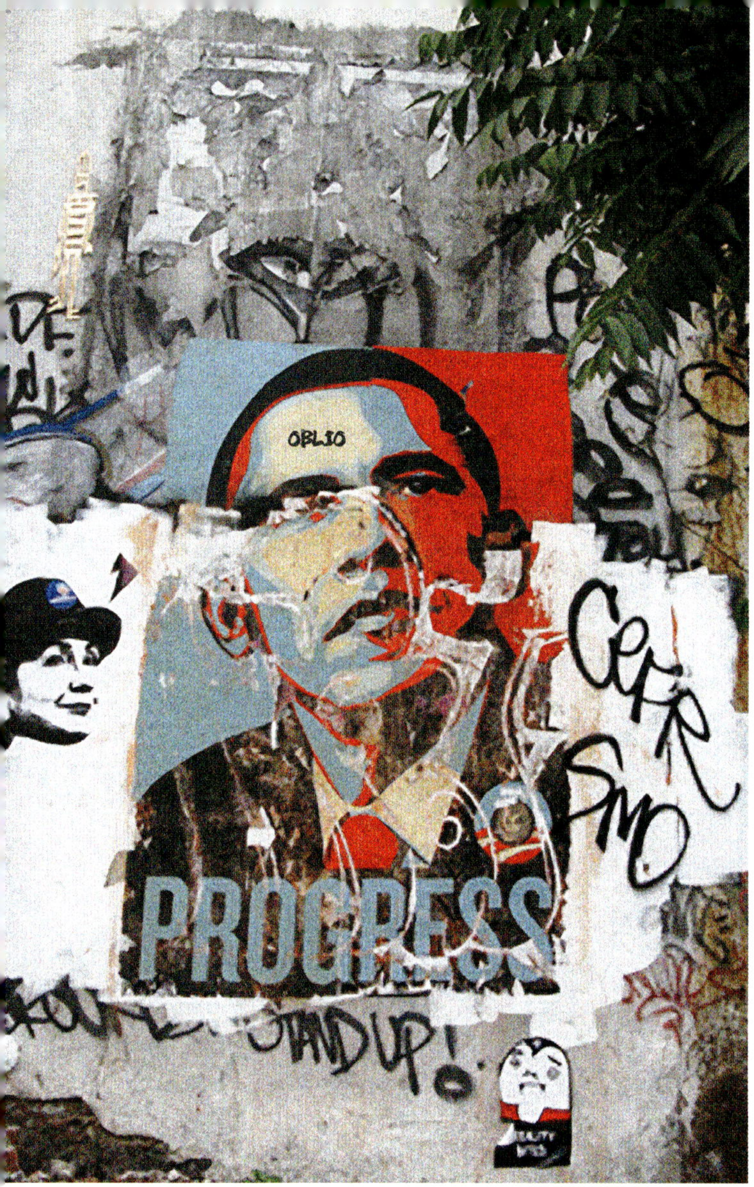
PROGRESS
STAND UP!

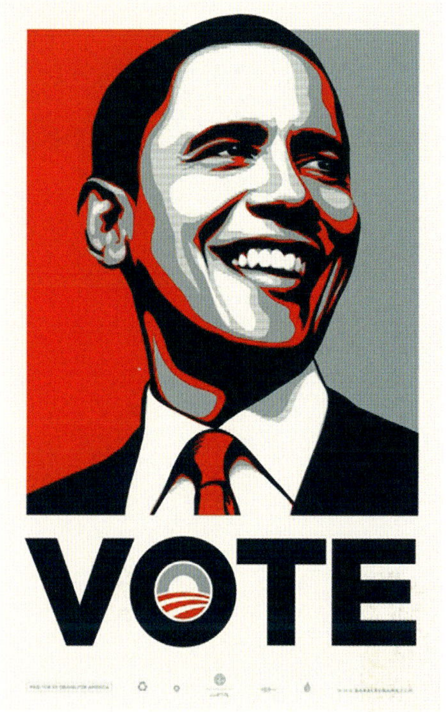
VOTE

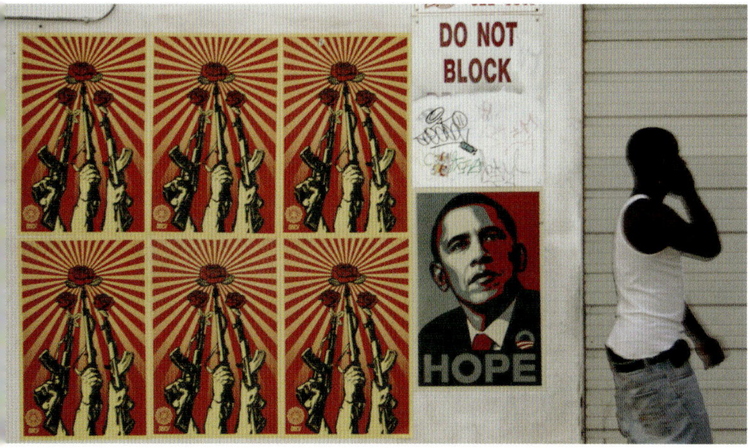
DO NOT
BLOCK
HOPE

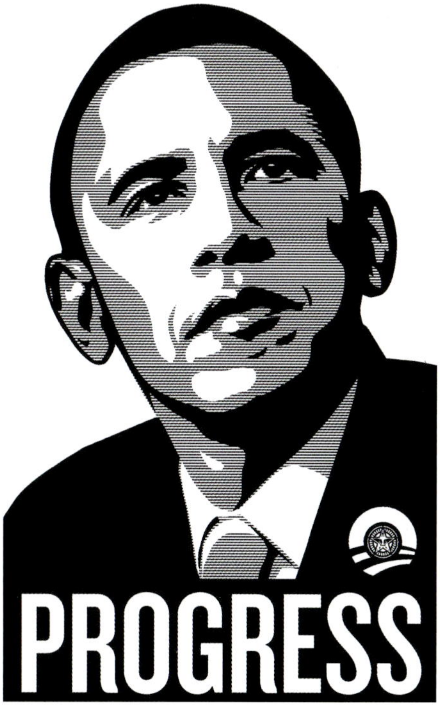
PROGRESS

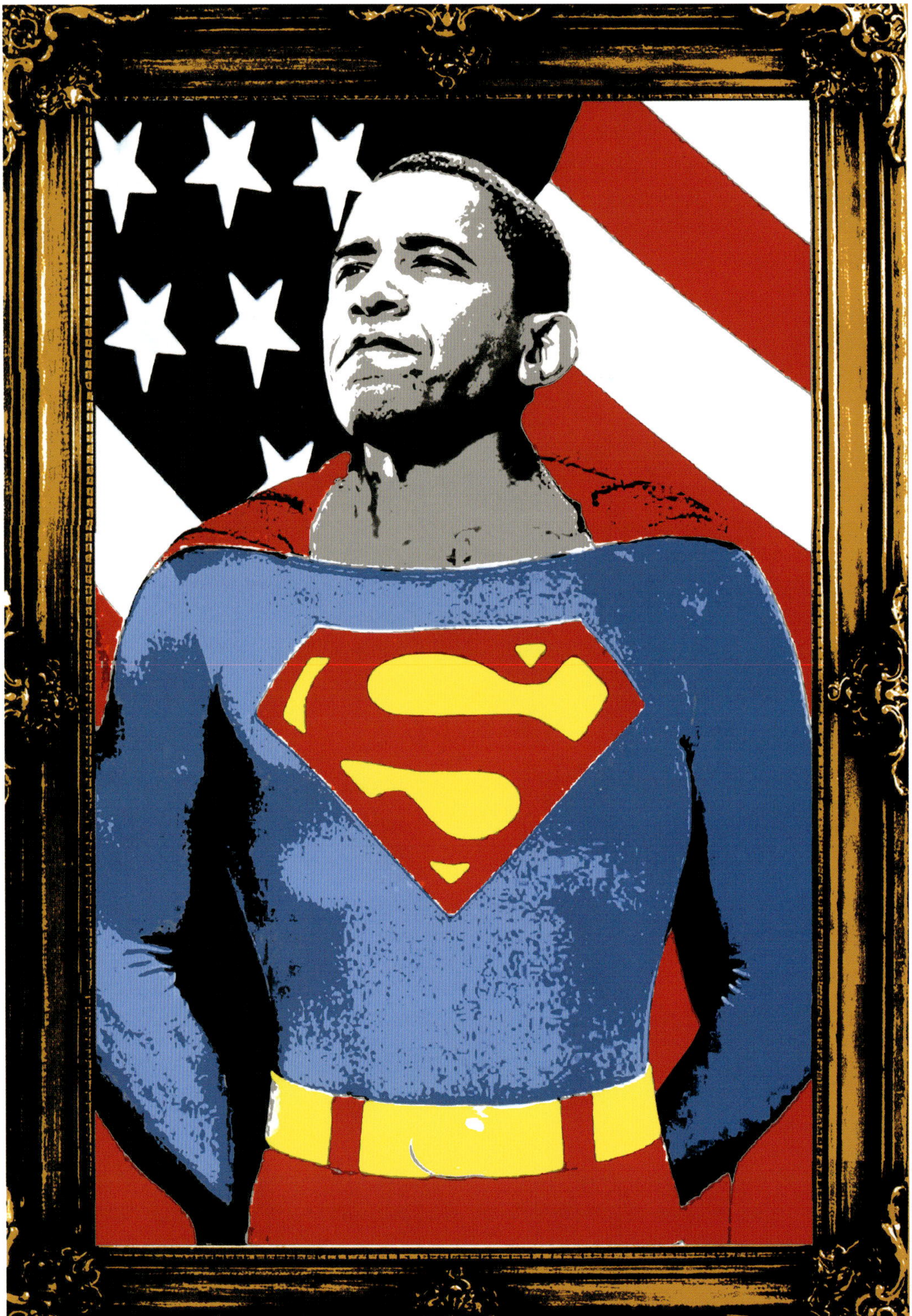

Mr. Brainwash

Mr. Brainwash

Mr. Brainwash or, as some call him, MBW, is the moniker of an eccentric filmmaker. He started painting back in 1989 and in the late 90s began filming the great street artists around the world. After years filming the likes of Bansky, Shepard Fairey, and many others, he has put down the camera and once again taken up the spray-can to become one of California's most prolific street artists. He became our street host, hooking us up with great opportunities for pasting AOs.
–DG

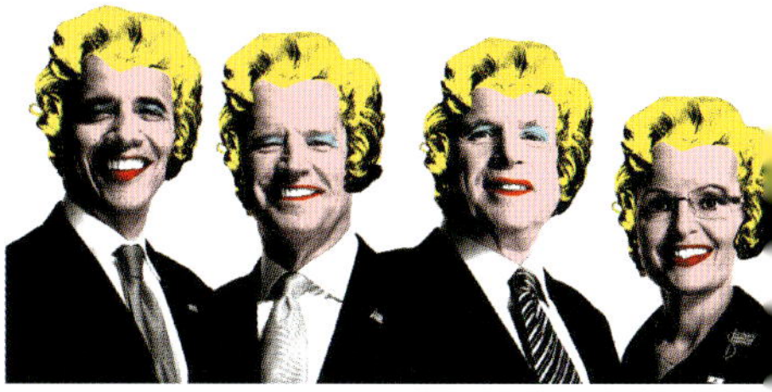

Mr. Brainwash

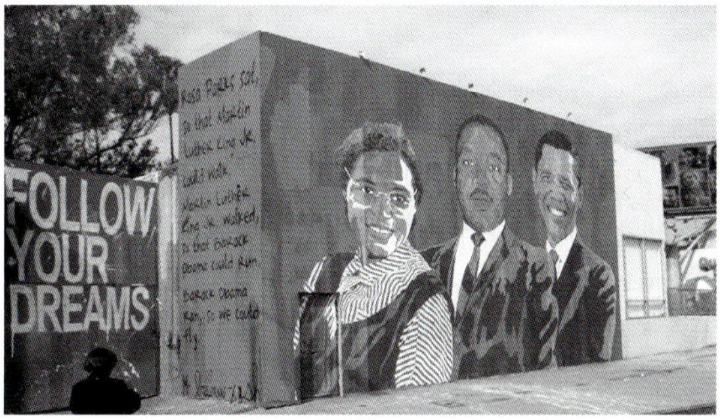

Mr. Brainwash

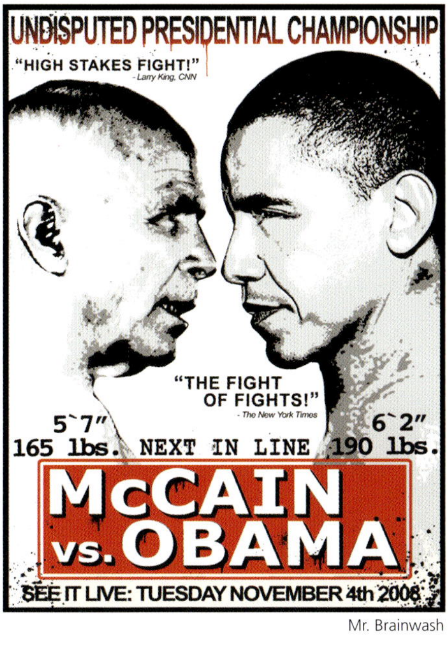

Mr. Brainwash

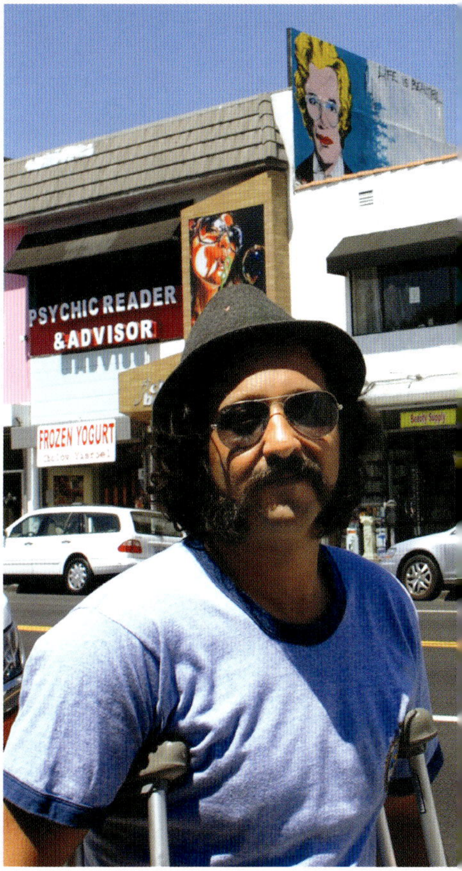

Mr. Brainwash in Los Angeles, just outside one of his Marilyn Warhol installations.

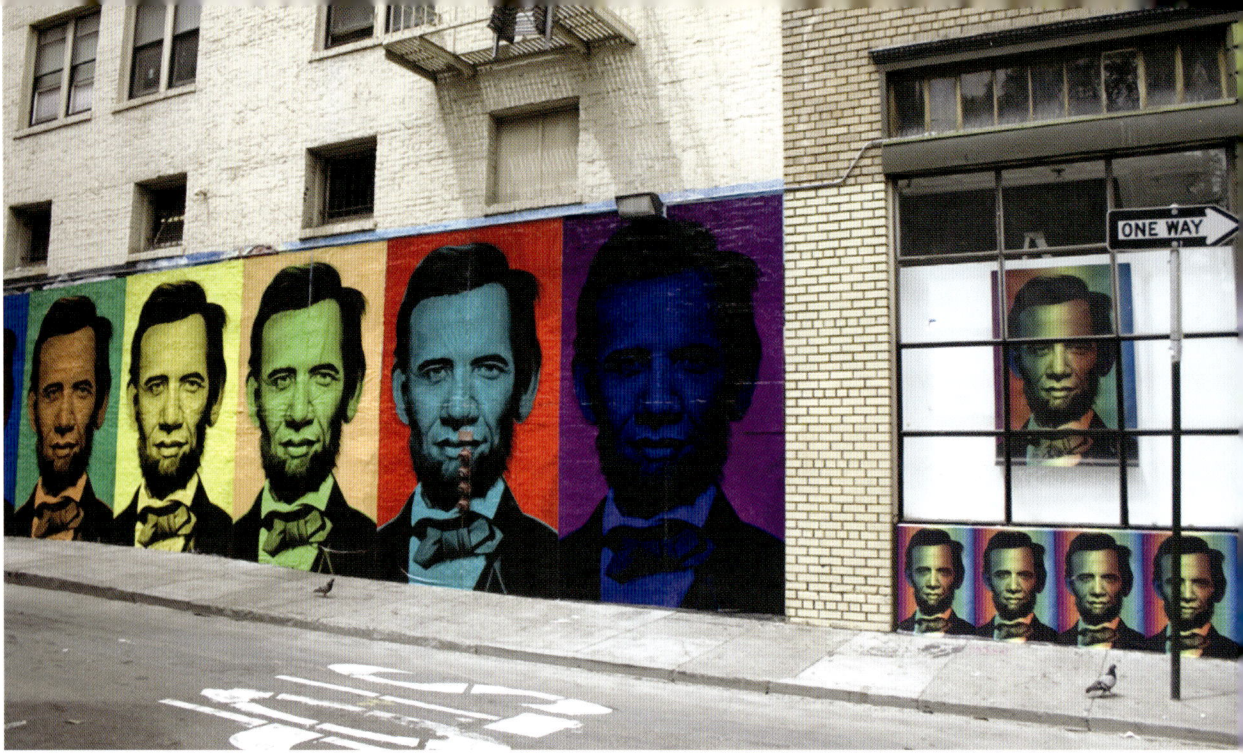

Left: Just outside The Shooting Gallery in the Tenderloin District.

Right: Gallery and club 111 Minna.

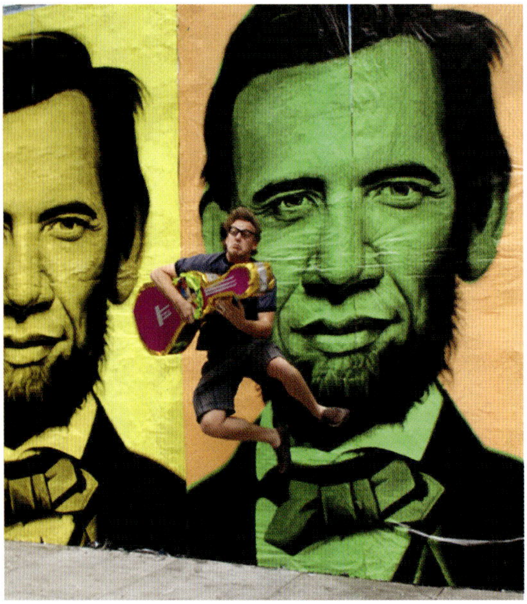

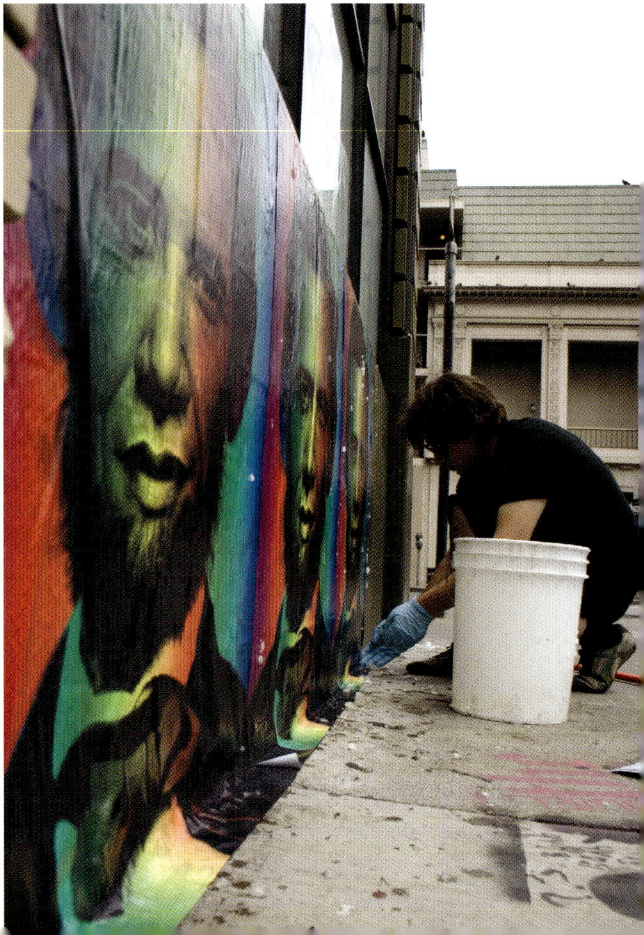

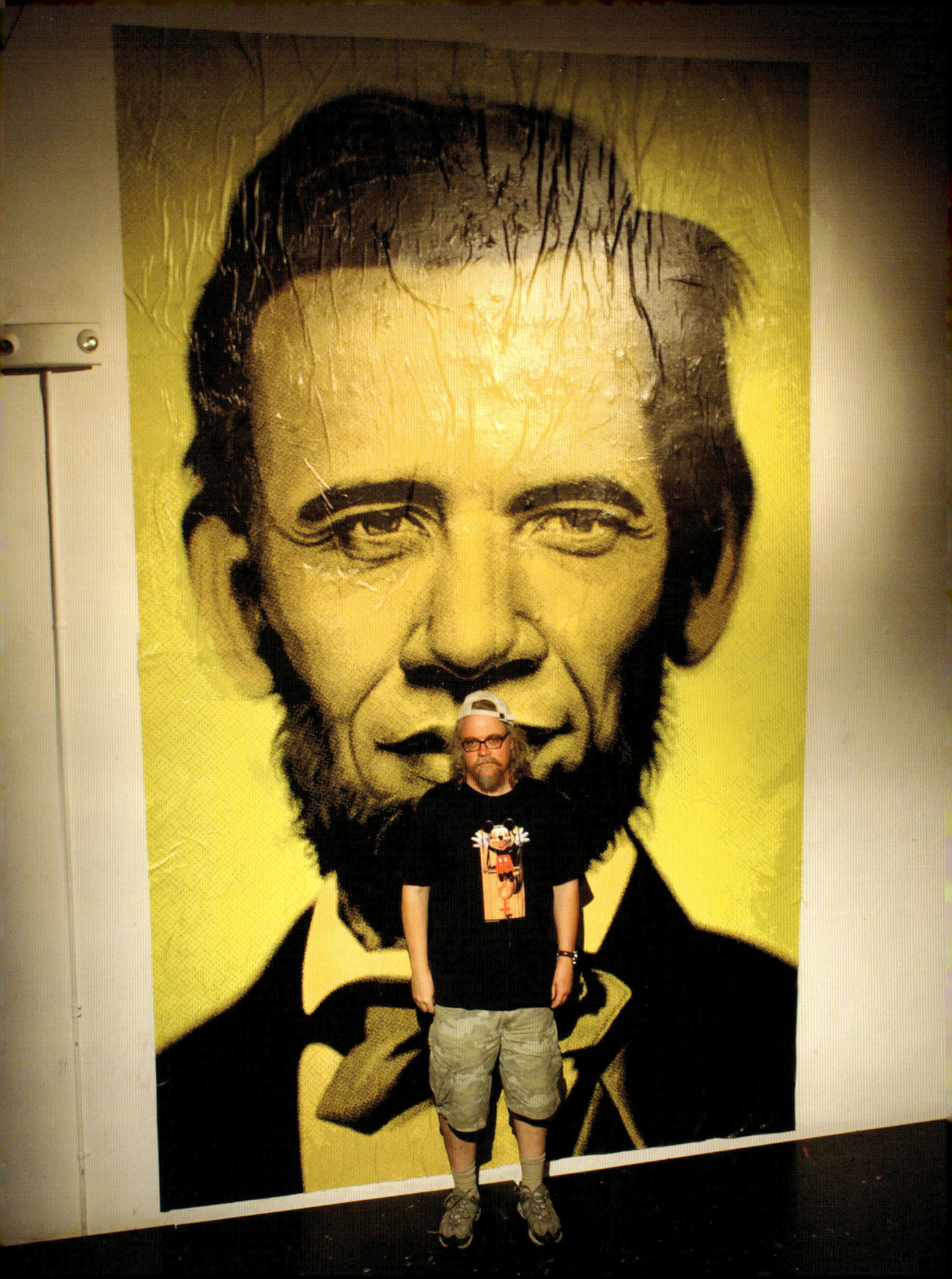

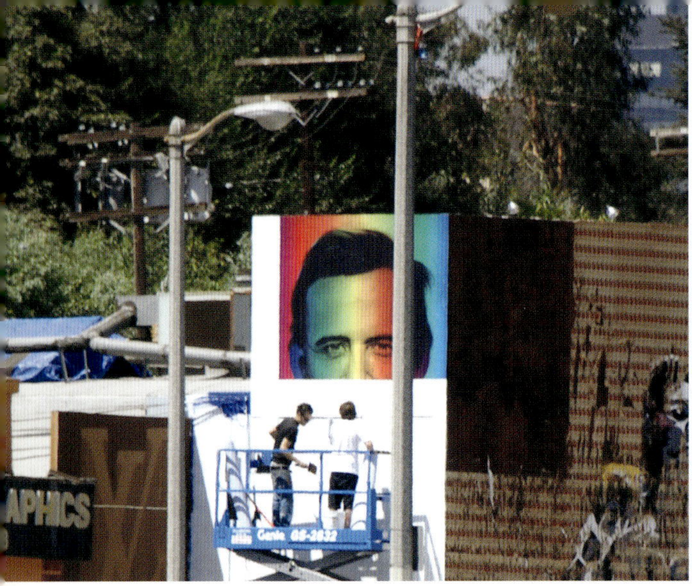
APHICS
Genie GS-2632

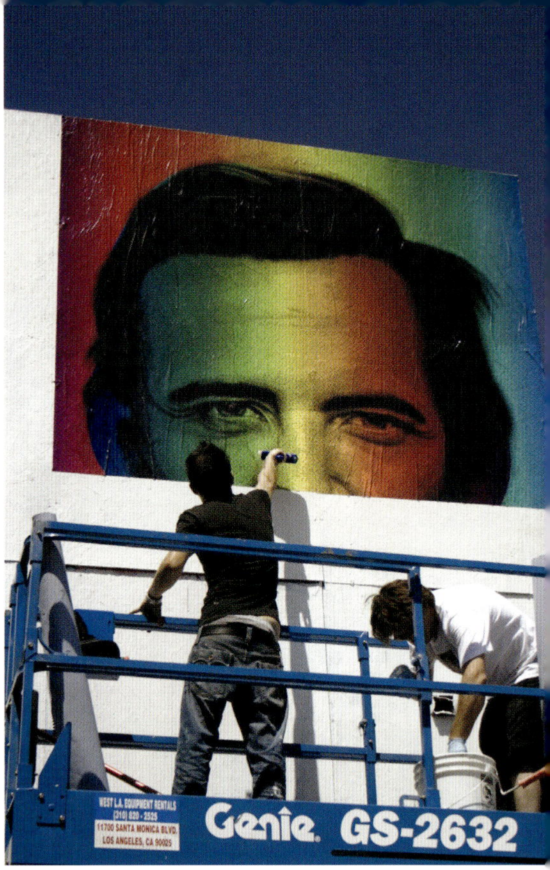
WEST L.A. EQUIPMENT RENTALS
(310) 820-2525
11700 SANTA MONICA BLVD.
LOS ANGELES, CA 90025
Genie GS-2632

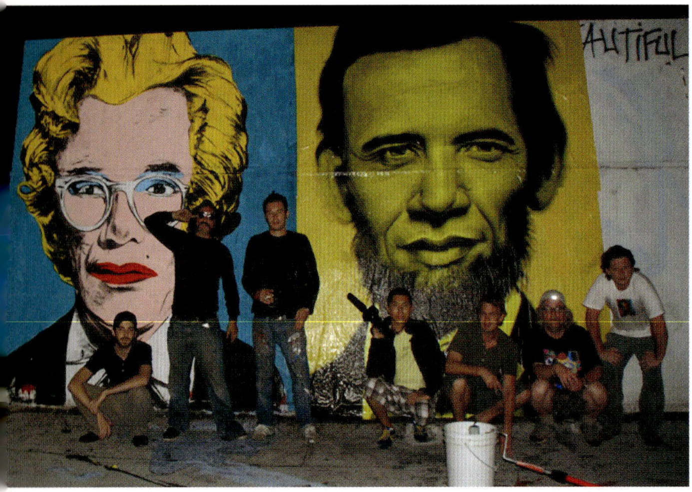
AUTIFUL

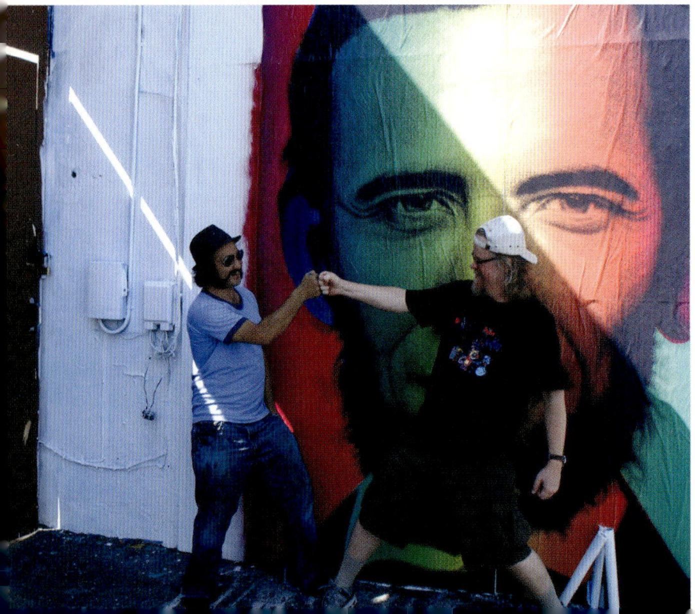

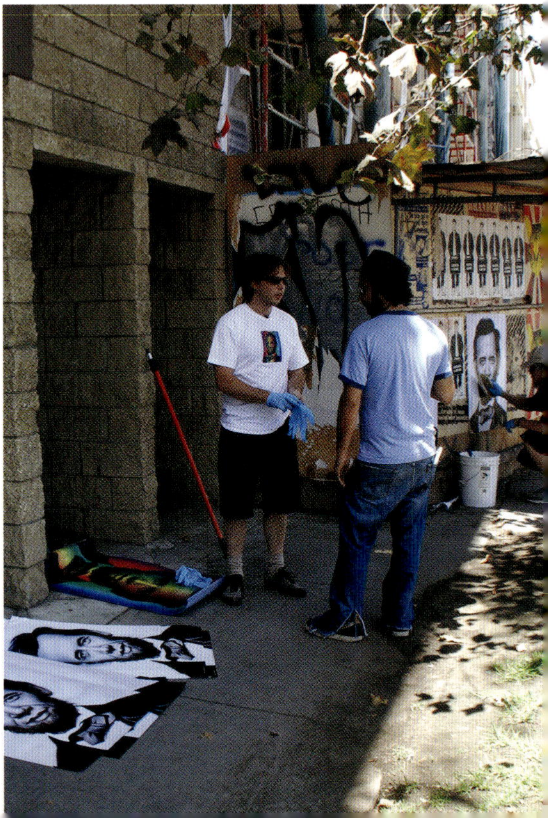

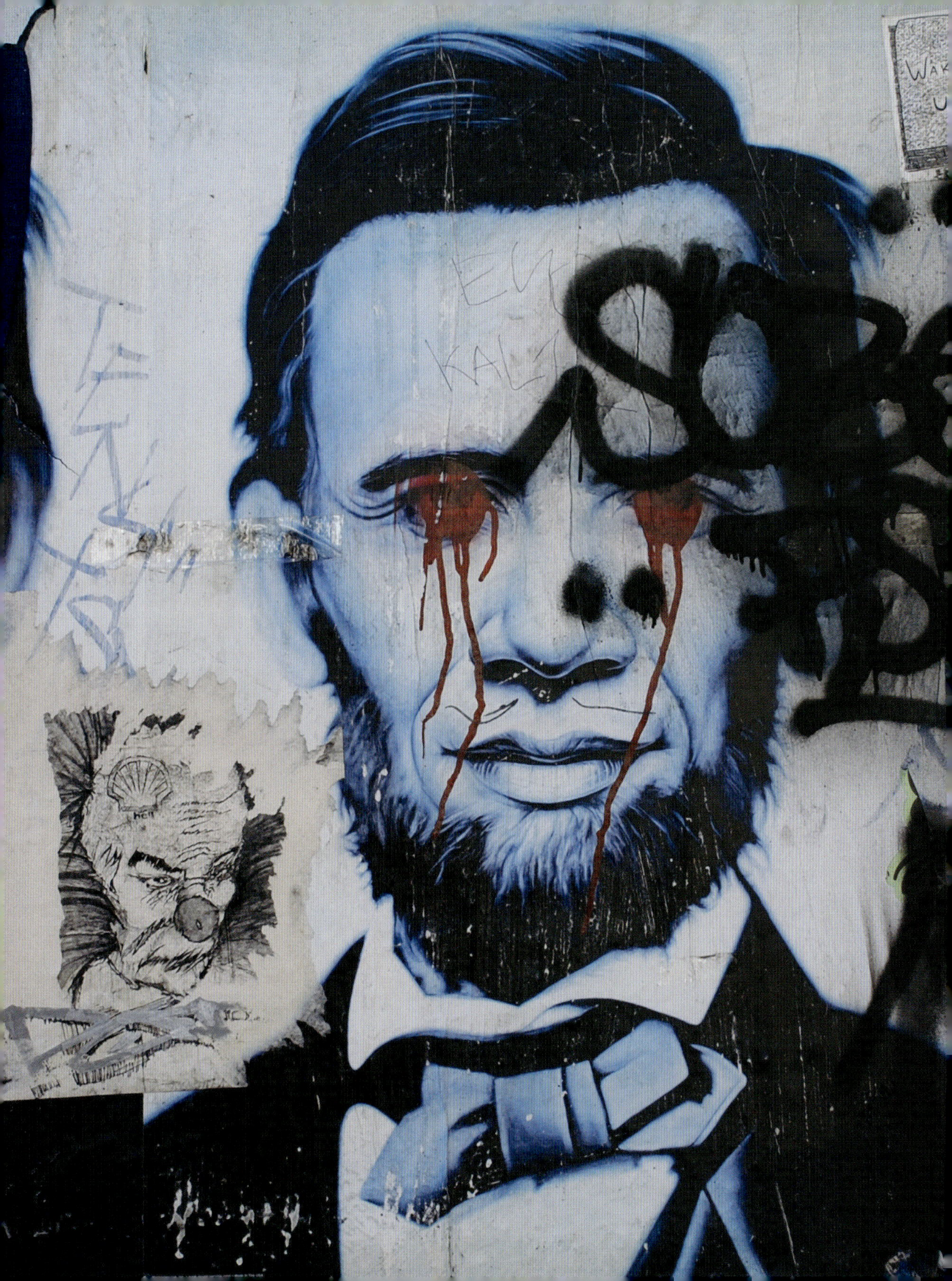

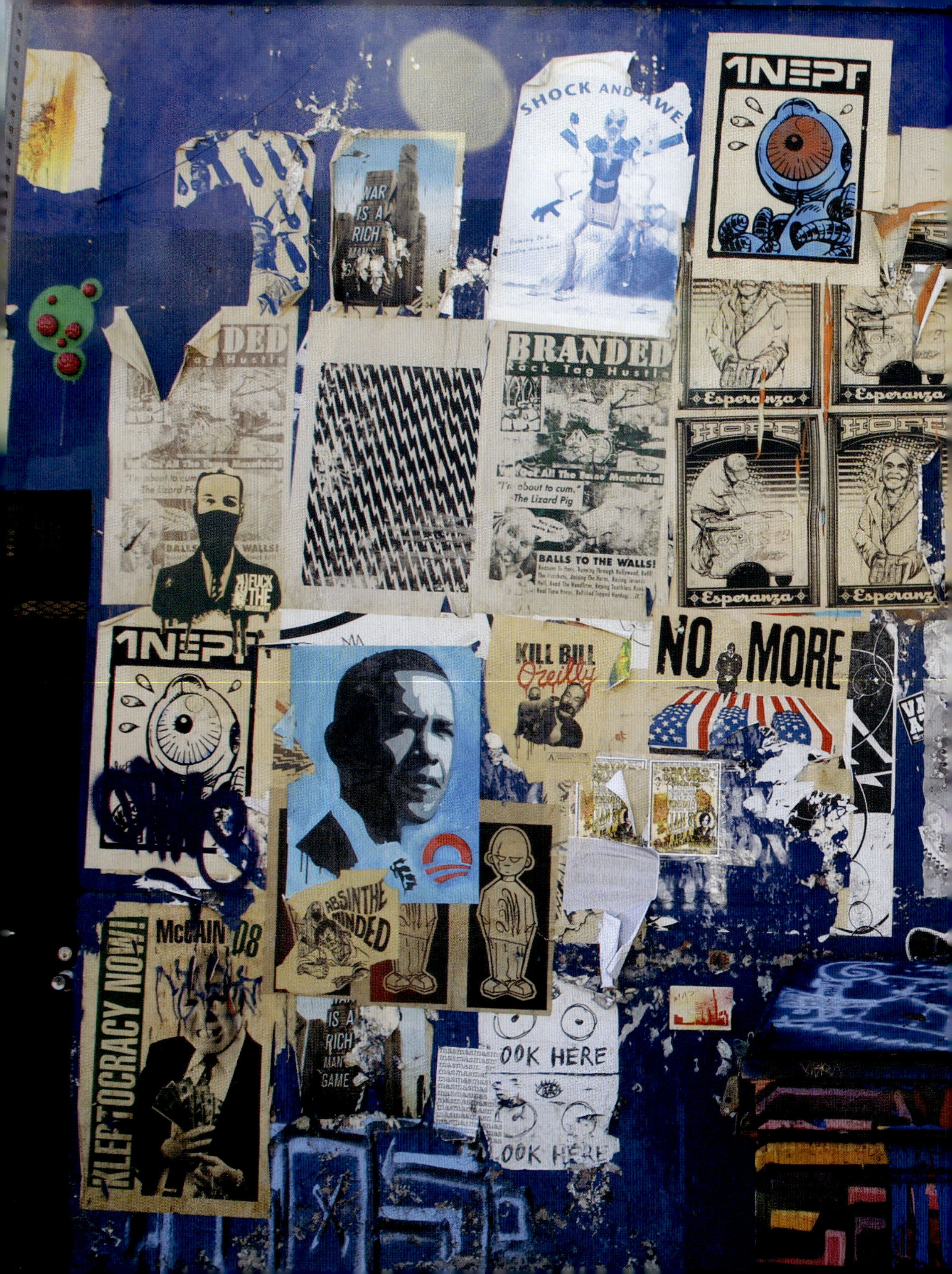

SHOCK AND AWE.
1NEPT
WAR IS A RICH
BRANDED
Rack Tag Hustl
"I'm about to cum."
-The Lizard Pig
BALLS TO THE WALLS!
Esperanza
HOPE
Esperanza
NO MORE
KILL BILL
O'reilly
1NEPT
ABSINTHE MINDED
McCAIN 08
KLEPTOCRACY NOW!
IS A RICH MAN'S GAME
OOK HERE
OOK HERE

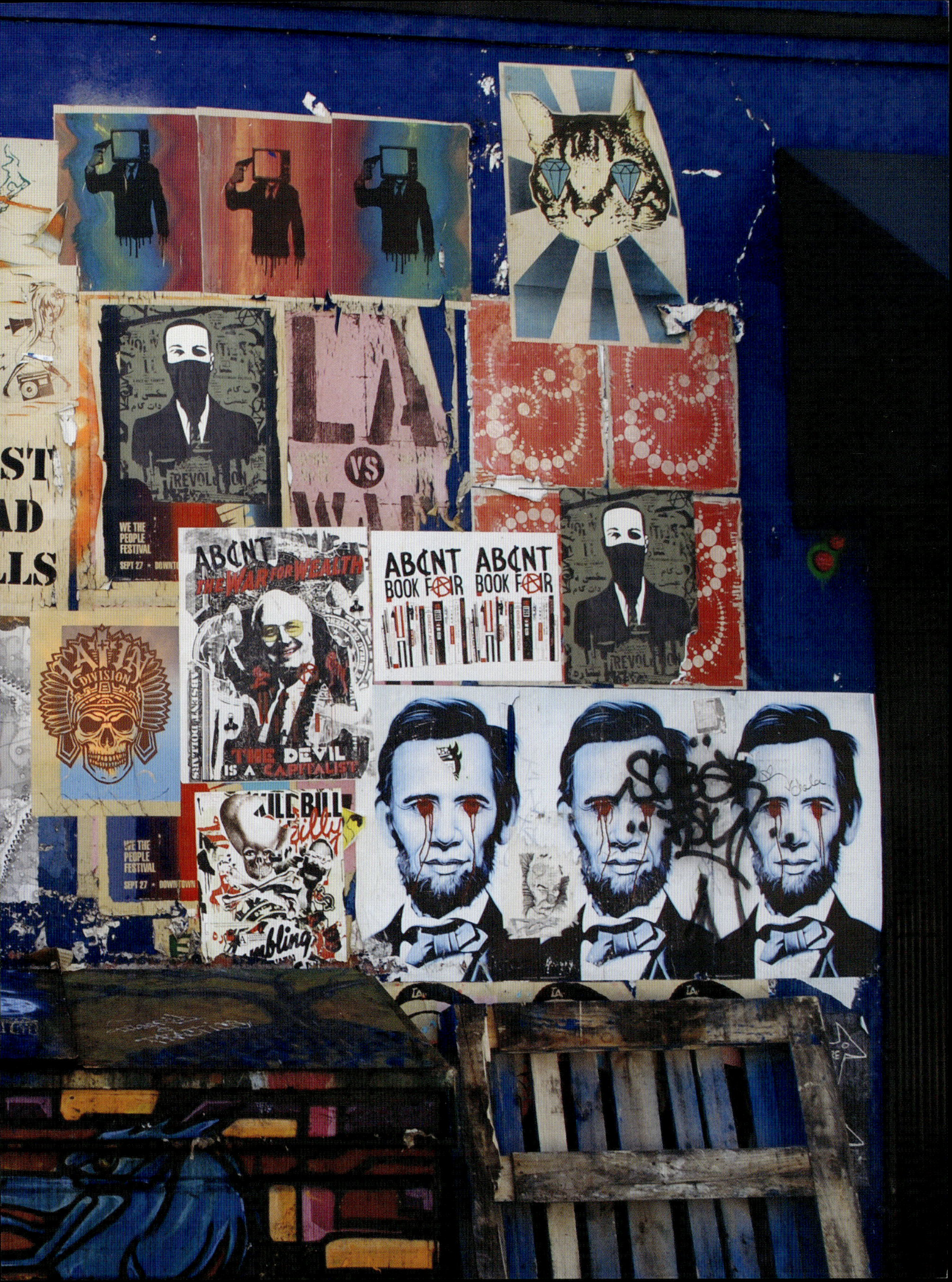
ABCNT
THE WAR FOR WEALTH
THE DEVIL
IS A CAPITALIST
ABCNT
BOOK FAIR
ABCNT
BOOK FAIR
VS
WE THE
PEOPLE
FESTIVAL
SEPT 27 • DOWNTOWN
WE THE
PEOPLE
FESTIVAL
SEPT 27 • DOWNTOWN
DIVISION

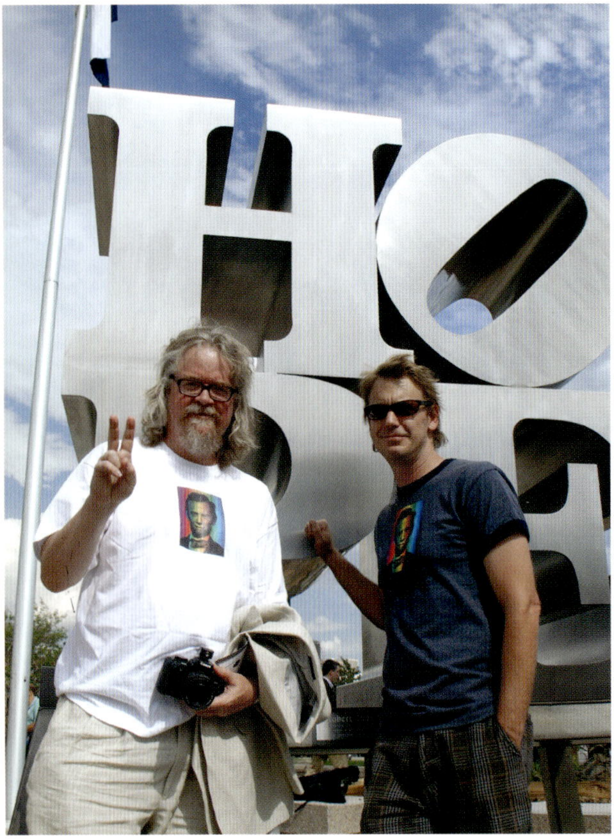

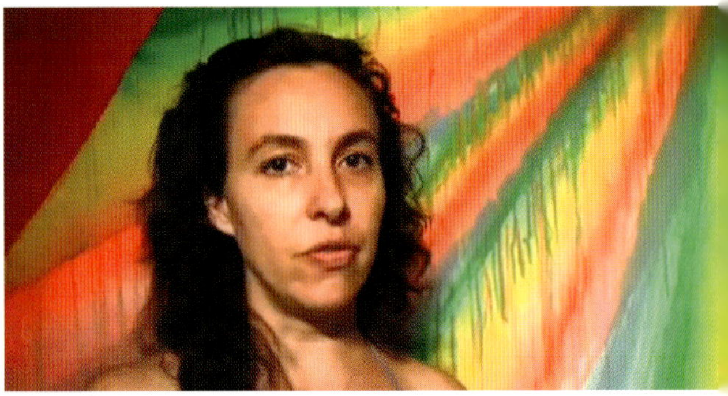

Maya Hayuk

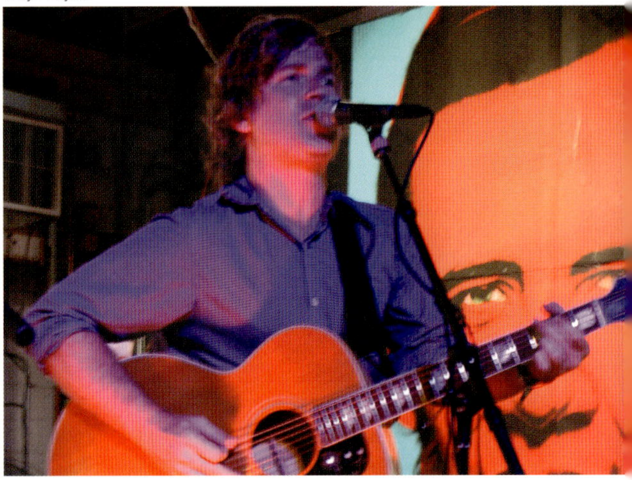

Matthew Caws

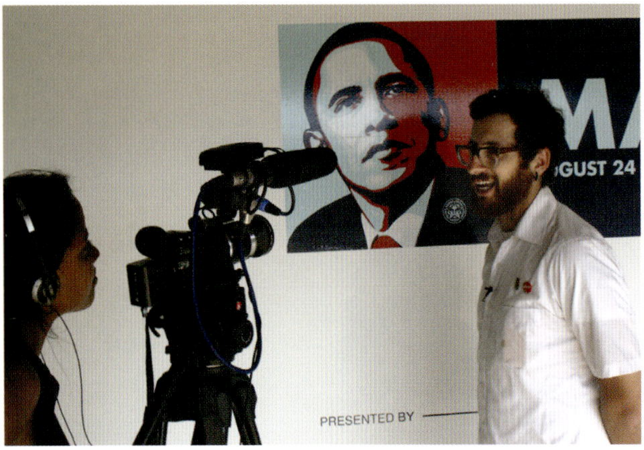

Yosi Sergant

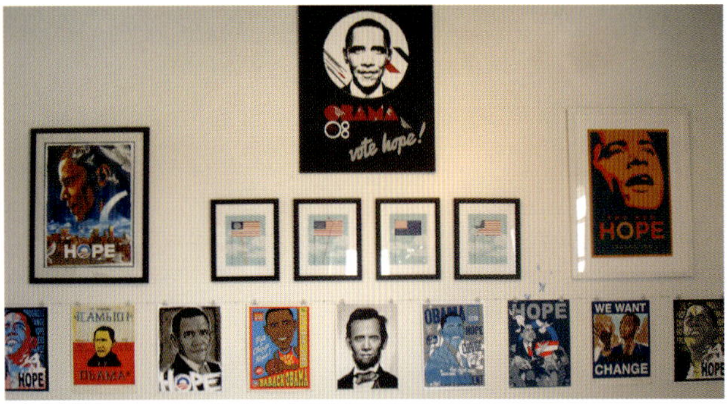

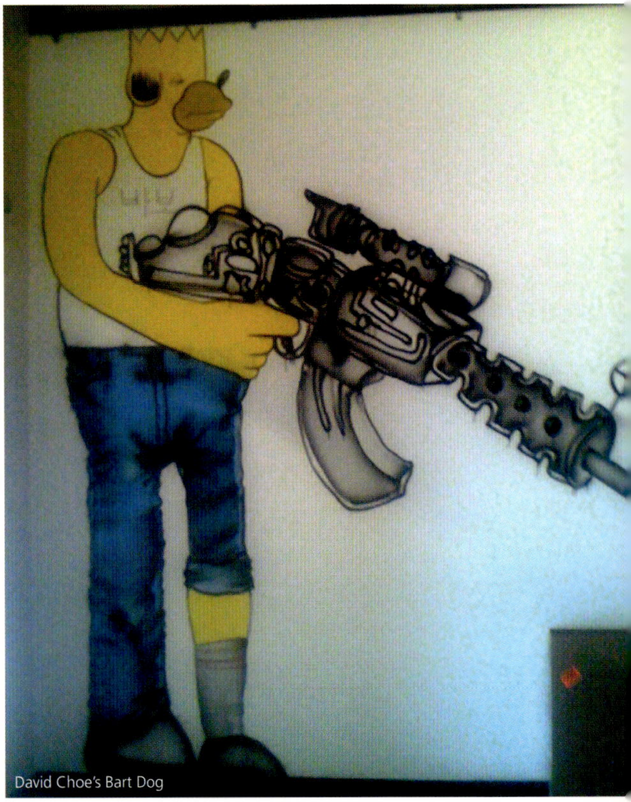

David Choe's Bart Dog

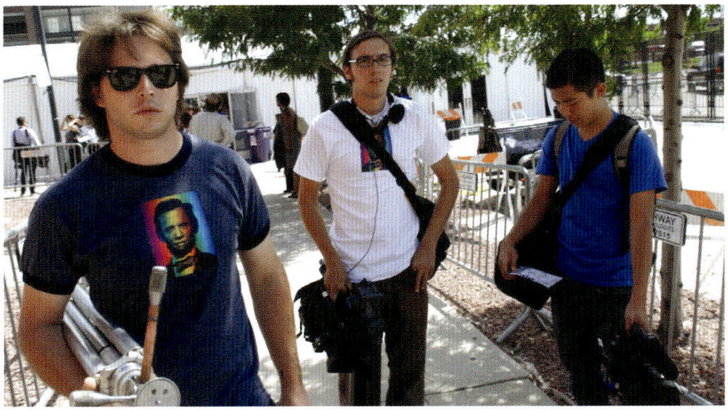

Denver

Democratic National Convention Manifest Hope

All I can really say about the DNC and Manifest Hope experience is it was pure and utter insanity (but in a good way). See the Abraham Obama movie if you don't believe me.
–DG

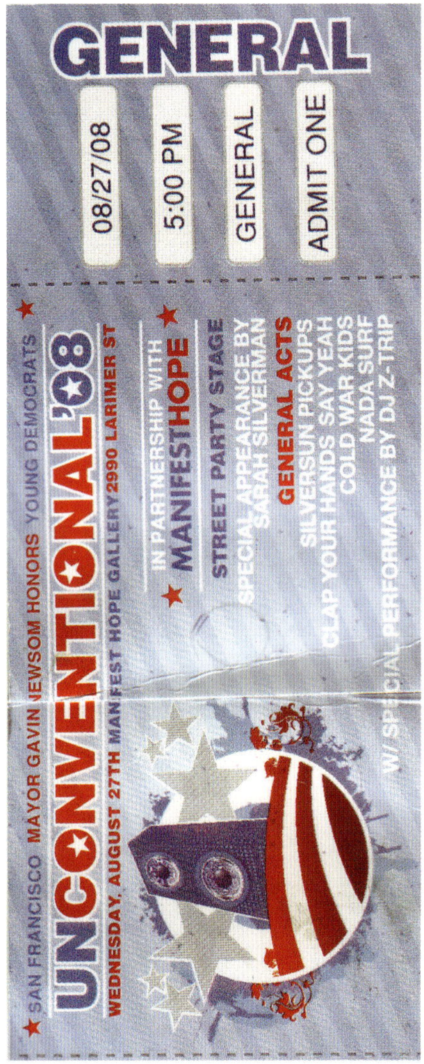

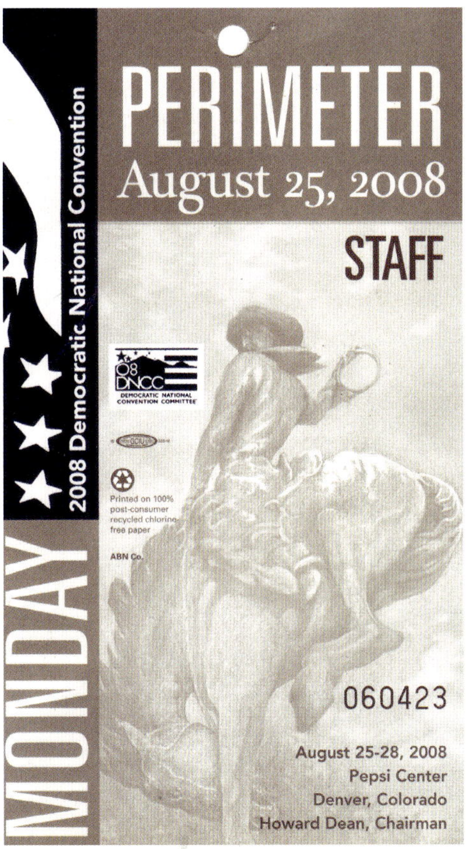

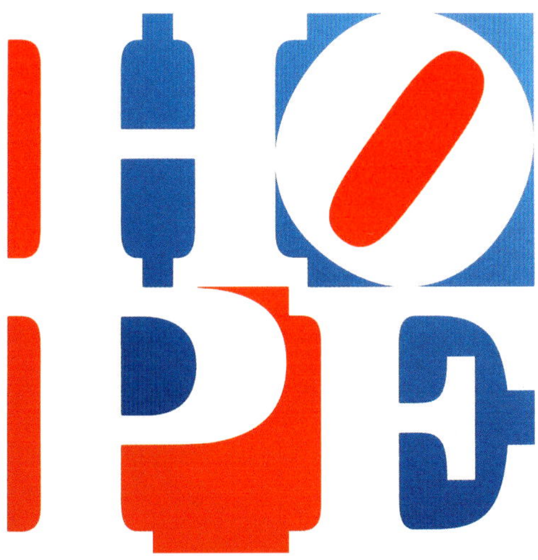

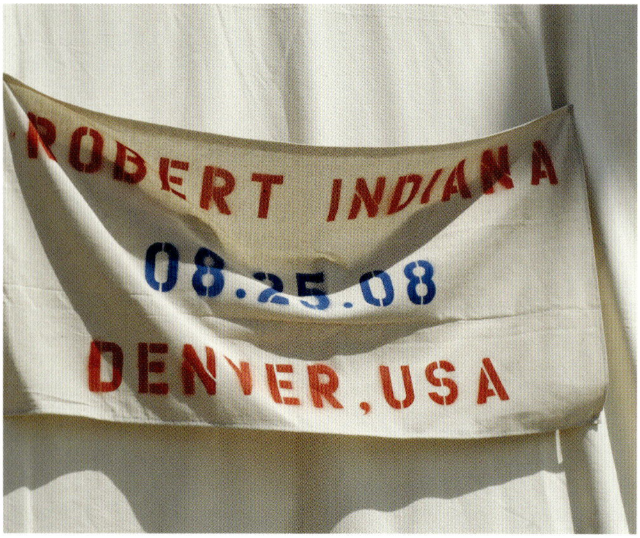

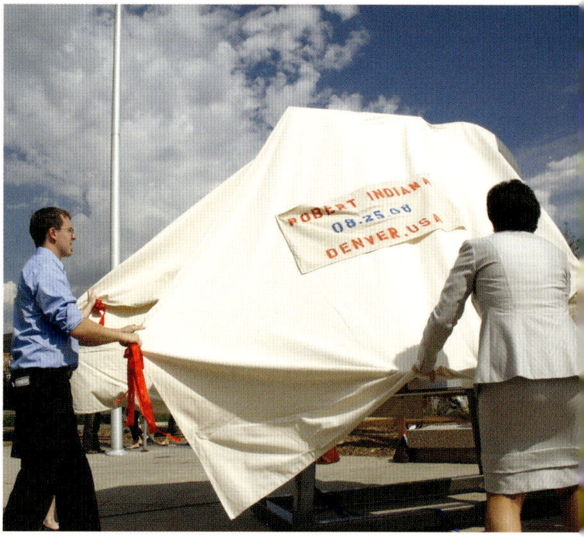

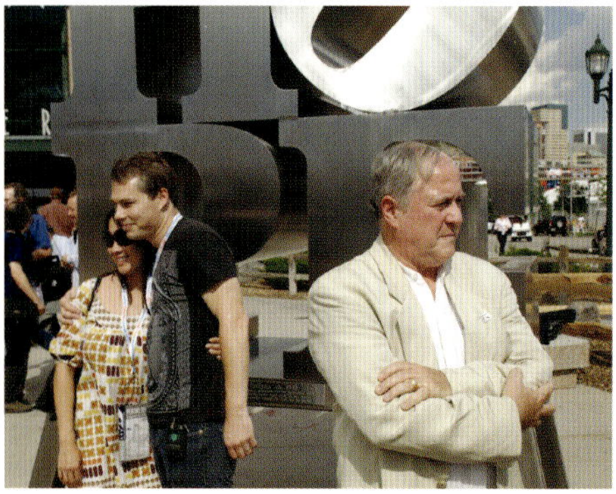

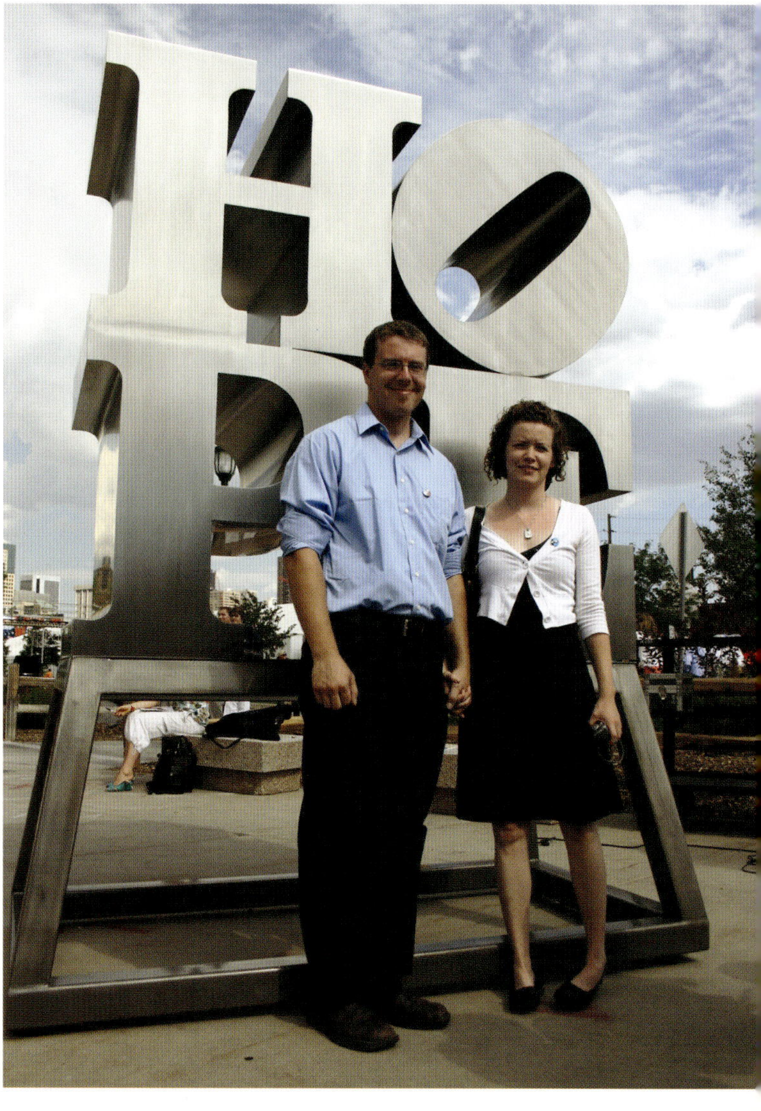

Left: From Robert Indiana's *Hope* sculpture installation fabricated by Lauren Holmgren and Josh Dow of Green Foundry to Shepard and Amanda Fairey.

Right: From the Reverend Al Sharpton's reaction to the Abraham Obama image and stickering with *The Daily Show* guys, there was never a dull moment at the DNC.

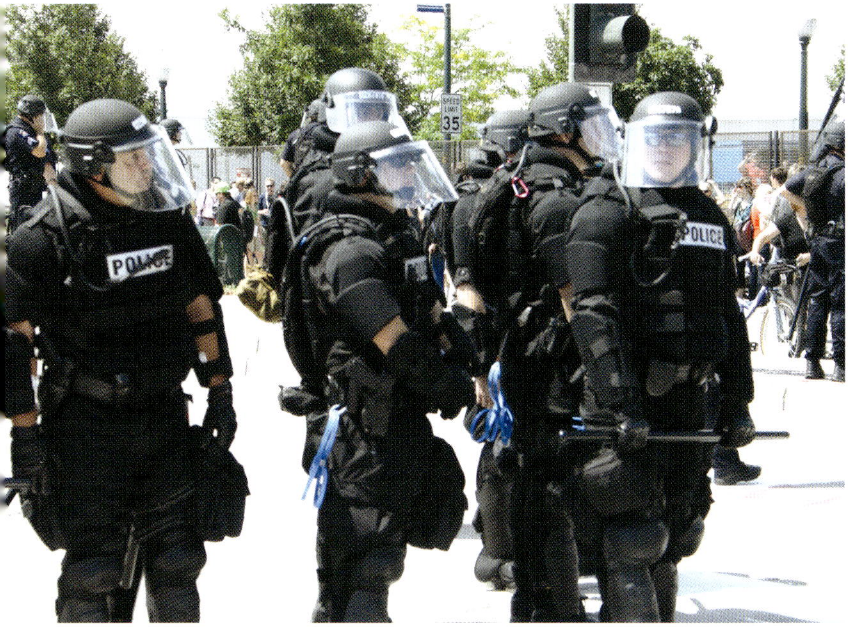
POLICE
POLICE
SPEED LIMIT
35

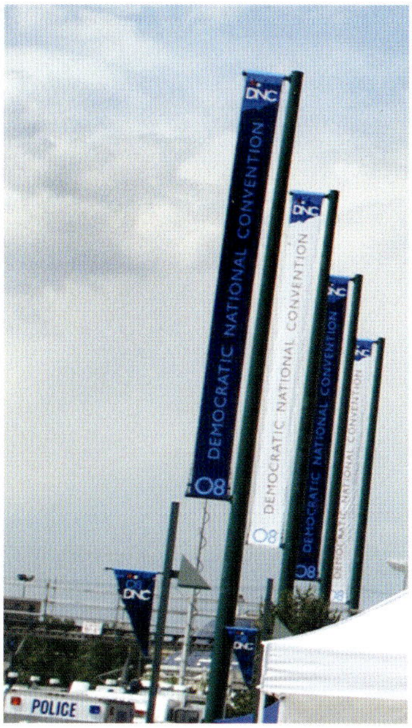
DNC
DEMOCRATIC NATIONAL CONVENTION
O8
POLICE

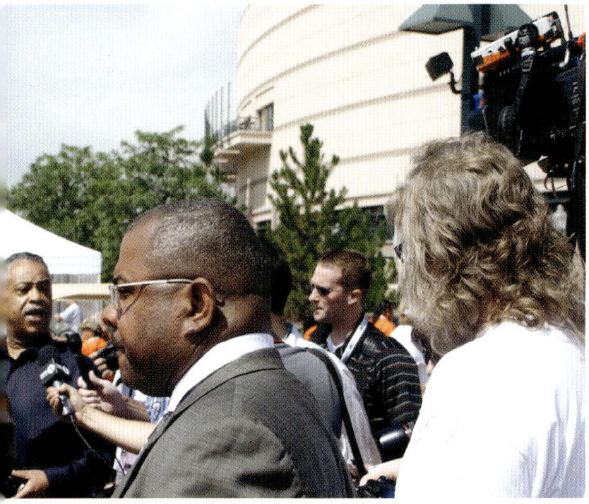

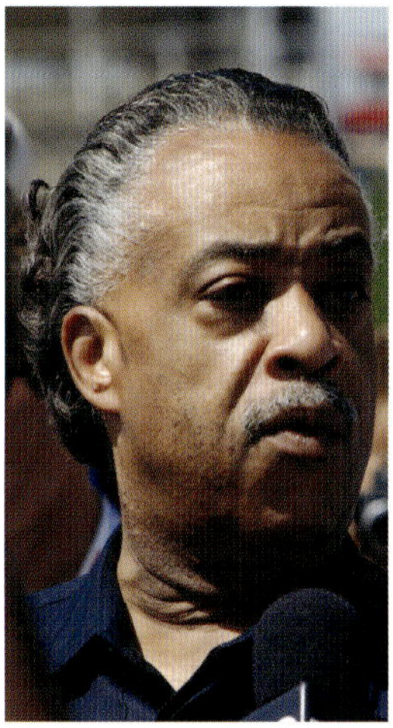

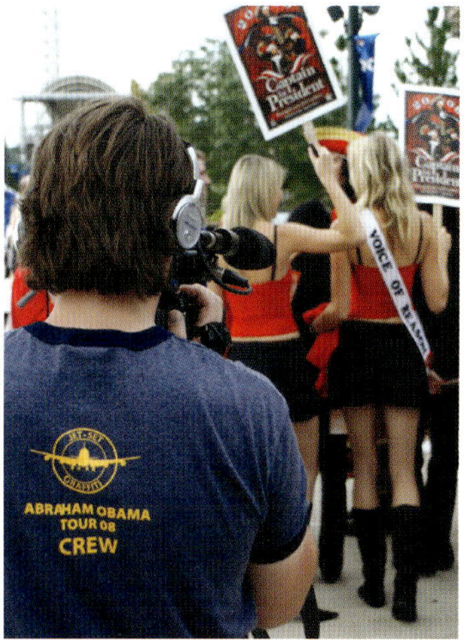
Captain President
ABRAHAM OBAMA
TOUR 08
CREW

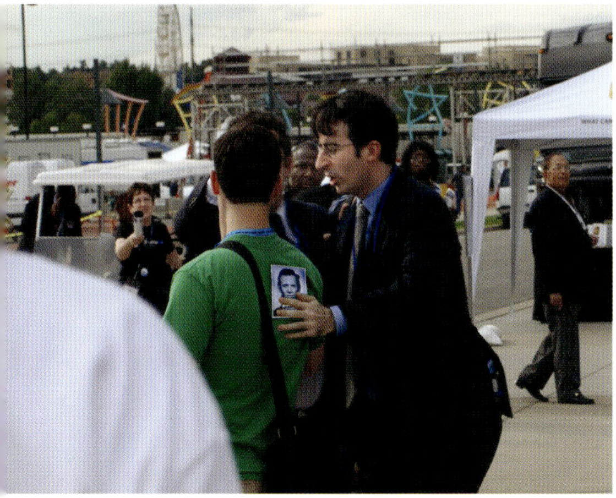

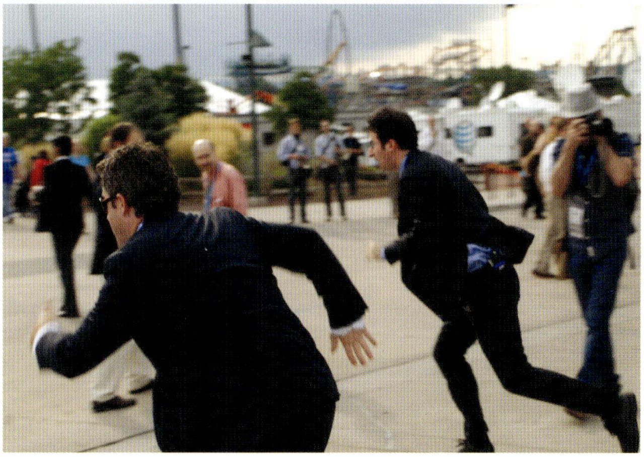

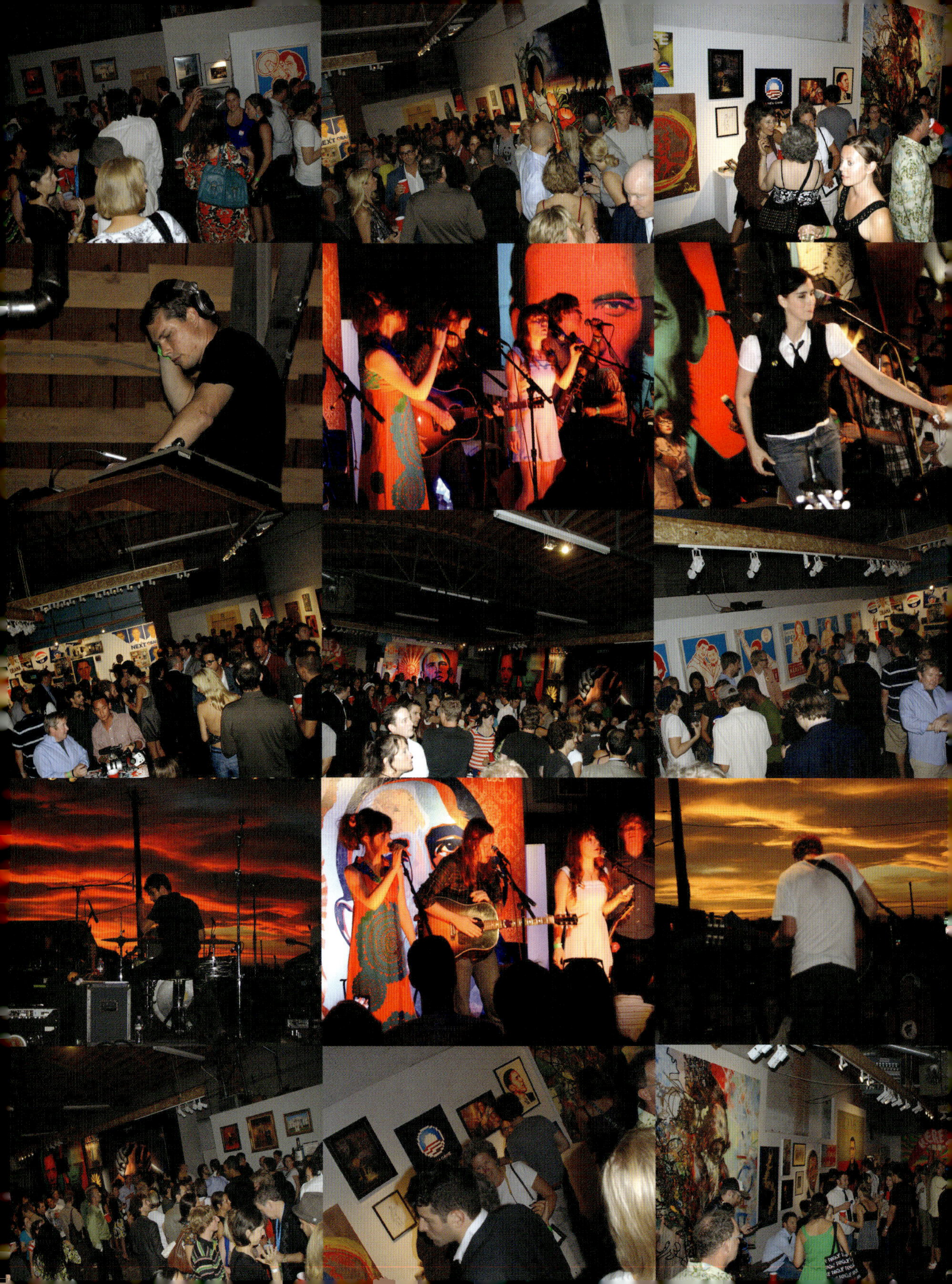

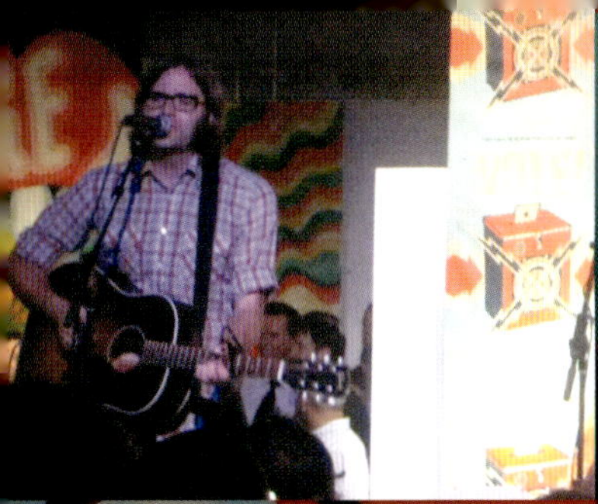
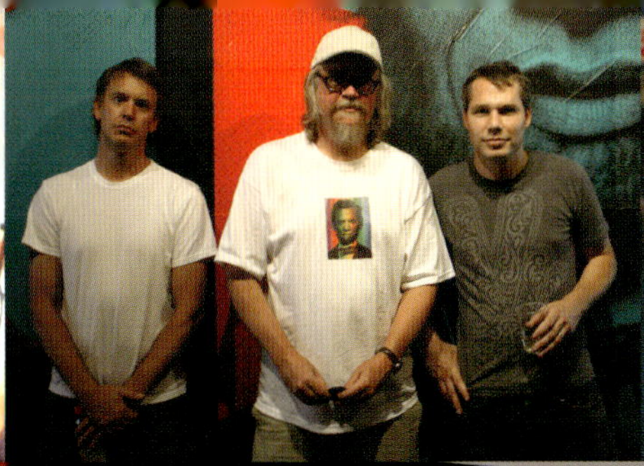
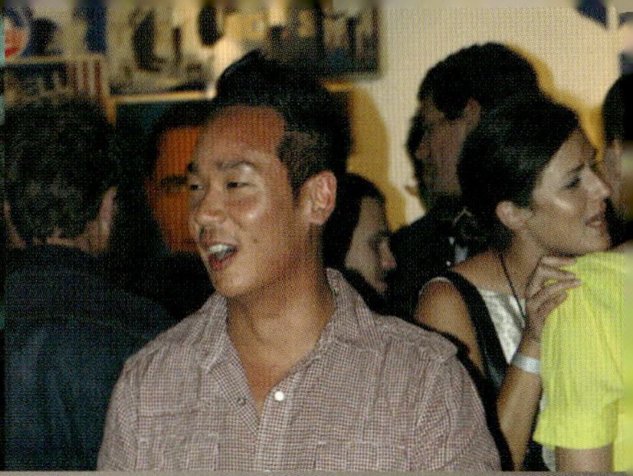
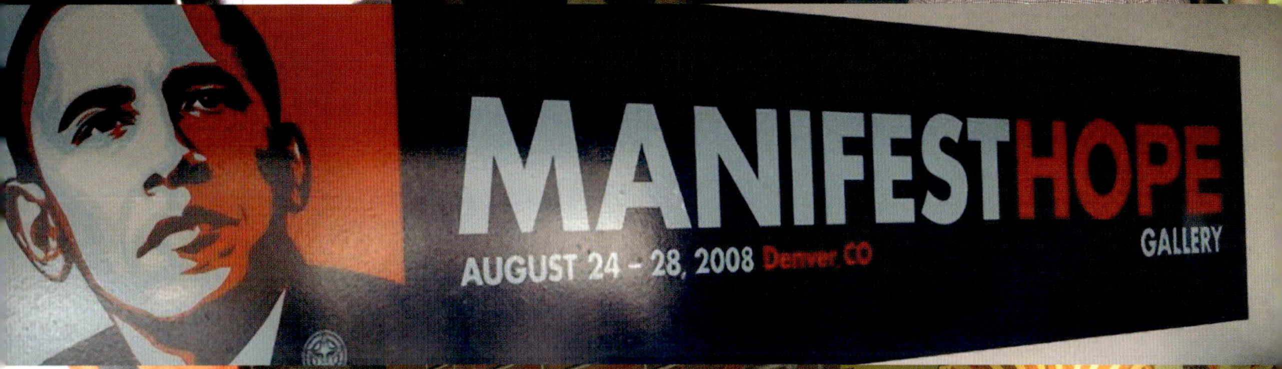
MANIFESTHOPE
GALLERY
AUGUST 24 – 28, 2008 Denver, CO
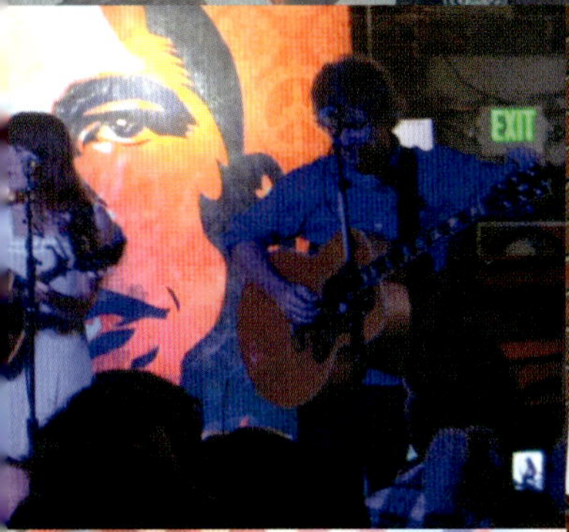
EXIT
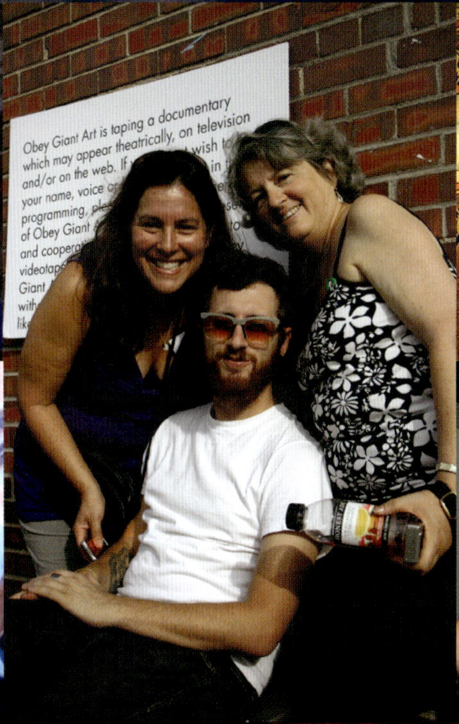
Obey Giant Art is taping a documentary
which may appear theatrically, on television
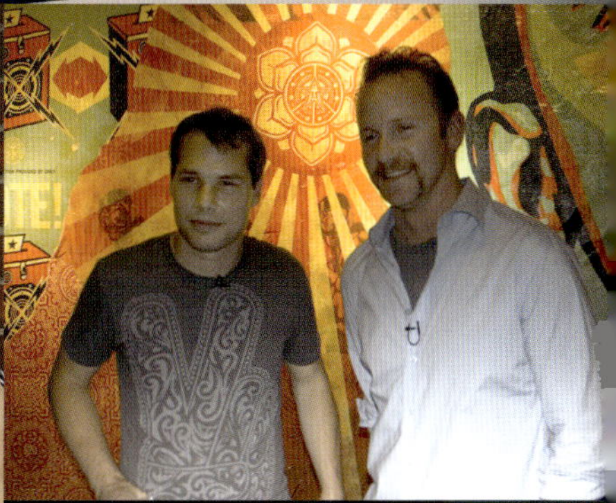
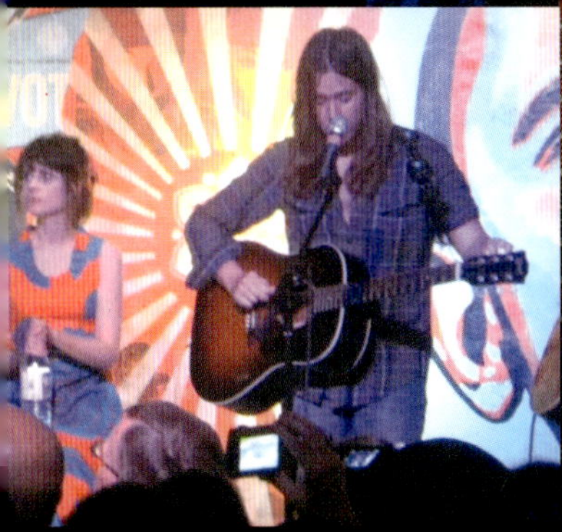
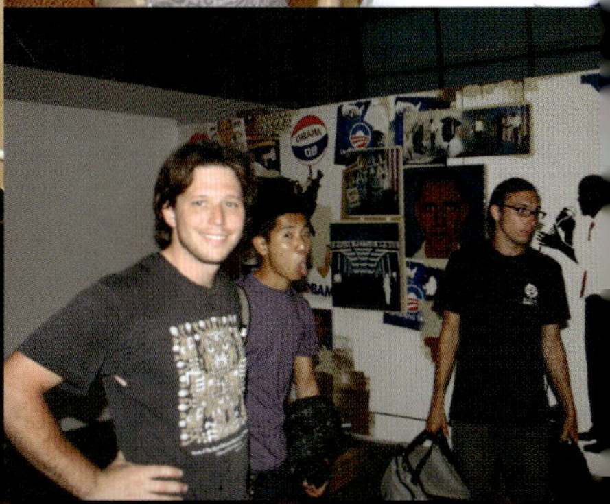

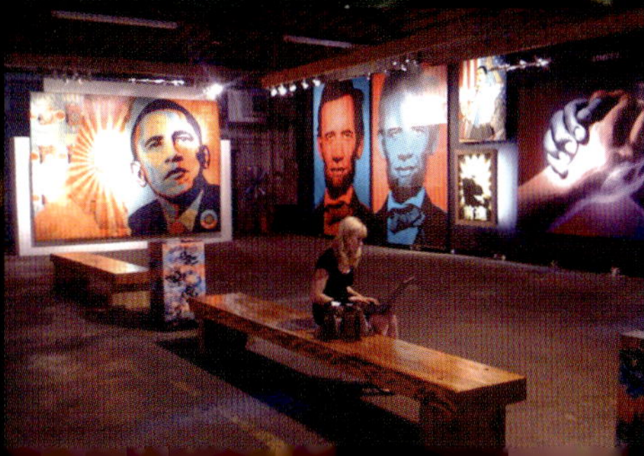
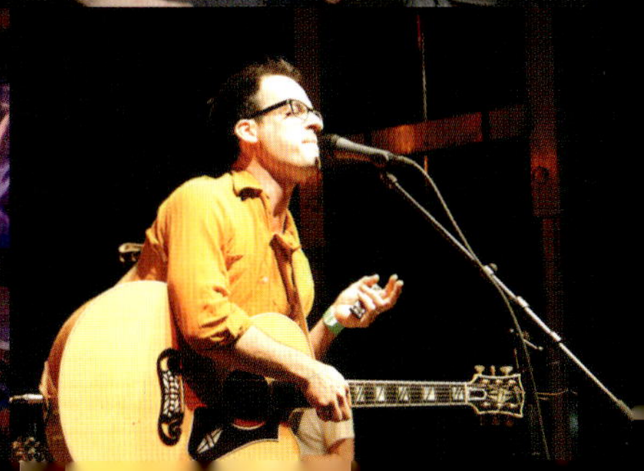

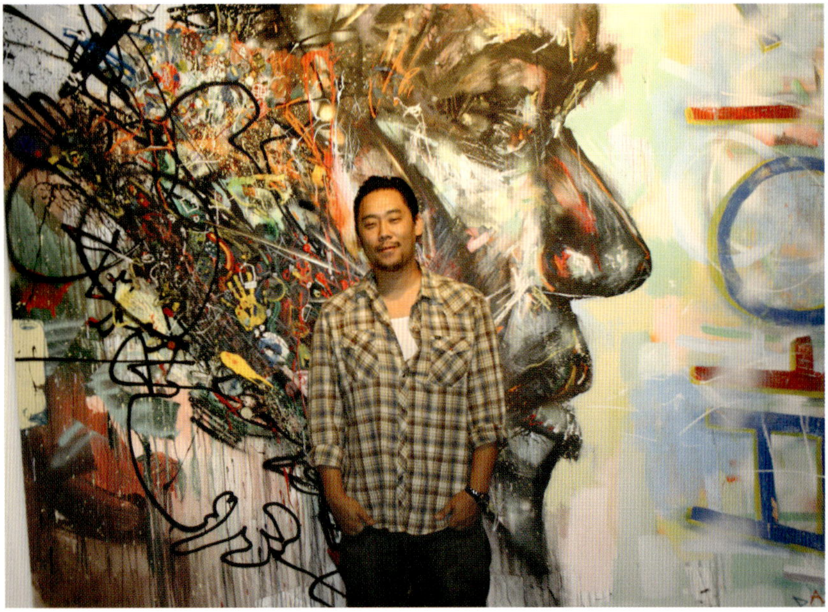

David Choe

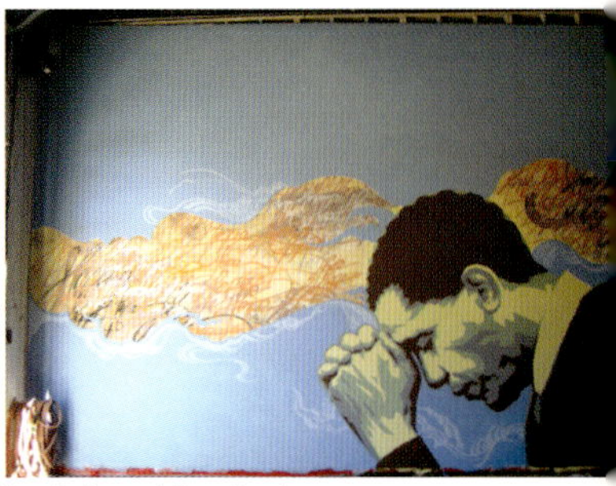

Dan Buller and Gene Pendon

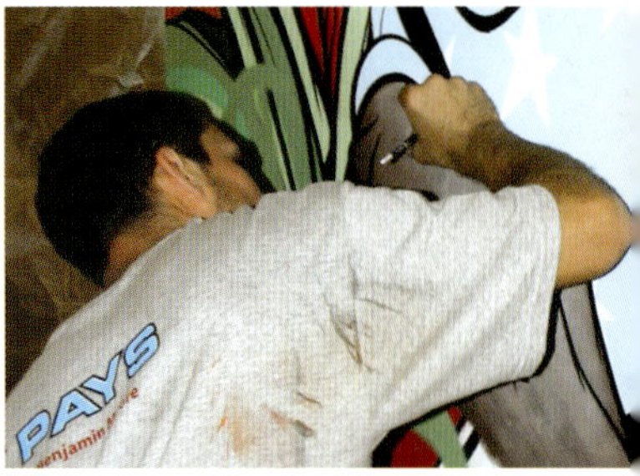

Sam Flores

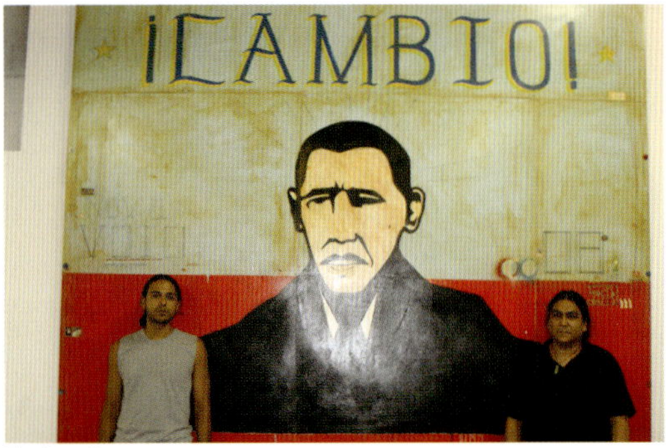

The Date Farmers

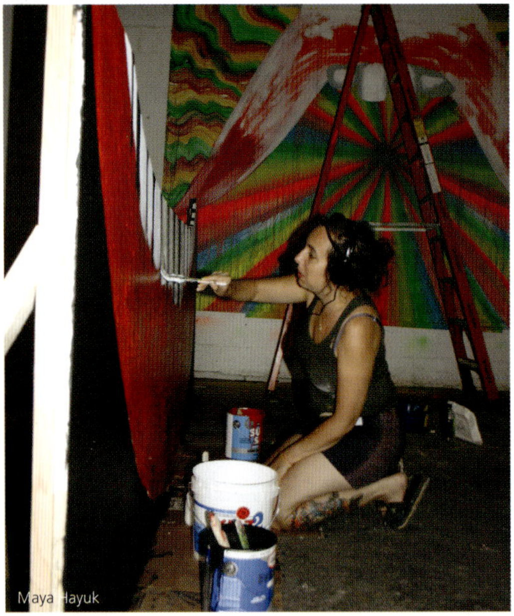

Maya Hayuk

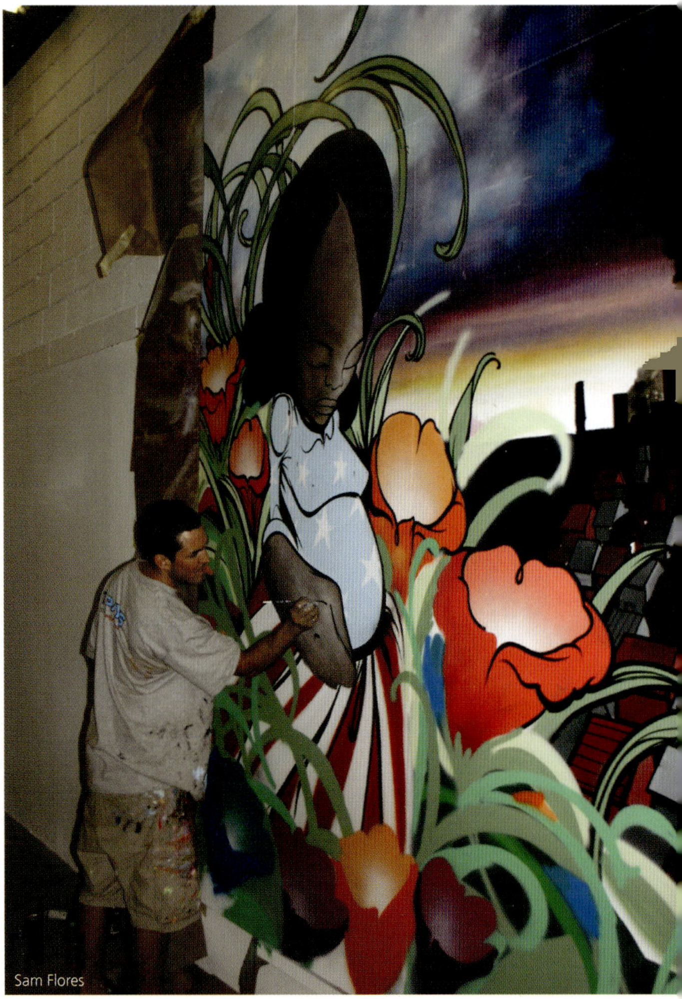

Sam Flores

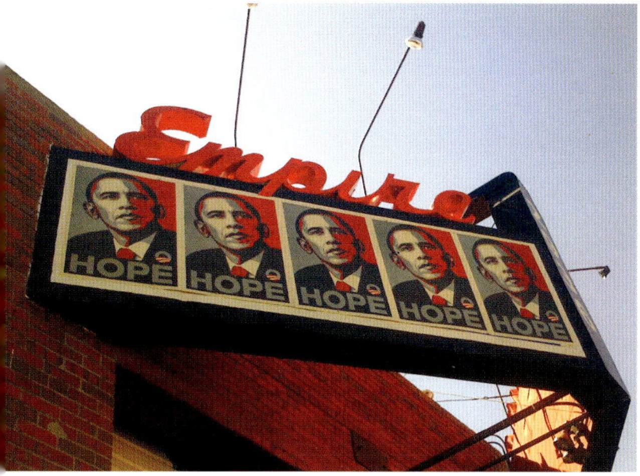

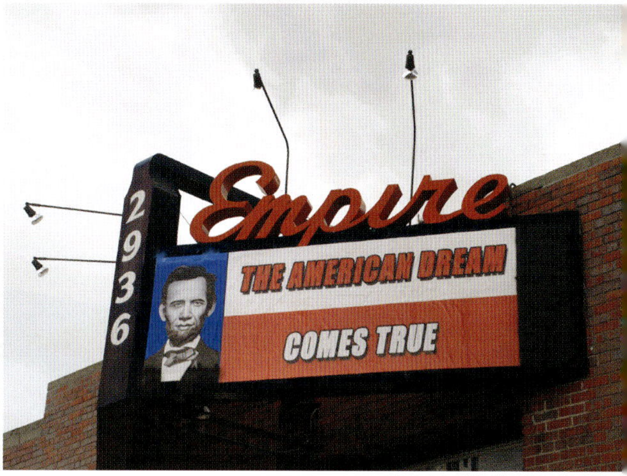

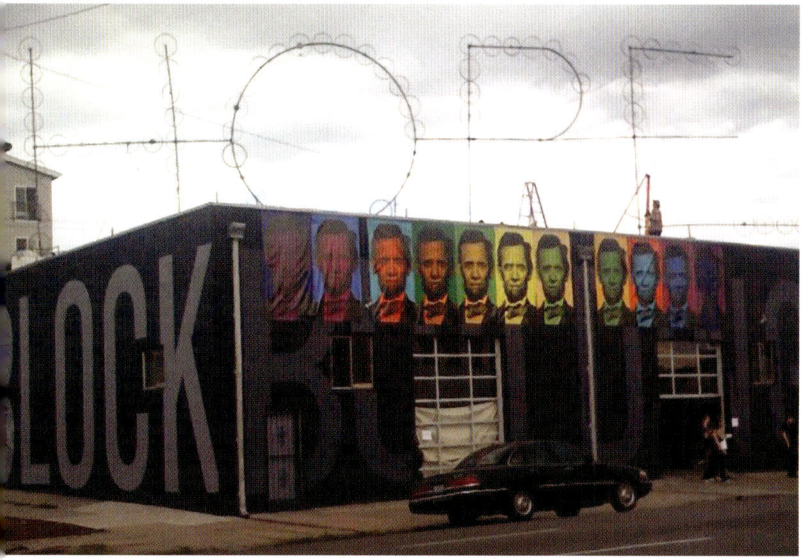

denken Gallery

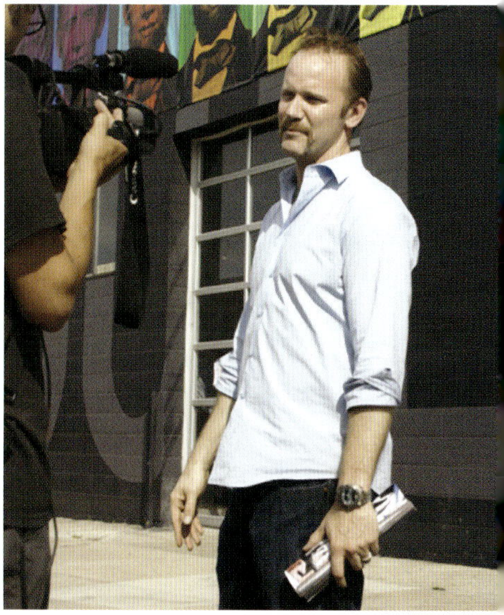
Morgan Spurlock

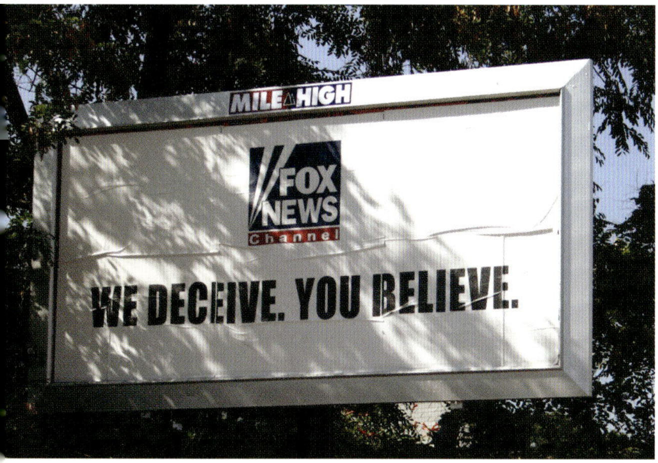

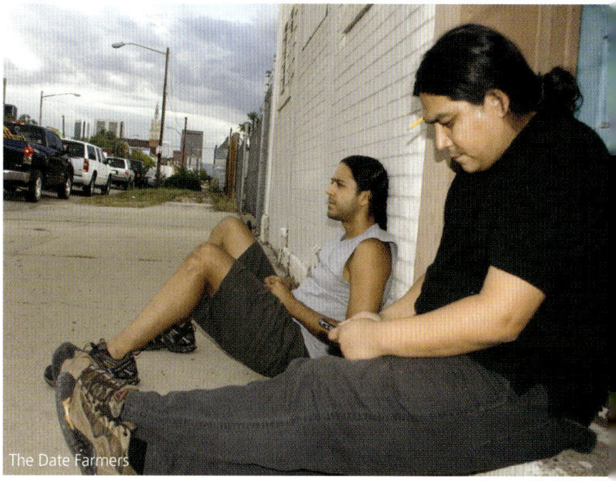
The Date Farmers

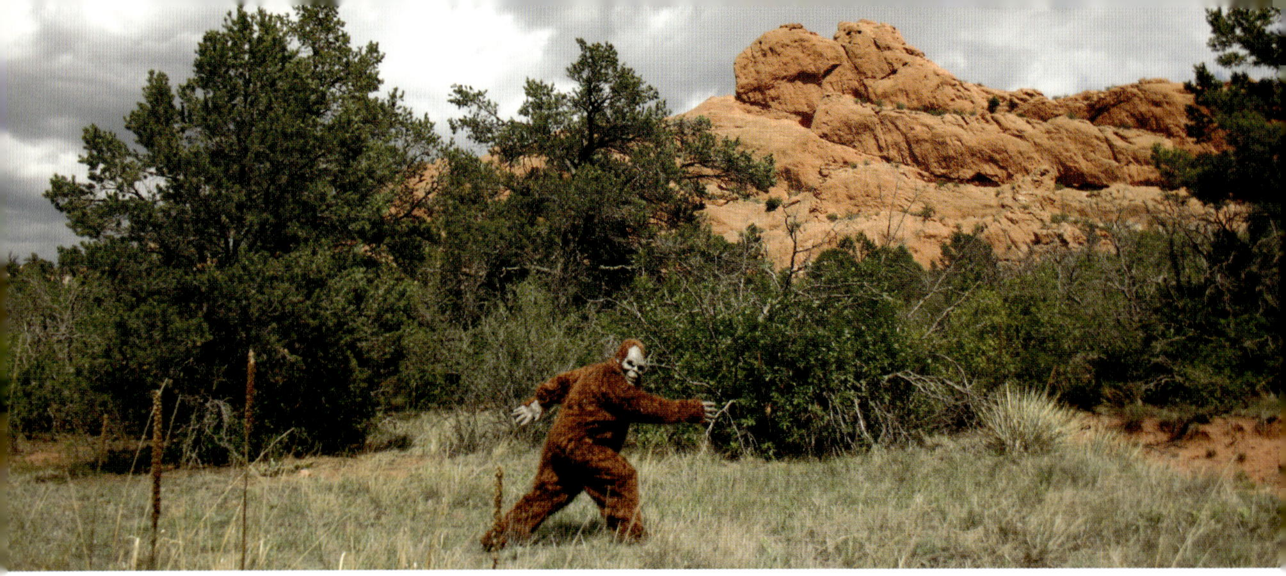

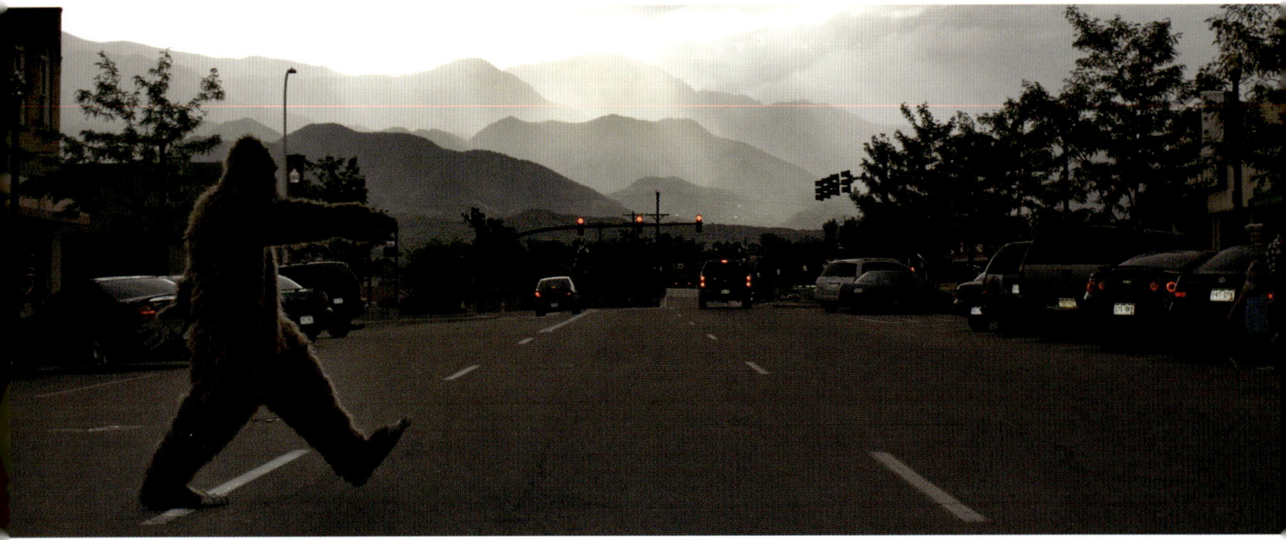

photo by Jeff Kall

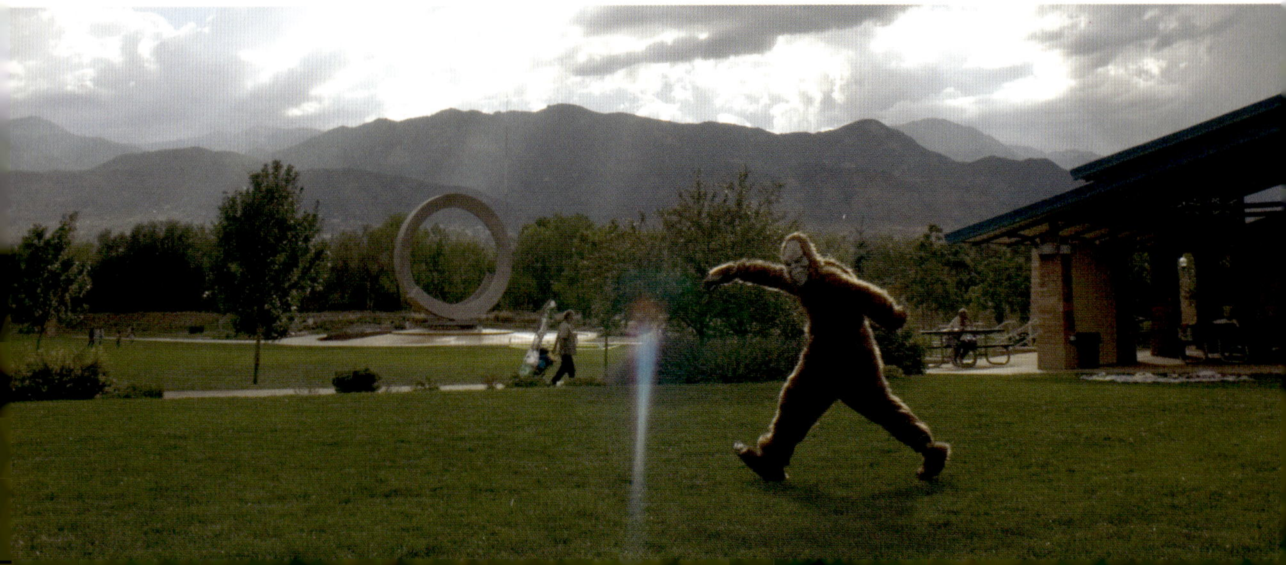

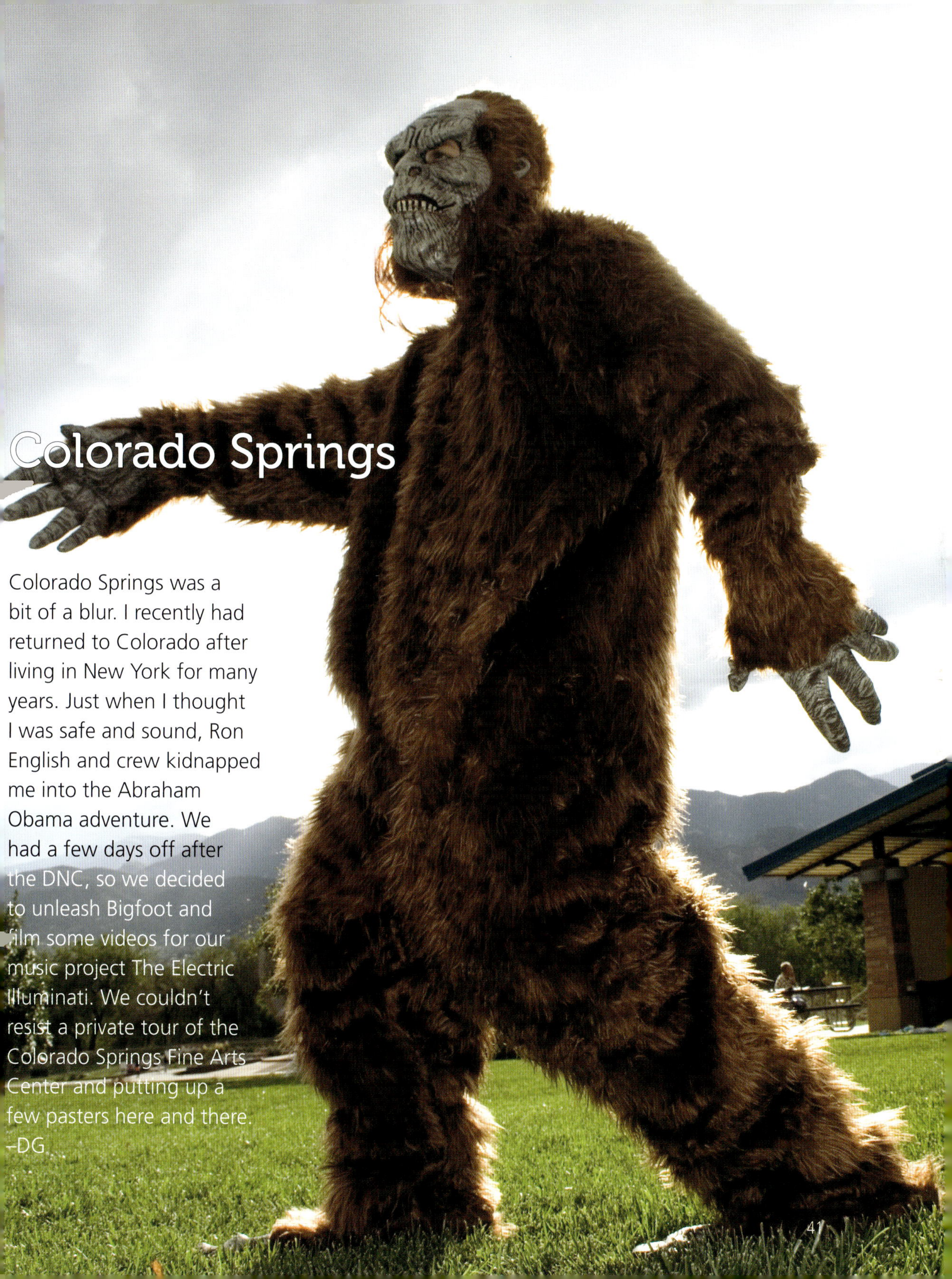

Colorado Springs

Colorado Springs was a bit of a blur. I recently had returned to Colorado after living in New York for many years. Just when I thought I was safe and sound, Ron English and crew kidnapped me into the Abraham Obama adventure. We had a few days off after the DNC, so we decided to unleash Bigfoot and film some videos for our music project The Electric Illuminati. We couldn't resist a private tour of the Colorado Springs Fine Arts Center and putting up a few pasters here and there. –DG

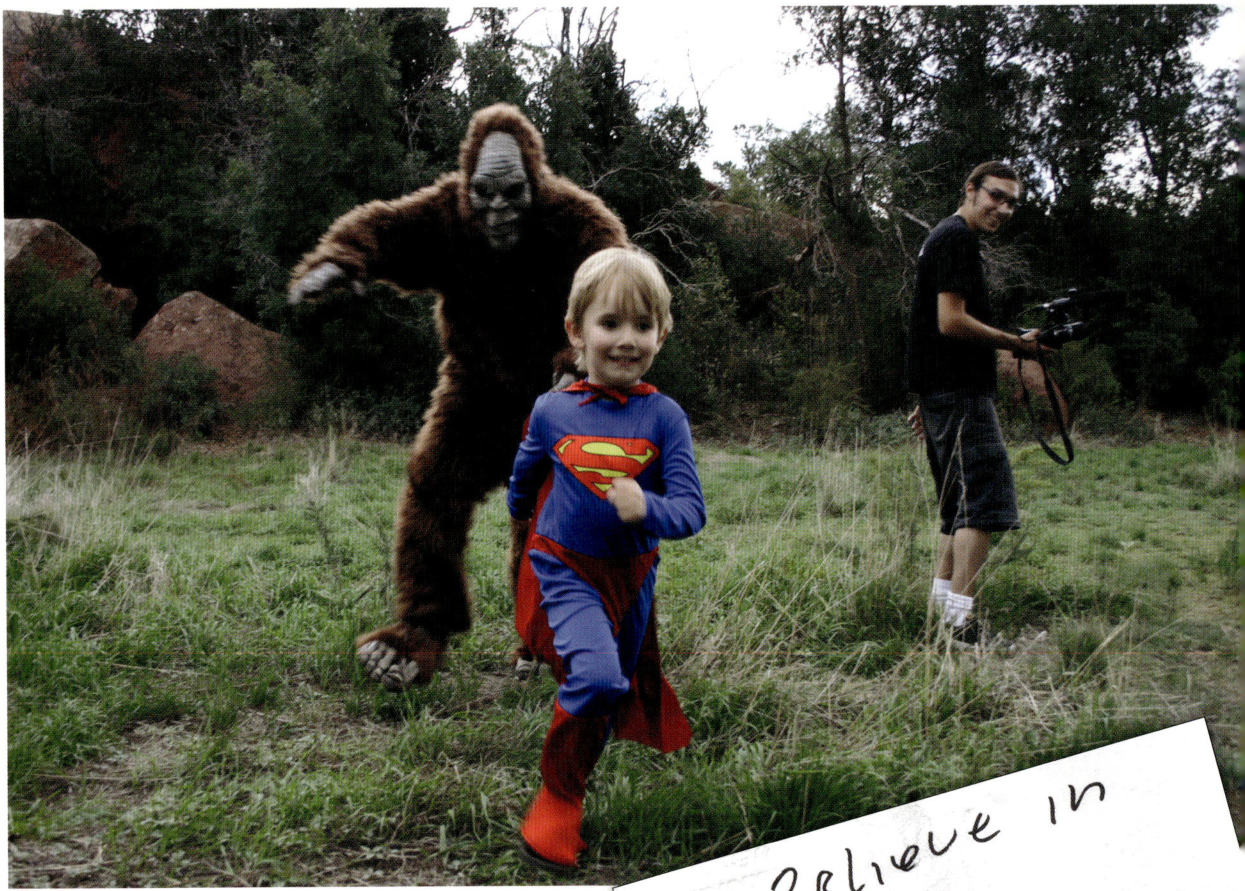

Left: Bigfoot and a very young Superman become part of the Abraham Obama tour in Garden of The Gods in Colorado Springs.

Right: The crew works out the song "I Believe In Bigfoot."

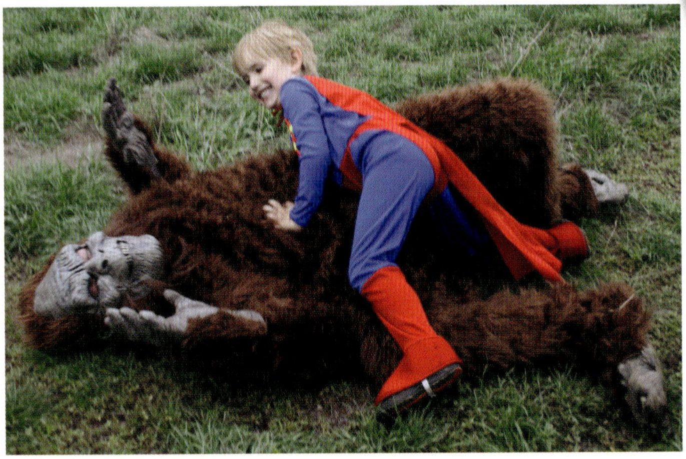

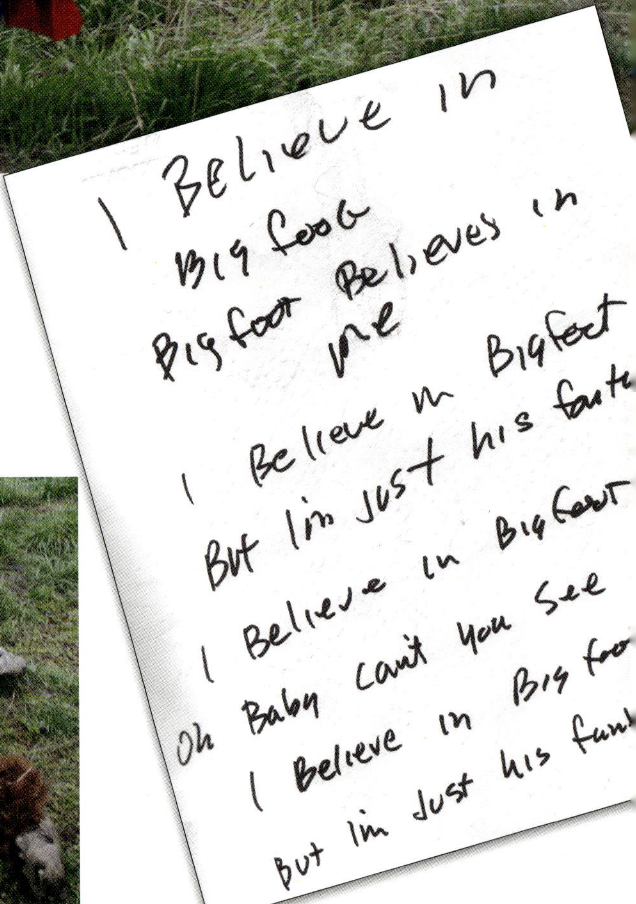

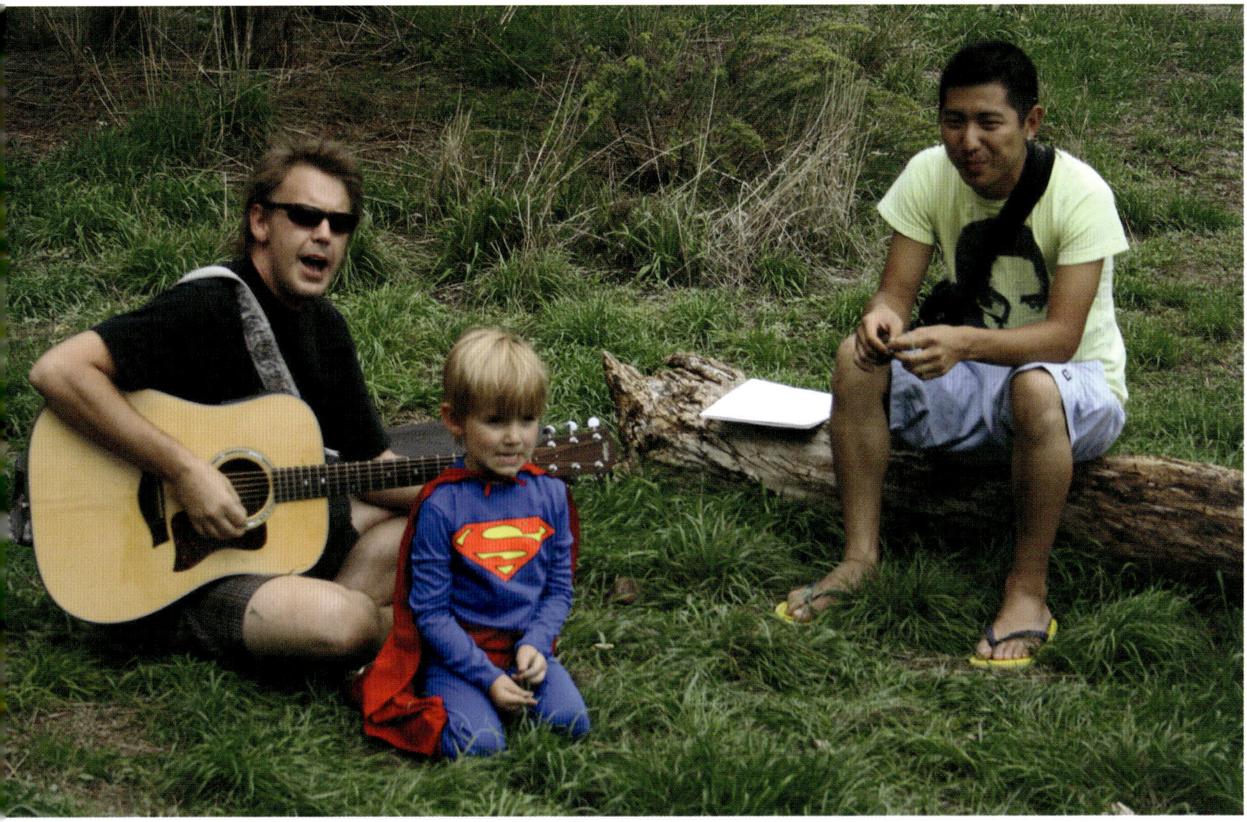

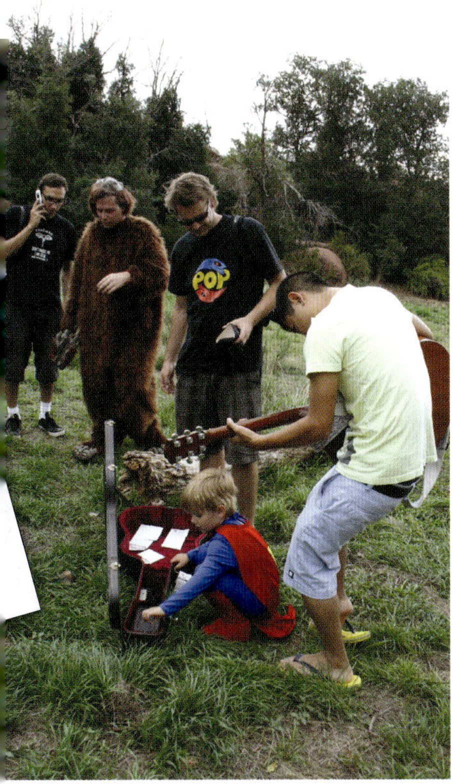
POP

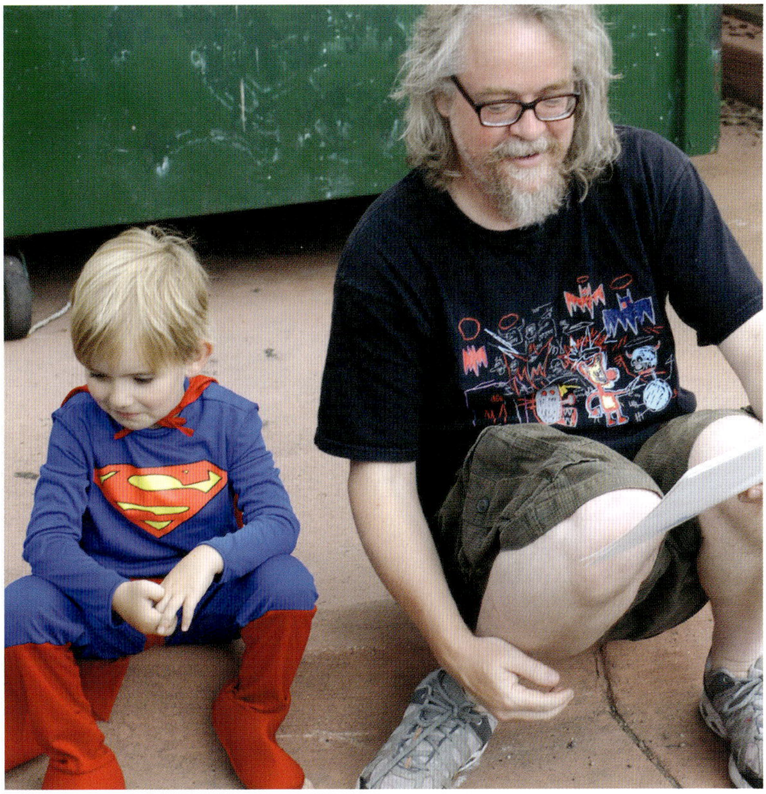

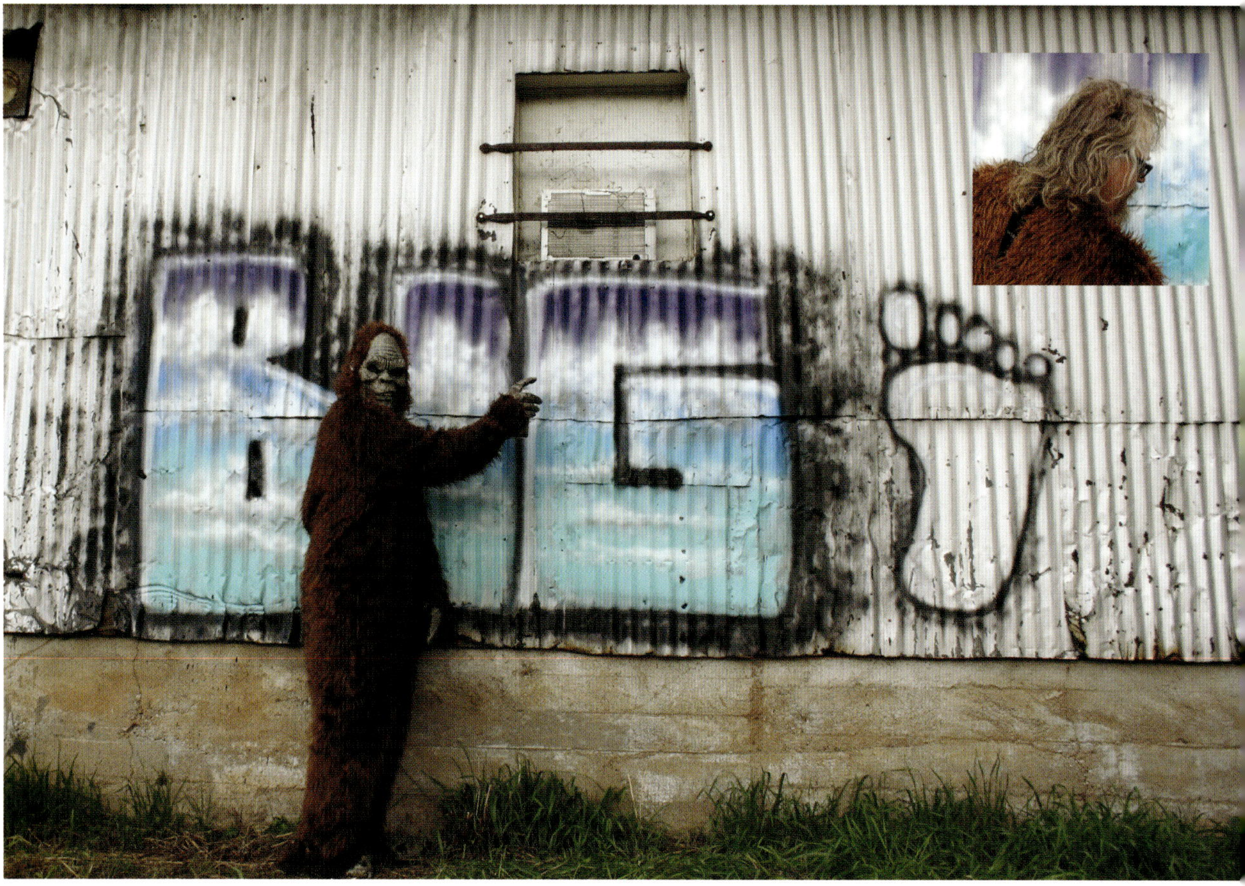
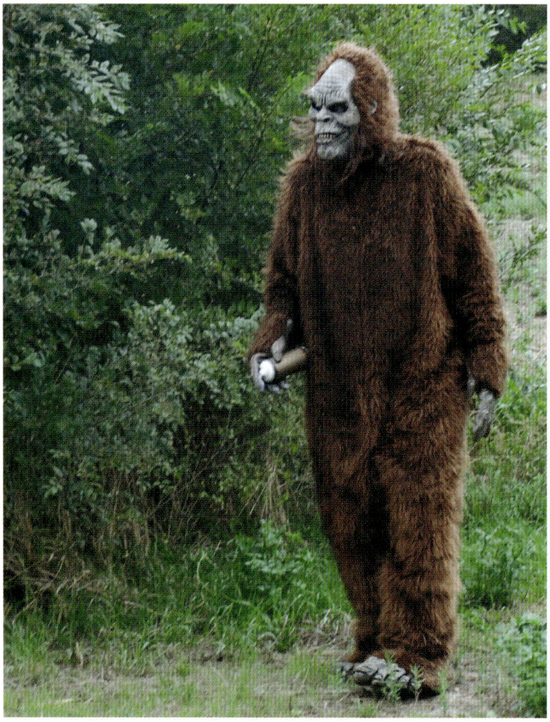
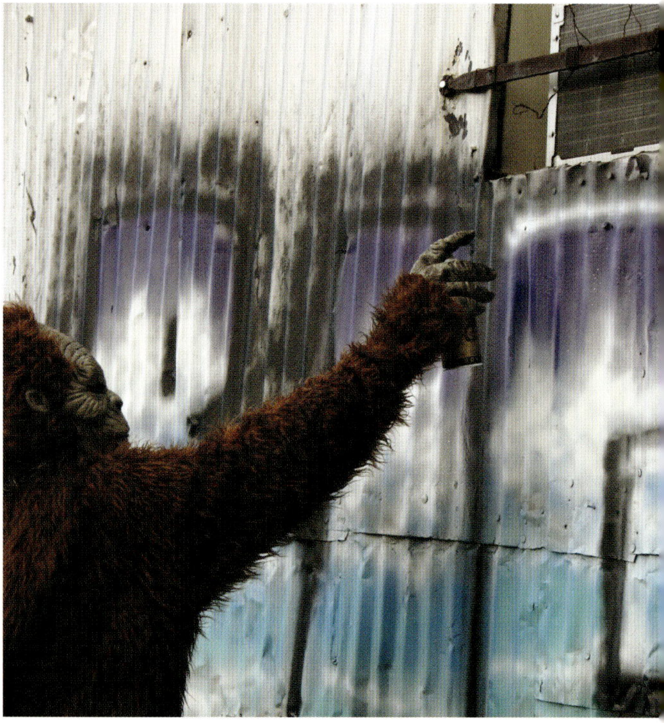

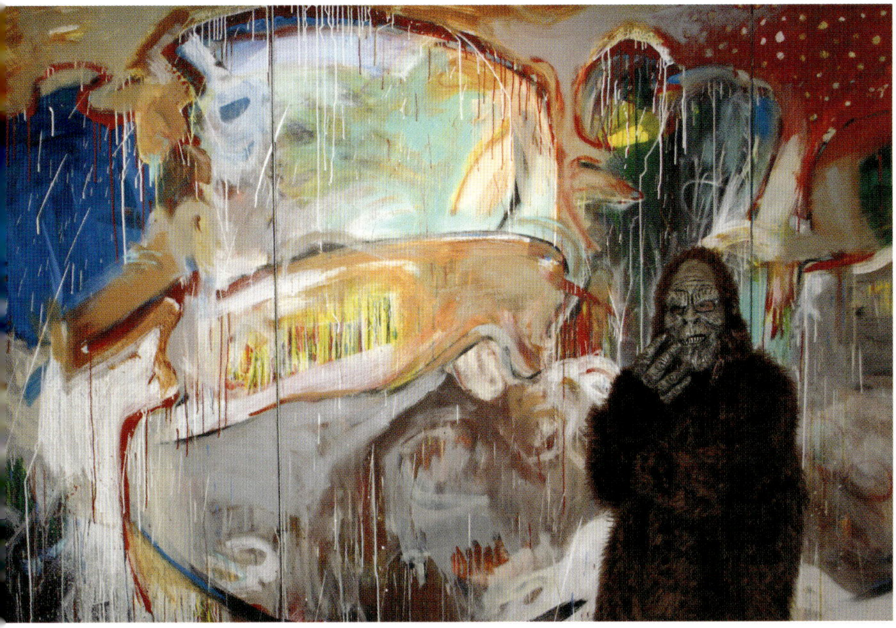

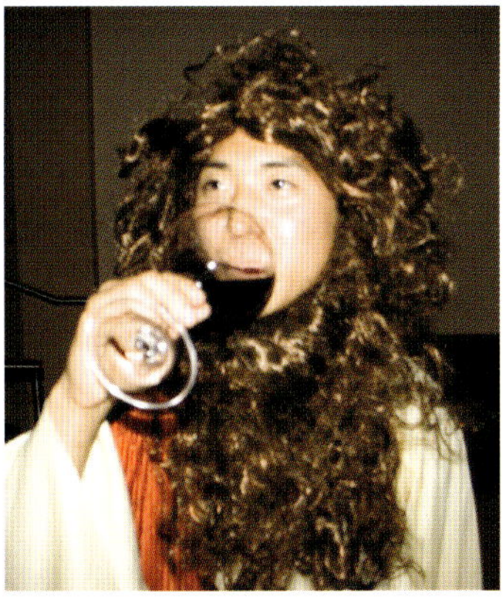

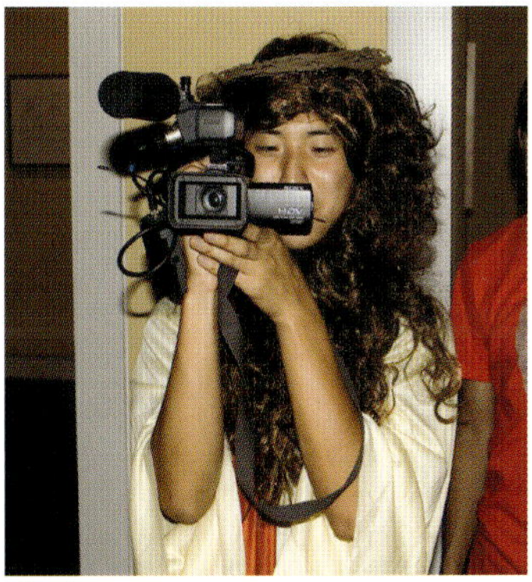

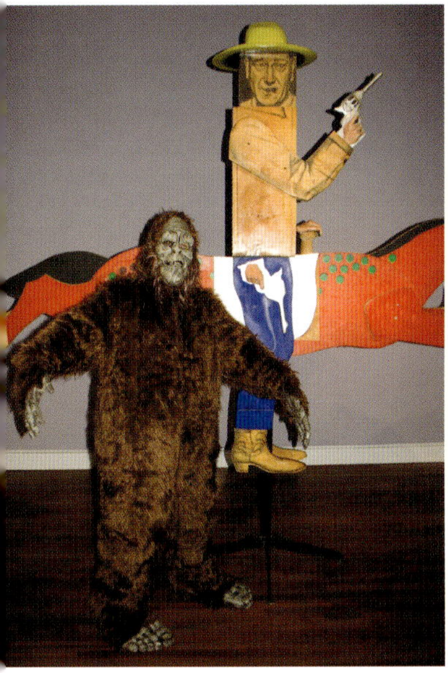

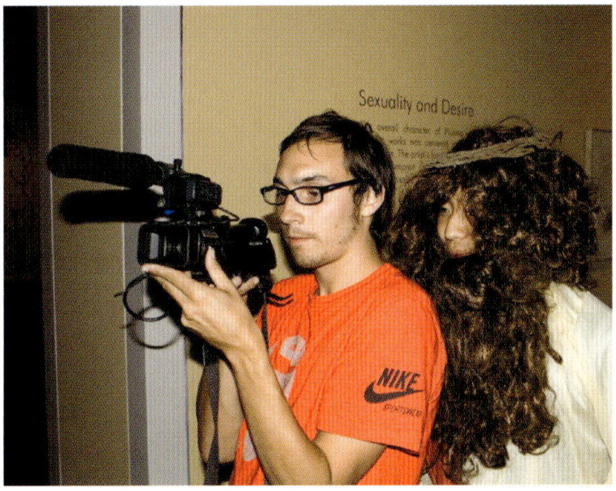

Left: Bigfoot caught doing graffiti in the Depot Arts District.

Bigfoot, Jesus, and crew at the Fine Arts Center right before crashing a high school reunion.

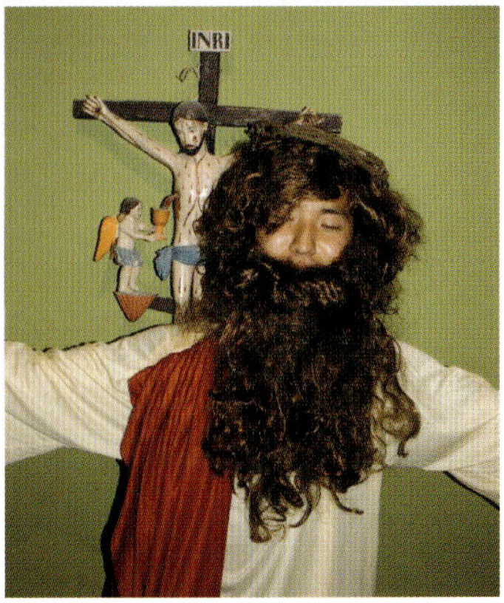

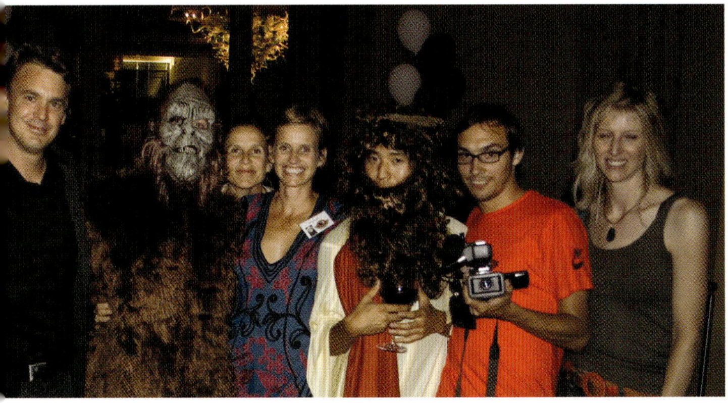

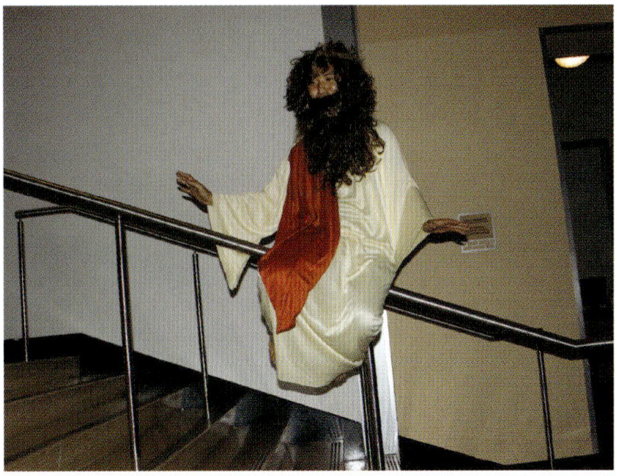

Which of these is not like the others?

Boston, Jersey City, Los Angeles, New York City, San Francisco, Denver, Colorado Springs

by Kat Tudor, Creative Director, Smokebrush Foundation For The Arts

I'm going to call Colorado Springs the outlier here. So how'd we even get in this book anyway? Why would Abraham Obama end up coming here, where seldom is heard a liberal word? We have nine local hipsters that I can think of, hardly enough to qualify for the Abraham Obama sweepstakes. But I think we wooed him here with our charm and chutzpah, refusing to believe or live up to our national reputation as conservative, Christianist, and crazy (although I can see how you might get that idea). I'll only say that we're scenic and sinful and right in the red, red heart of America. And where do you think an image like Abraham Obama might have more impact–in San Francisco, where there are thousands of progressives per square inch of cutting-edge art, or Colorado Springs, where–well, not so much. Abraham Obama, at first glance, does not seem to be a good fit for our community, but that is exactly why he's a perfect fit. We welcomed him here to galvanize conversation and controversy and a civic investigation into what is art. The Art Commission determined that AO was art, not politics, so he didn't have to be fined and immediately removed.

Both Ted Haggard and Nikola Tesla have lived in Colorado Springs, drawn here by strong currents. Both electrified the city. Both left town in disgrace, told to go and take their experiments elsewhere. Abraham Obama is a hybrid concept, kind of like Ted/Tesla. Sometimes the strong currents are shifted here by the arrival of a mad genius to the area. Who knows if the real Obama would have gotten the 40% of the vote in El Paso County that he needed to win the state and turn Colorado blue if Abraham Obama had not gotten here first? He looked out over the city from 25 locations and anybody who looked back was compelled to imagine a hybrid thought: black man/president.

I once heard a man call a local talk radio show and say (regarding a controversial piece of public art), "If God had wanted us to have art, he would have made some." That sounds about right to me. So let's call Abraham Obama divinely inspired and watch as he slowly peels away and disappears. At least he wasn't driven out of town like those other bad boys.

Above: Outside The Smokebrush Foundation For The Arts.
Right: Inside The Smokebrush Gallery, Ron signs the vinyl Abraham Obamas.

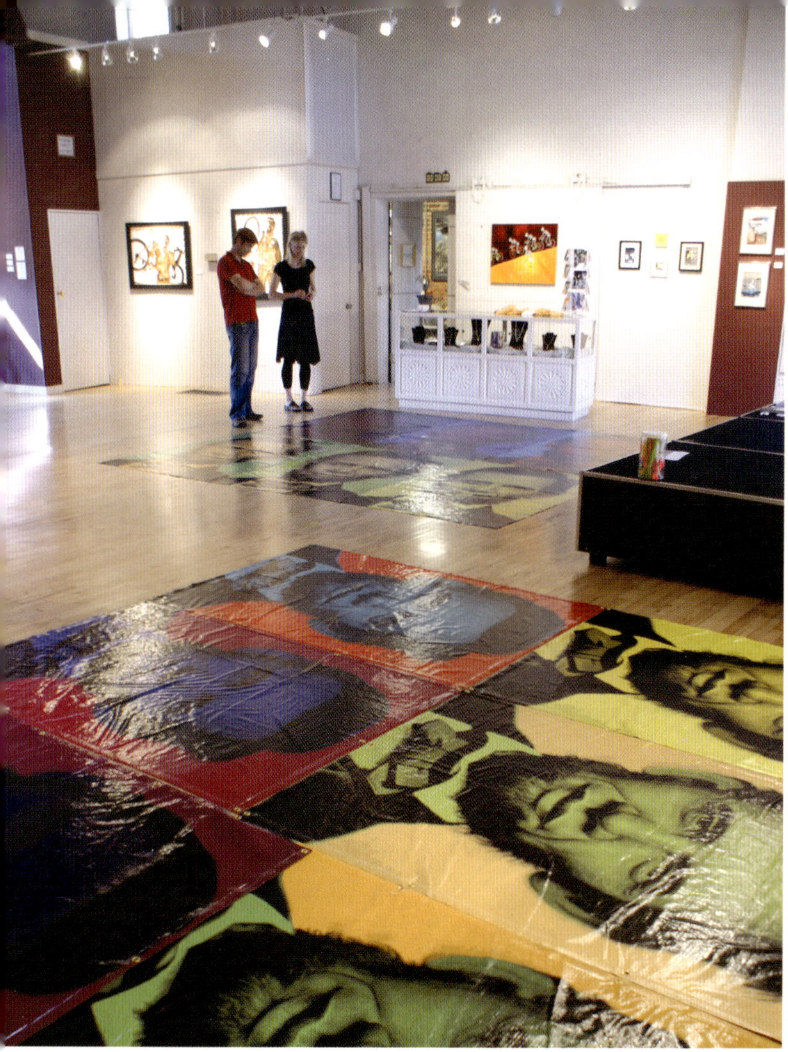

photo by Jeff Kallaus

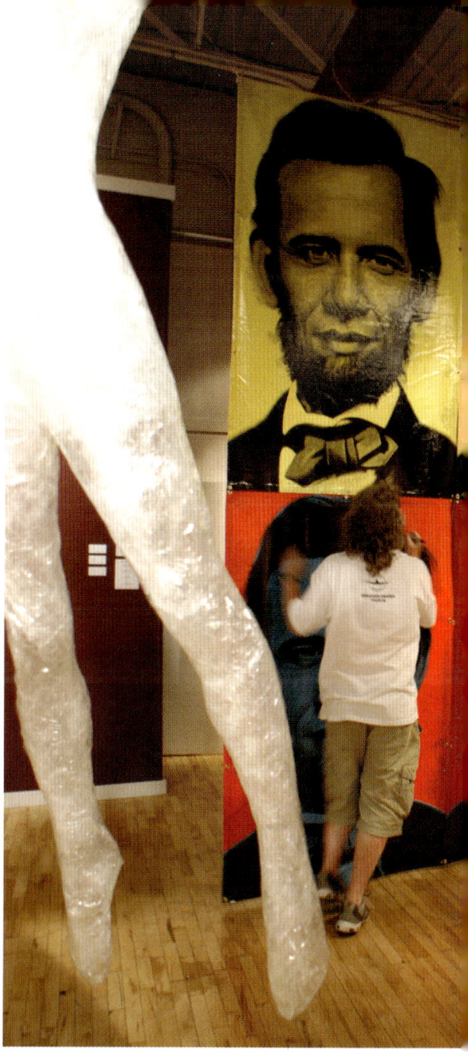

photo by Jeff Kallaus

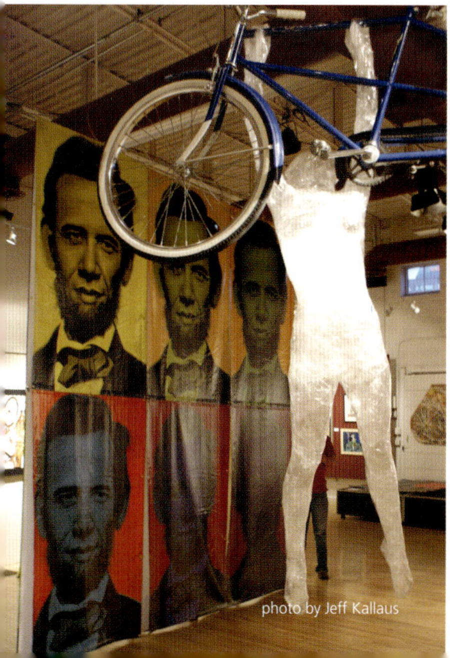

photo by Jeff Kallaus

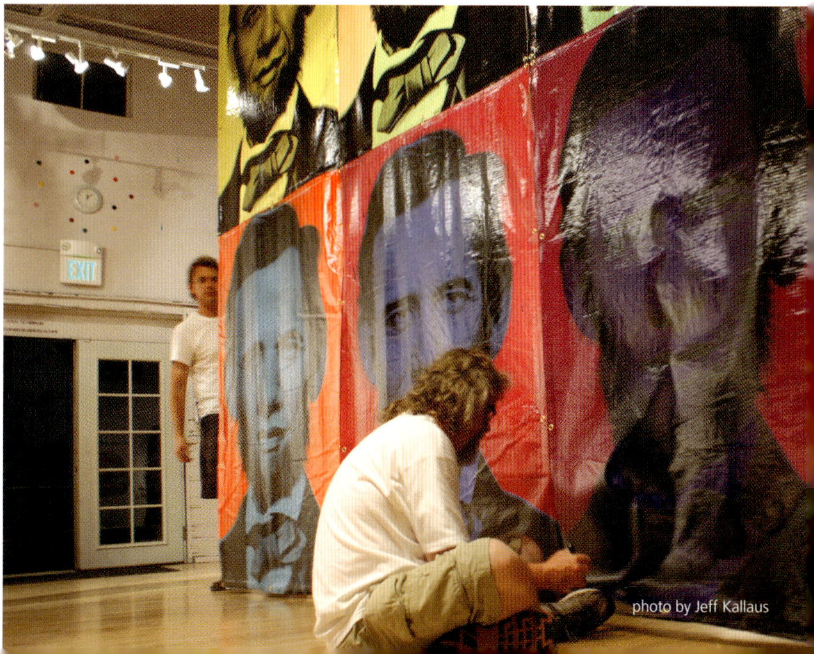

photo by Jeff Kallaus

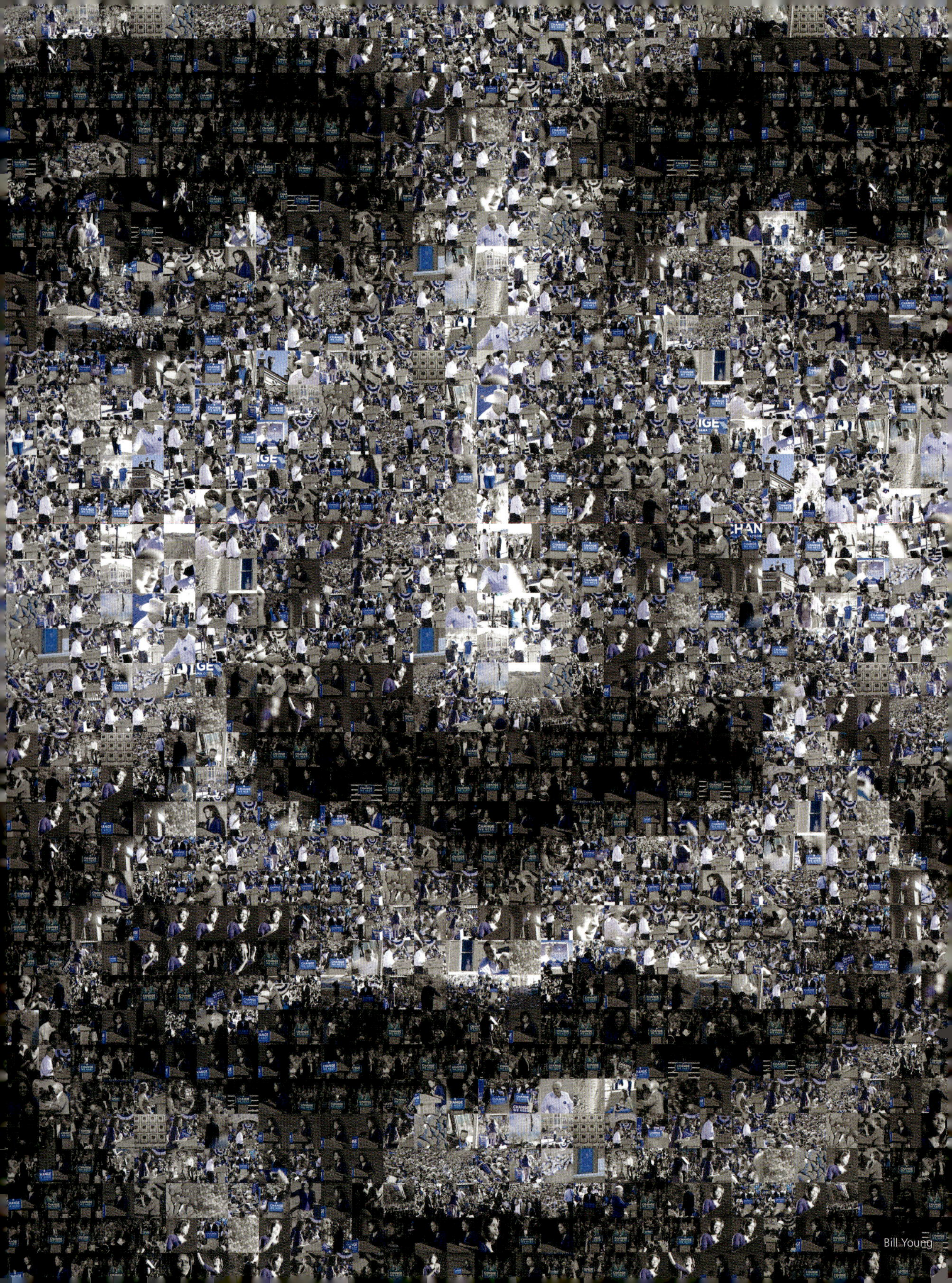

Bill Young

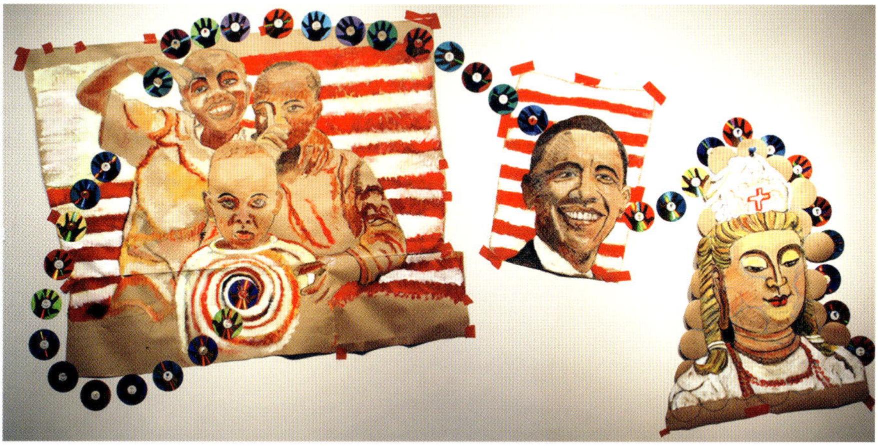

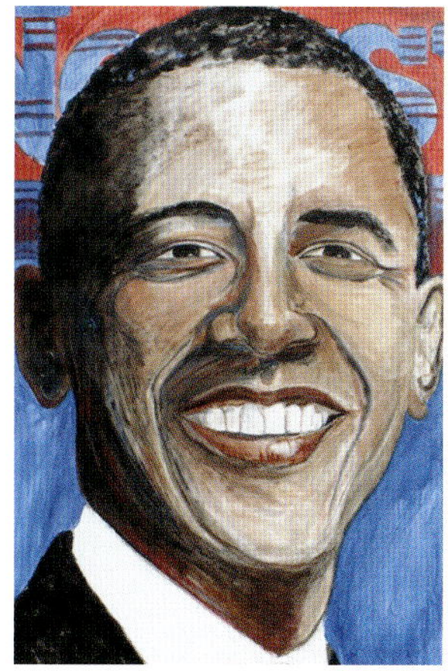

Kat and Bob Tudor

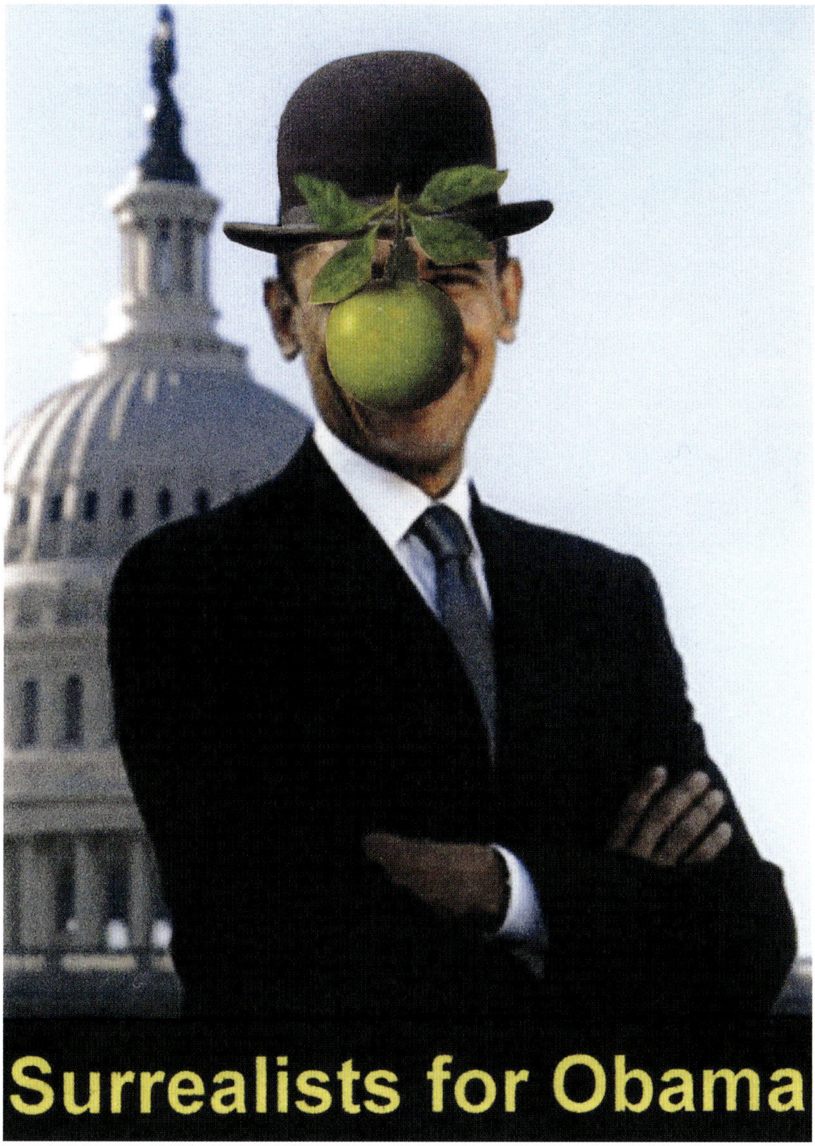

Dave Armstrong

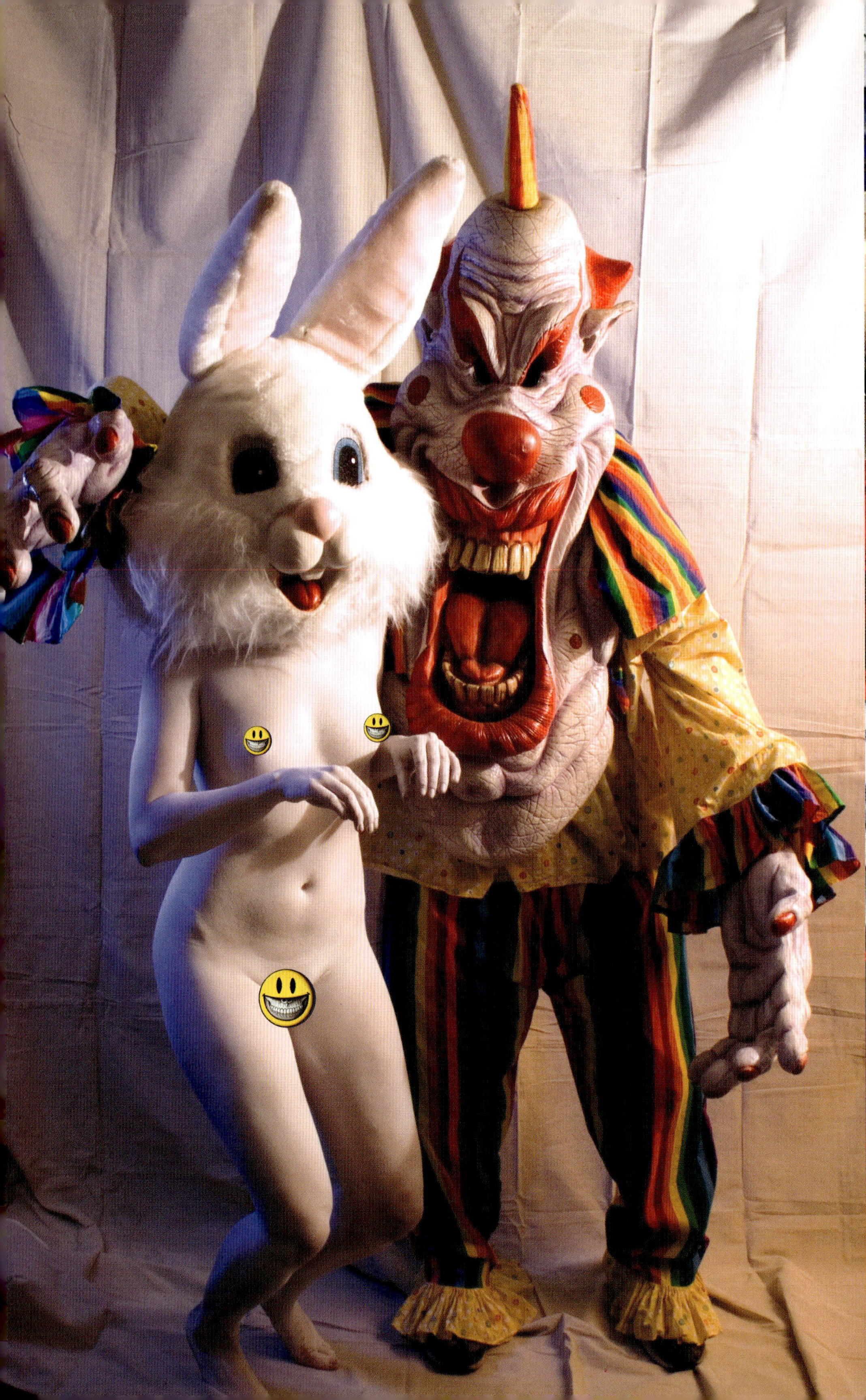
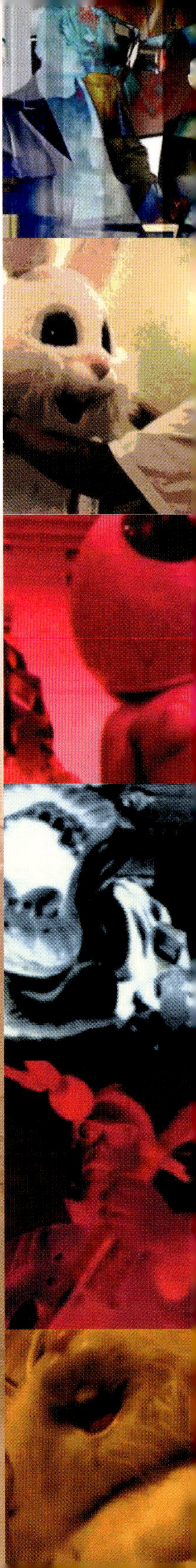

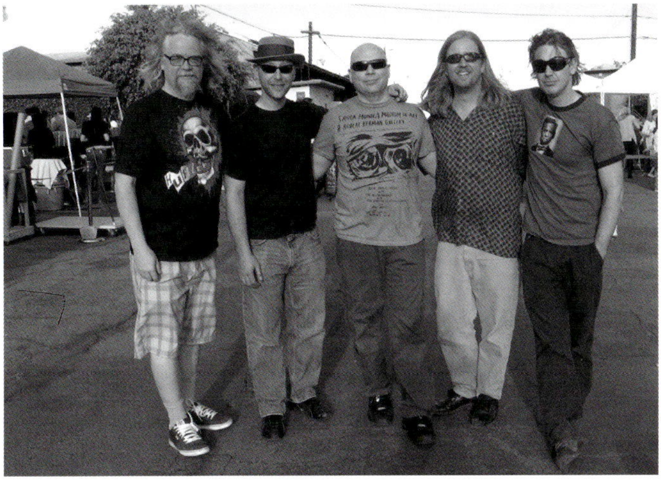

The Electric Illuminati

The Electric Illuminati is a music project started by Ron English and Jack Medicine (me). We collaborated with Daniel Johnston with the bands Hyperjinx Tricycle and Hyperjinx Four (with added member famed Indie producer Kramer). Ron writes the lyrics, which are equally as thought-provoking as his paintings and Jack writes the music. The rest of the band makes them sound great. We all got together on the AO tour in Colorado Springs for a video shoot of the song *The New Fool On The Hill*, a follow-up to the **YouTube** sensation *The Obama Song*.
–DG

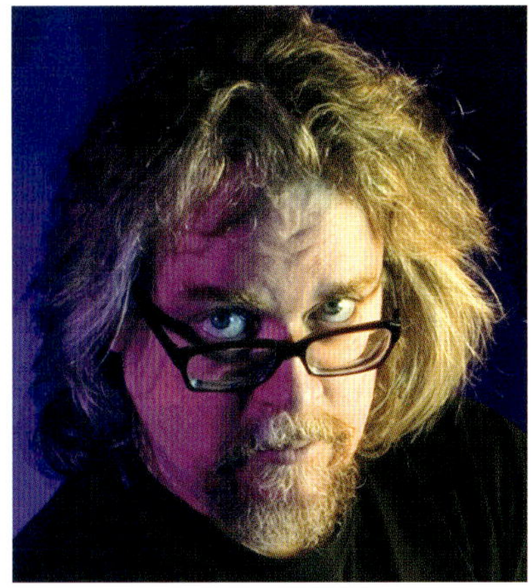

Ron English

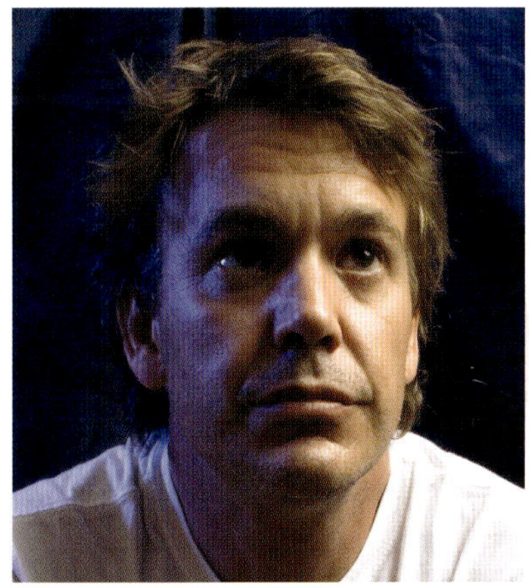

Jack Medicine

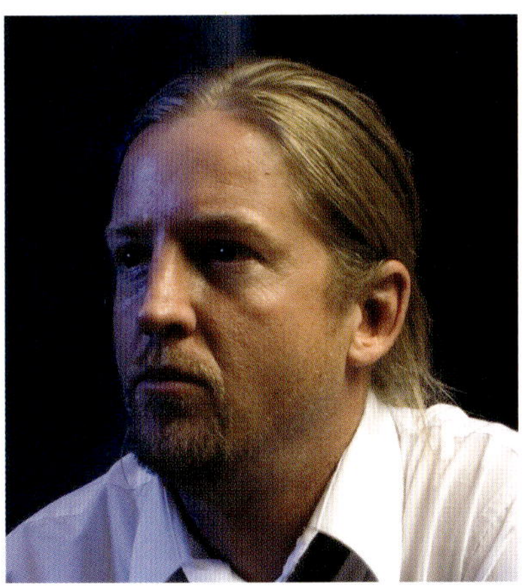

Jaq Kennedy

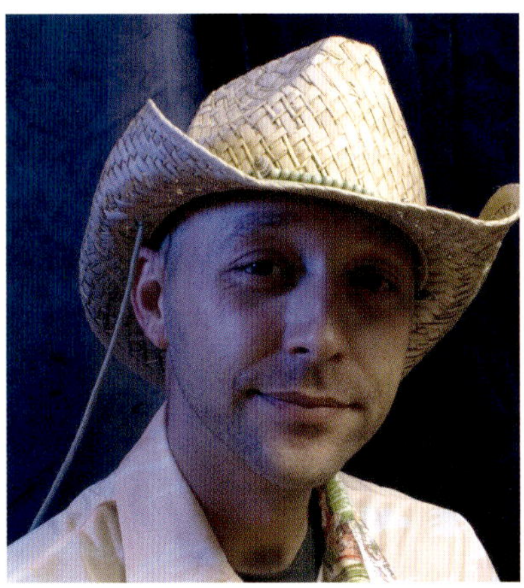

Craig Haughton

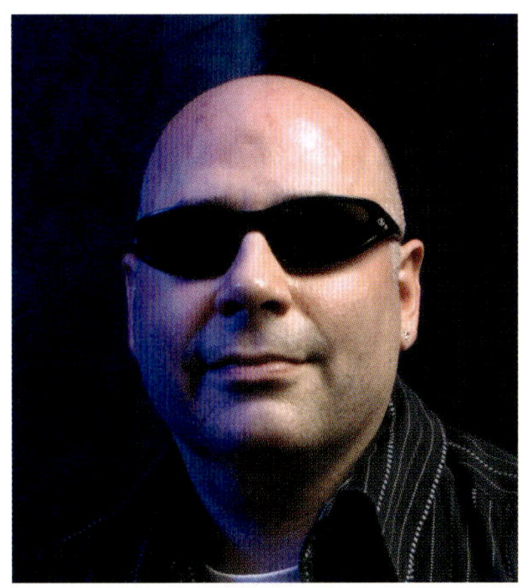

Michael Kimbrell

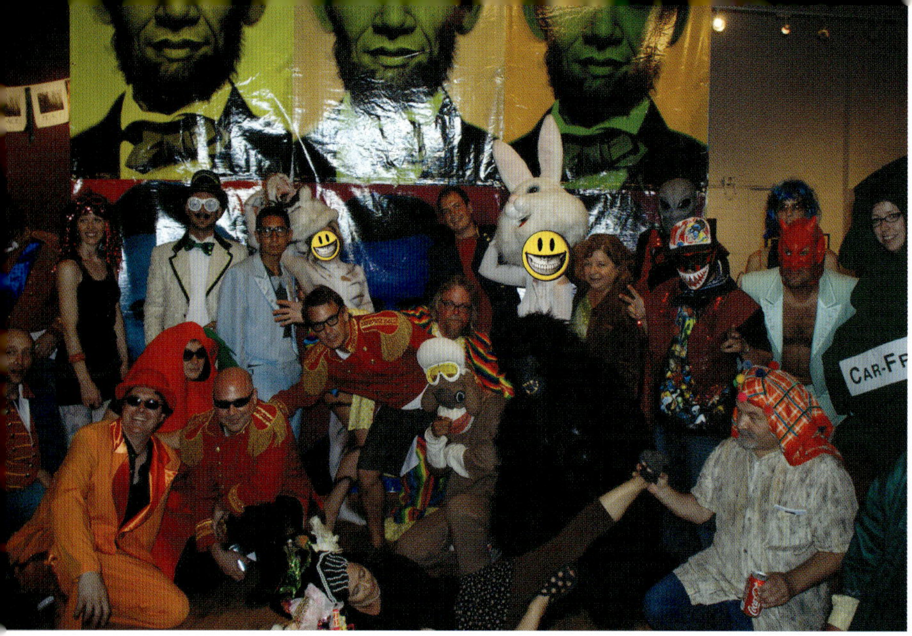

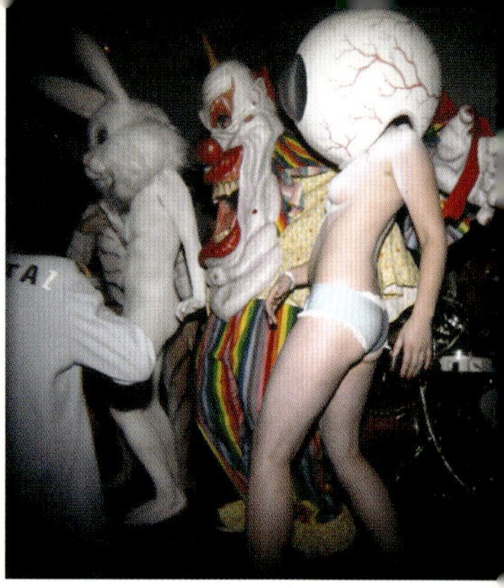

photo by Heather Oelkla

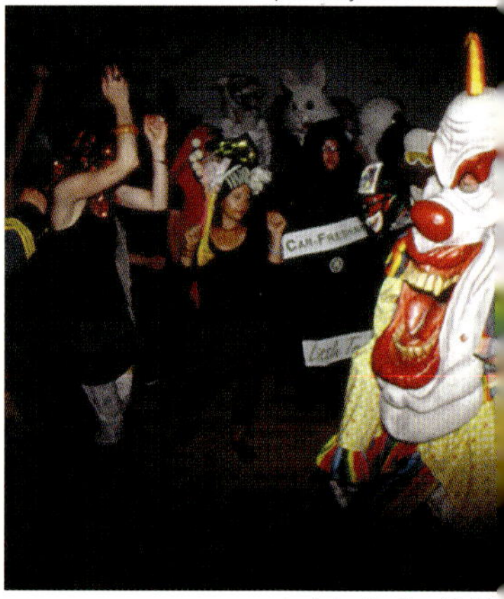

photo by Heather Oelkla

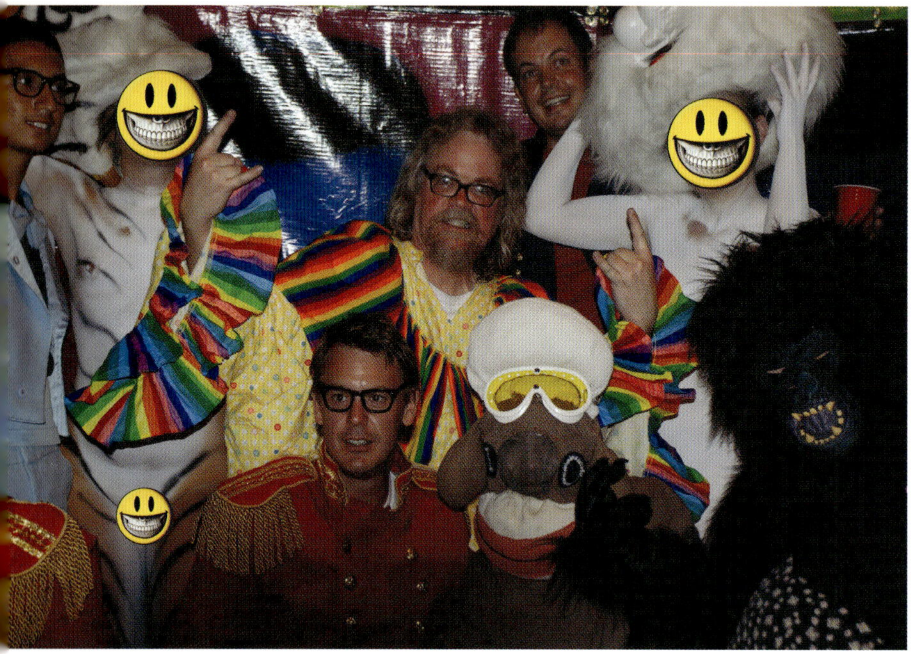

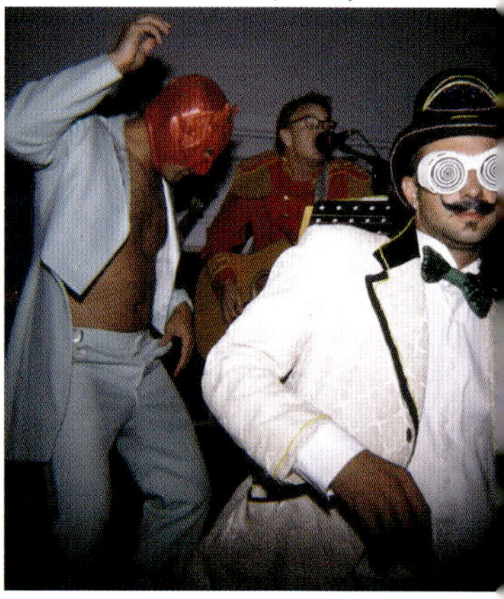

photo by Heather Oelkla

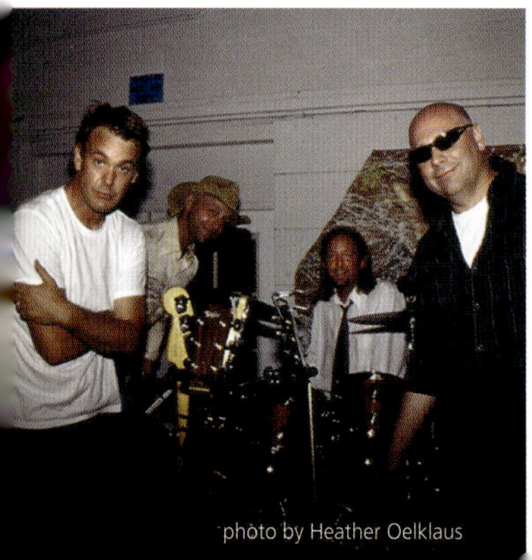

photo by Heather Oelklaus

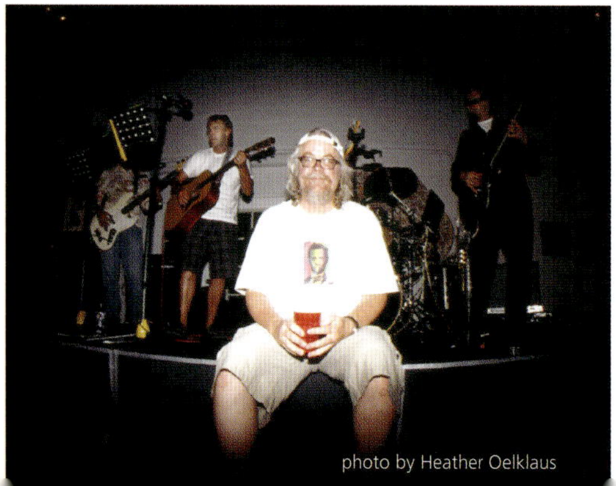

photo by Heather Oelklaus

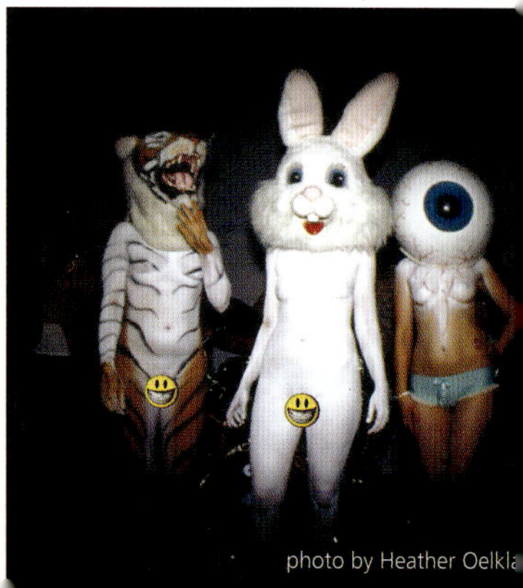

photo by Heather Oelkla

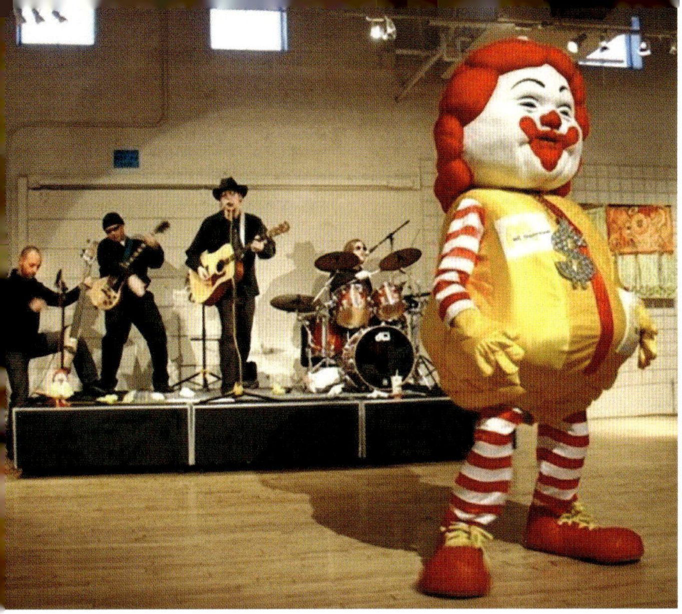

photo by Jeff Kallaus

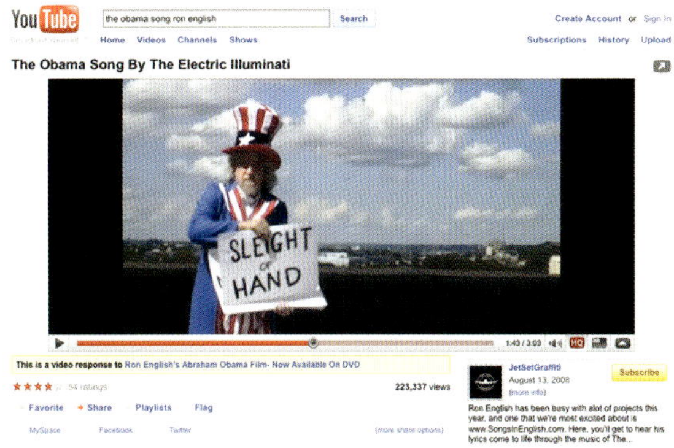

The Obama Song

Chaos, destruction
Death and Disorder
Fences and walls, barriers and borders
Mullahs and ministers
Diplomats and lawyers
Malcontents and terrorists
Bigoted governments

Propaganda dissonance
Ruling class extravagance
Narrow minds intolerance
Aggression vs. self defense
Misguided reverence
Self deluded arrogance
Ignorance and violence
& things, that we can't put behind us
Degradations, Dogma
Khamenei, Osama
And America, just wants to believe in
Barack Obama
Revelations, dharma
Shariah Law and Karma
and America, just wants to believe
in Barack Obama

Iran, Afghanistan
Taliban, Klu Klux Clan
Christian, Muslim
Secular Utopian
Mythical Holy Land
Magical sleight of hand
Neo Con Barbarians
Starting wars without a plan

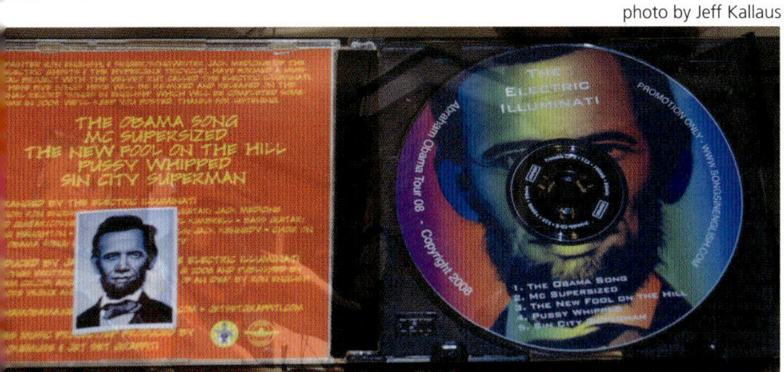

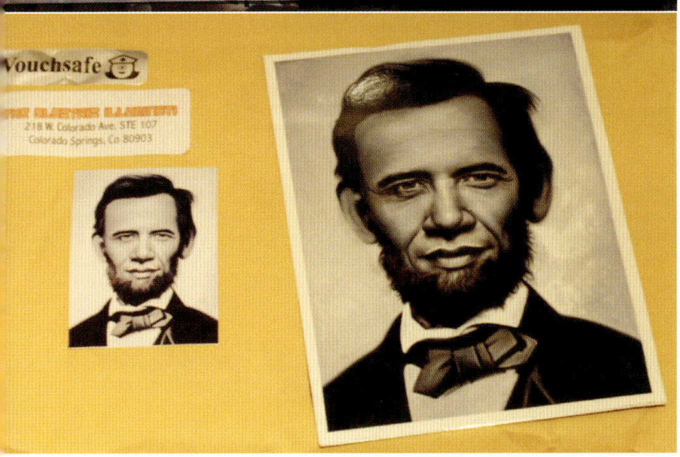

ectric Illuminati care packages for college radio during the tour.

ft: Various photographs from the Colorado Springs video shoot th Ron English and The Electric Illuminati.

ght: Various screen shots from Electric Illuminati music videos cluding Ron English's lyrics to The Obama Song, the official Abram Obama song. More at songsinenglish.com.

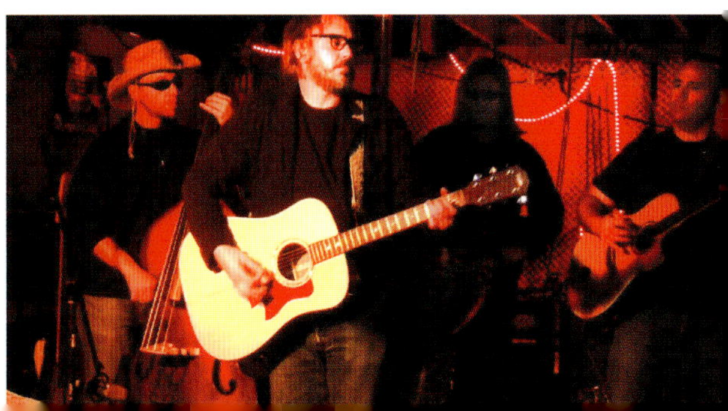

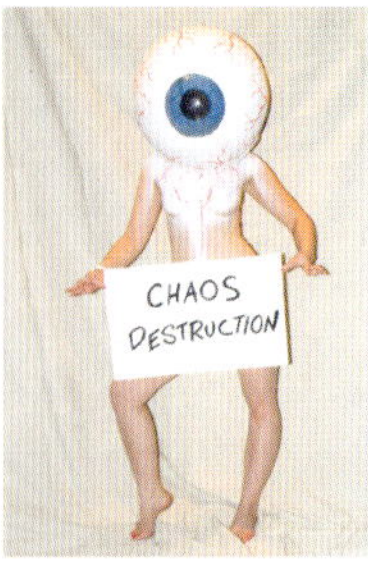
CHAOS
DESTRUCTION
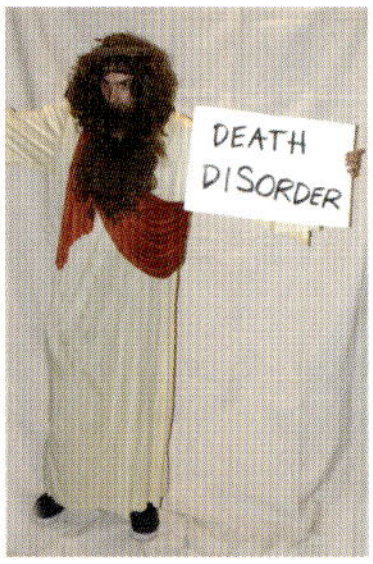
DEATH
DISORDER
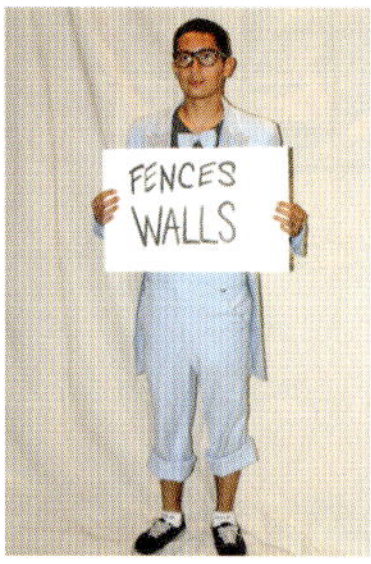
FENCES
WALLS
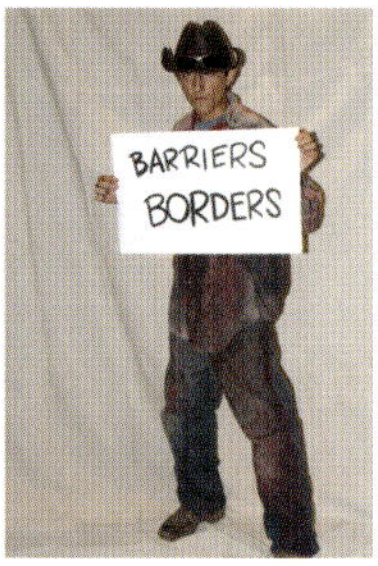
BARRIERS
BORDERS
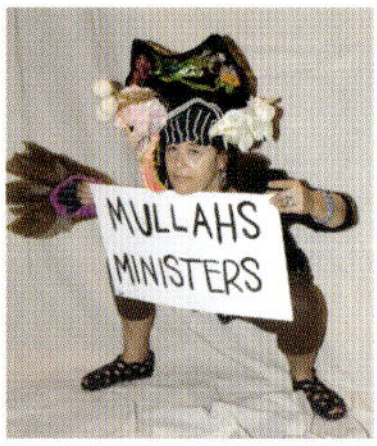
MULLAHS
MINISTERS
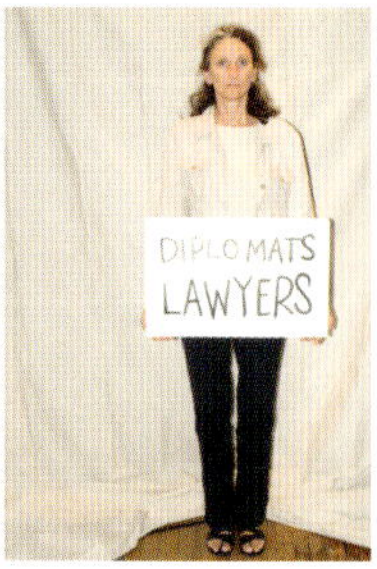
DIPLOMATS
LAWYERS
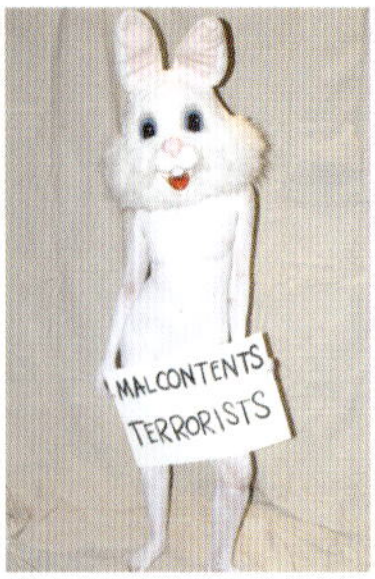
MALCONTENTS
TERRORISTS
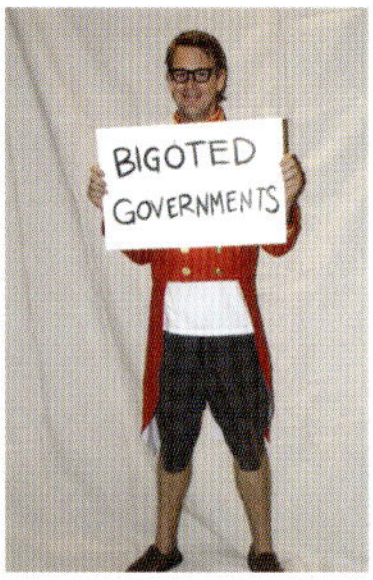
BIGOTED
GOVERNMENTS
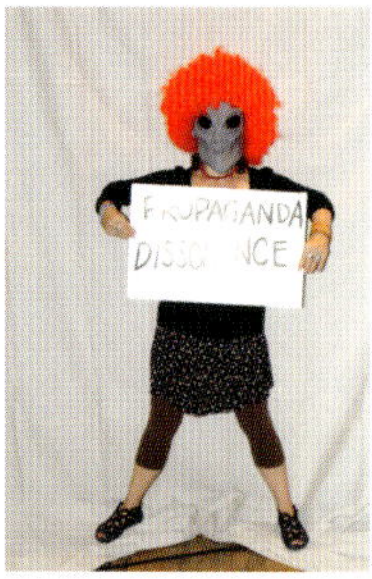
PROPAGANDA
DISSO NCE
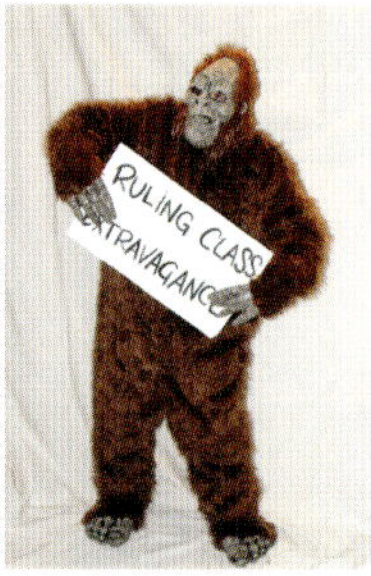
RULING CLASS
EXTRAVAGANCE
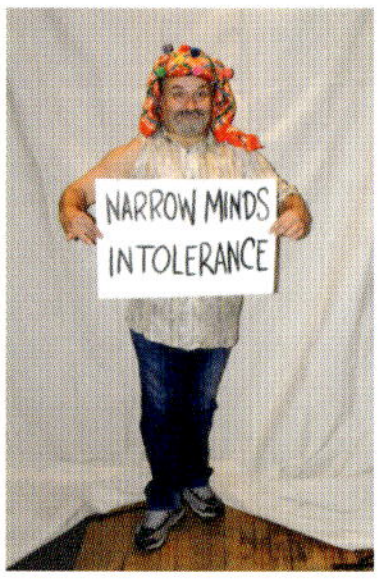
NARROW MINDS
INTOLERANCE
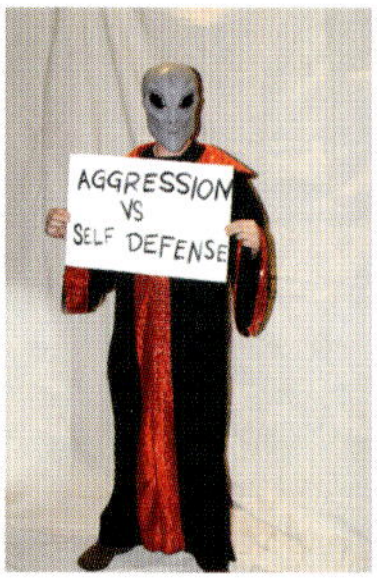
AGGRESSION
VS
SELF DEFENSE
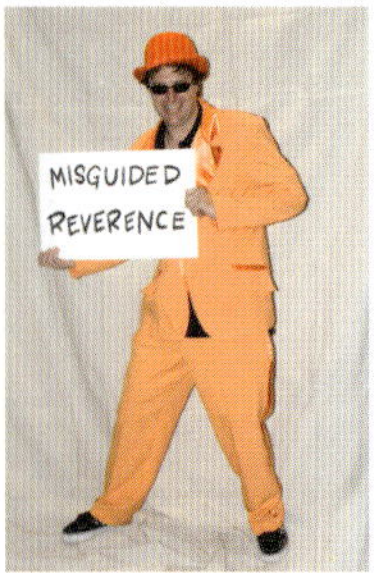
MISGUIDED
REVERENCE
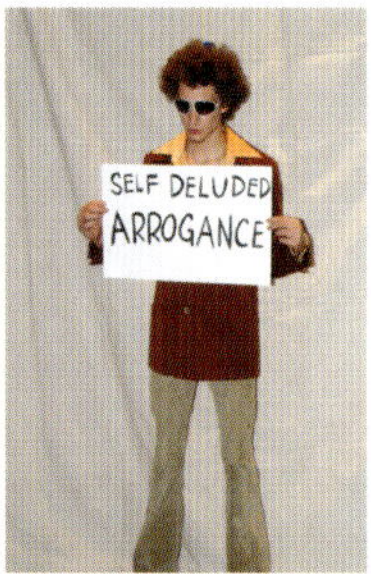
SELF DELUDED
ARROGANCE
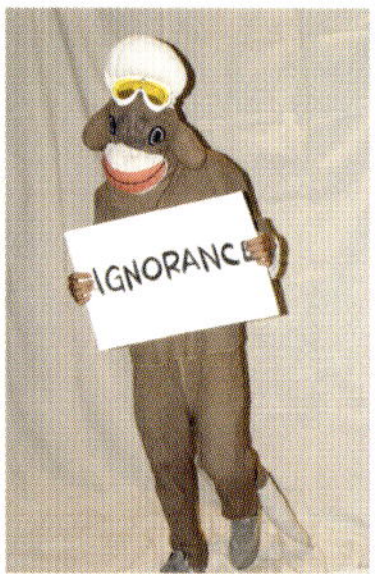
IGNORANCE
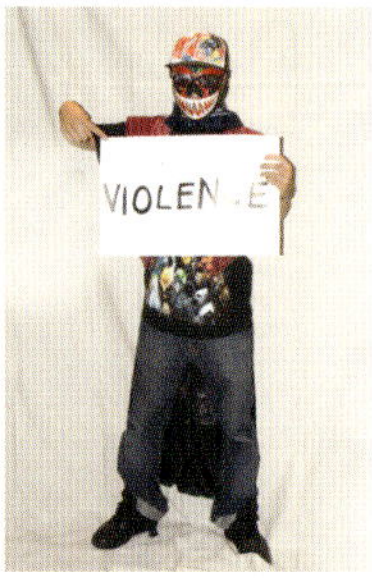
VIOLEN E
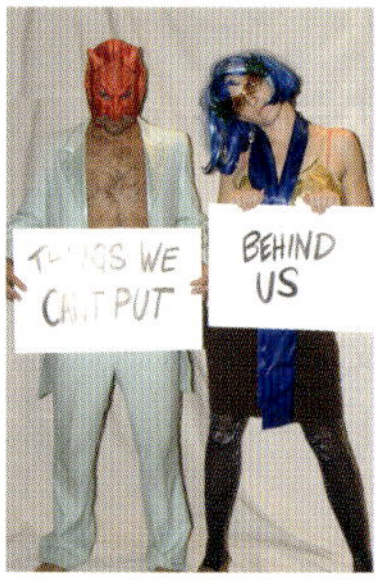
WE
PUT
BEHIND
US
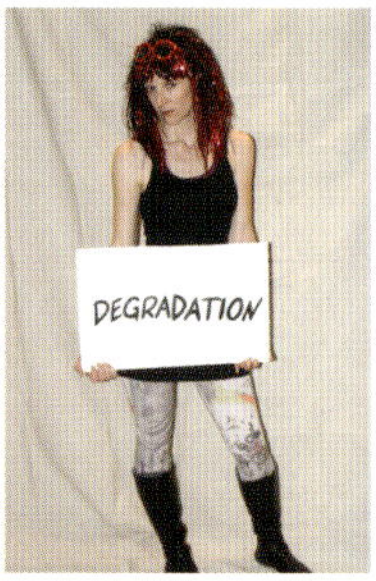
DEGRADATION
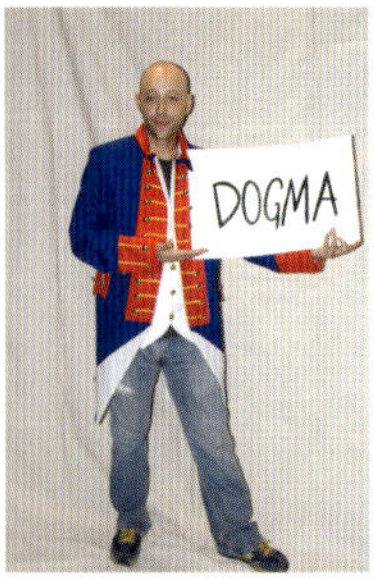
DOGMA
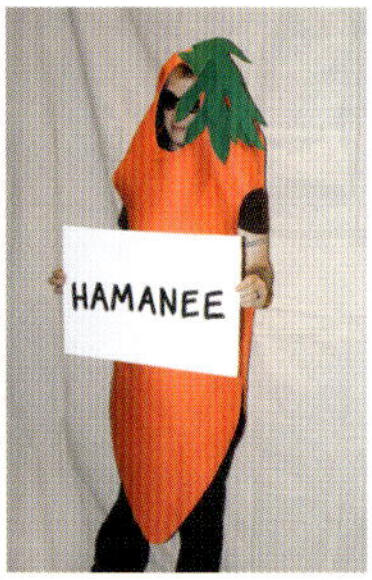
HAMANEE
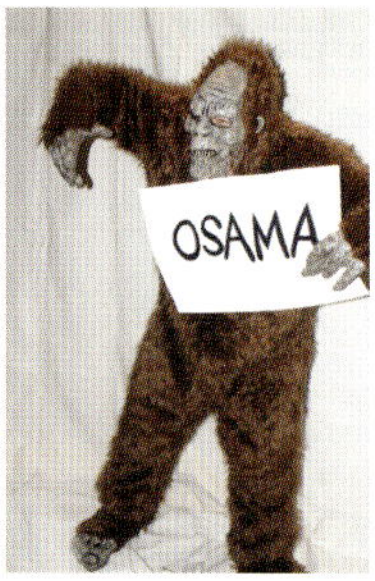
OSAMA
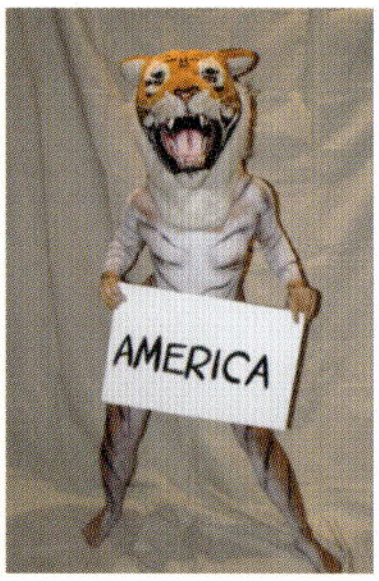
AMERICA
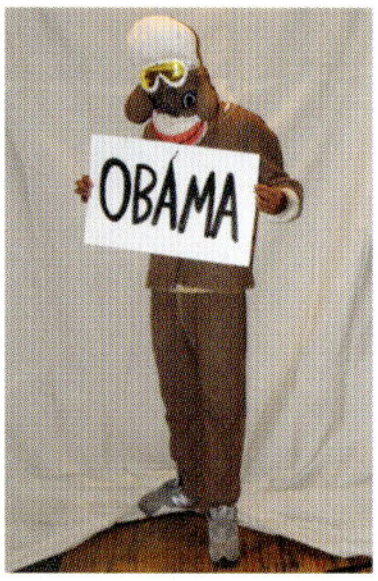
OBAMA
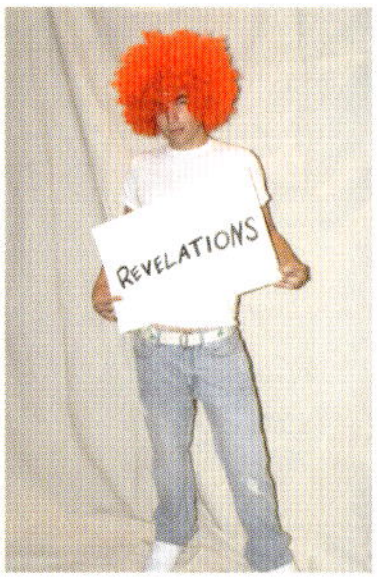
REVELATIONS
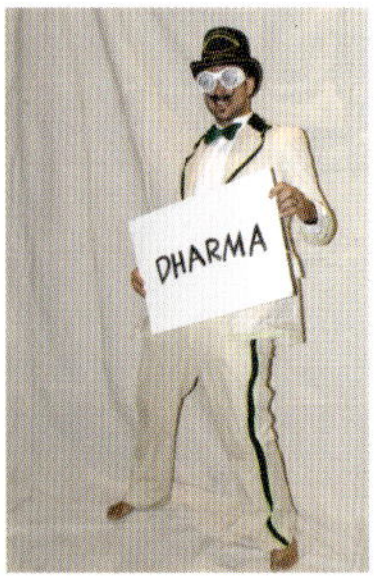
DHARMA
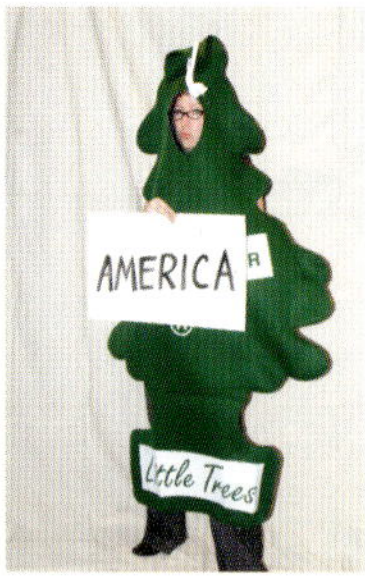
AMERICA
Little Trees
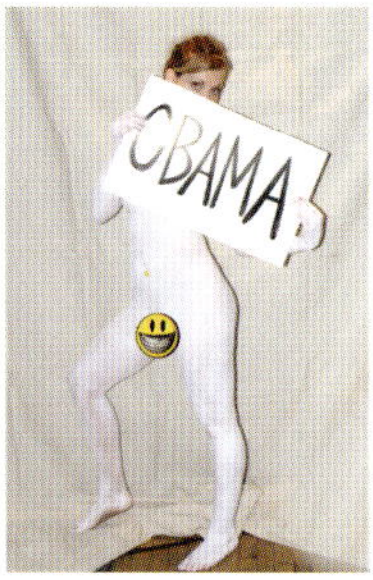
OBAMA
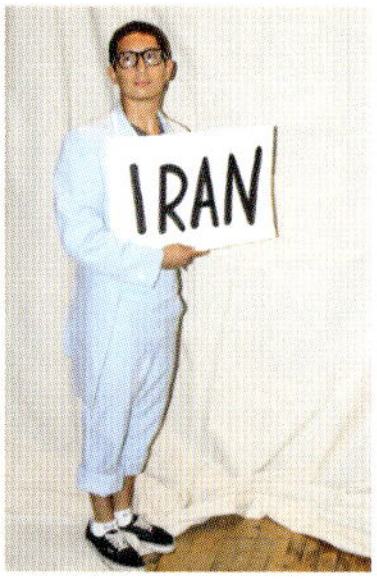
IRAN
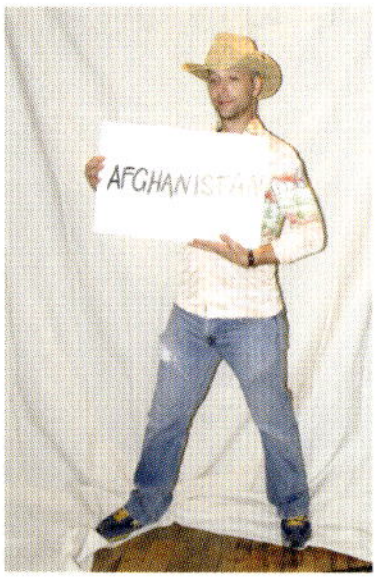
AFGHANIST
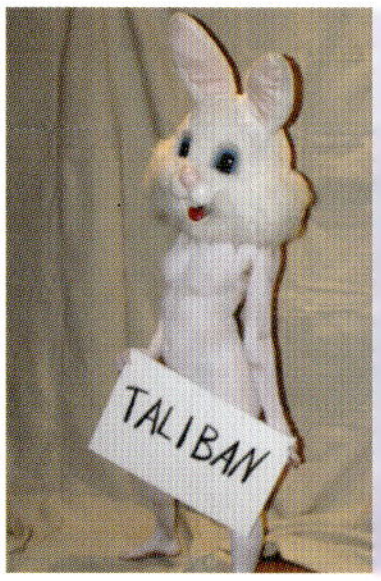
TALIBAN

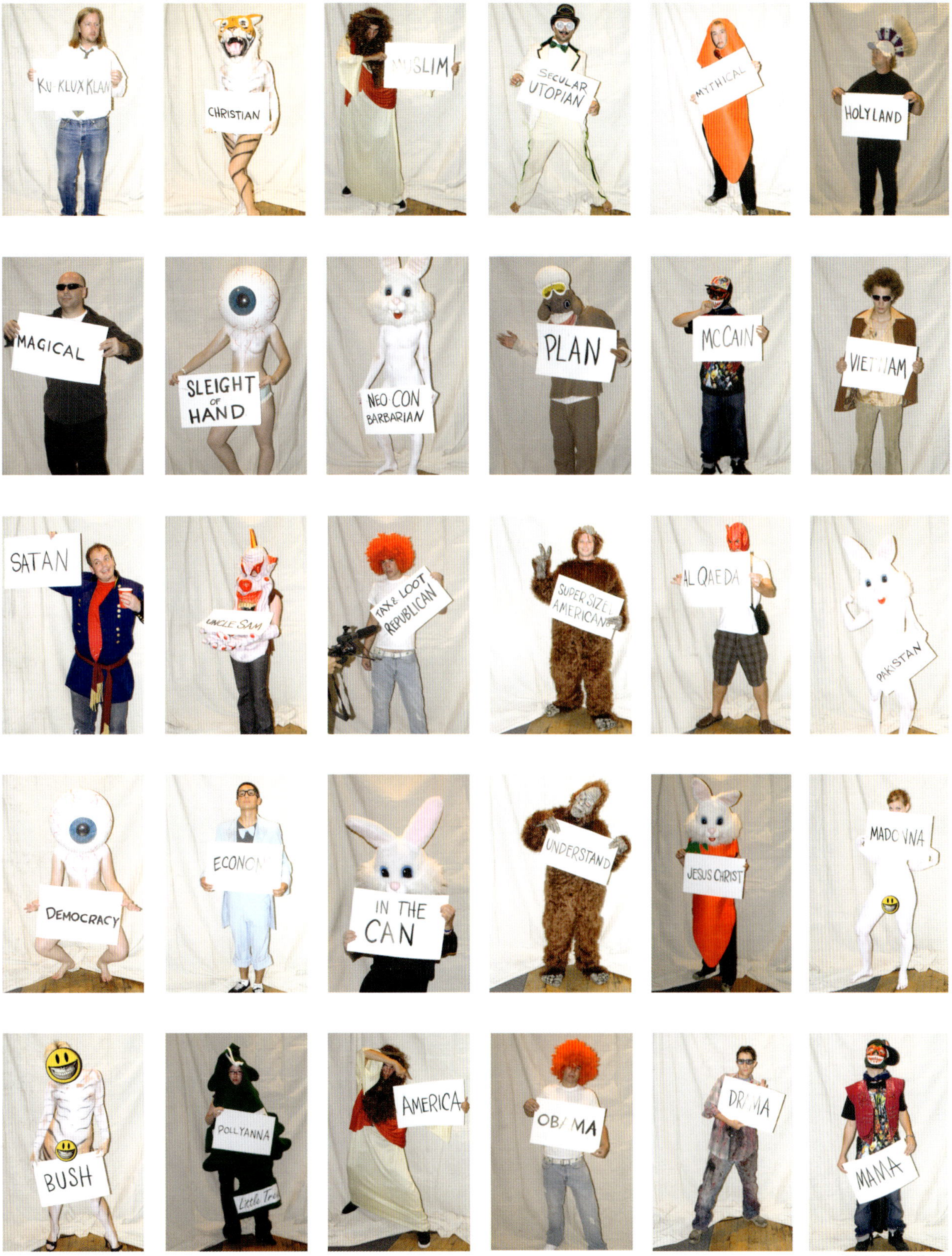

All photos Bill Young

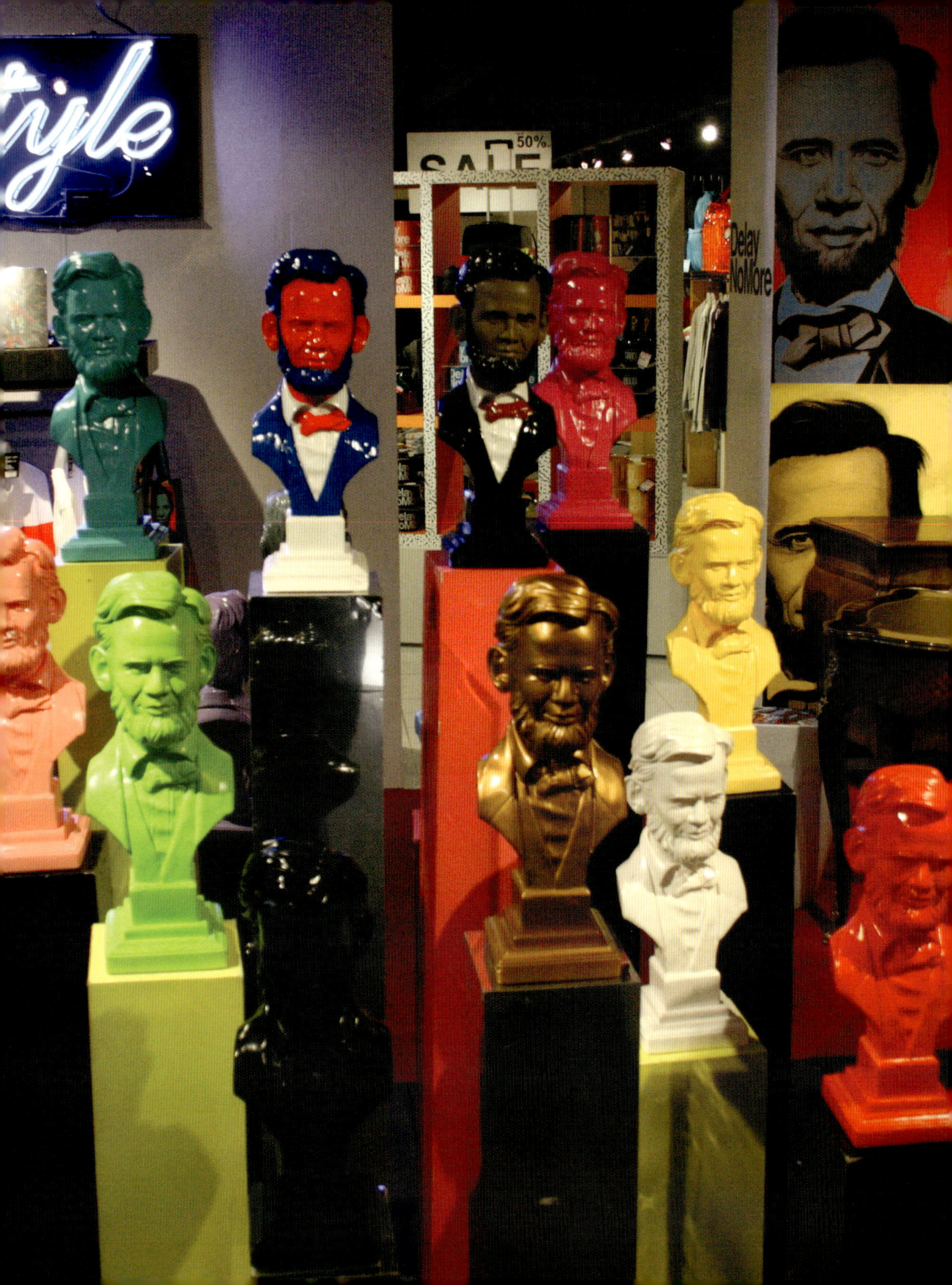
tyle
50%
SALE
Delay NoMore

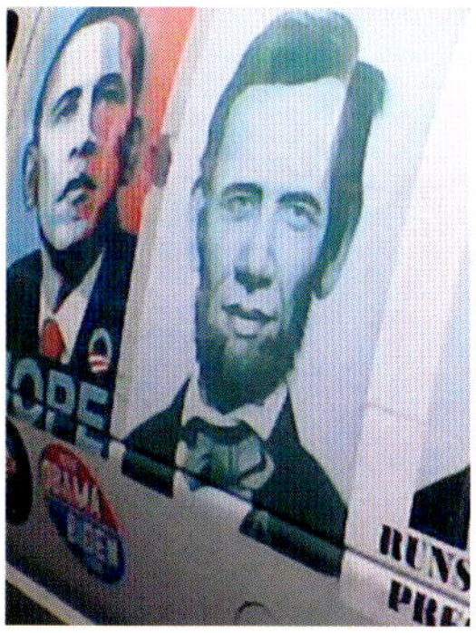

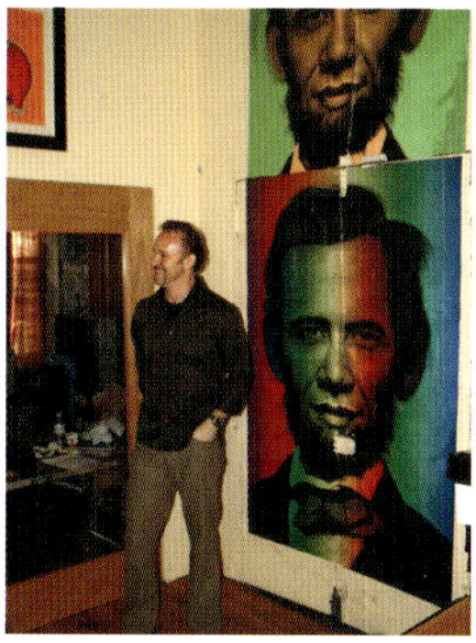

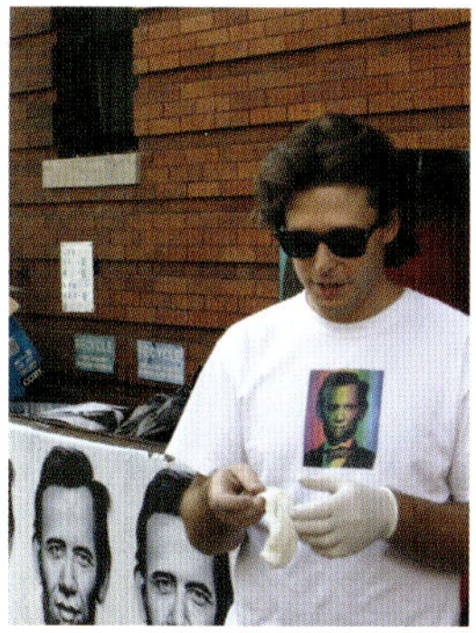

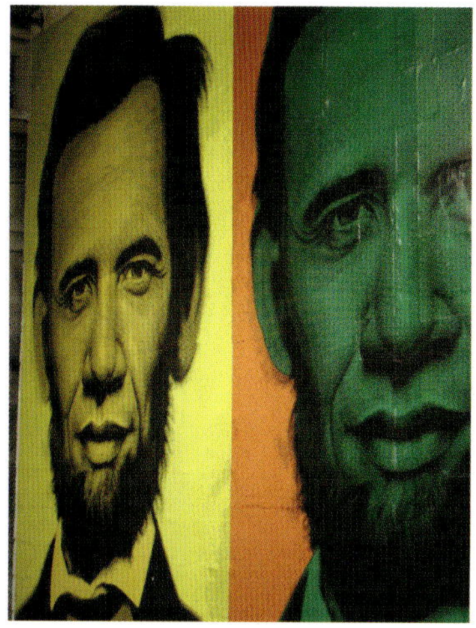

After The Tour

Colorado Springs • NYC • Brooklyn Jersey City • Los Angeles • Hong Kong

So the tour was over but we were all still on an Abraham Obama adrenaline rush. It was still a month before the election, so since we had tons (literally) of posters left over, big and small, we all decided to continue pasting where and when we could. It quickly turned into a friendly competition. There were bets on who could do the most, who could paste the highest, etc. So we were off. The following chapter is a visual documentary of what went down.
–DG

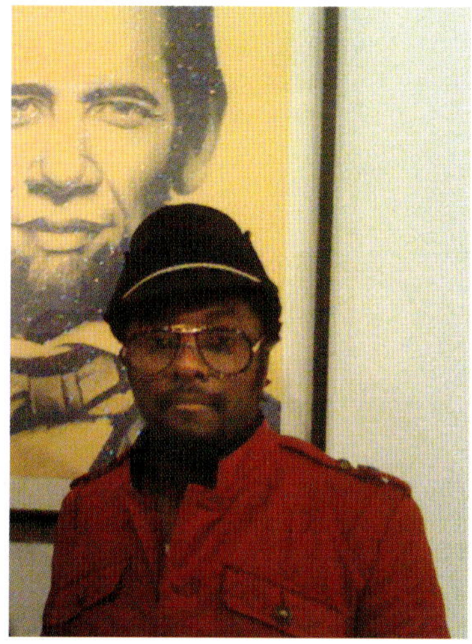

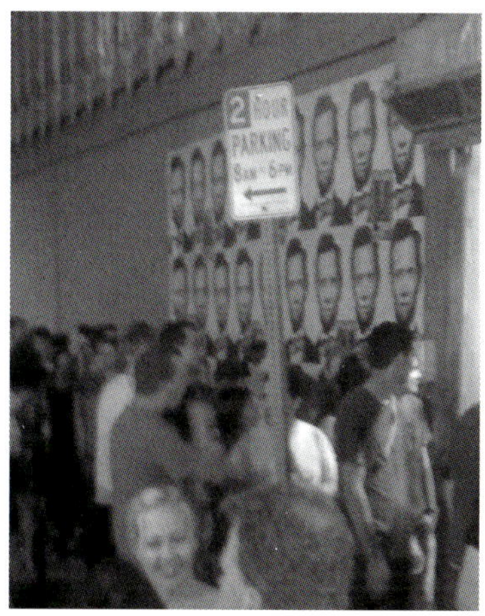

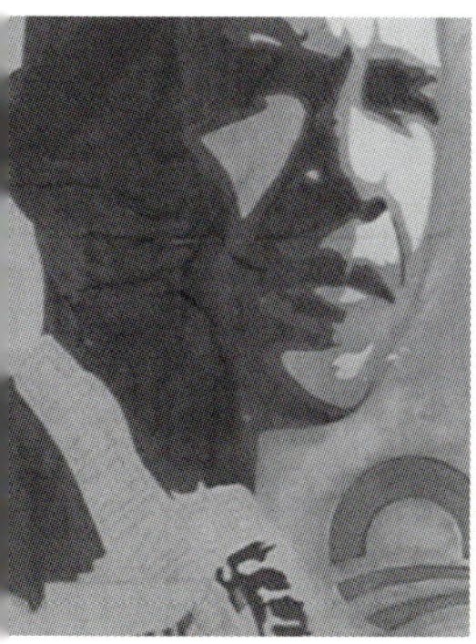

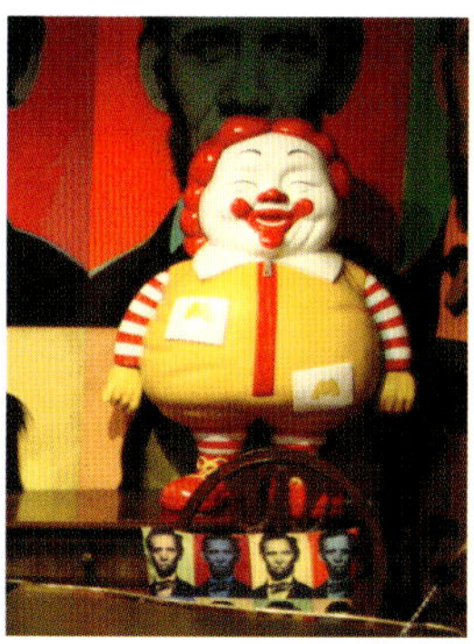

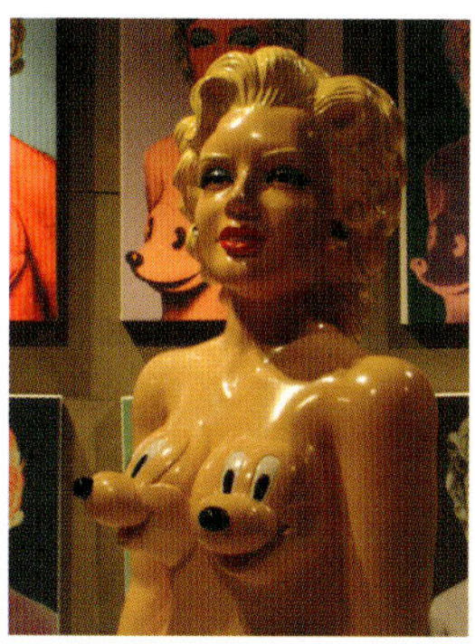

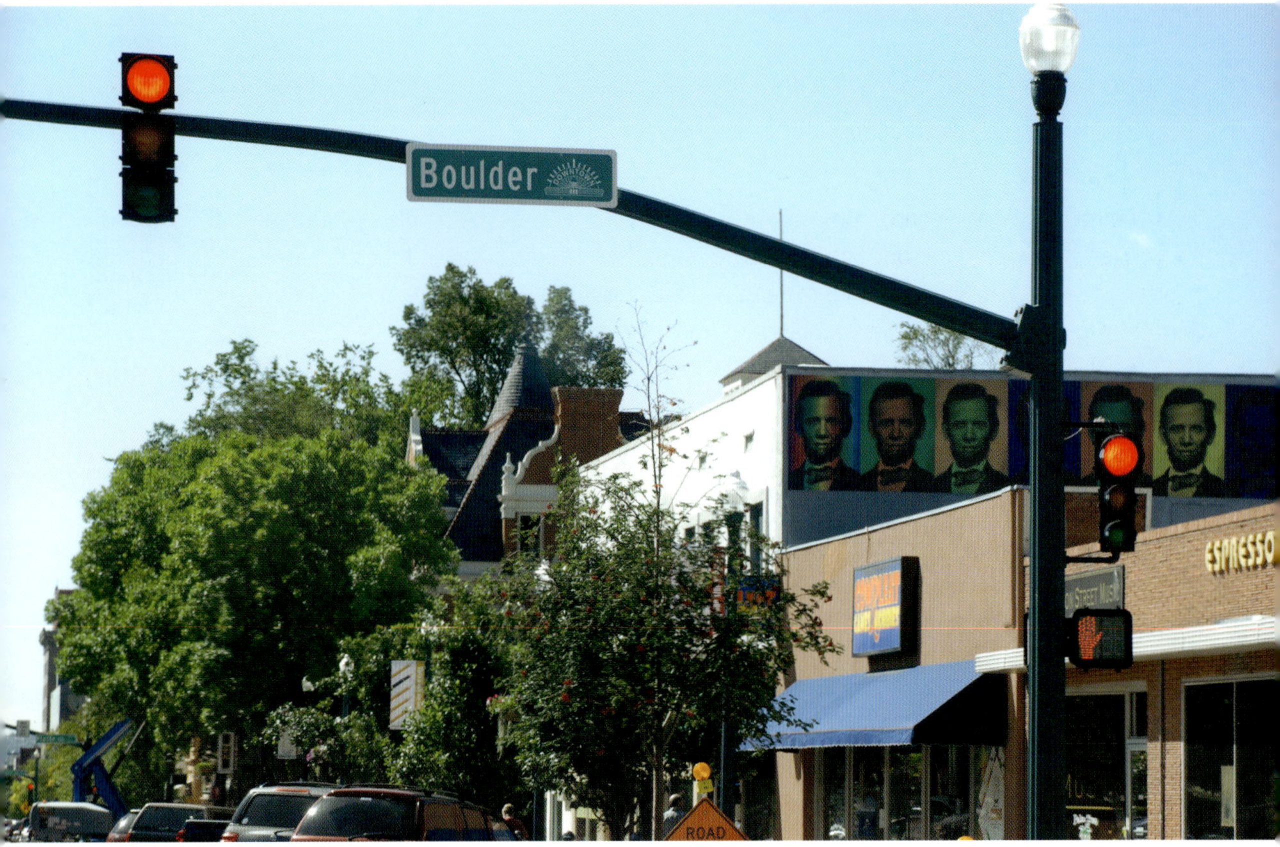

It started as a simple Abraham Obama installation but quickly became a rooftop Rorschach tes

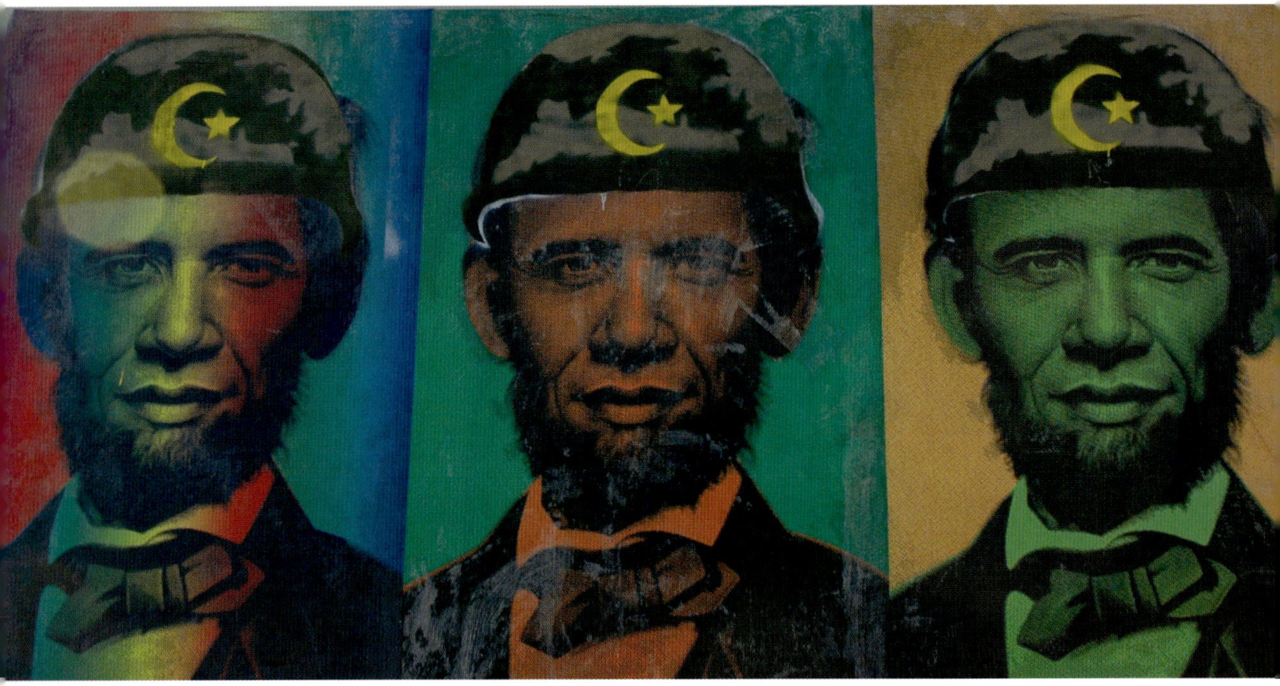

Colorado Springs

Riffing on a Roof, by Kat Tudor

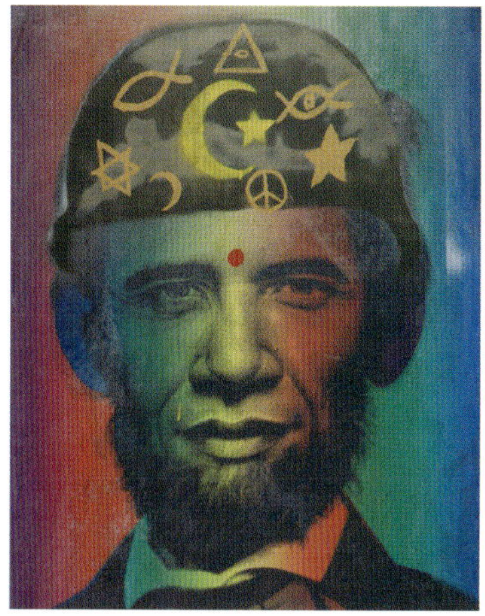

When I heard that the Abraham Obama posters hanging over the roof of Poor Richard's Restaurant had been vandalized, I expected a crude response to this subtle art piece, but that's not what I found. Instead of defacing Abraham Obama, this so-called vandal had transformed him, giving him a gold helmet and a celestial environment and doing so carefully, with stencils and shiny color. I admired the artistry, if not the sentiment of the work (my guess was that our boy was now supposed to be a Muslim terrorist). This deft design deserved a considered response, not the usual knee-jerk reaction to public graffiti–cover it up as soon as possible and pretend it was never there in the first place. We had a little public conversation going on, up on the roof, right before the election.

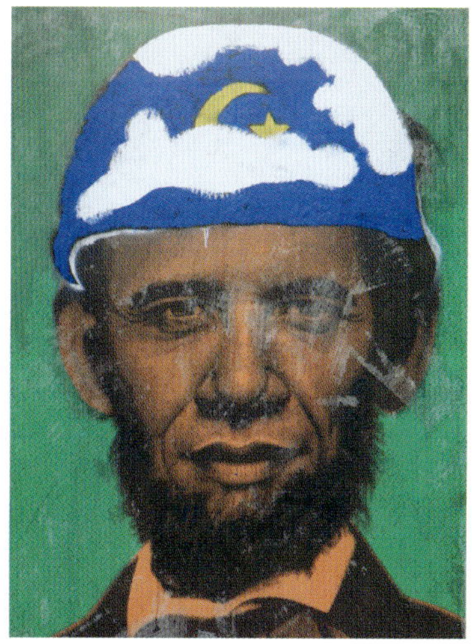

I, too, love to riff on someone else's creation. I share a habit with my husband, Bob, of fixing up odd artworks from the Arc thriftstore. We buy velvet paintings, family portraits, other-worldly landscapes, discarded and discredited art and have fun reimagining, rearranging, and repurposing them. So I felt right at home becoming a serial vandal of both Ron English's and the mystery artist's work.

I started thinking that if Obama was perceived as a Muslim terrorist by some, there were many other perceptions of him out there as well–too white, a black revolutionary, an Abe-like savior of the nation, an alien. So I gave everybody their own worst fears or greatest hopes to look up to, a rooftop Rorschach test.

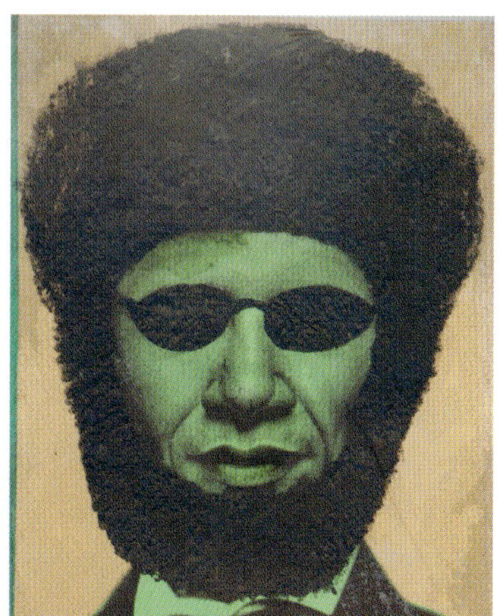

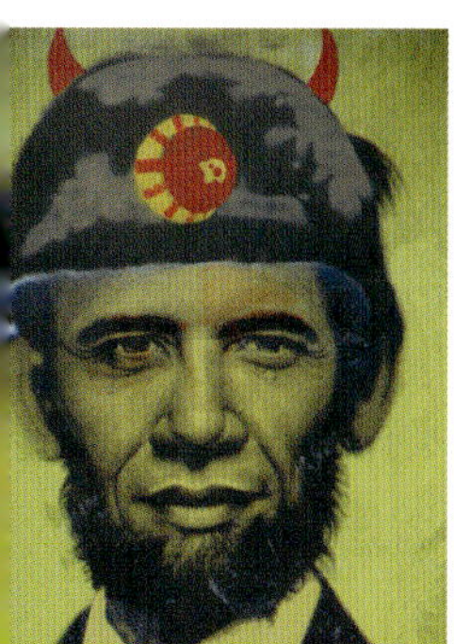

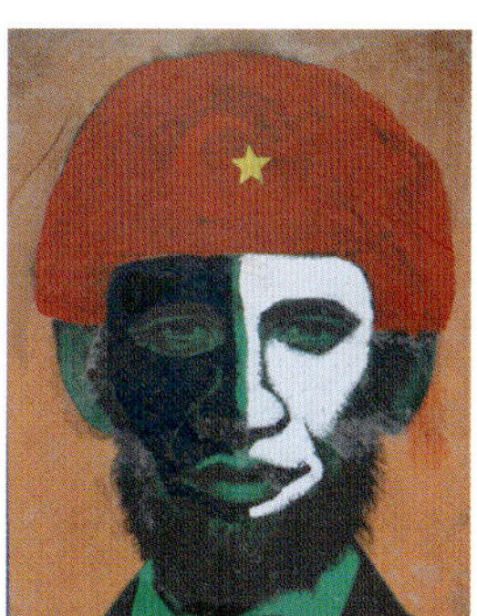

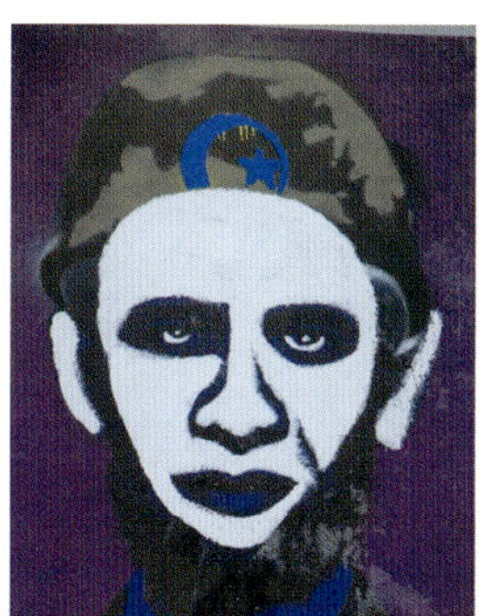

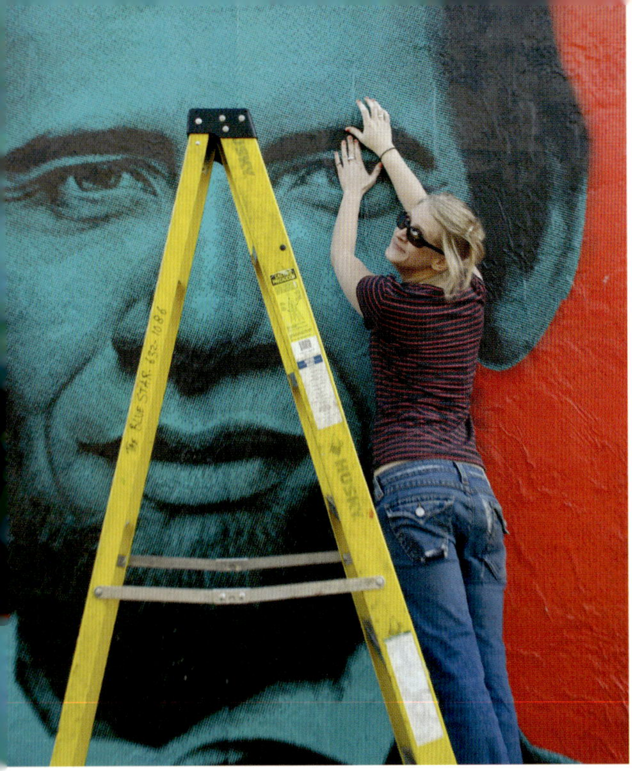

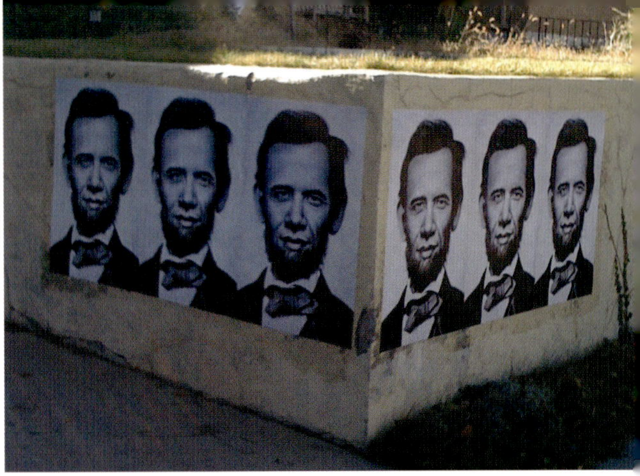

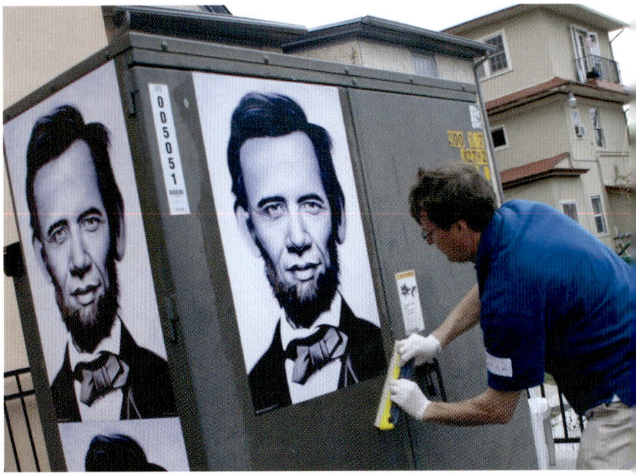

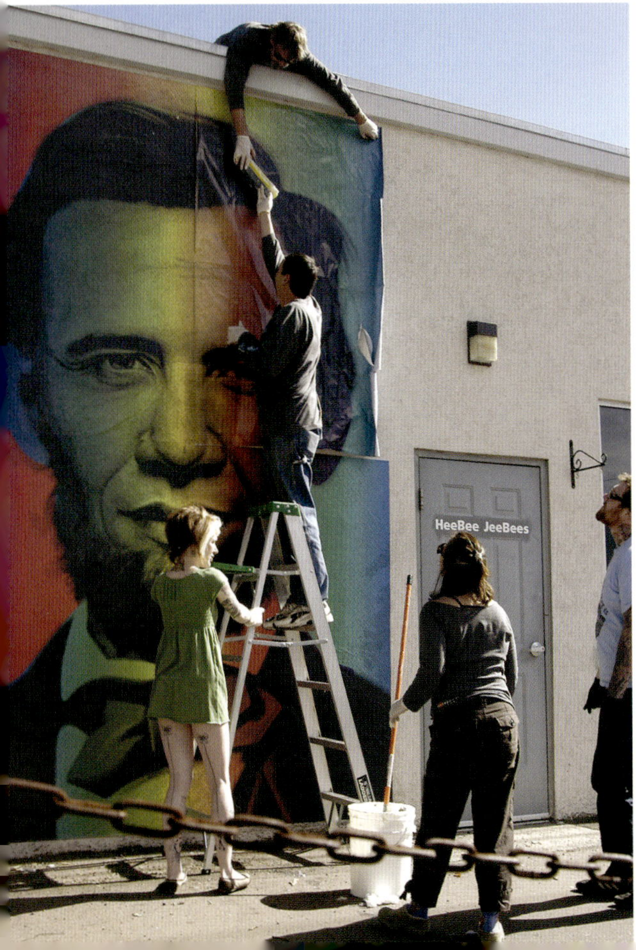

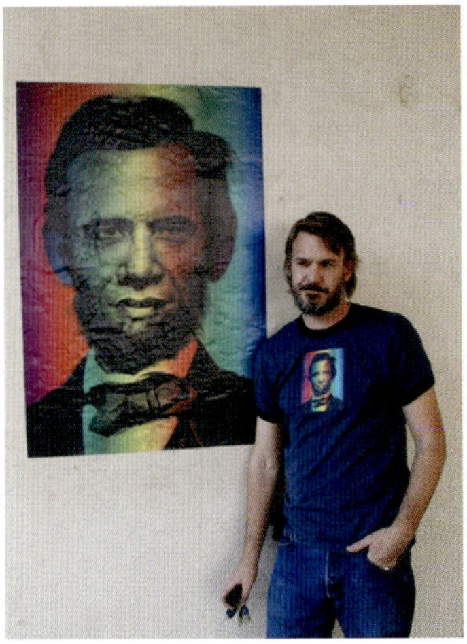

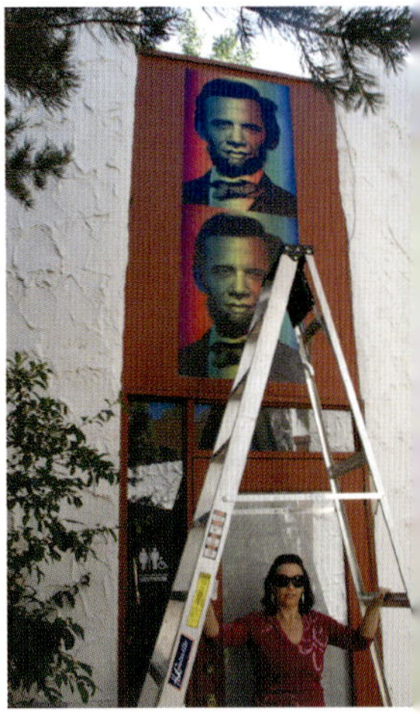

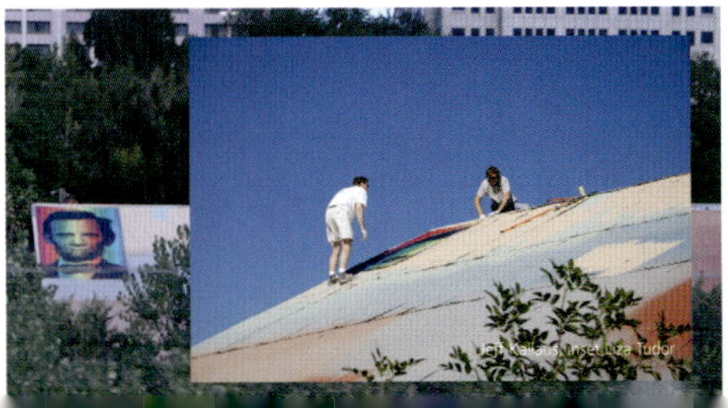

Jeff Kallaus; Inset Liza Tudor

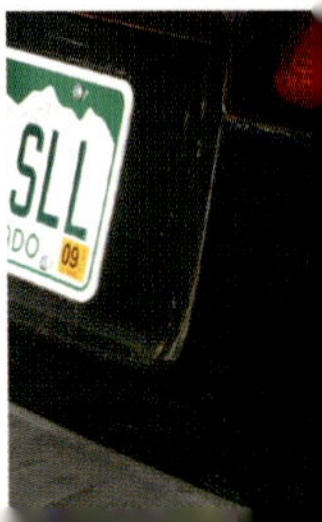

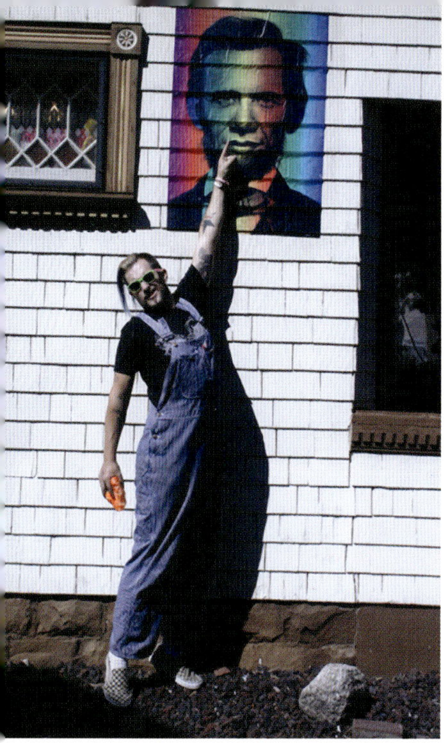

Jeff Kallaus

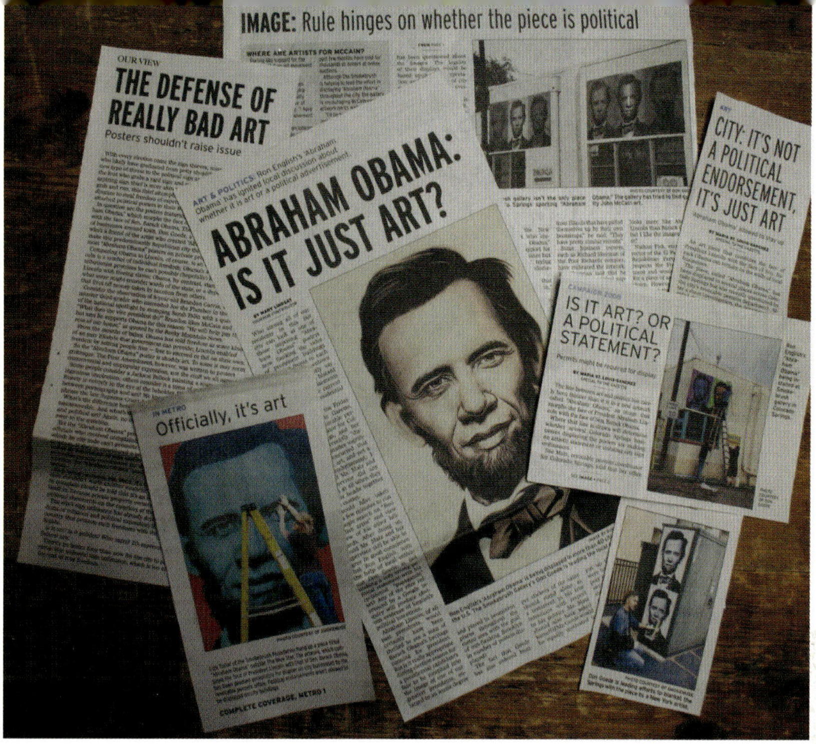

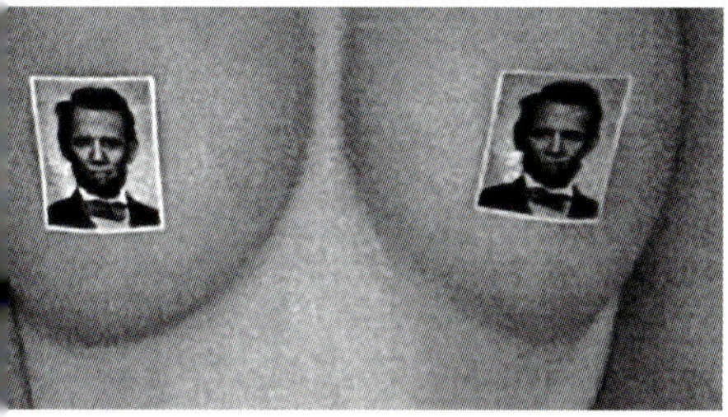

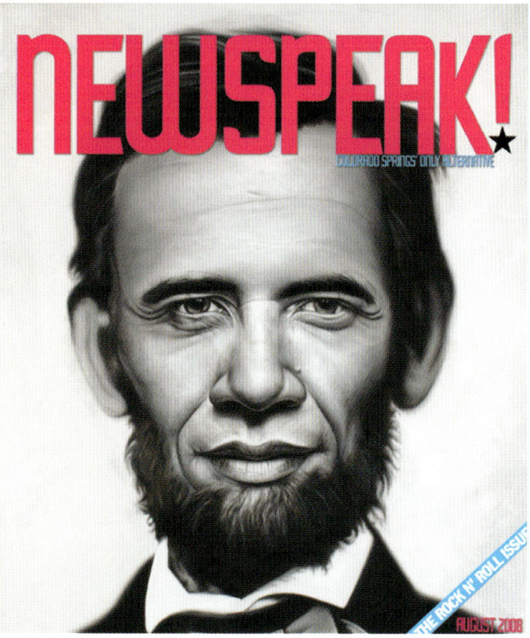

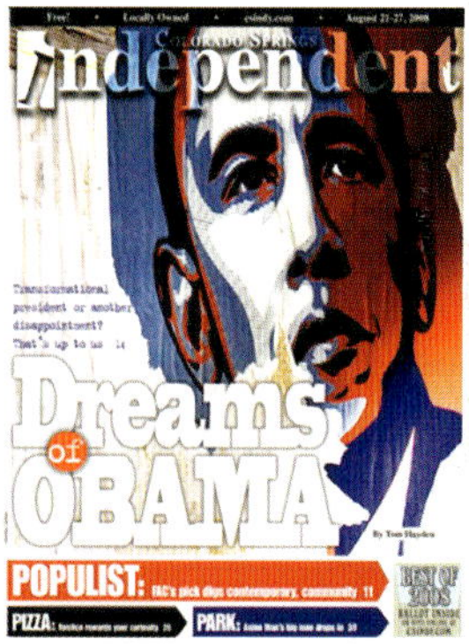

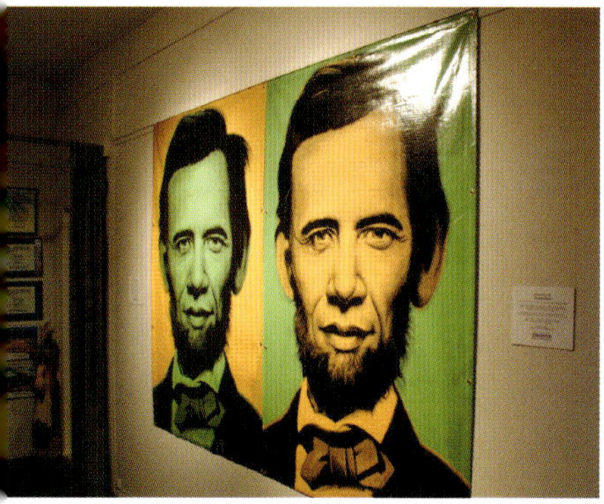

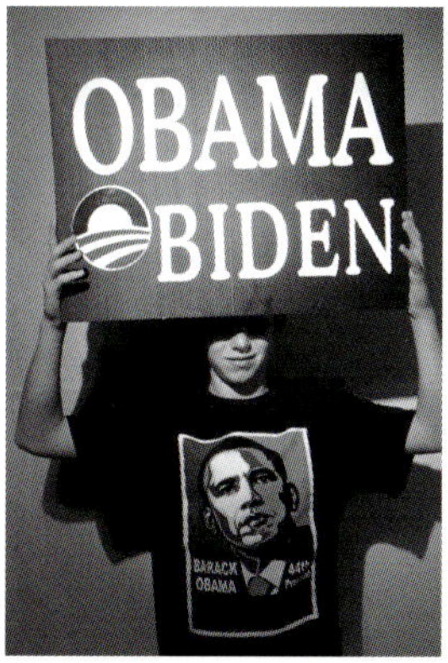

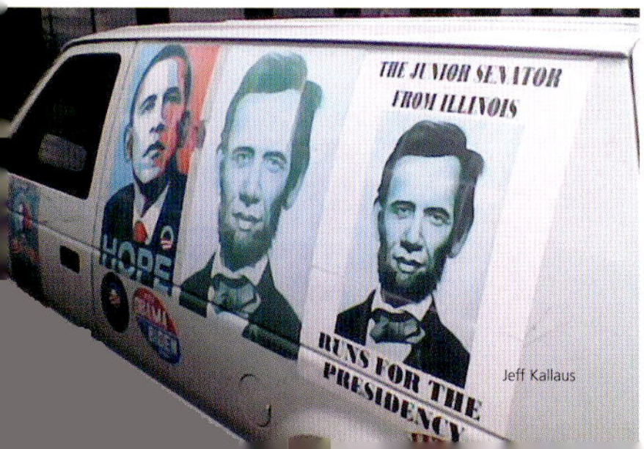

Jeff Kallaus

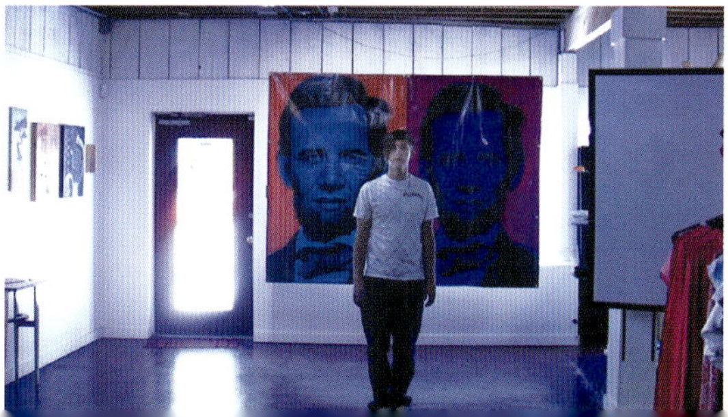

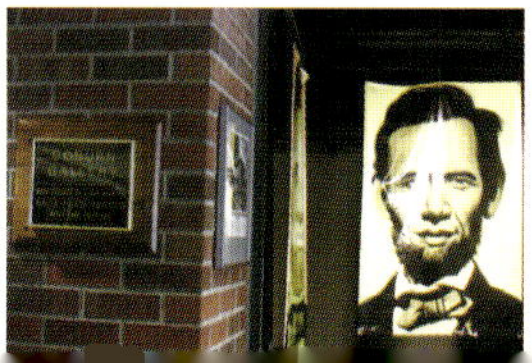

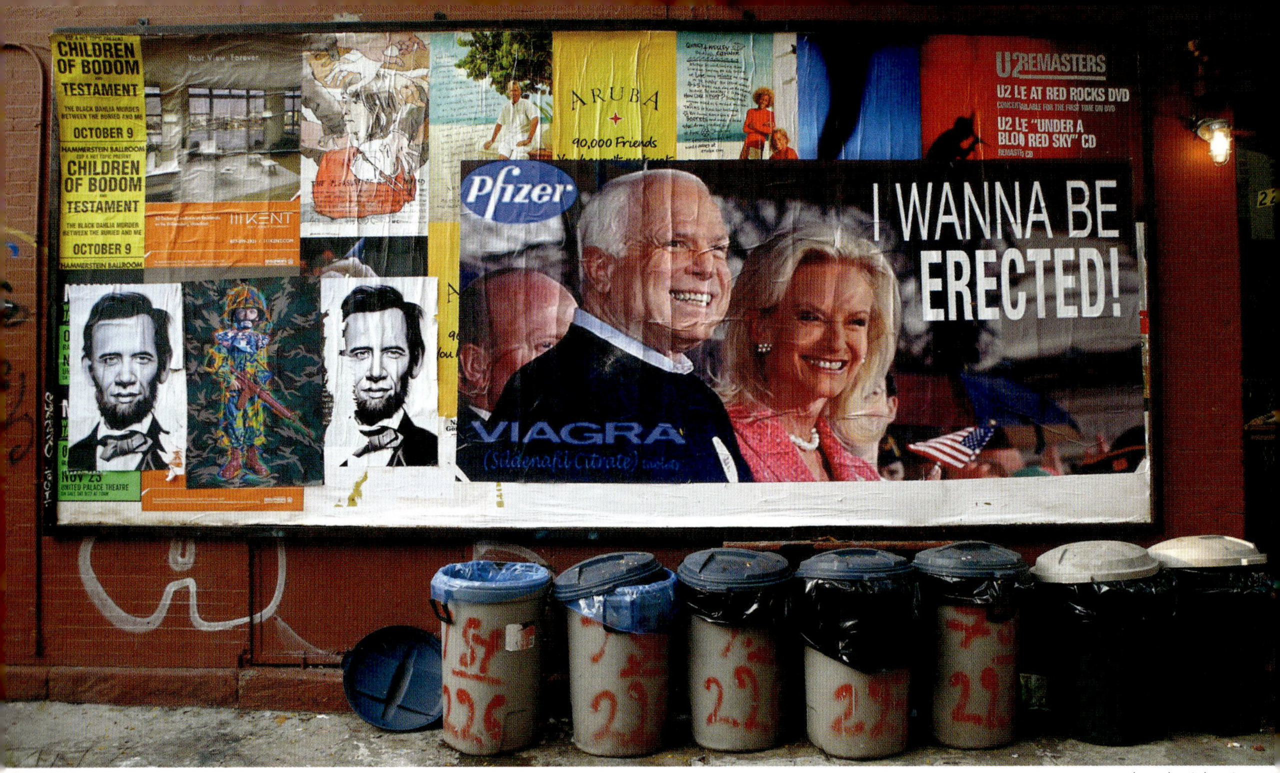

photo by Adam Lawrer

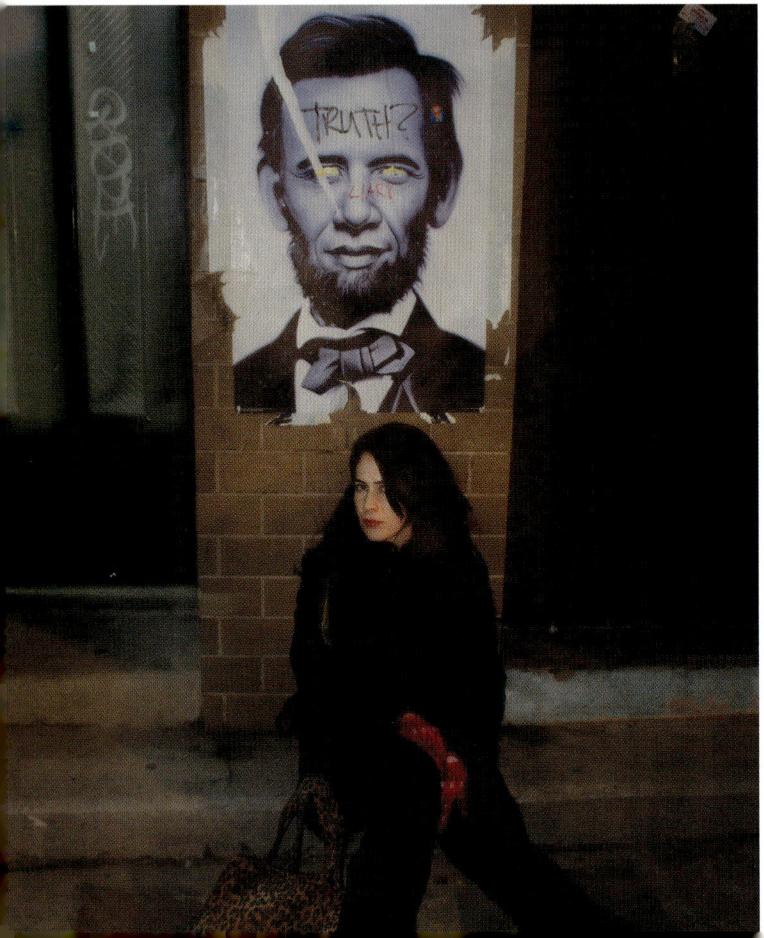

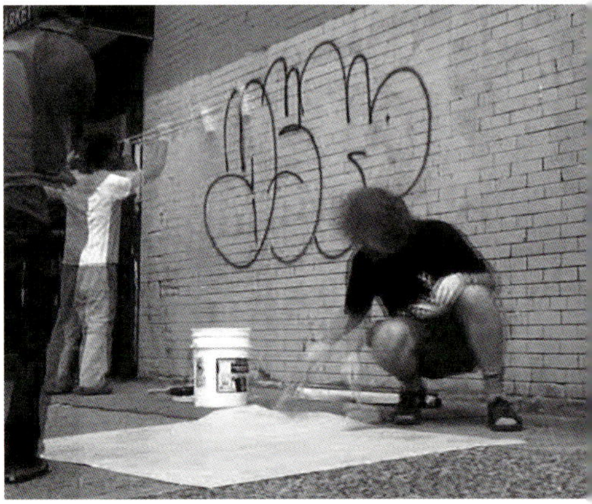

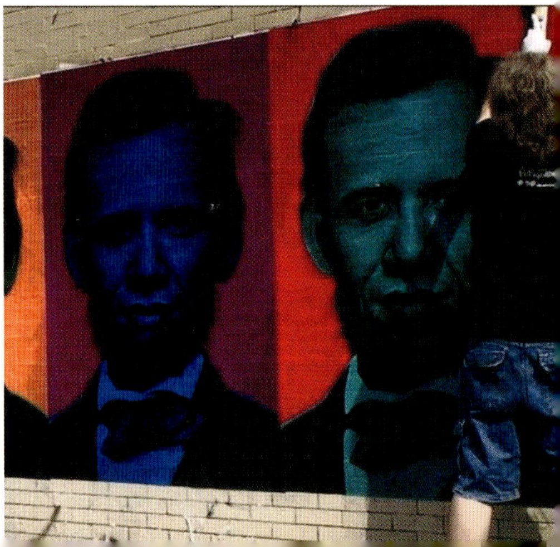

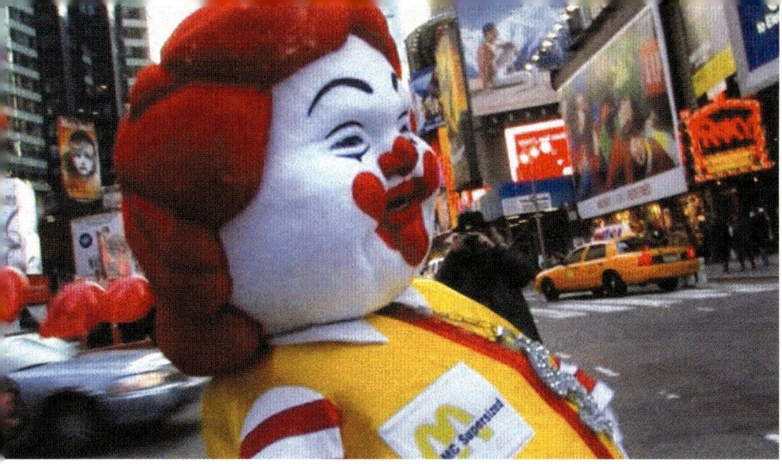

New York City

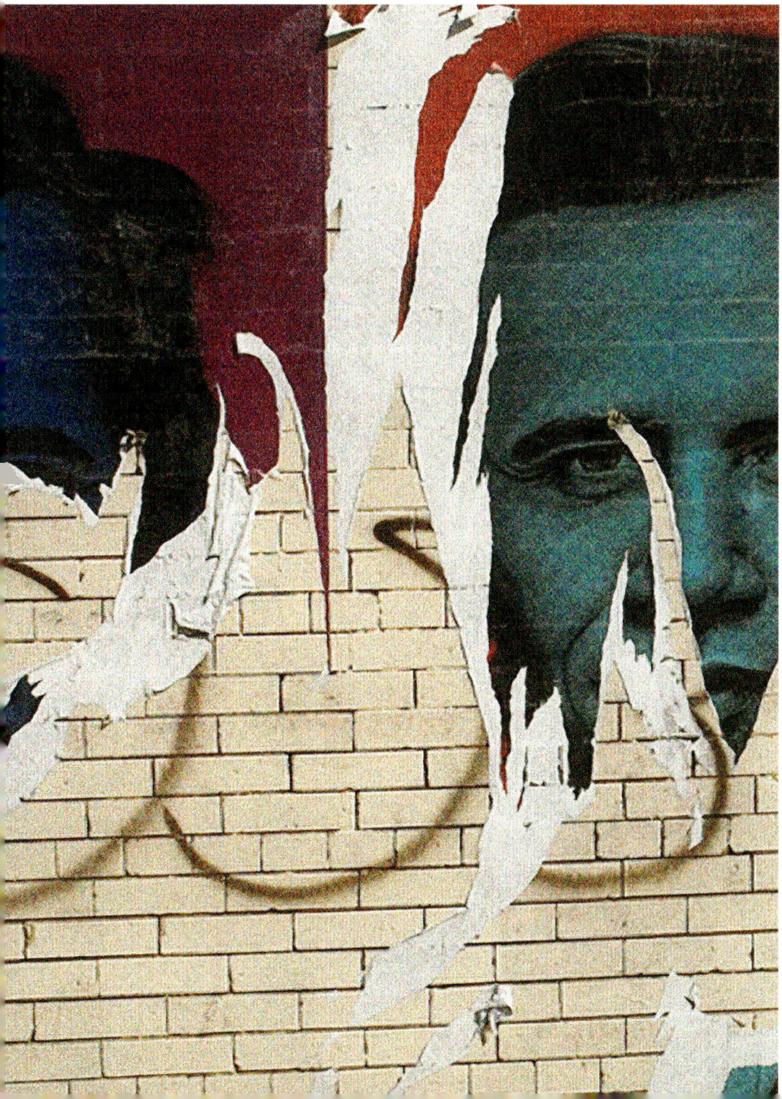

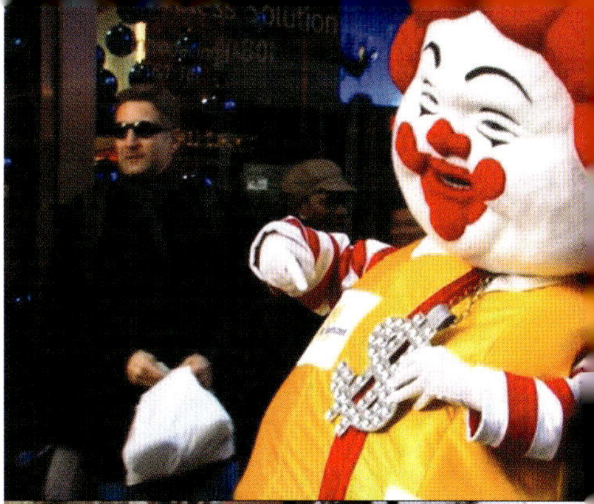

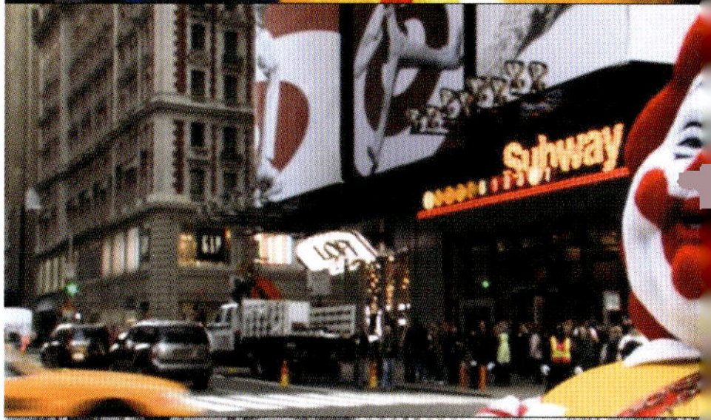

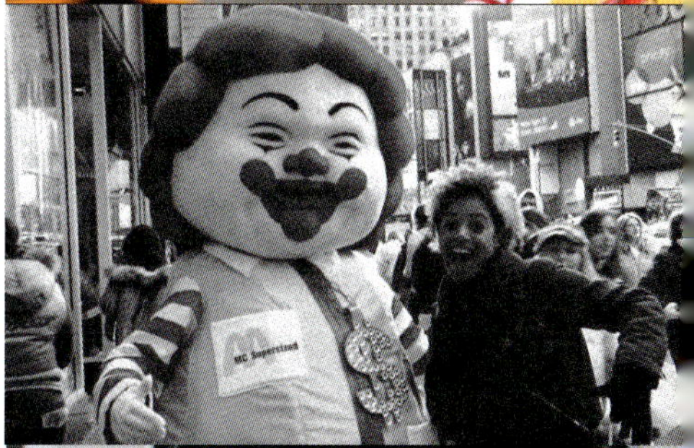

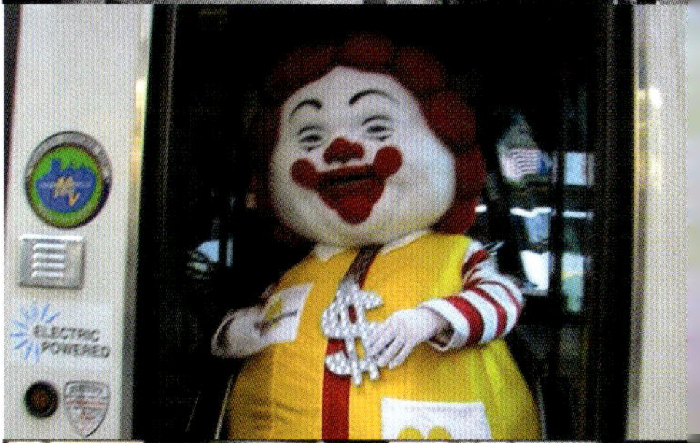

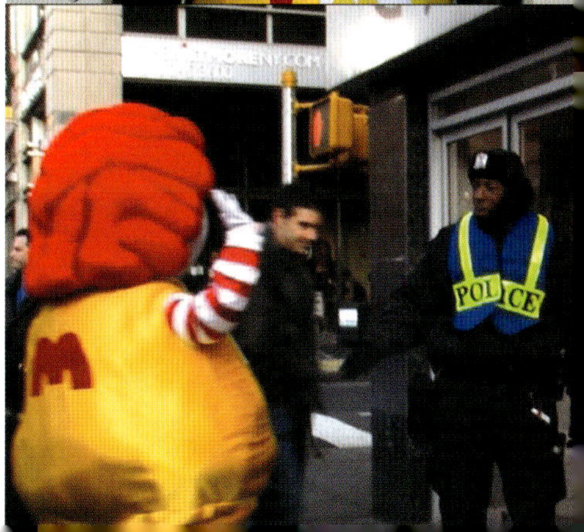

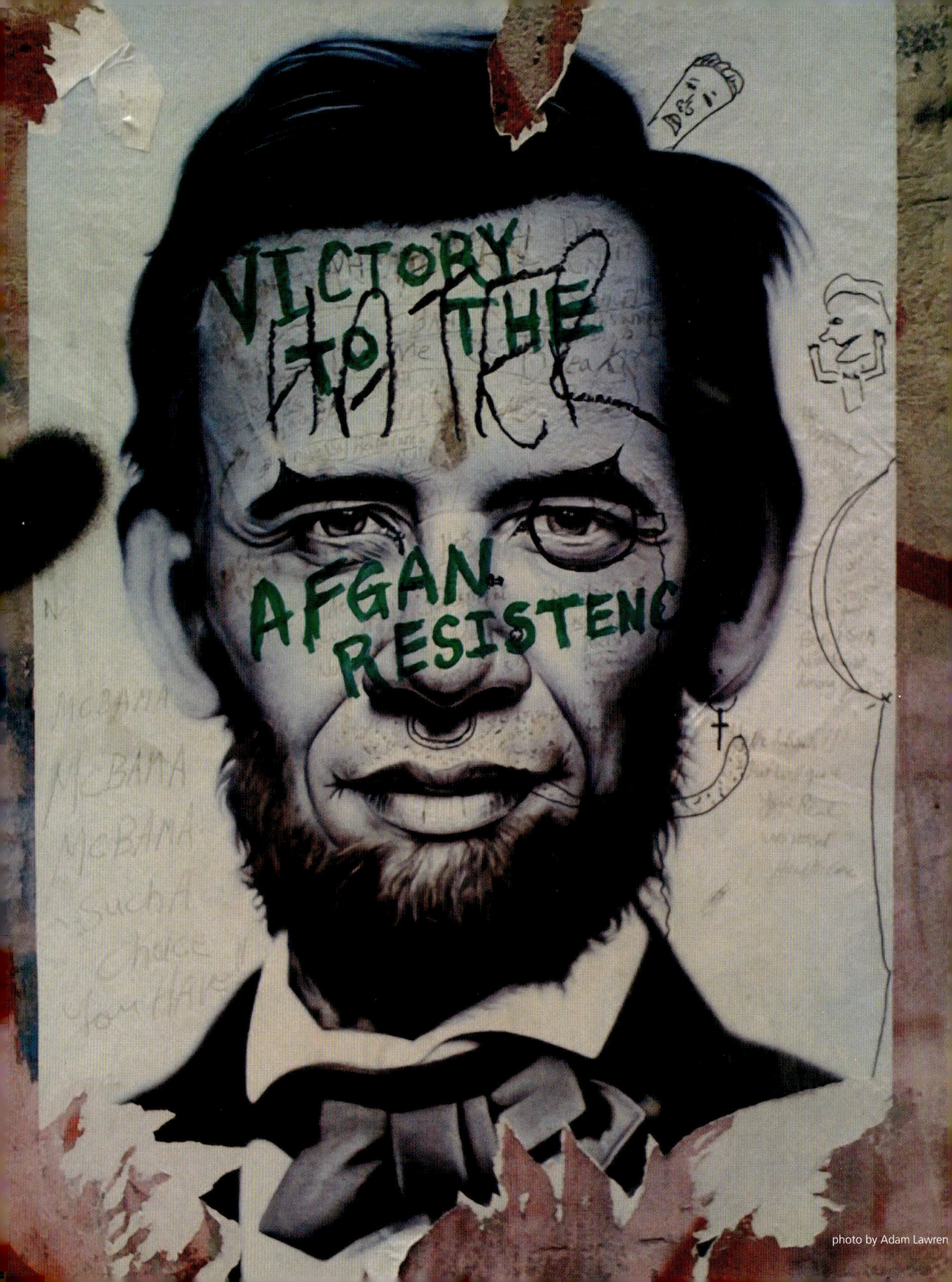

photo by Adam Lawren

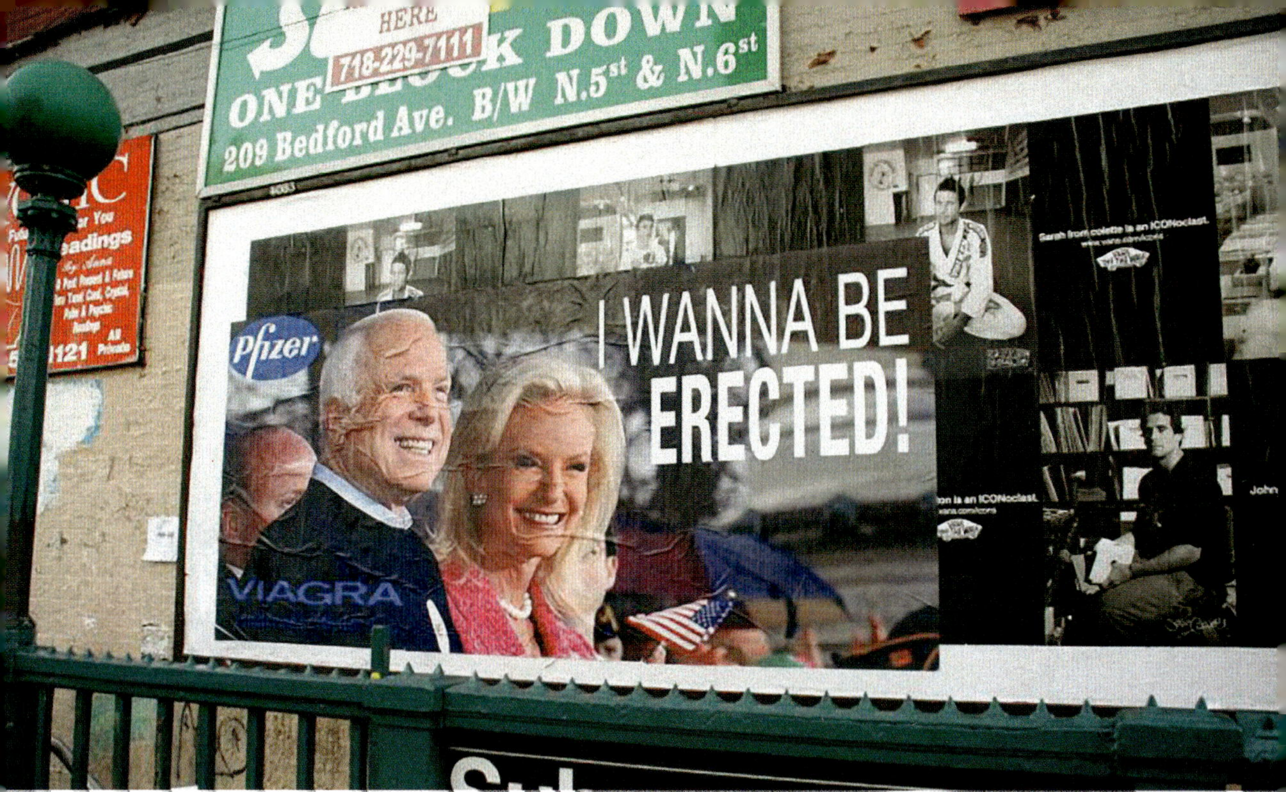

Brooklyn Subway

photo by Paolo Mastrangelo

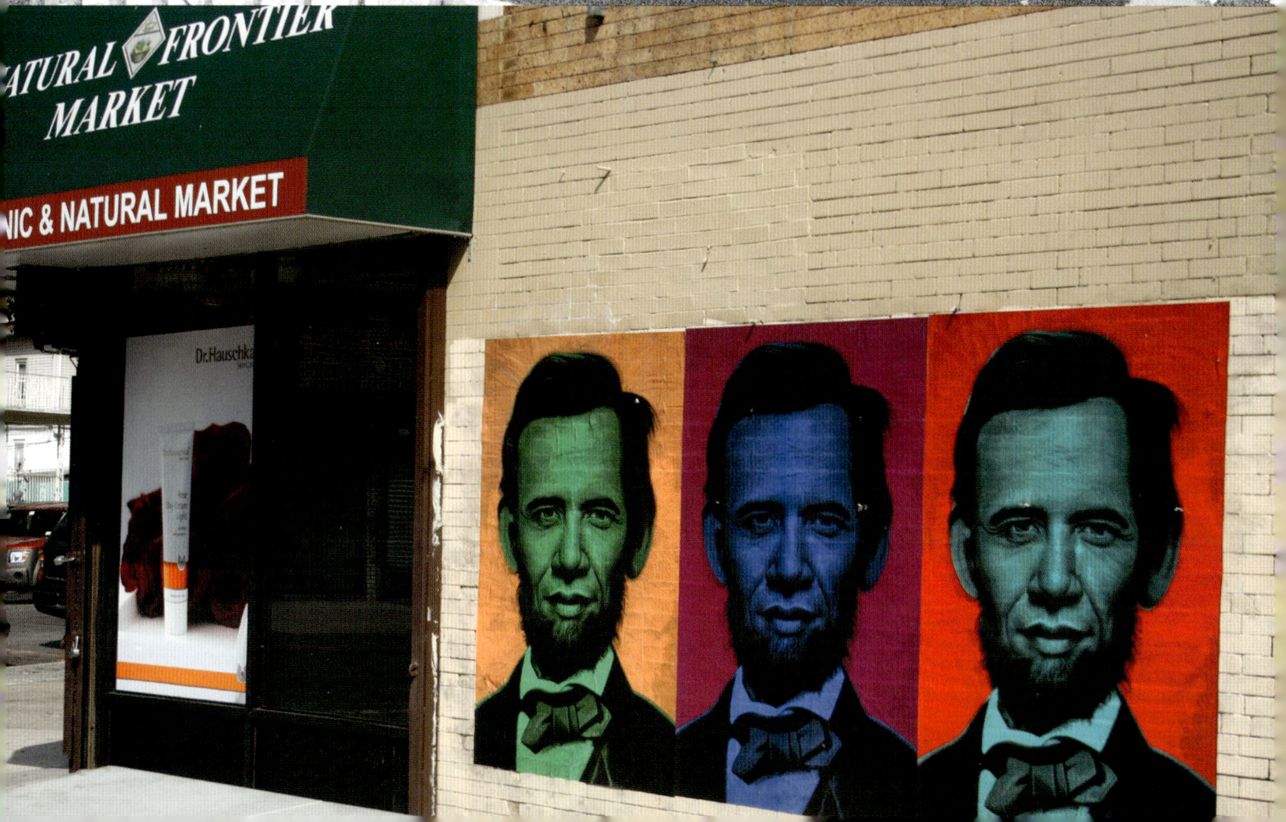

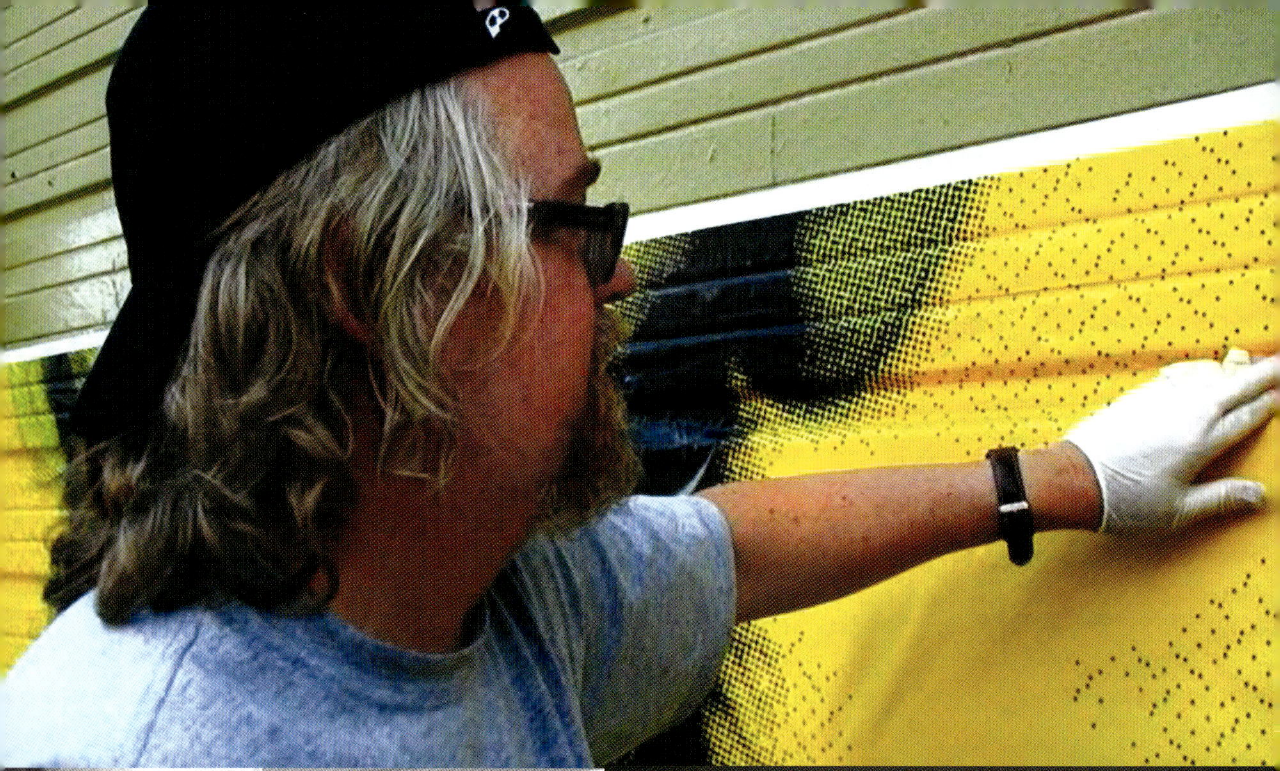

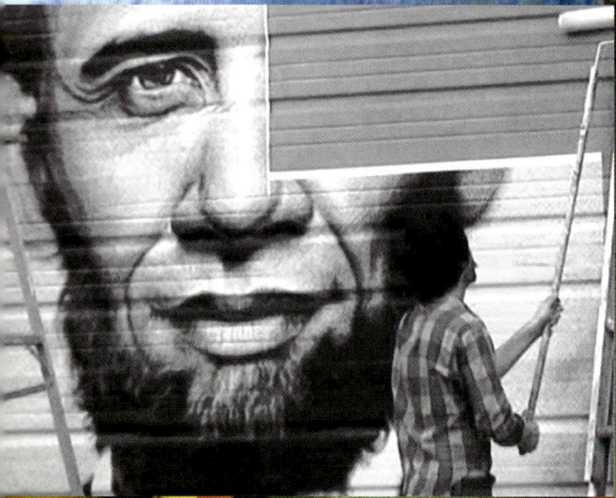

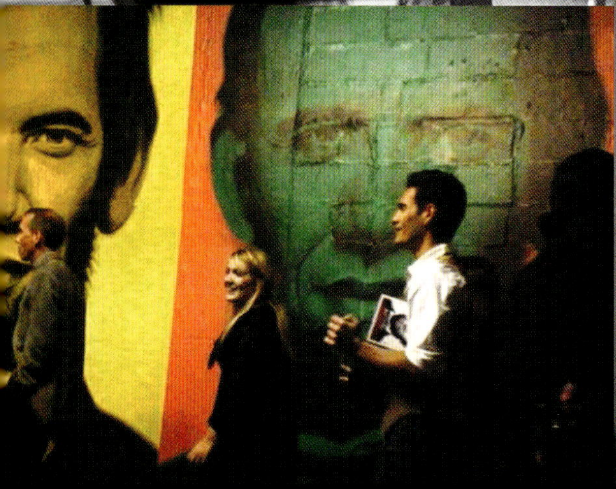

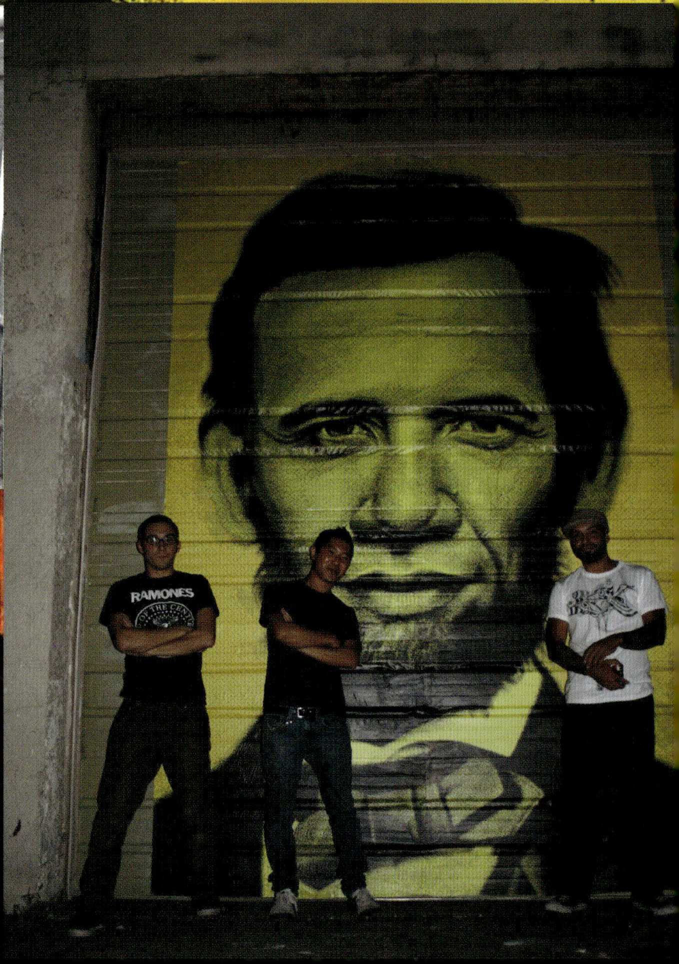
RAMONES

Jersey City

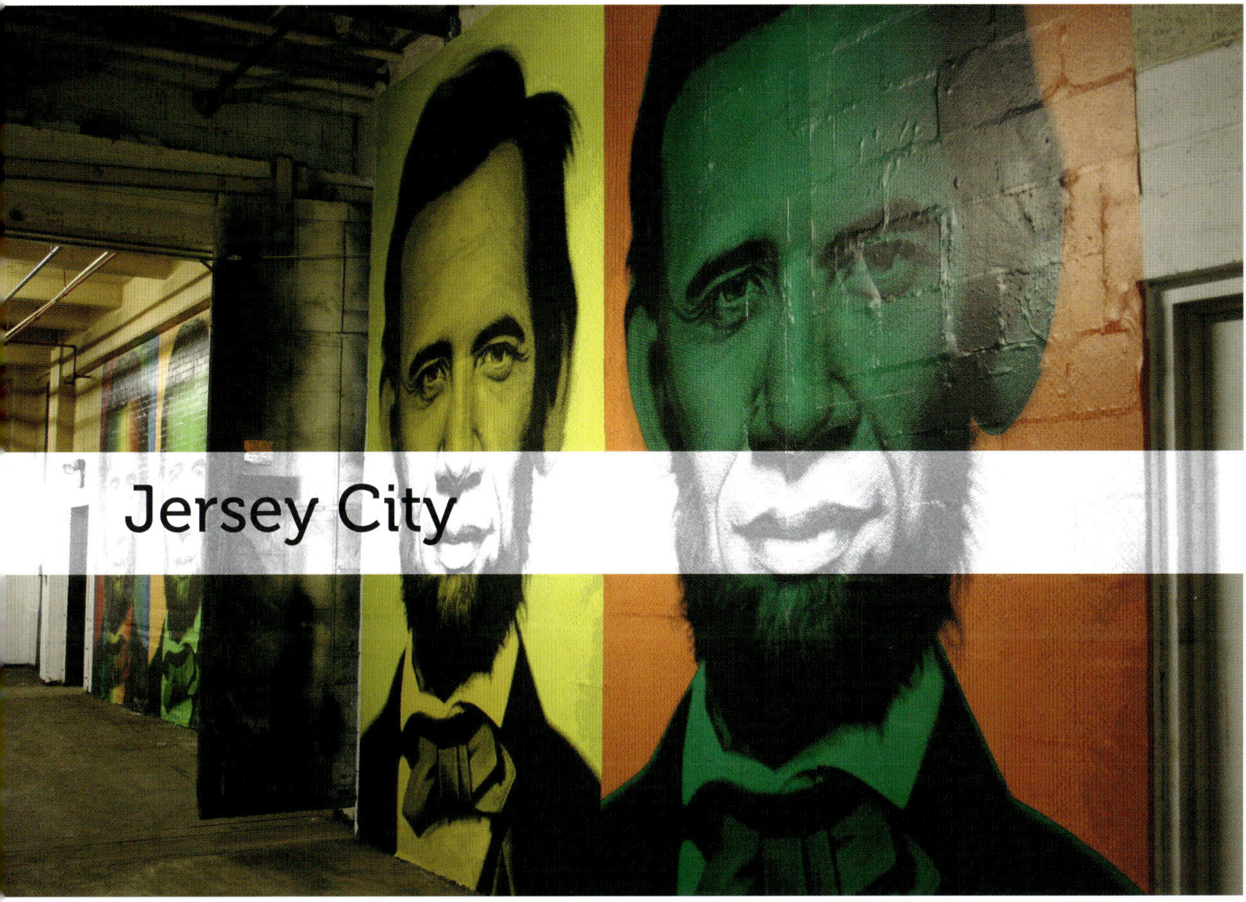

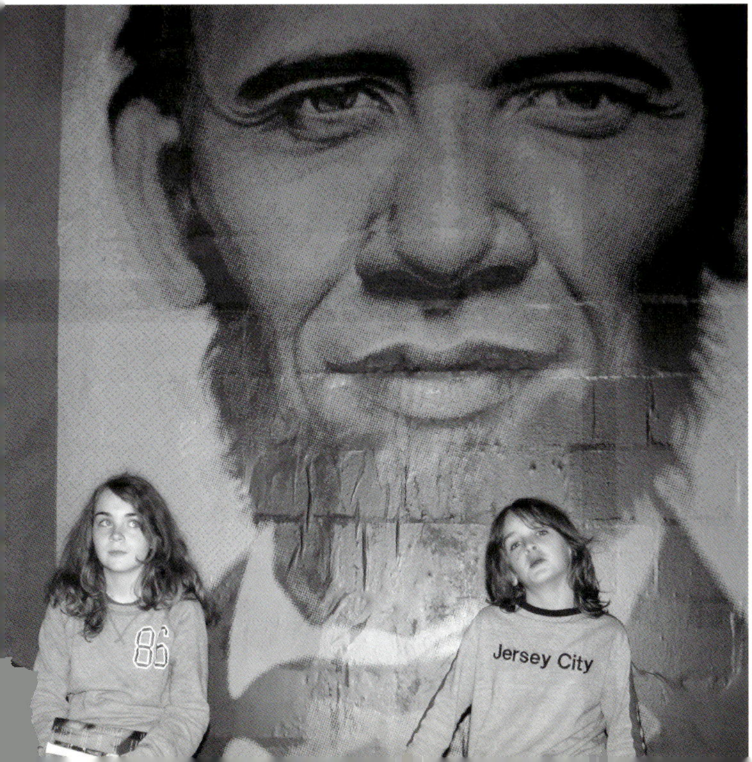

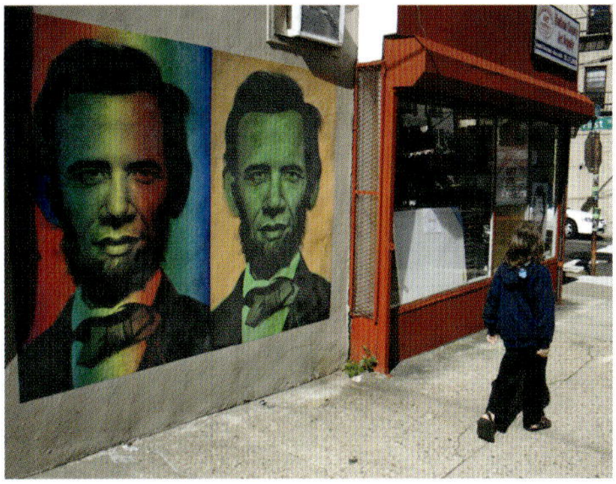

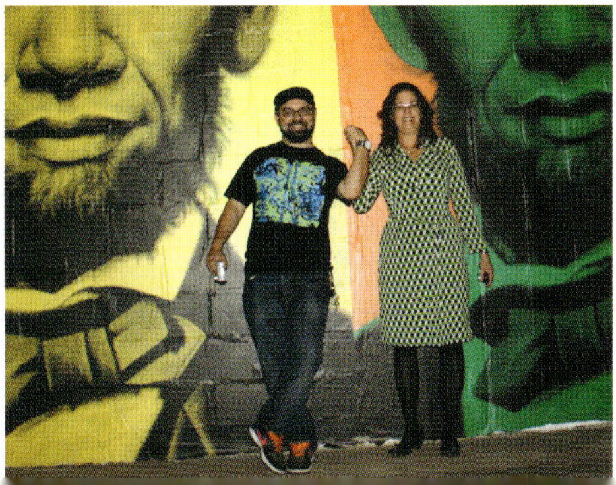

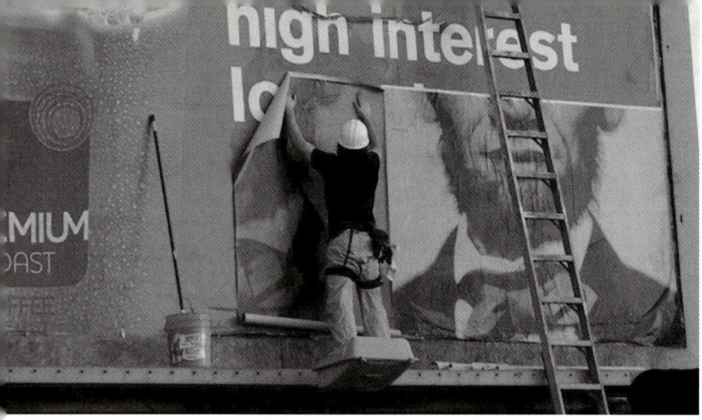
high interest

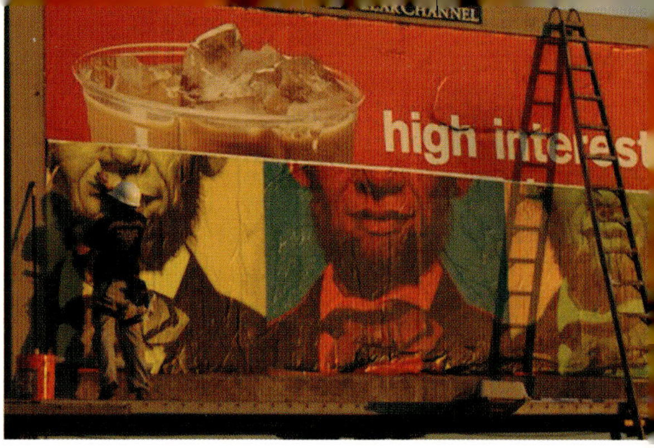
high interest

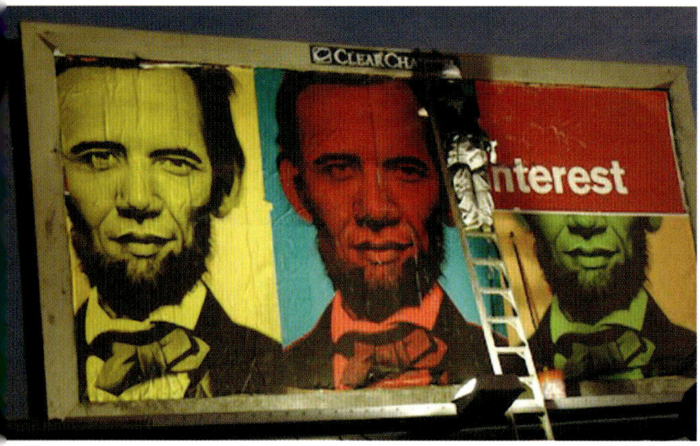
interest

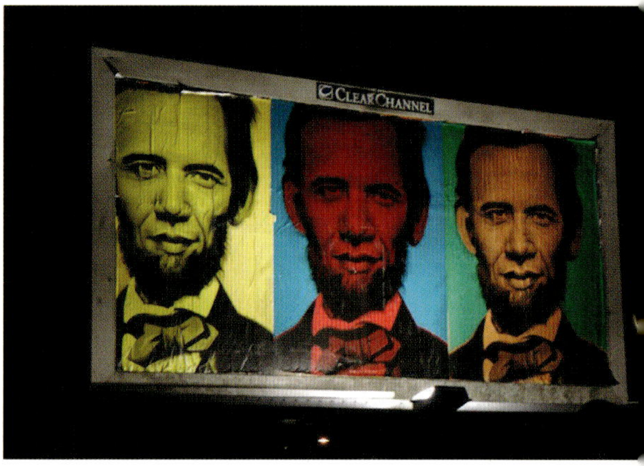
CLEAR CHANNEL

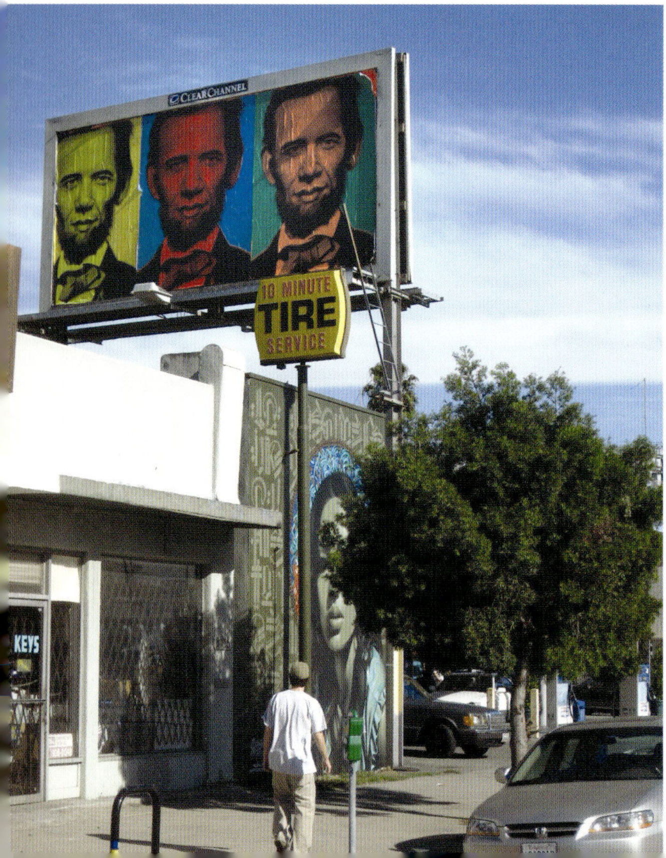
10 MINUTE
TIRE
SERVICE
KEYS

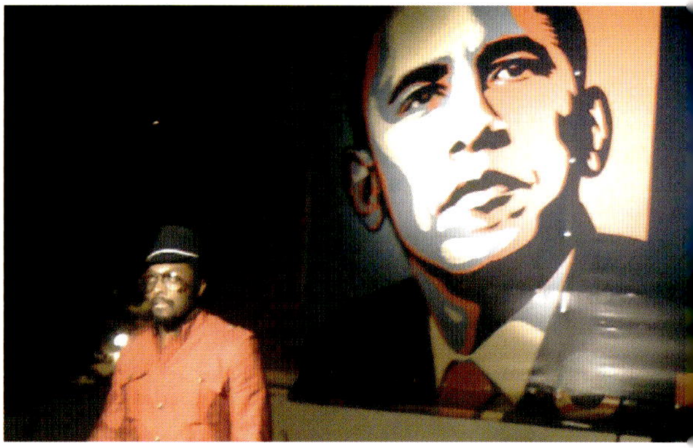

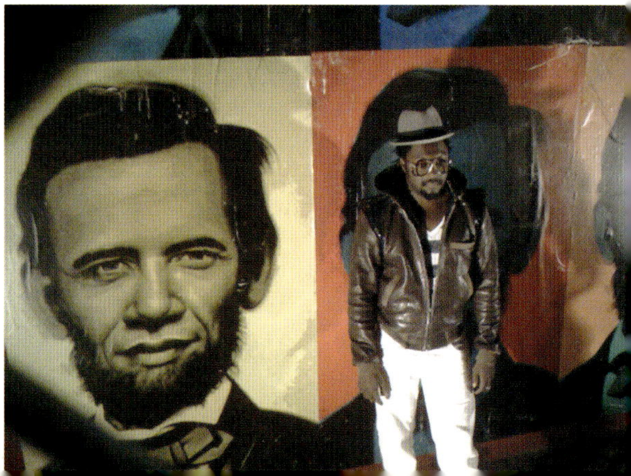

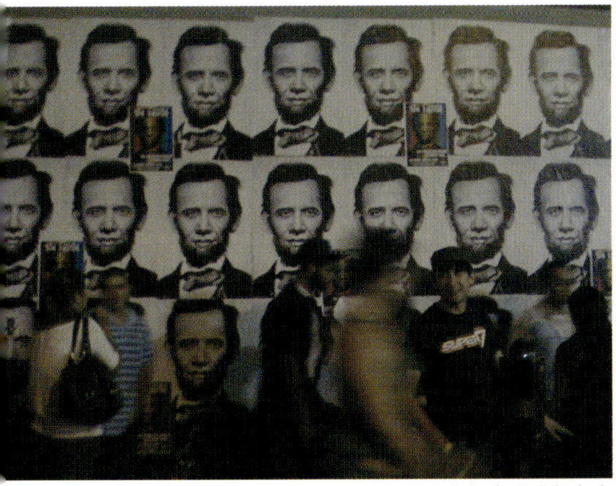

photos by Daniel Lahoda

Los Angeles

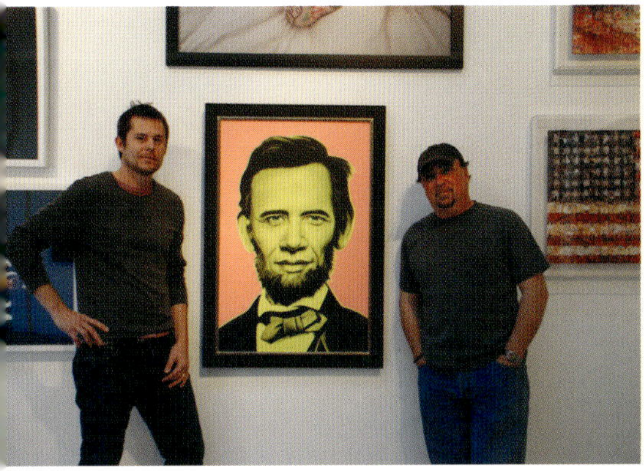

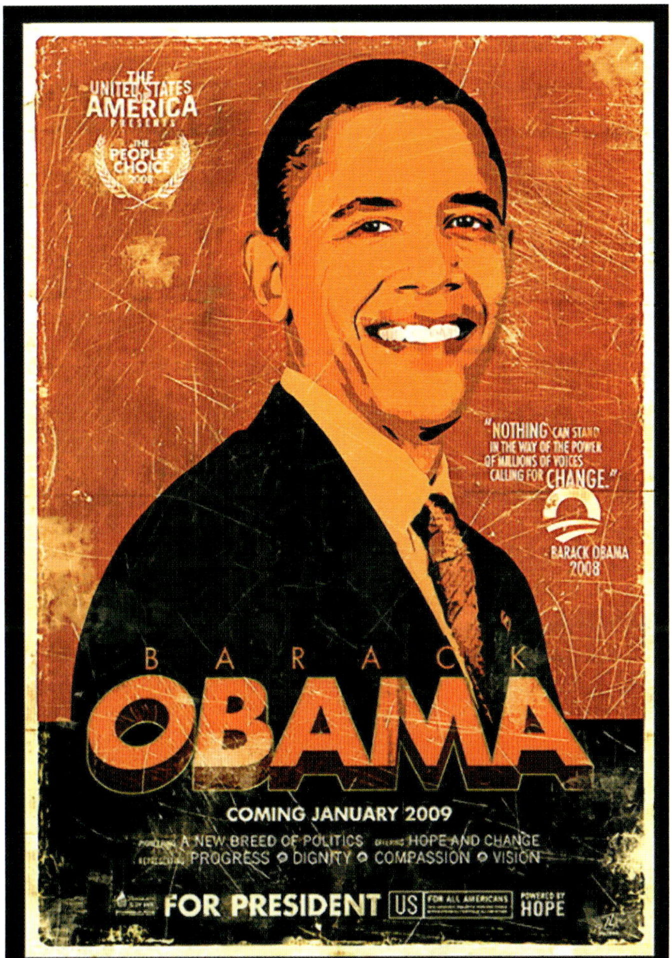

Artist Unknown

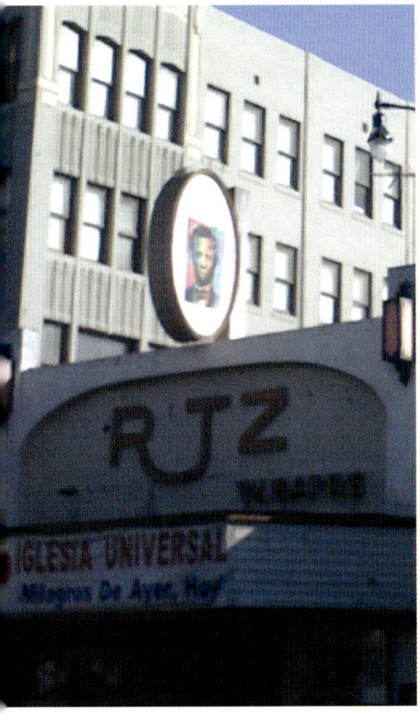

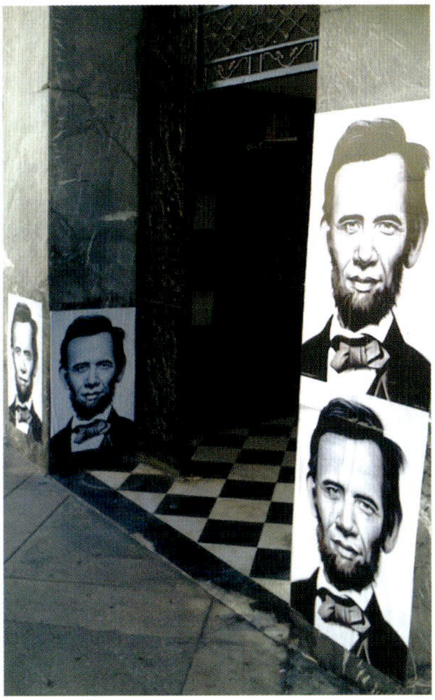

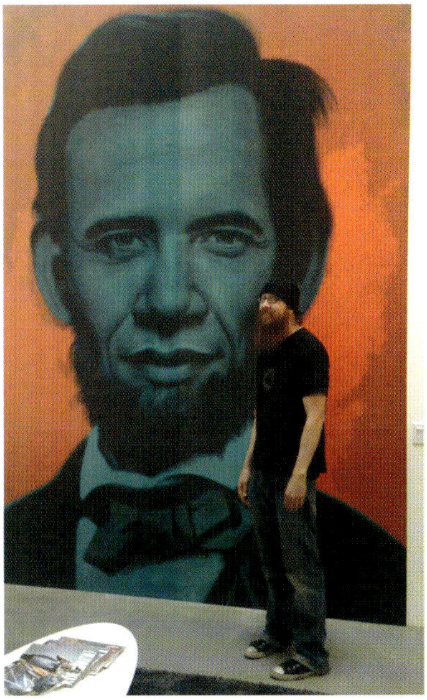

photo by Jon Cournoyor

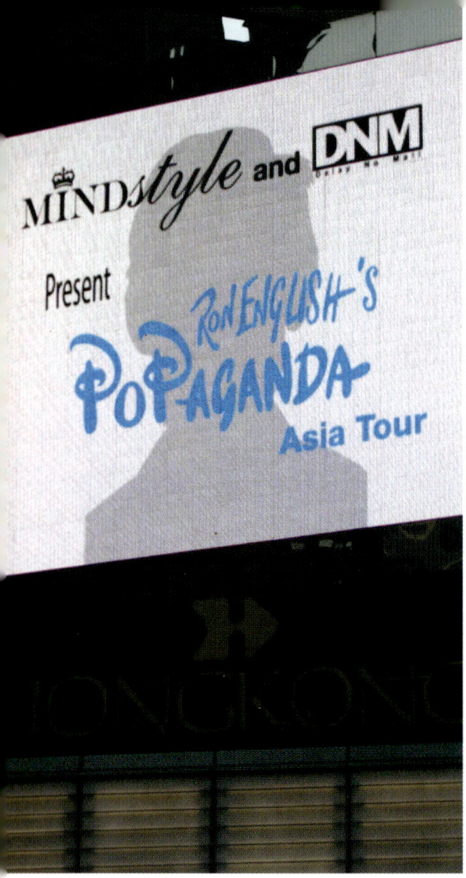
MINDstyle and DNM
Present
RON ENGLISH's
POPAGANDA
Asia Tour

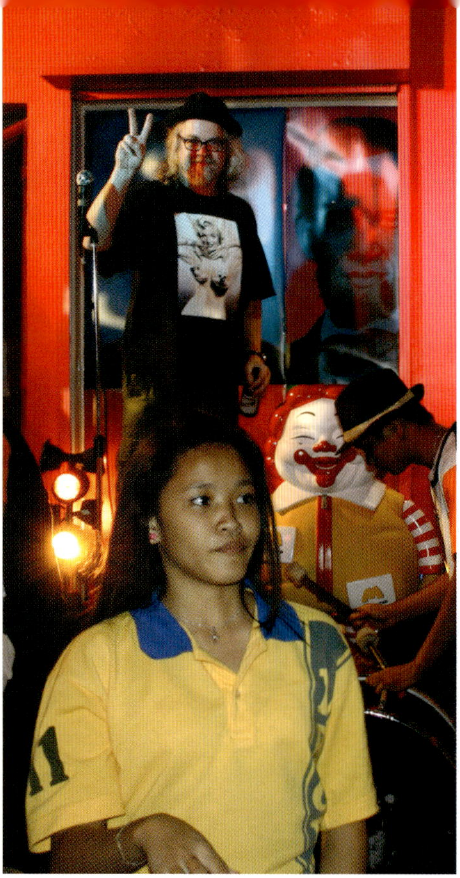

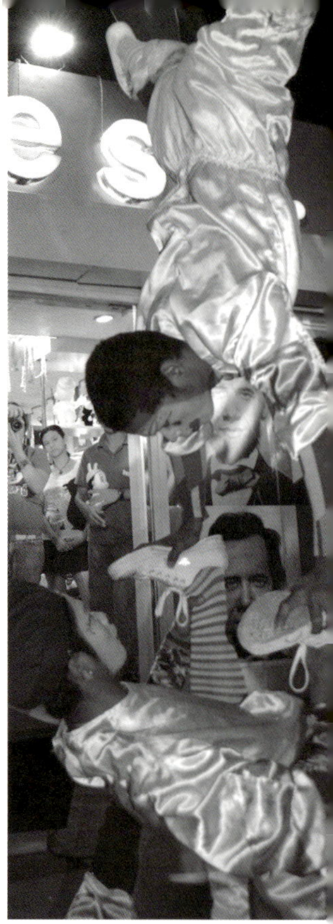

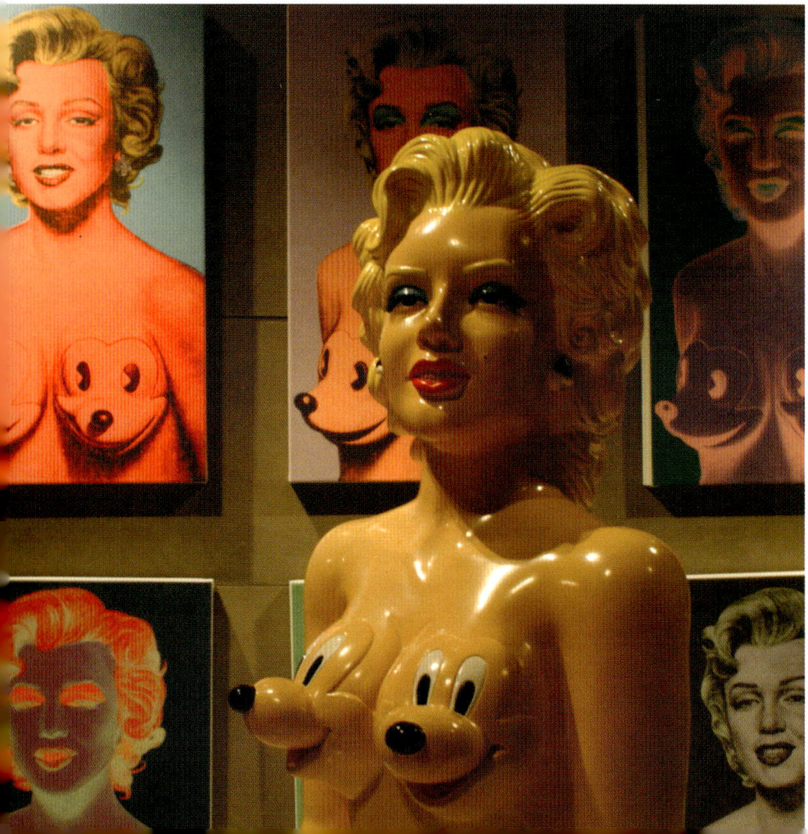

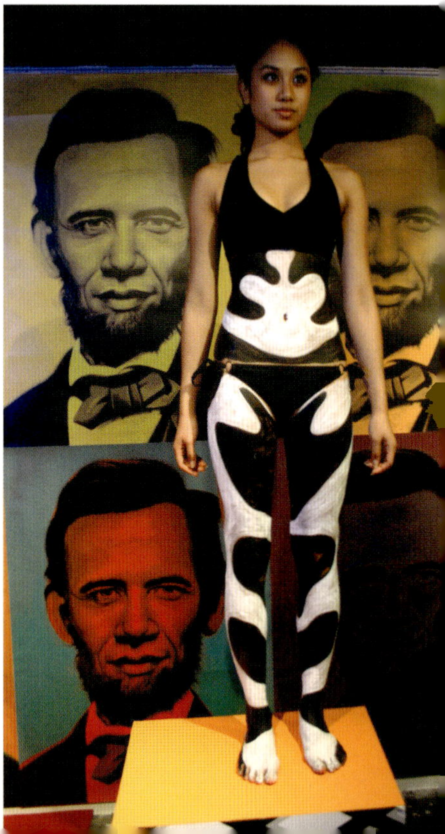

Hong Kong

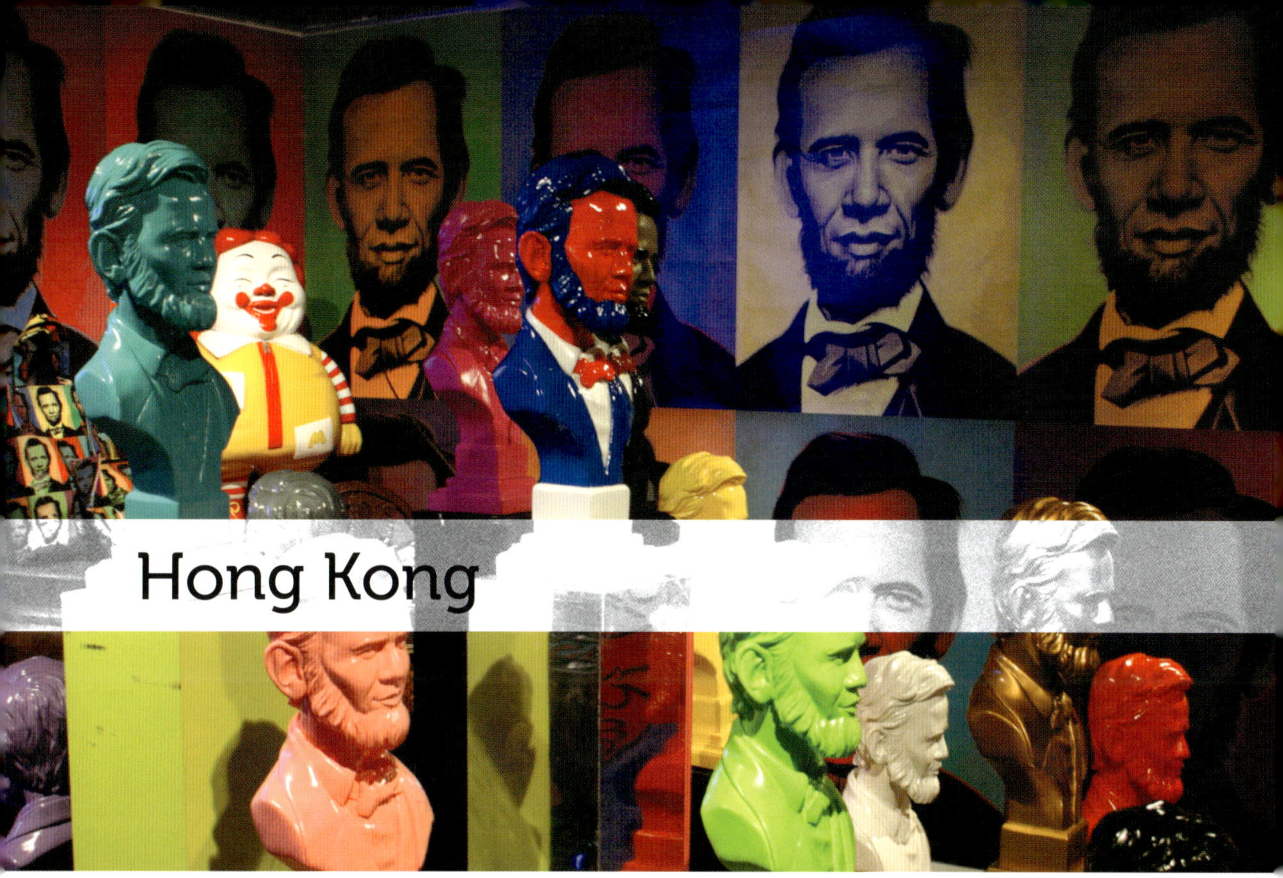

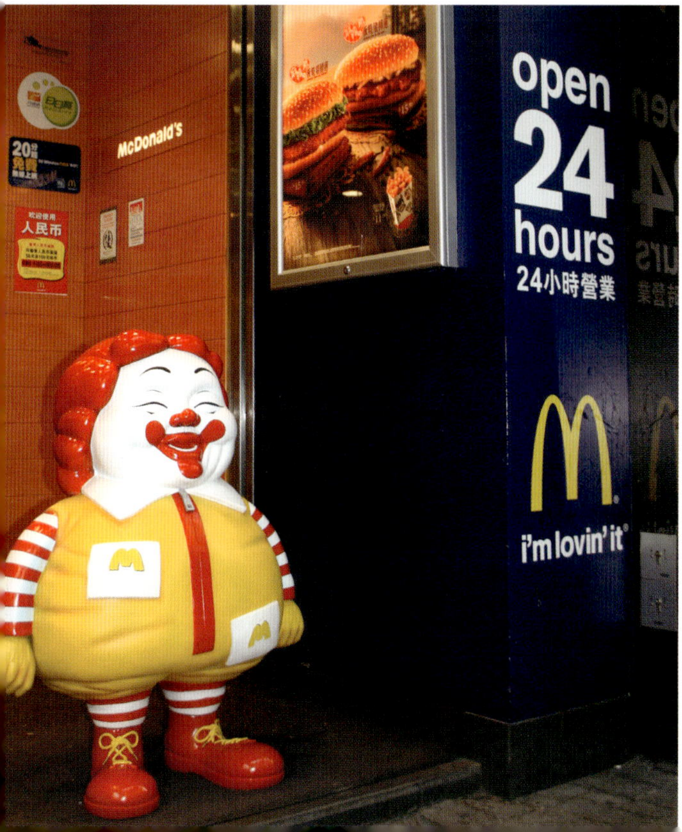
McDonald's
open
24
hours
24小時營業
i'm lovin' it
人民币

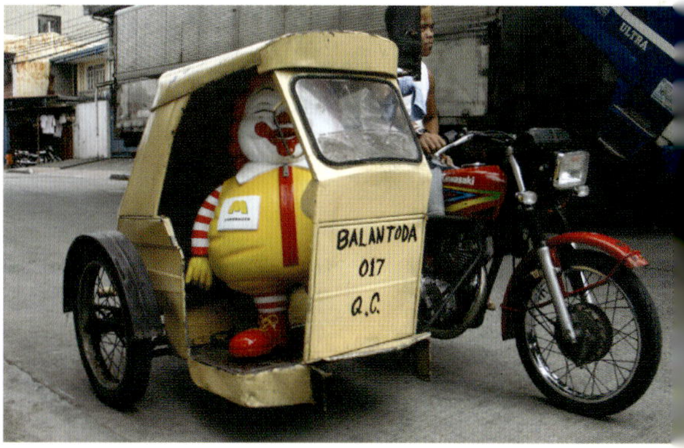
BALANTODA
017
Q.C.

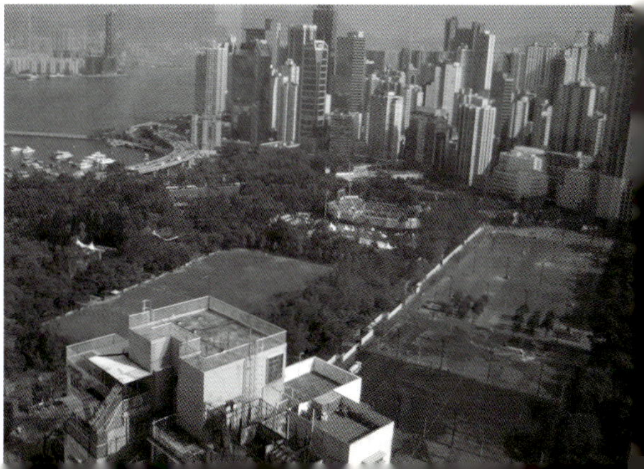

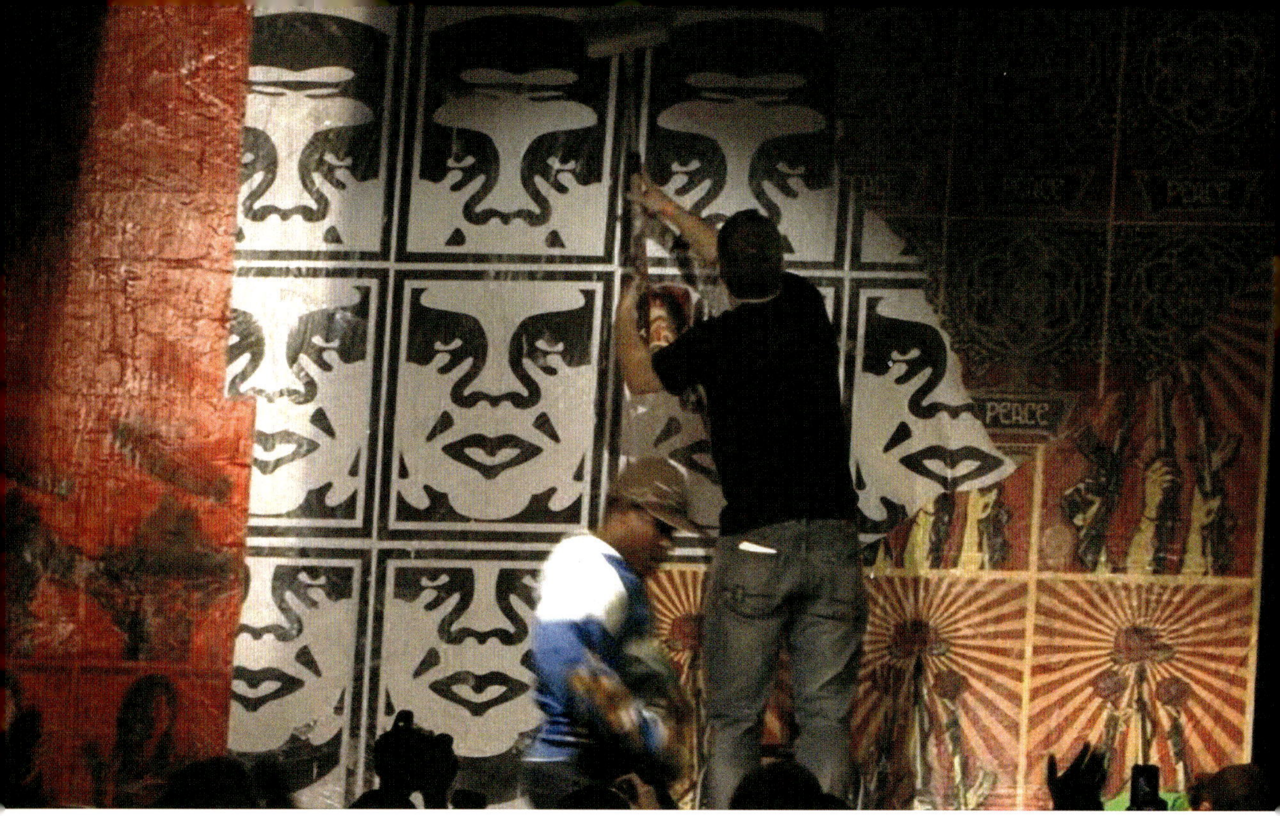
PEACE
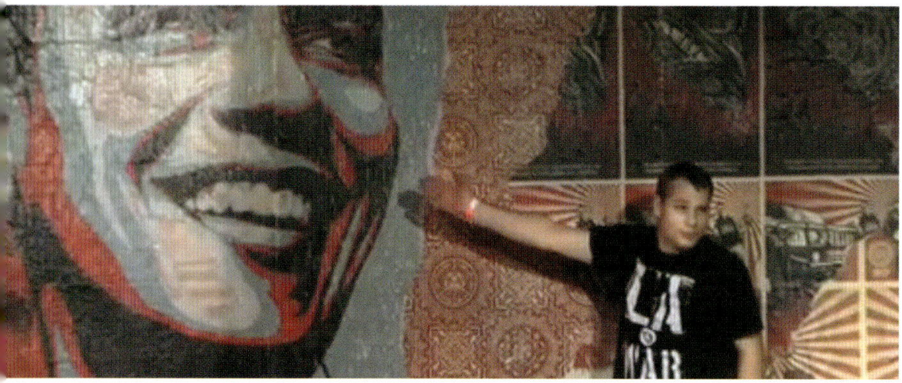
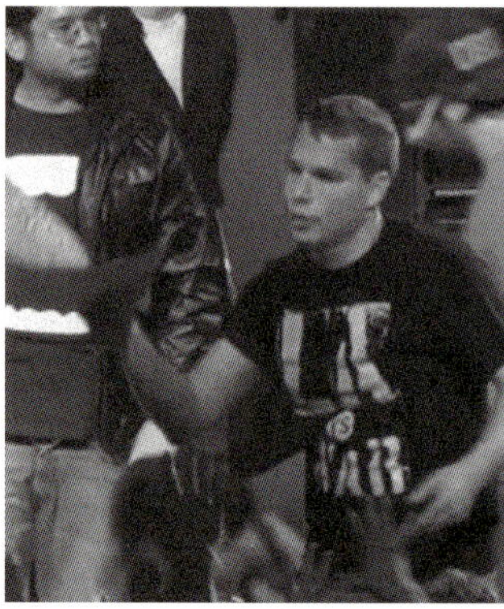
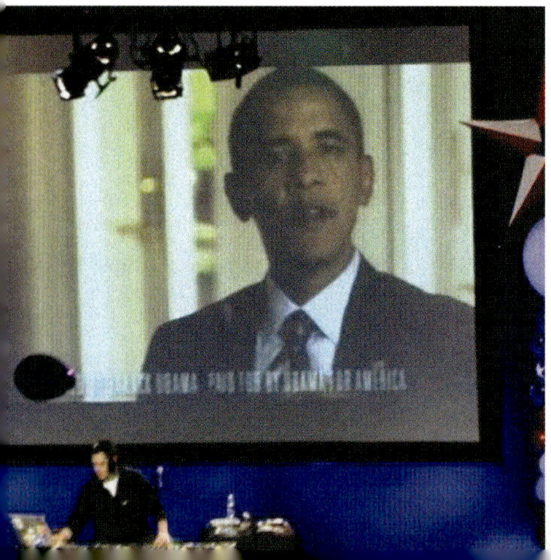
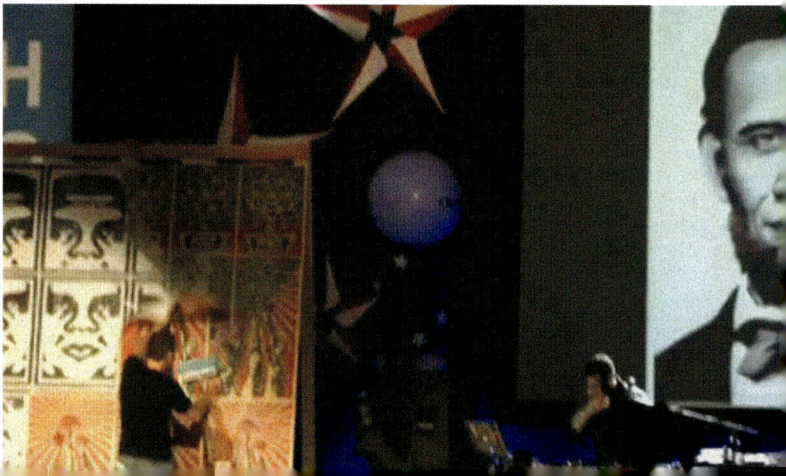

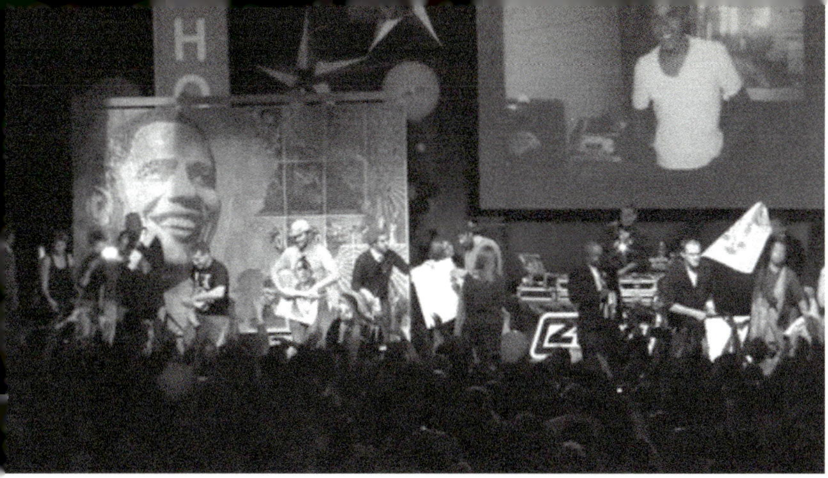

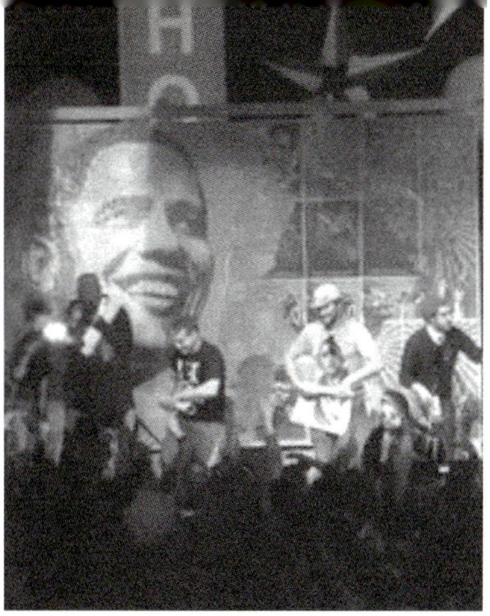

Election Night

Ron was home sick with exhaustion watching the election on TV. Kevin was trying to get into any election party he could in New York. Chunwoo was bombing the East Village. Daniel Lahoda was at the official California election night party watching Shepard Fairey install his final iconic Hope mural while filming the final scenes for the movie Abraham Obama. I was recording a song called "America's Back" with The Electric Illuminati.
–DG

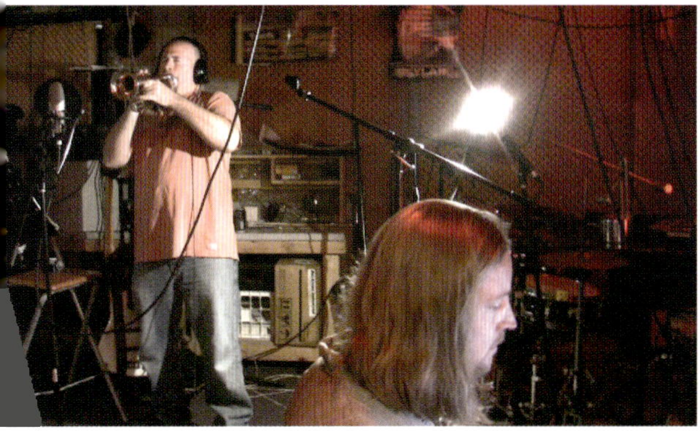

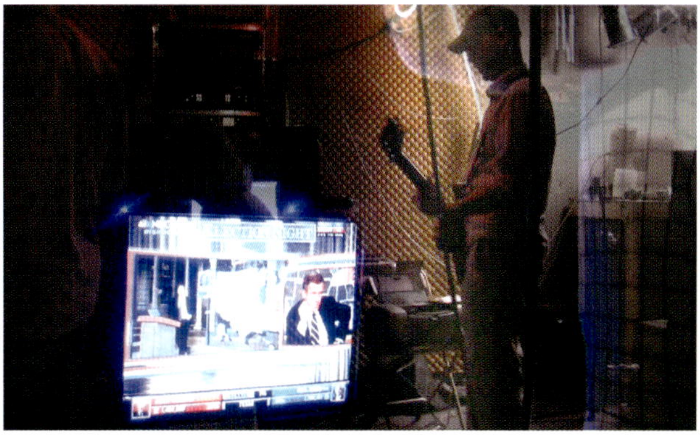

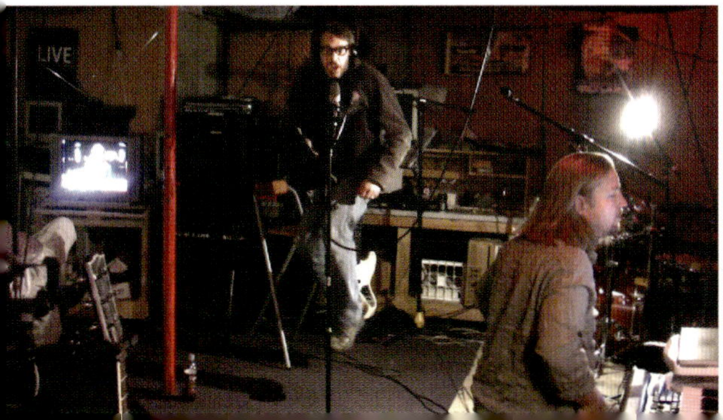

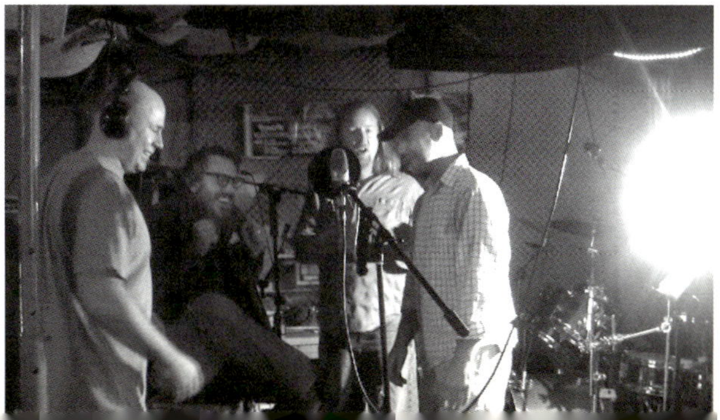

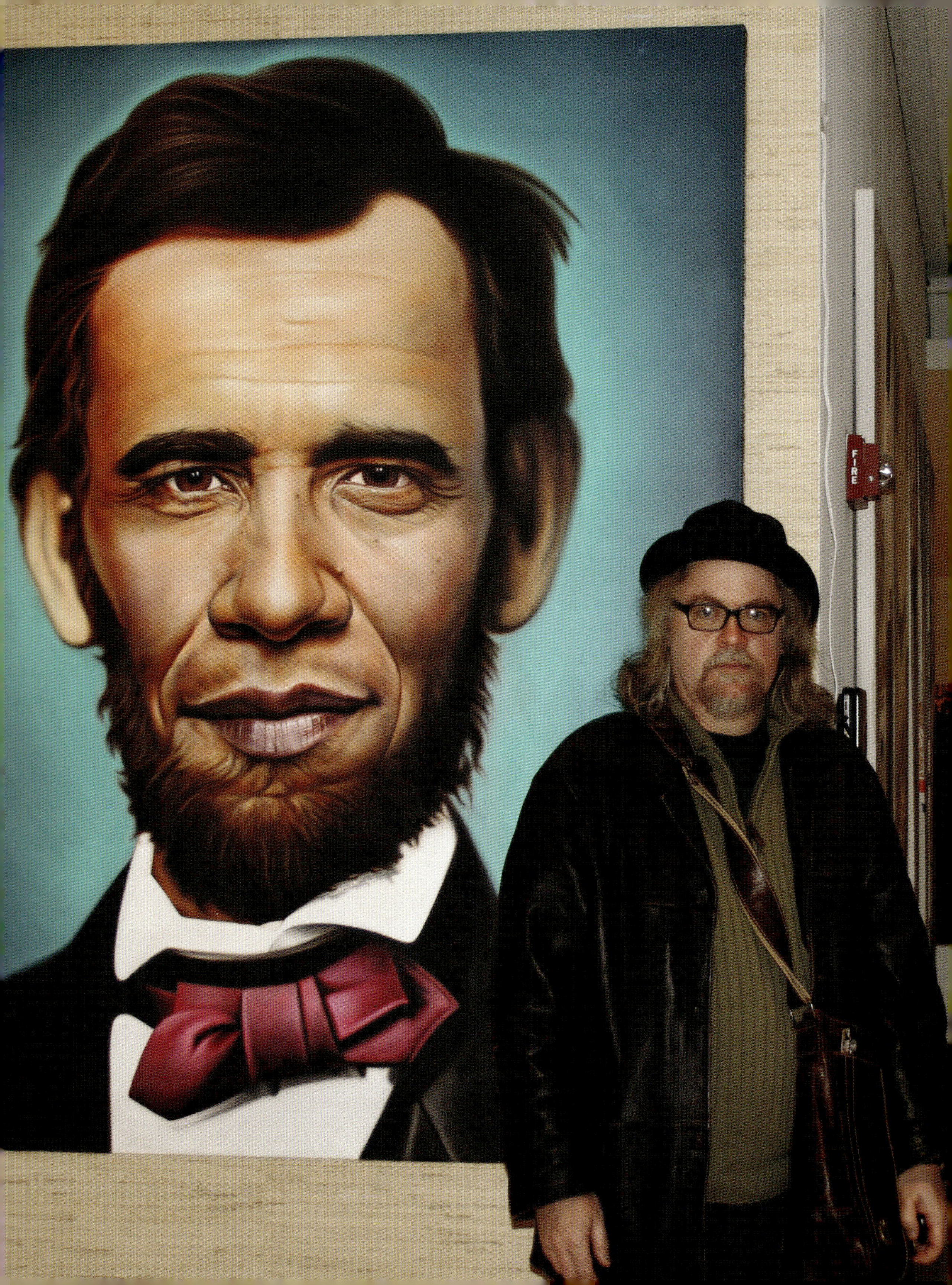
FIRE

Manifest Hope: DC

Words and photos by Jean Aw from NOTCOT.com

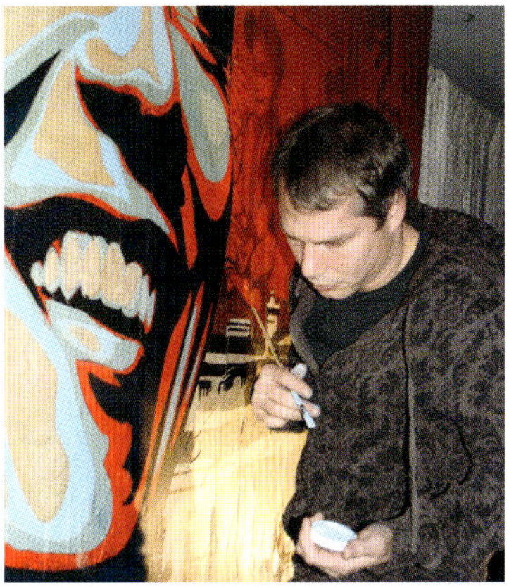

Wow. Yosi Sergant (along with his whole team at the awesome Evolutionary Media Group) and Shepard Fairey sure knew how to put on a hell of an art show, raise spirits, and pull off a ridiculously nonchalant, humble adorableness. It was an absolute honor to be able to watch such influential folks put their powers to use for good in the election of Obama from such a close distance, and personally, their ability to bring the creative community together so strongly and visually was numbing. I went back to my hotel, mind spinning, and a CF card loaded with over 100 amazing pictures.

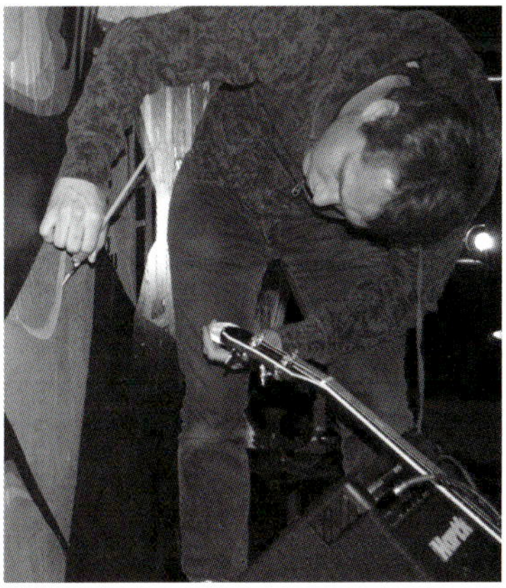

Manifest Hope: DC was absolutely incredible, regardless of how you may feel about Obama, or the visual idolization of our new icon–the quality of art in this show and the amount of art in this show was absolutely stunning. The focus of Manifest Hope: DC was three themes… Manifest Change–Health Care Reform, Manifest Unity–Workers' Rights, and Manifest Opportunity–The Green Economy.

All photos by Jean Aw except left photograph by Tarssa Yazdani and two upper right photographs by Ron English

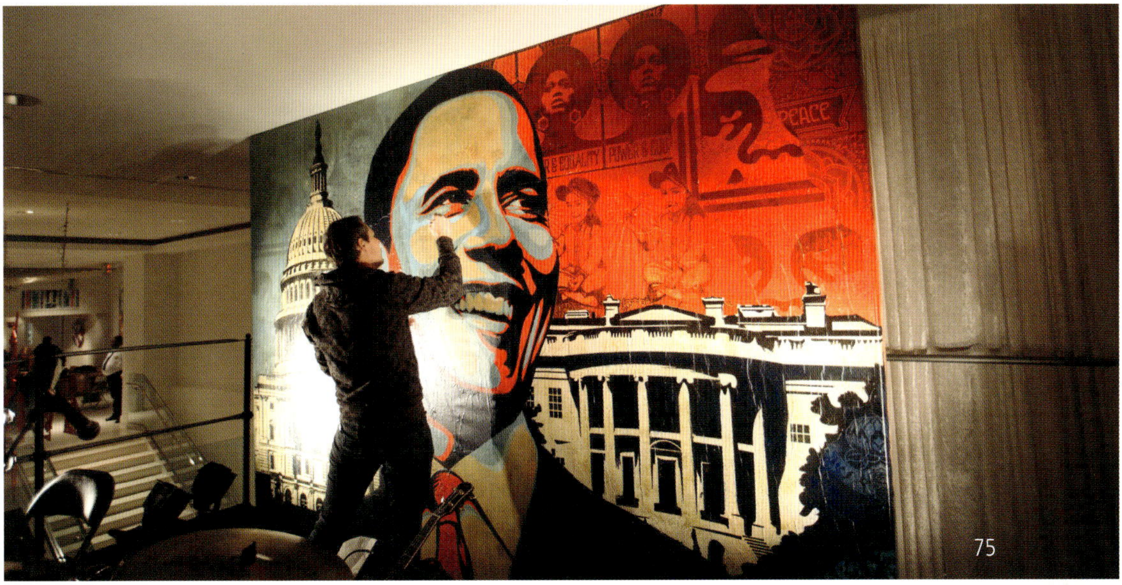

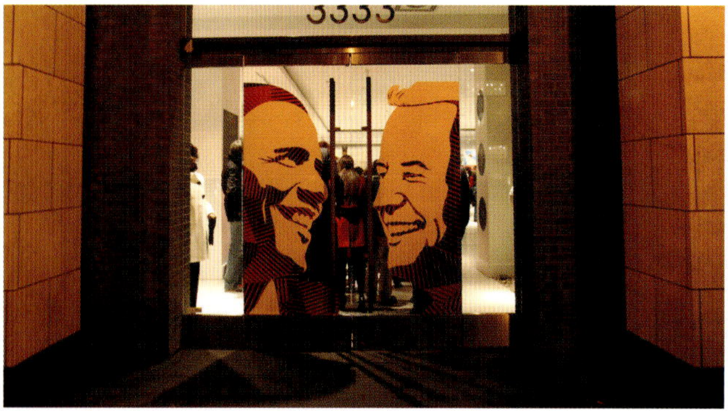

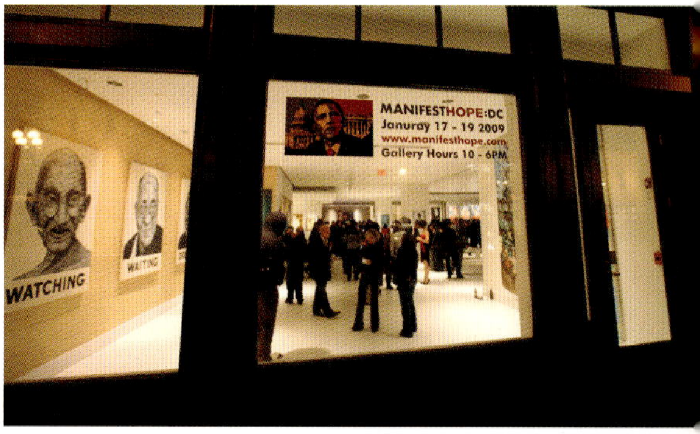
MANIFESTHOPE:DC
Janurary 17 - 19 2009
www.manifesthope.com
Gallery Hours 10 - 6PM
WATCHING
WAITING

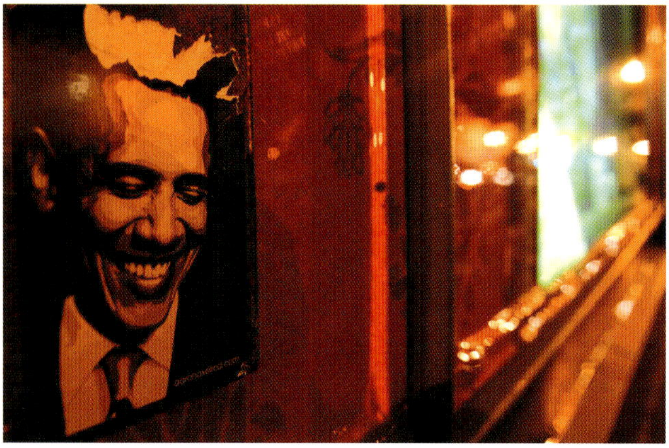

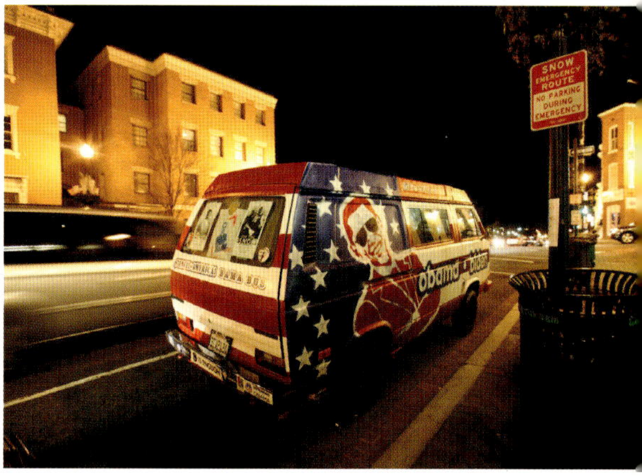
SNOW EMERGENCY ROUTE
NO PARKING DURING EMERGENCY

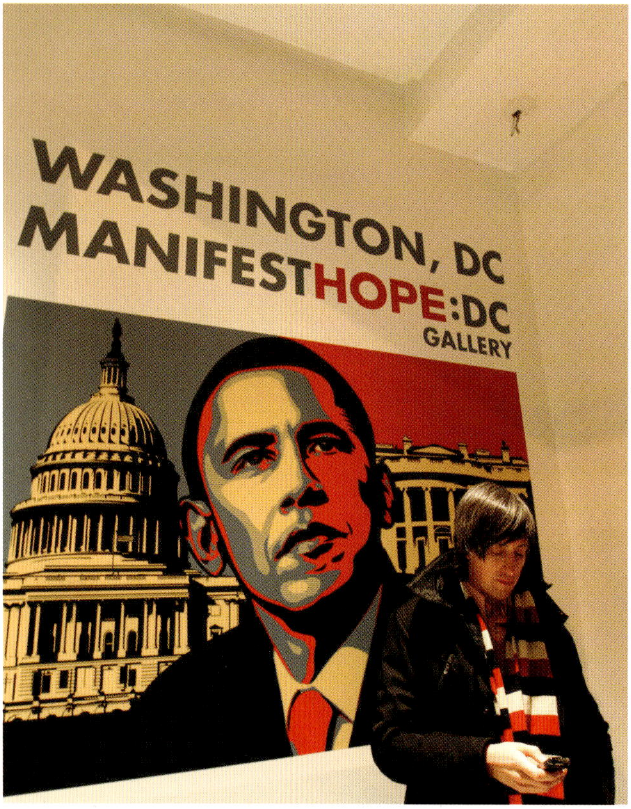
WASHINGTON, DC
MANIFESTHOPE:DC
GALLERY

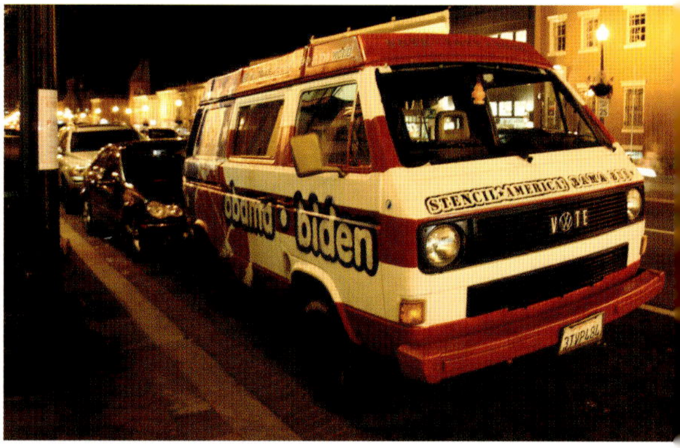
obama biden
VOTE

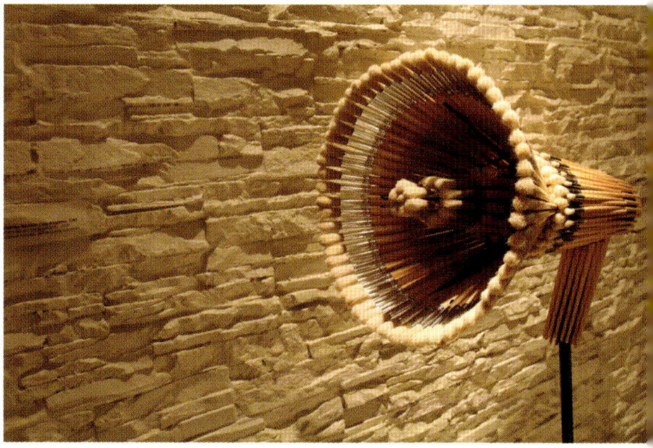

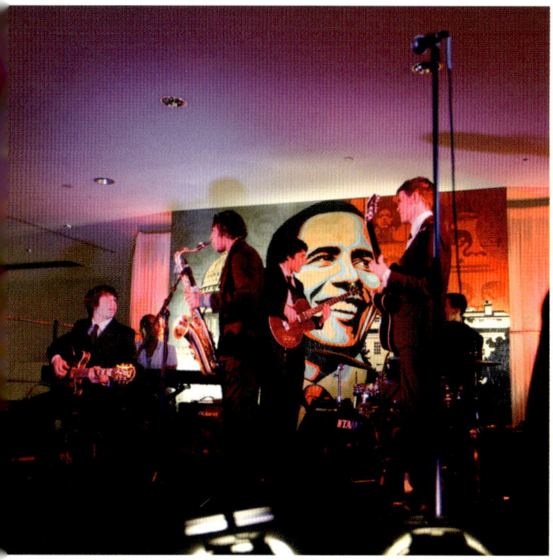

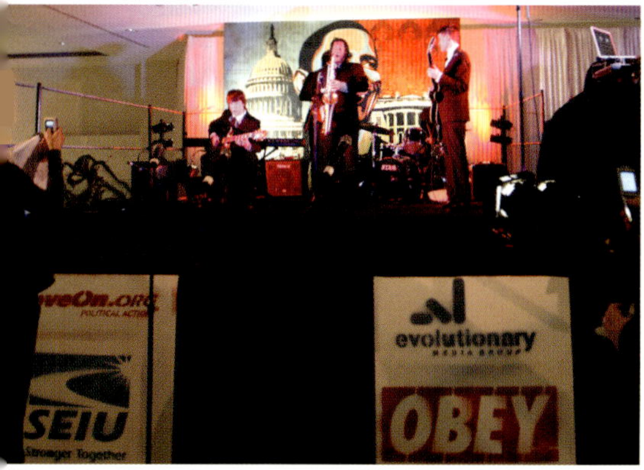
SEIU
Stronger Together
evolutionary
OBEY

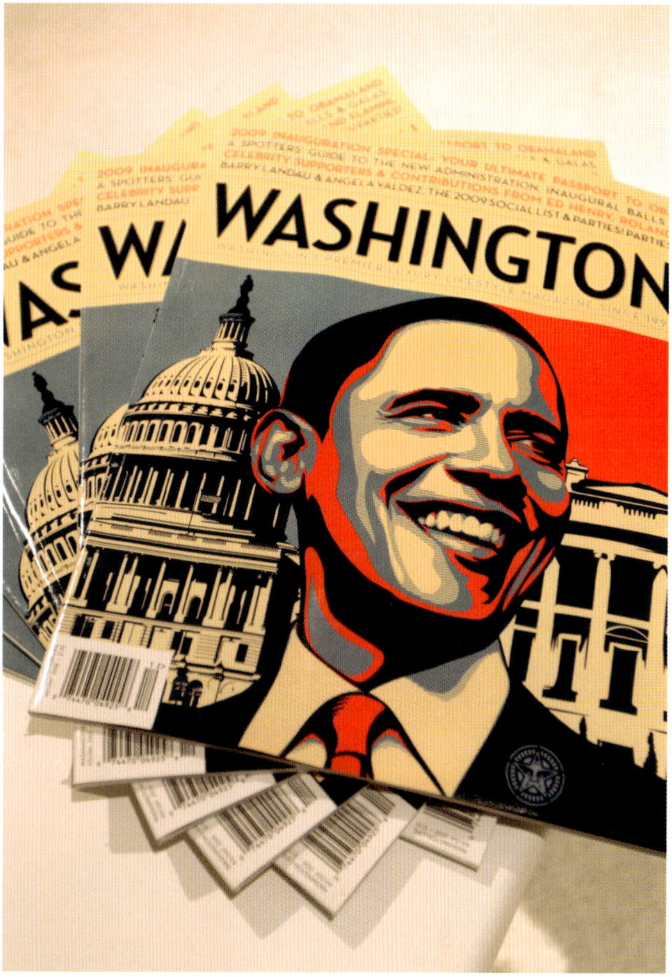
WASHINGTON
A SPOTTERS' GUIDE TO THE NEW ADMINISTRATION, INAUGURAL BALLS

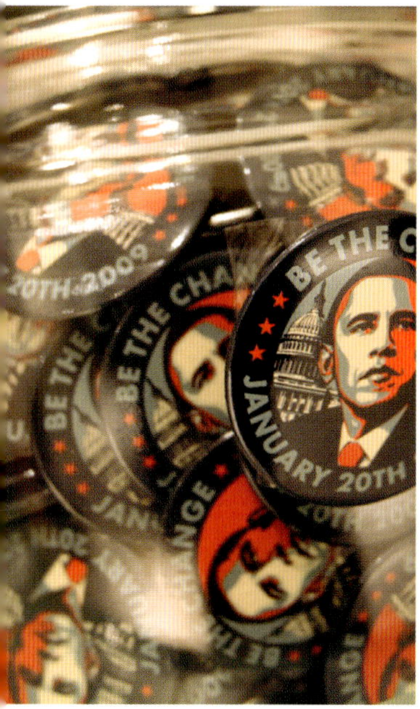
JANUARY 20TH

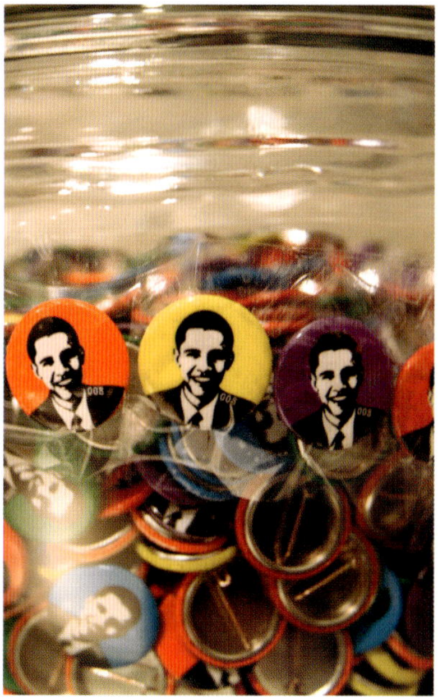

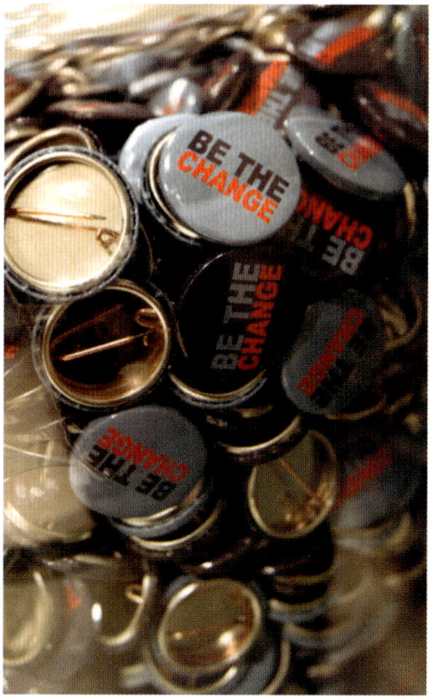
BE THE CHANGE

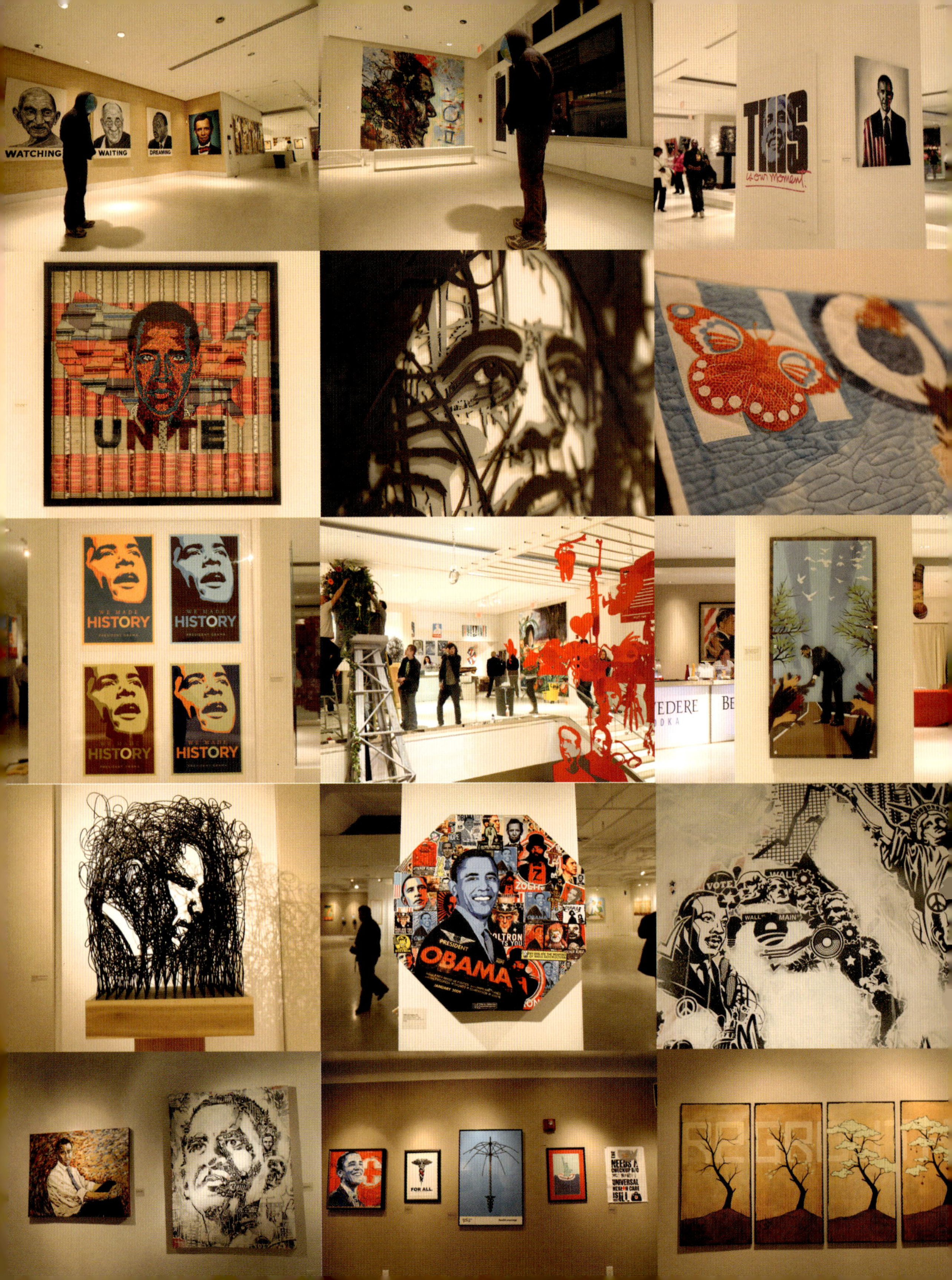
WATCHING
WAITING
DREAMING
THIS
UNITE
HISTORY
HISTORY
HISTORY
HISTORY
PRESIDENT
OBAMA
VOTE
WALL
MAIN
FOR ALL.

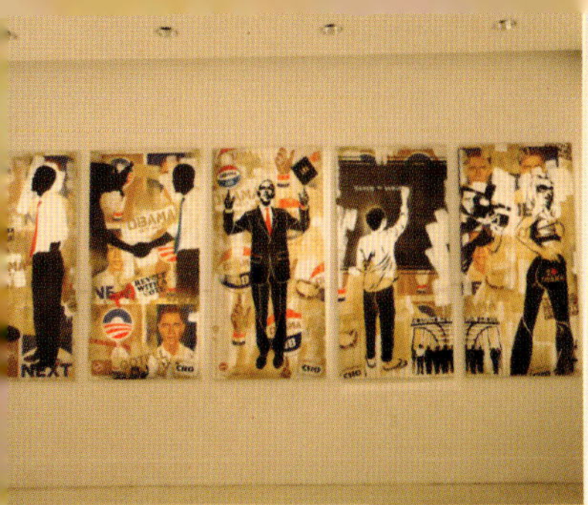
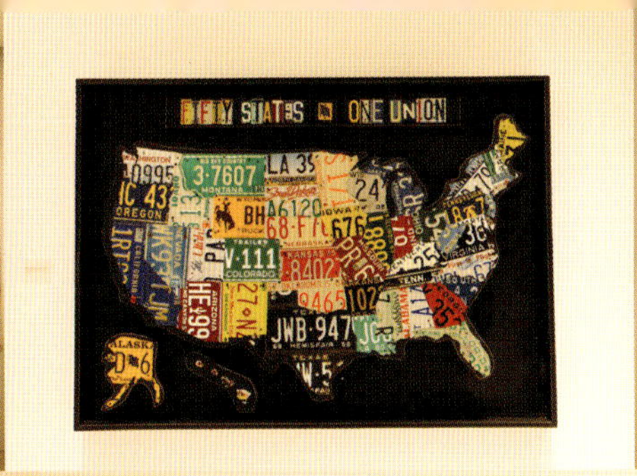
STATES
ONE UNION
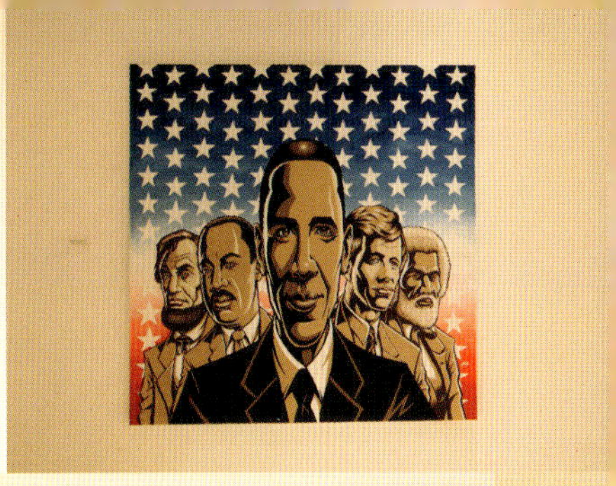
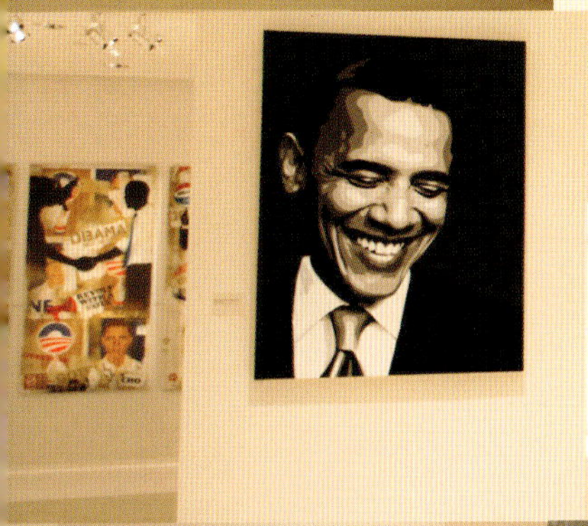
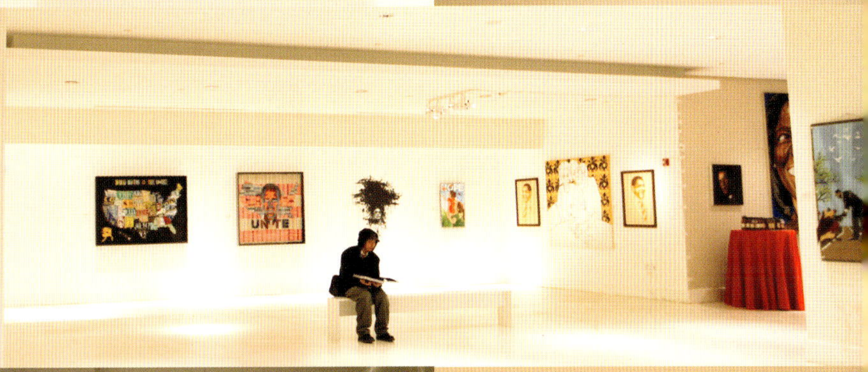
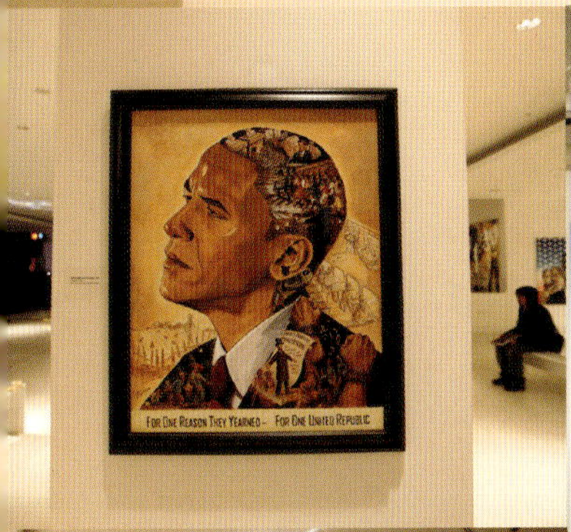
For One Reason They Yearned— For One United Republic
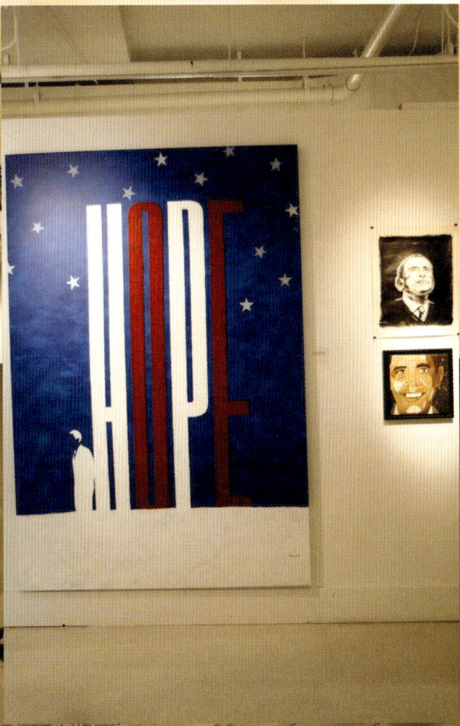
HOPE
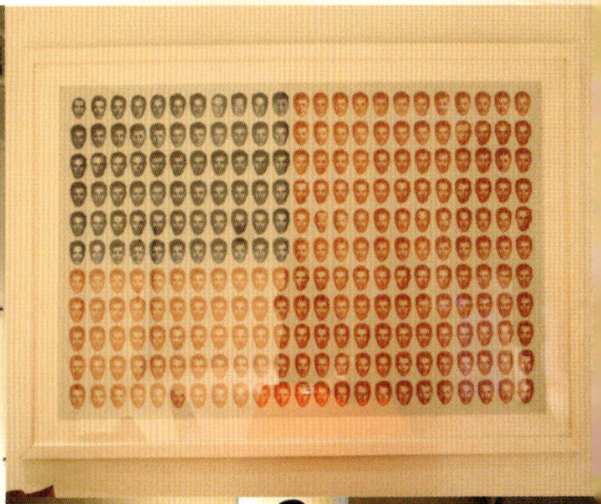
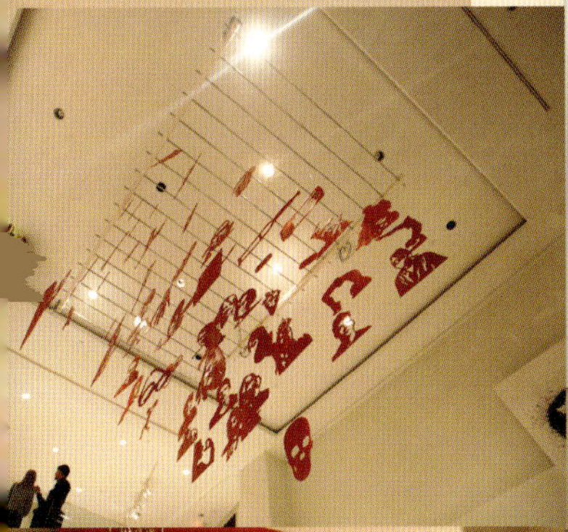
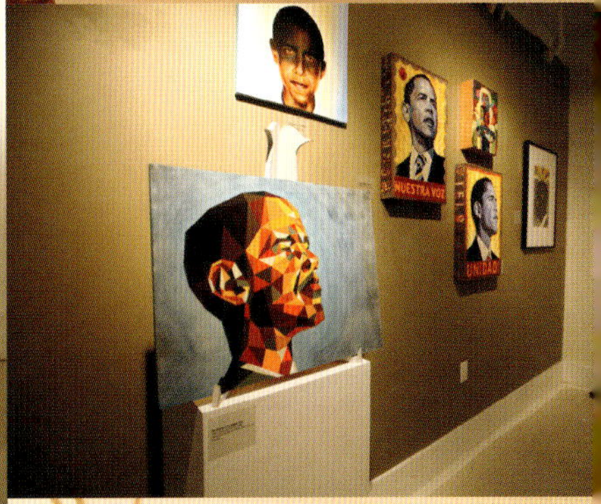
NUESTRA VOZ
UNIDAD
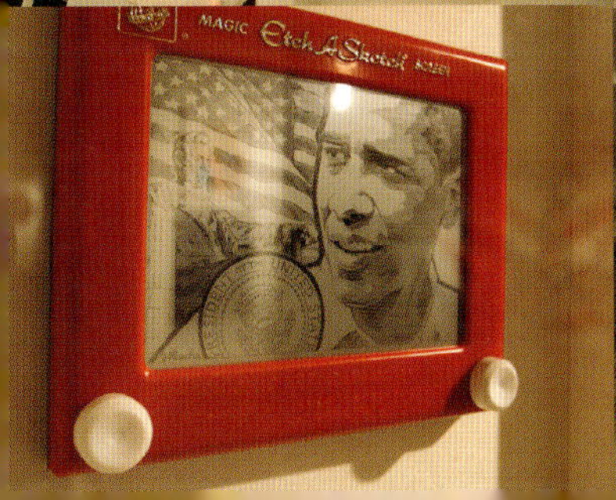
MAGIC Etch A Sketch
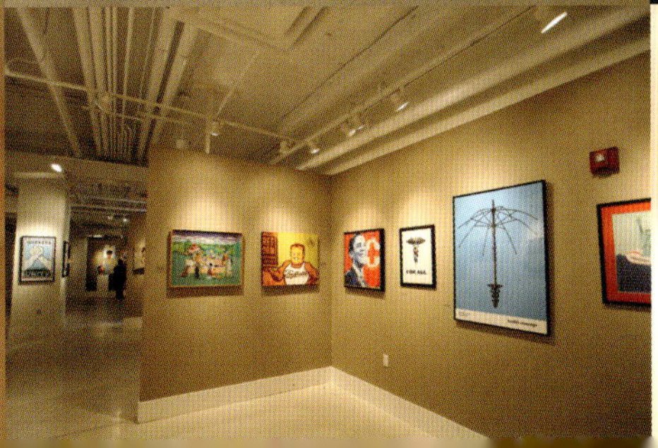
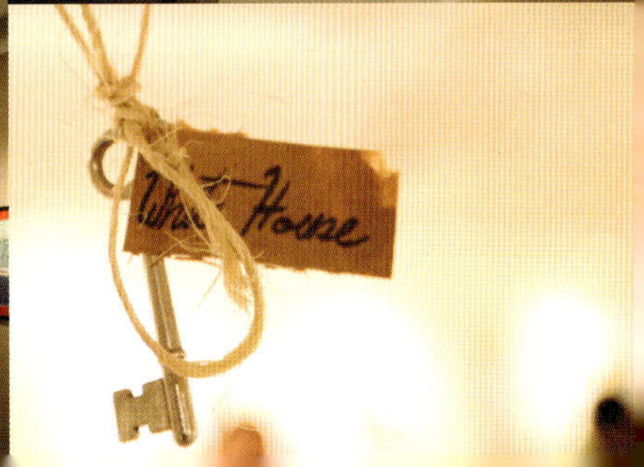
White House

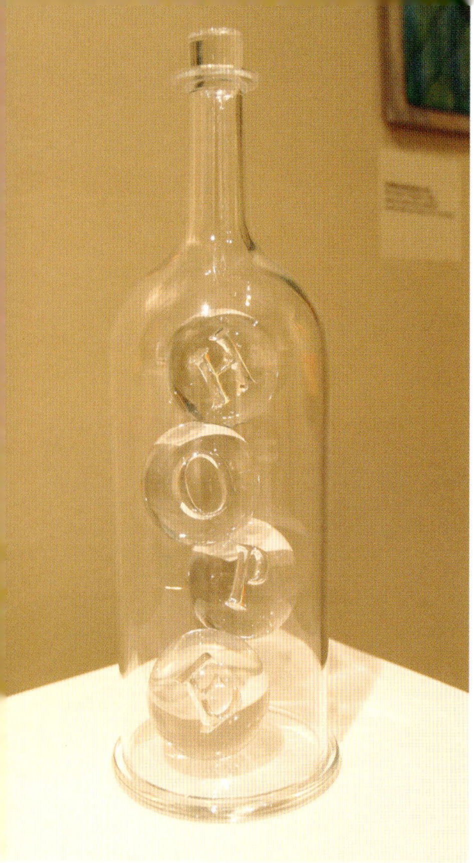

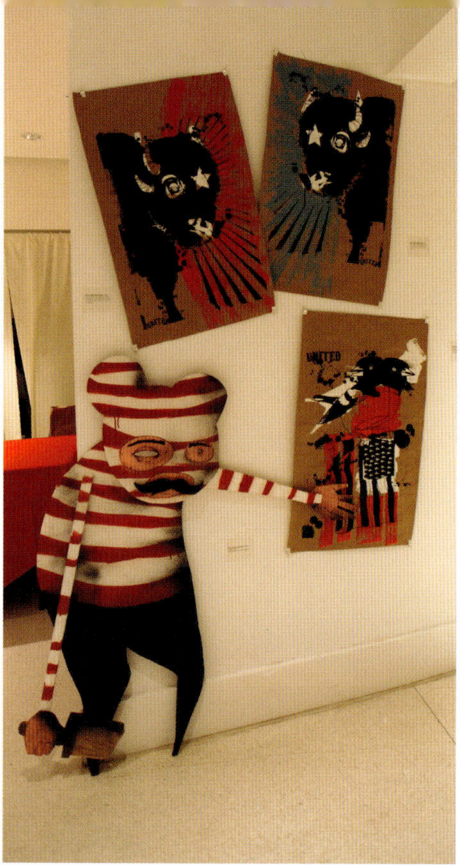

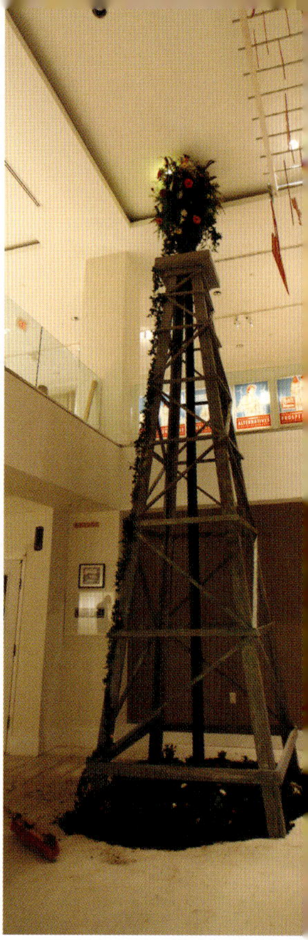

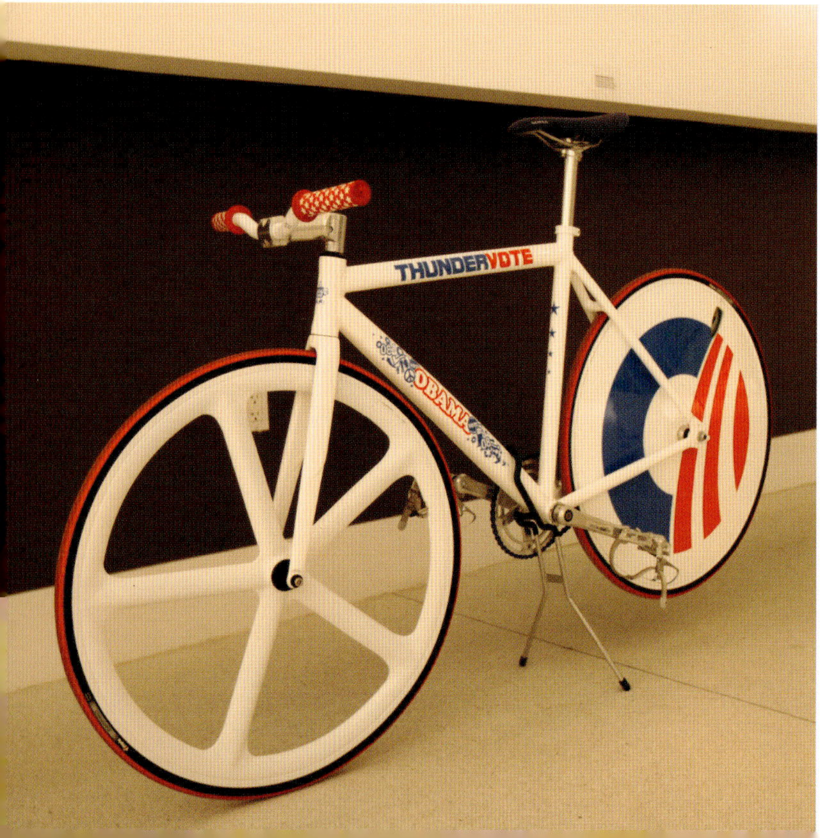
THUNDERVOTE
OBAMA

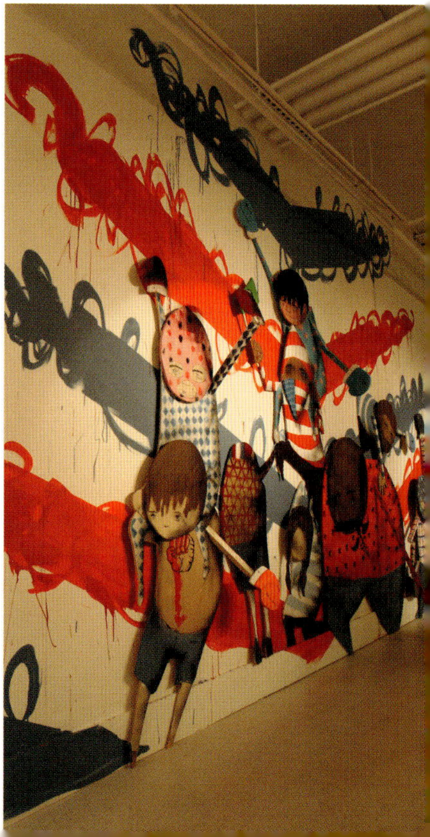

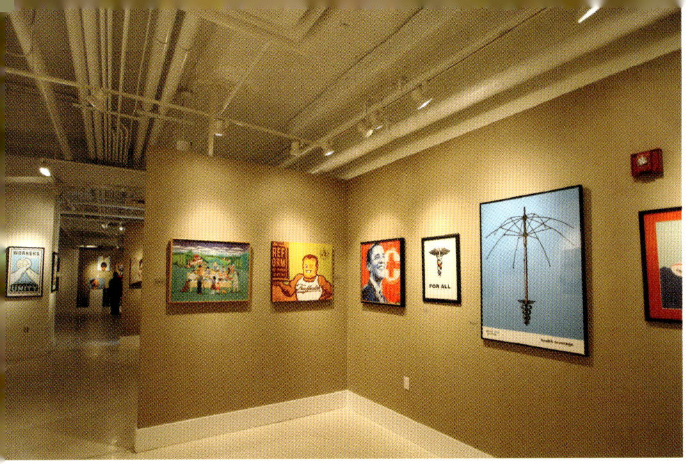
FOR ALL

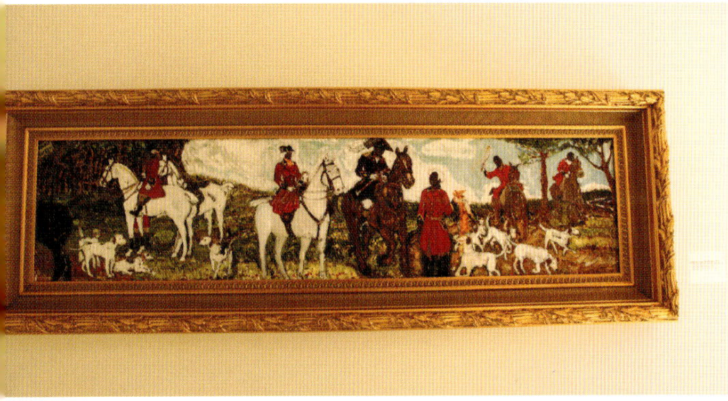

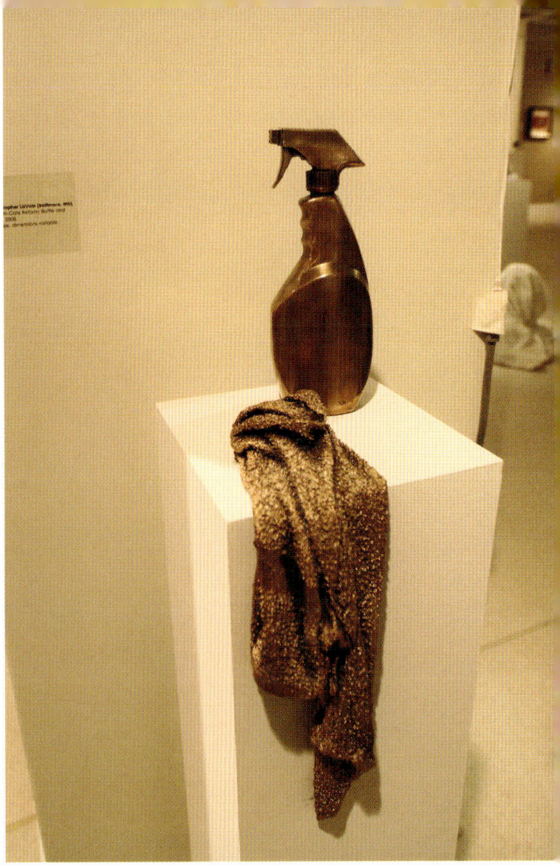

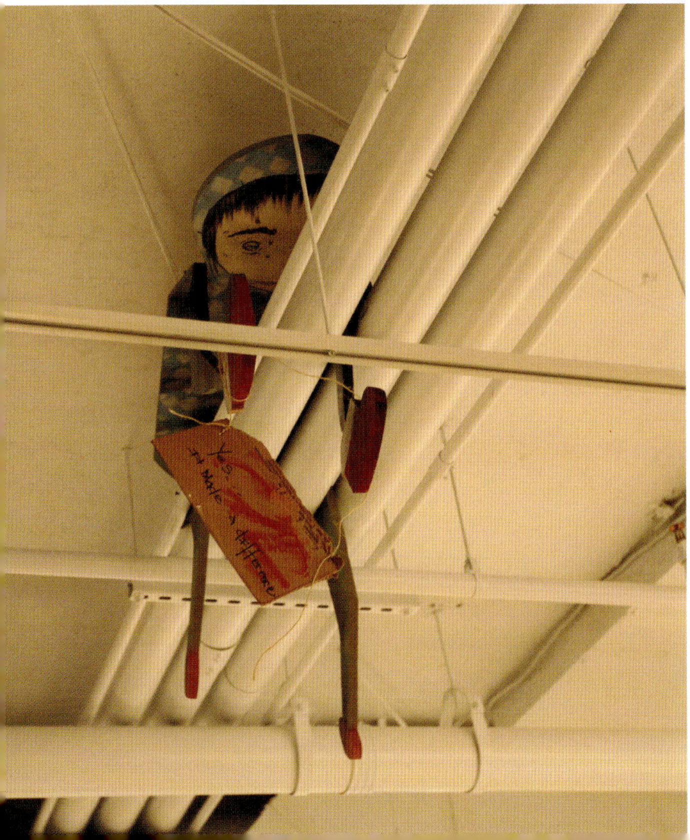

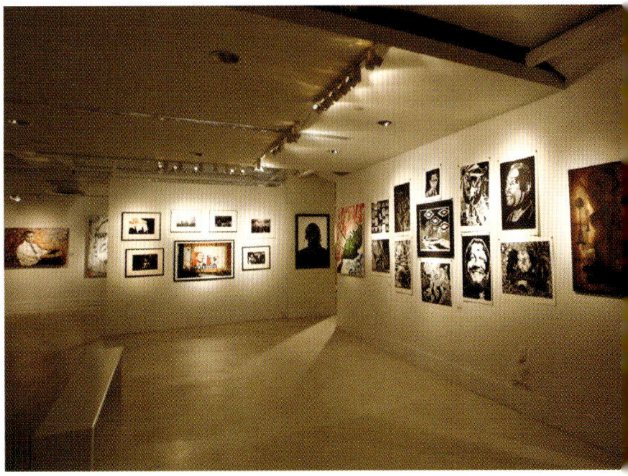

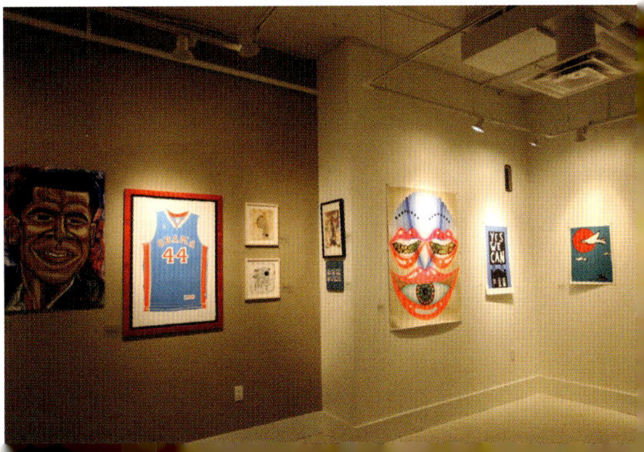
44

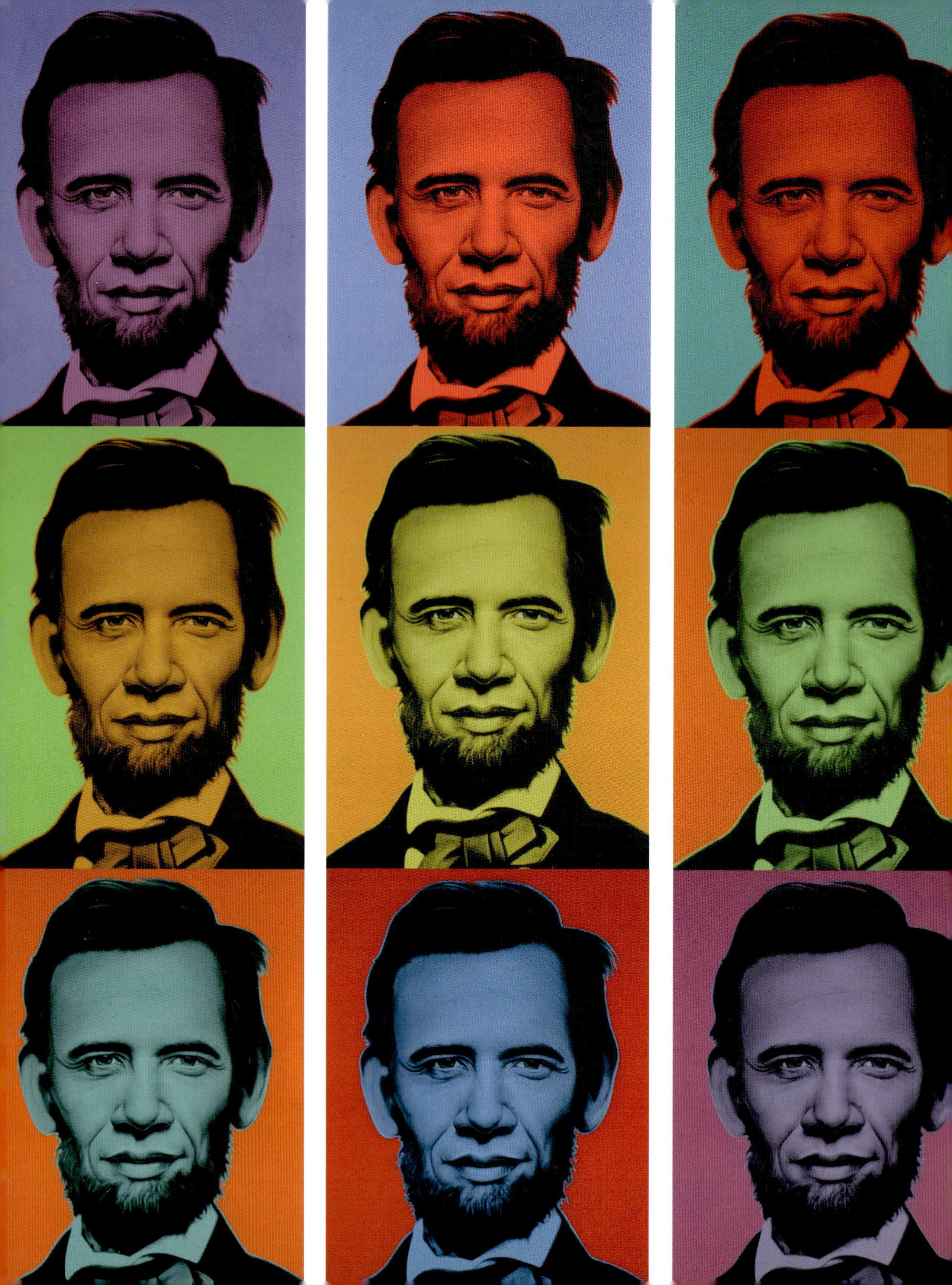

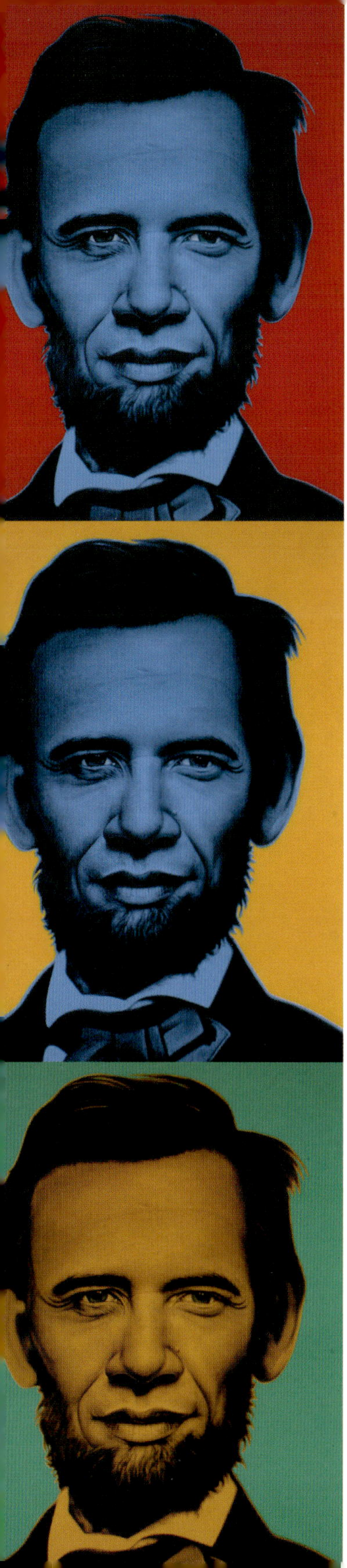

Myth & Metaphor

By Carlo McCormick

Myth is the glue that holds together the tattered American Dream. Barack Obama knows that, and so do artists here, which may very well be why at this particular historical moment they seem to understand and appreciate one another better than most other recent relationships between a president and the creative community. For Americans to do something so radical that it goes against their nature and history, they need a narrative, a good story to believe in. And because, let's face it, we're not the most literate people, we do best when our stories have pictures. The way in which the arts were employed as an aesthetic tool of social propaganda by Obama in the primaries and presidential election of 2008, and the nature of that empowerment through grassroots street-level visual activism, offers the quintessential model for delivering the new–wrap it up in the familiar, giving novelty the metaphorical context of history through the persistent myths of yore. Much in the same way as our affections turned around the figure of Obama, the visual signifiers created by the arts community around him were at once immediate classics, songs you can sing along to on the first listening, innovations so redolent of the return to old school values that you knew right away, that's just what you were thinking all along.

In that delicate interstice between public commissions versus what is tacitly permitted–so hypothetical a space that it could only have been mapped in the political geography where spin becomes truth–the insertion of artists who work on the street, often in criminalized forms, as master interrogators of the status quo to speak as surrogates for a dream too abstract for governmental discourse was a triumph of the creative over the consensus. Street artists are not only well-versed in the common and coded vernaculars of the street. They are, in fact, by virtue of their propensity for media hijacking, masters in the language of coercion and control. But as good as this work may well have been for the Obama campaign, conversely it was as a subject that Obama proved to be great for the artists themselves. So much of the skills and strategies that were brought to visualizing him–or shall we say representing what he represents–were engendered and honed in critique. The transformation in many of these artists from an inherently critical and antagonistic position to one of advocacy, the turn, if you will, from negative to positive information, not only echoed Obama's urgency of change born out of dissatisfaction with the status quo way of doing things, it goes to prove that at the heart of the culture wars, the fallacy in the assertion that those who question and protest our policies are somehow un-American. From Mark Twain to Thomas Nast to *Mad Magazine*, the satirical voice has proven to be a most American parlance. The problem for artists such as Ron English, who practice mutant forms of deviant mimicry, mediated appropriation, and grotesque parody, becomes how to translate the visual lampooning of one's disputes into a pictorial advocacy of mutual agreements, shared values, and nobler aspirations. And more importantly, how to take the image of another as a true expression of one's self.

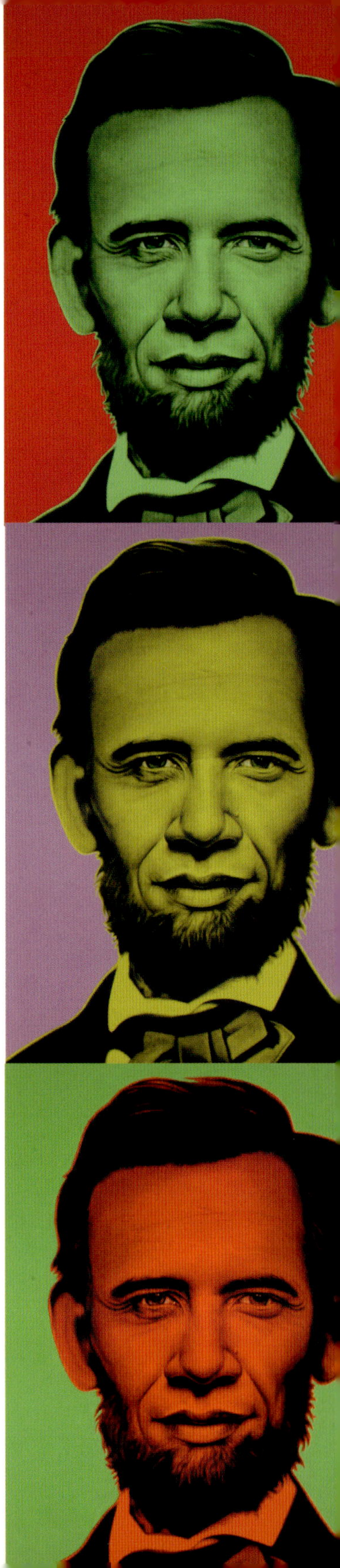

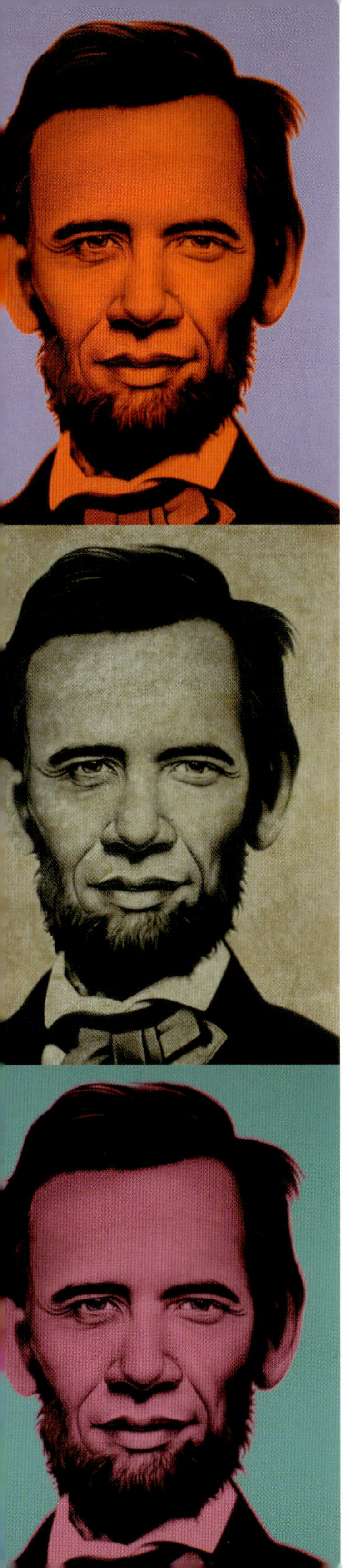

A skinny lawyer from the state of Illinois becomes, in turn, lawyer for that state, president of his country, and ultimately, the signifier for mass social redemption on a scale that is historically both epic and heroic; we need a certain symmetry to justify anything unordinary as much as we need precedent to measure the extraordinary. Legacy plays well in those critical moments when we as a society come to seek a new start, which is why the utopian and idyllic are so often intertwined with the Arcadian. With a presumed base that was demographically urban and multicultural, Barack Obama–from his announcement of candidacy upon the same site as Lincoln's to his inaugural speech at his memorial–well understood how Lincoln could embody a broader body politic reconfigured to a rural, log cabin white man. Through sleight of hand and slant of history, Ron English actualized the absurdity and believability of this comparison, because yes he does believe, but–well, his greatest faith is in the willful power by which we must all suspend our belief. It is, when you think about it, a very peculiar place for art, politics, and history to meet. Because the strength of any idea depends deeply on its capacity to be envisioned by others and the popularity of any public figure will be some quotient of the curious science regarding image, Obama–through the hands of artists like Ron English–was able to manifest something greater than the frailty of his humanness or the gentle humor of his humility by the convergence of personal attributes and beloved national myths upon that metaphorical dimension of the iconic.

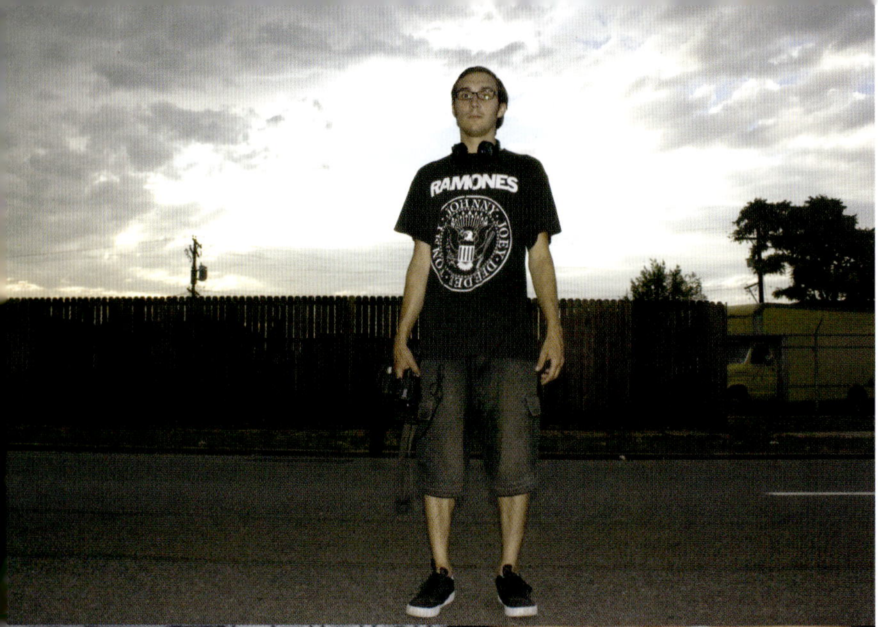
RAMONES
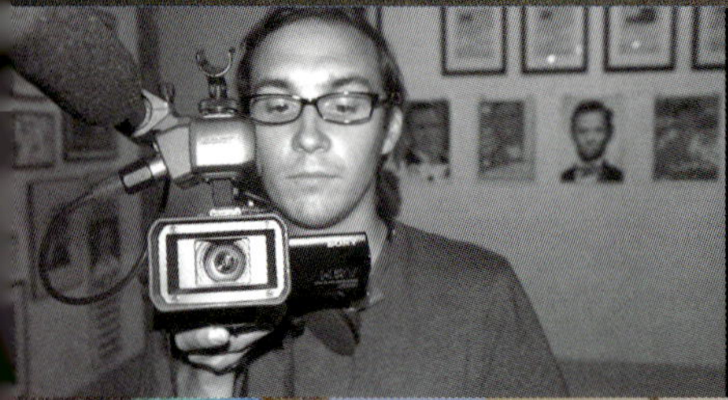
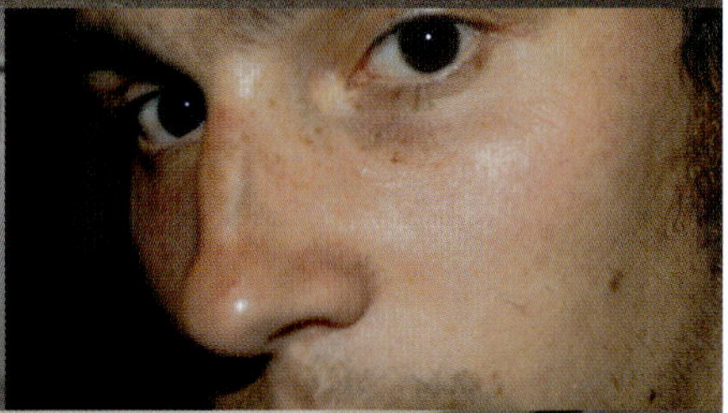
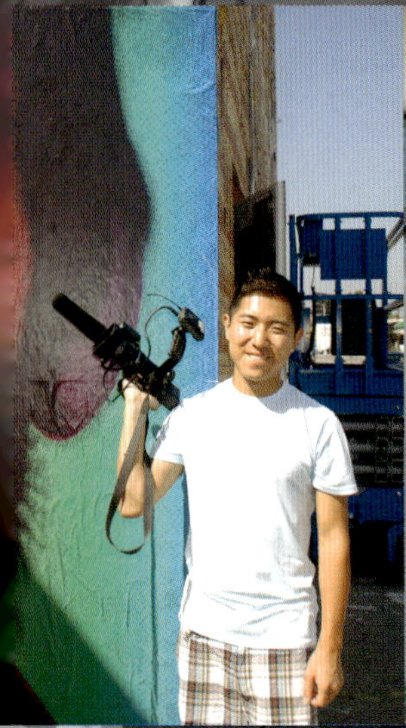
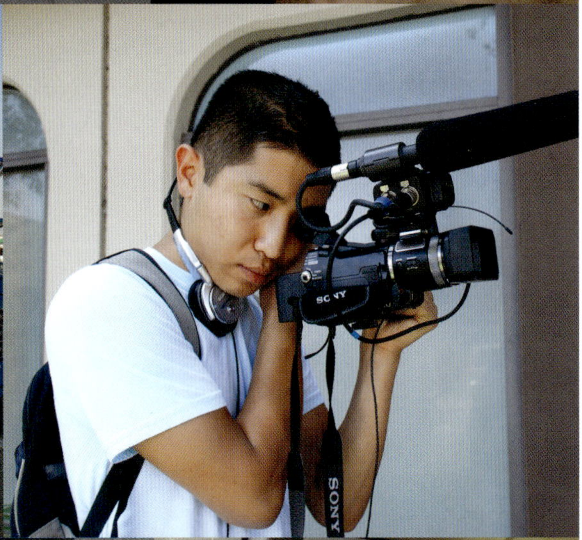
SONY
SONY
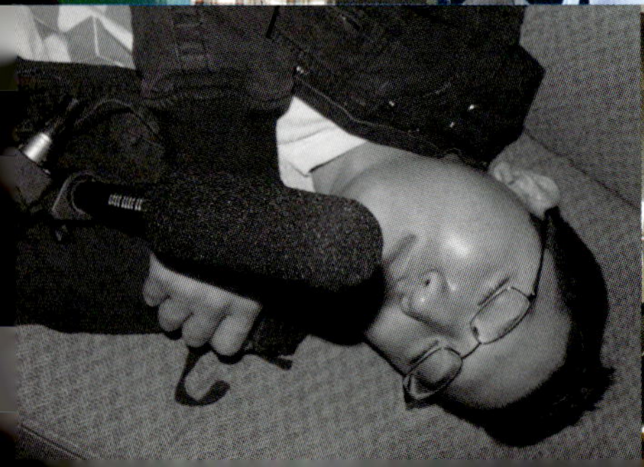
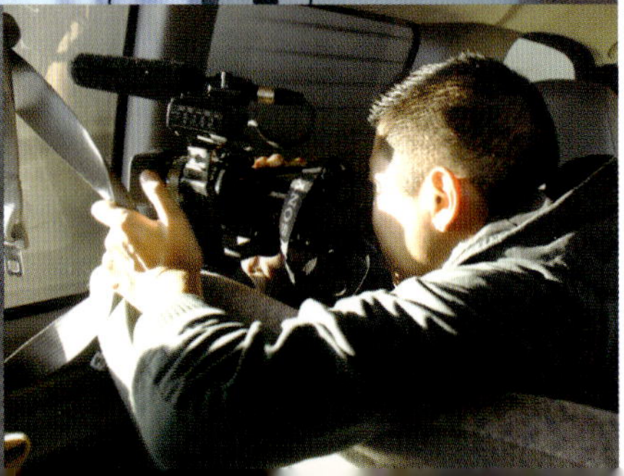
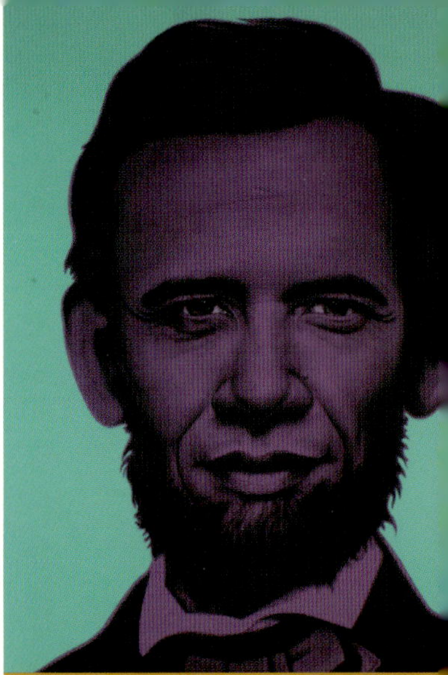
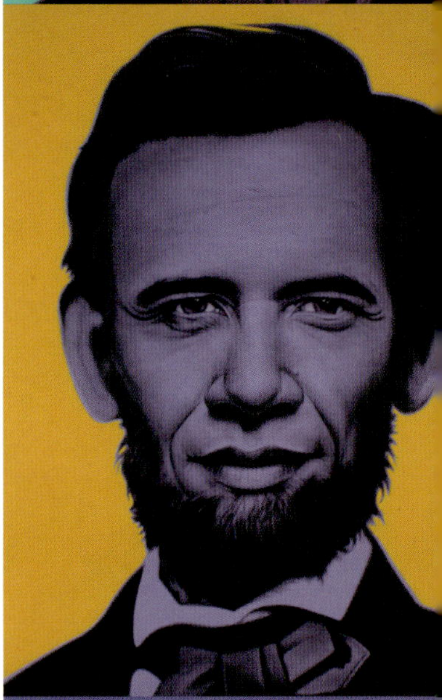
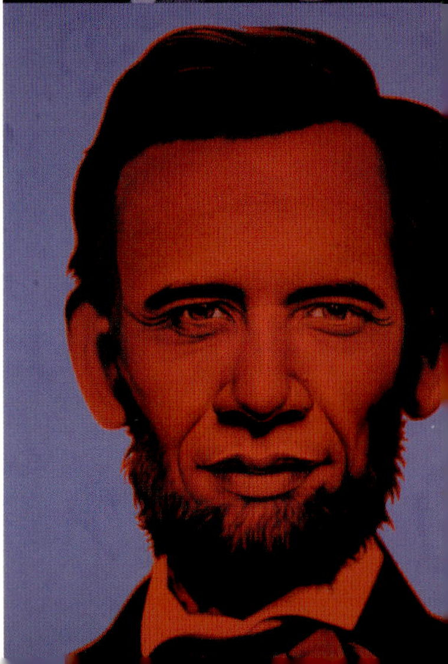

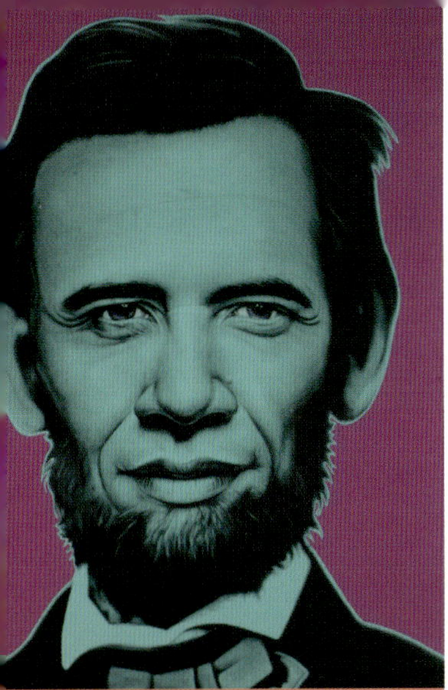

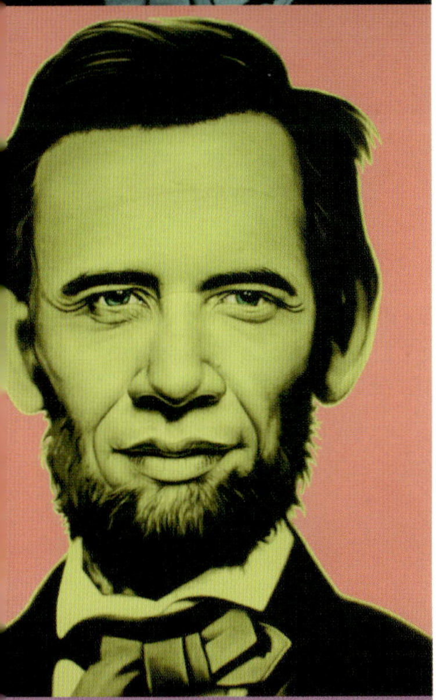

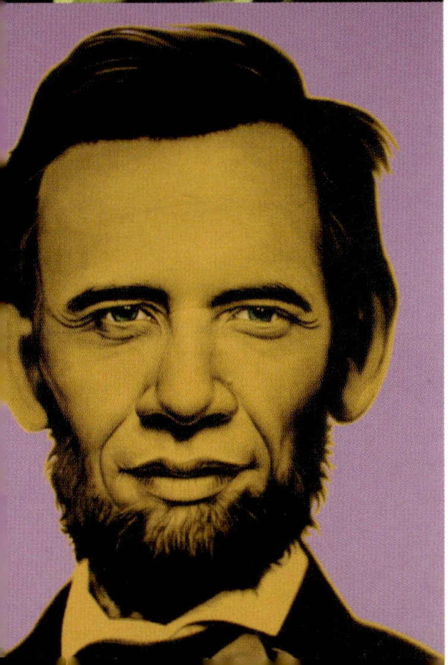

The Crew

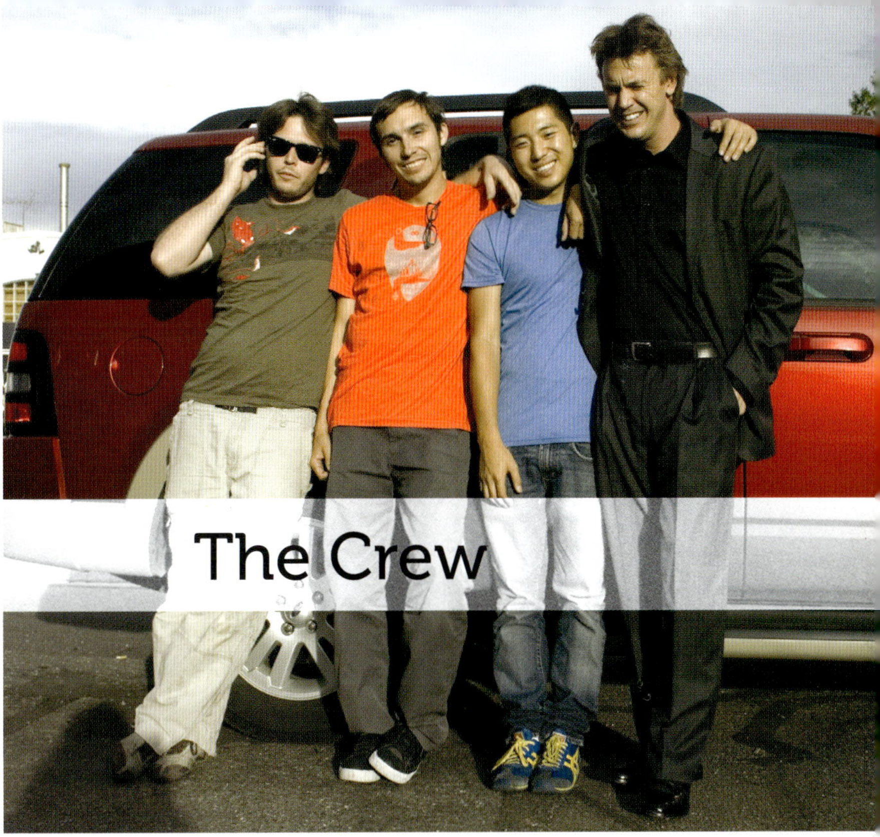

Ron English (shadow) • Daniel Lahoda • Kevin Chapados • Chunwoo Kae • Don Goede

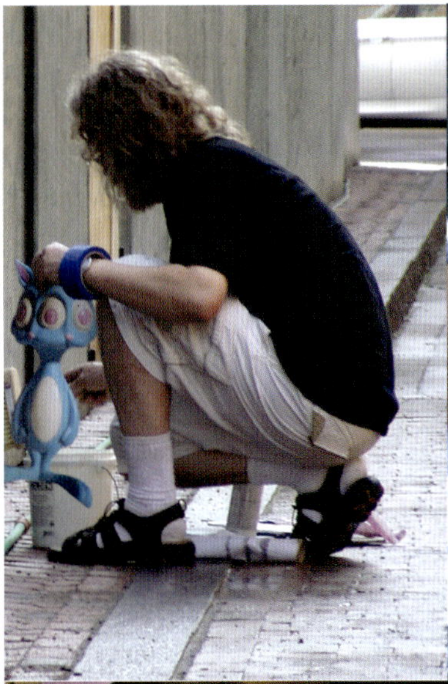

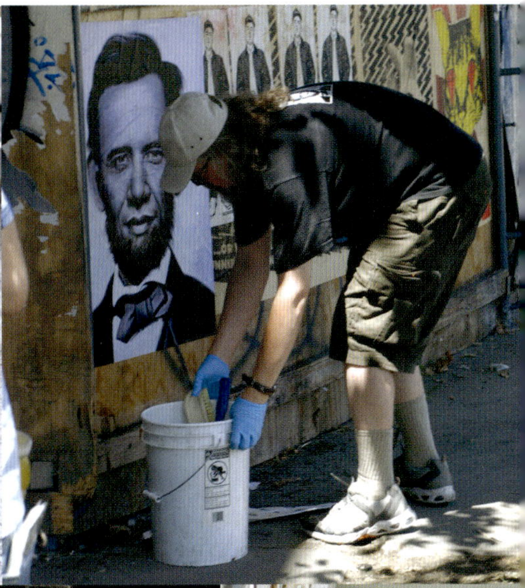

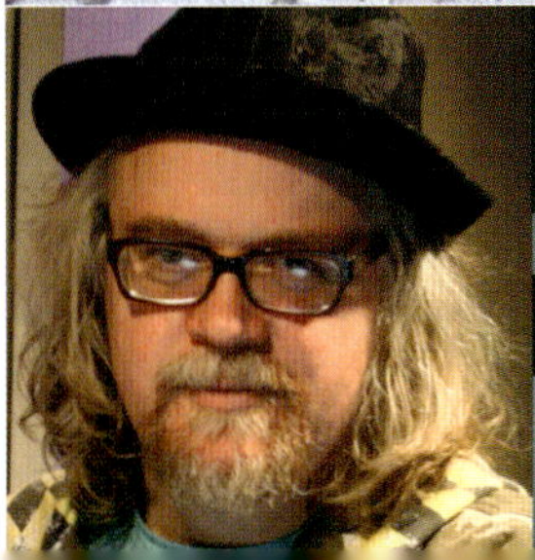

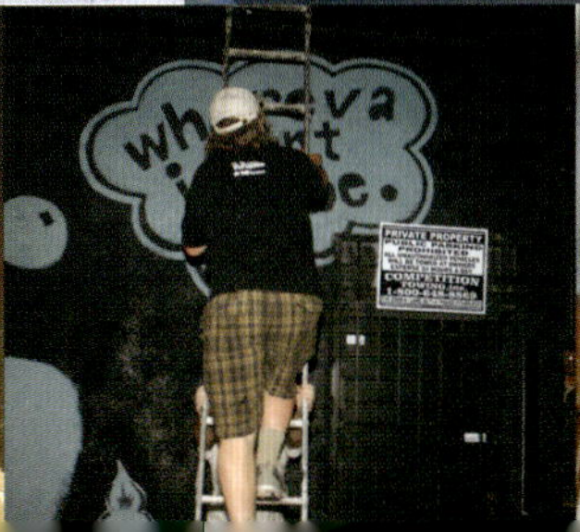

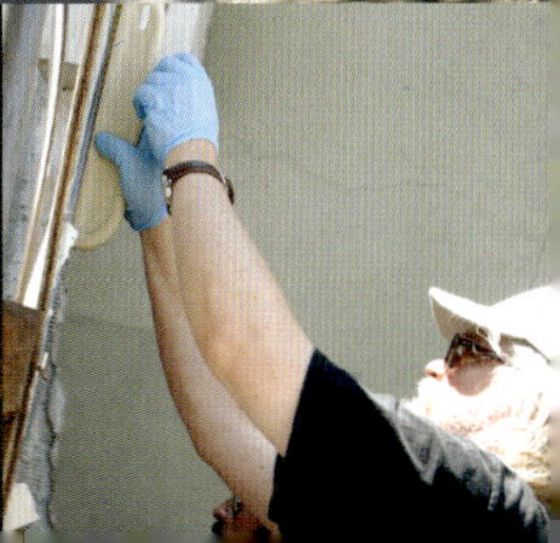

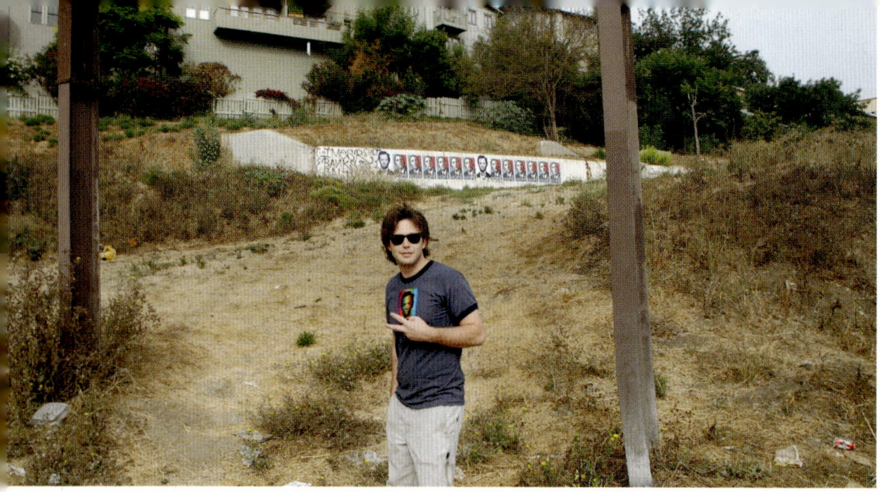
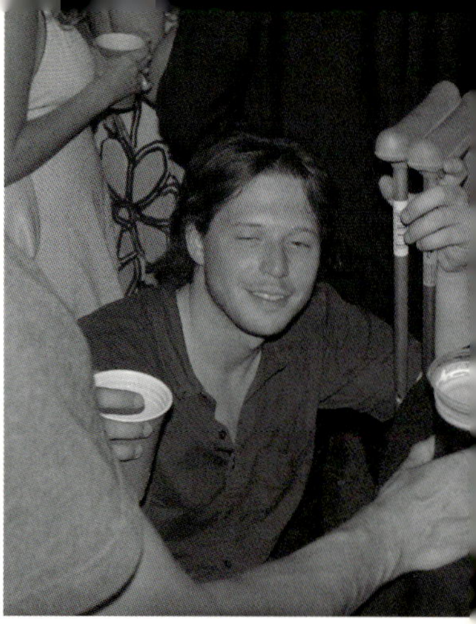
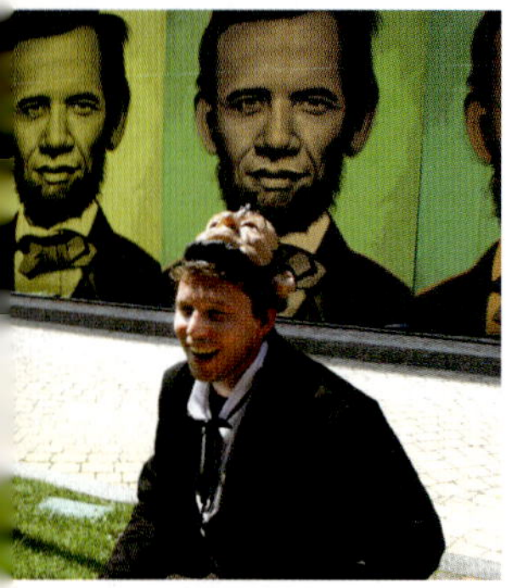
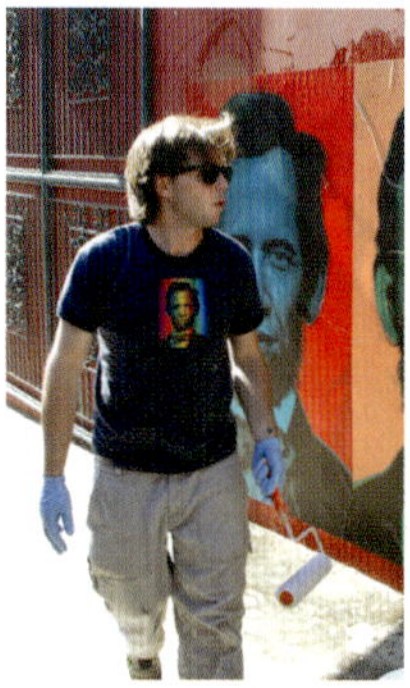
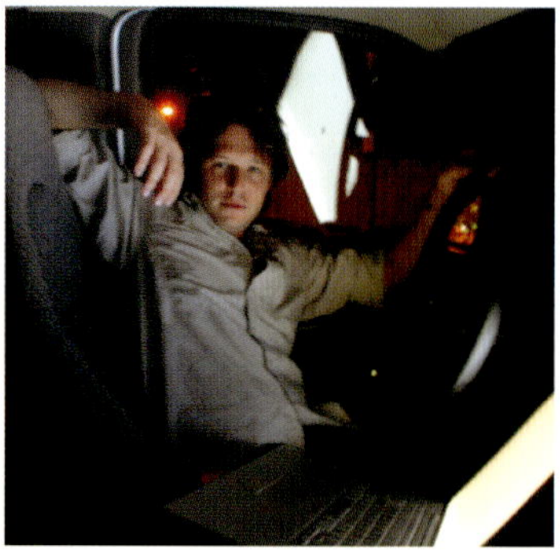
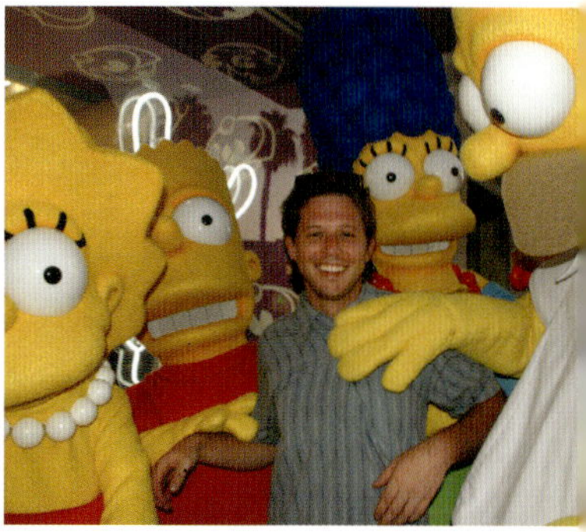
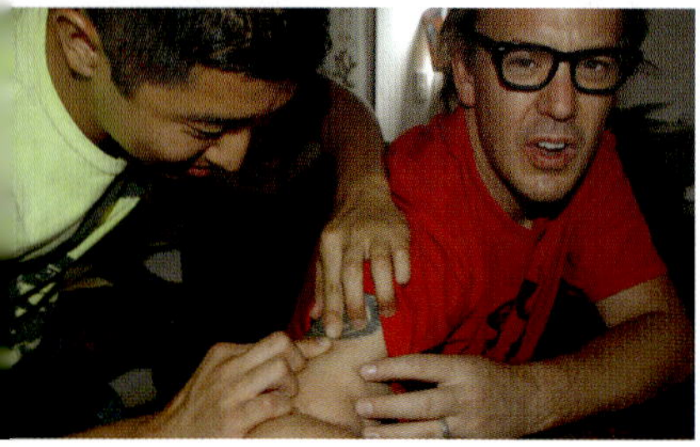
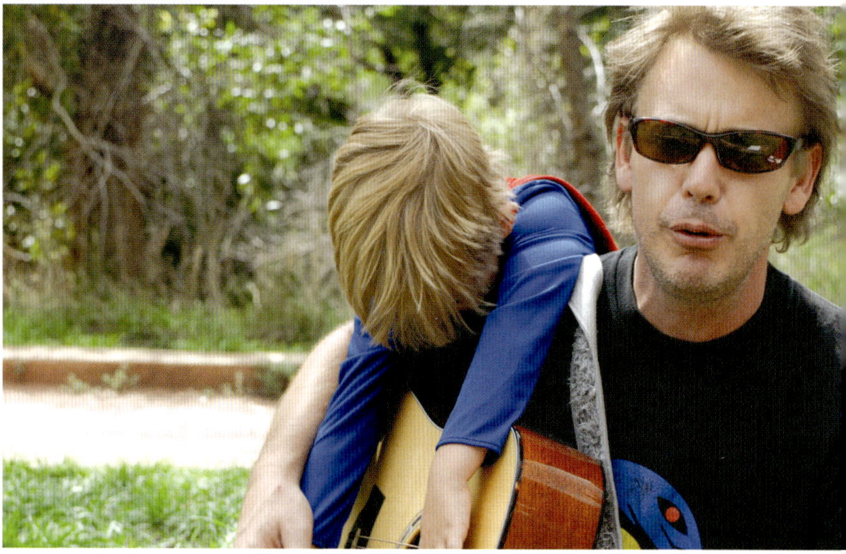
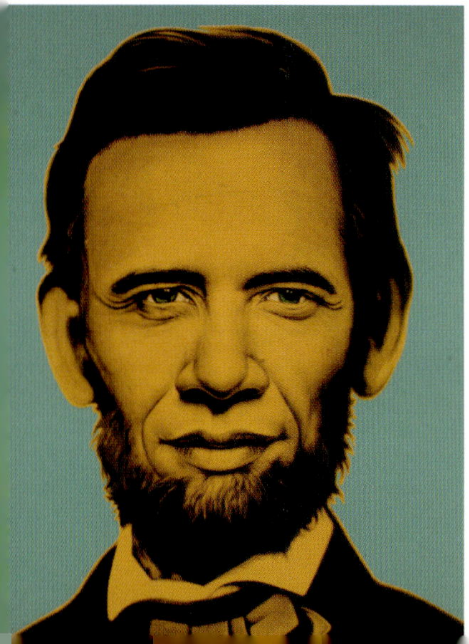
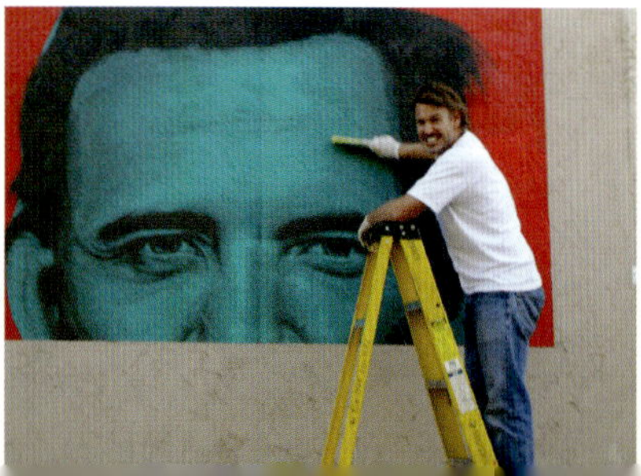
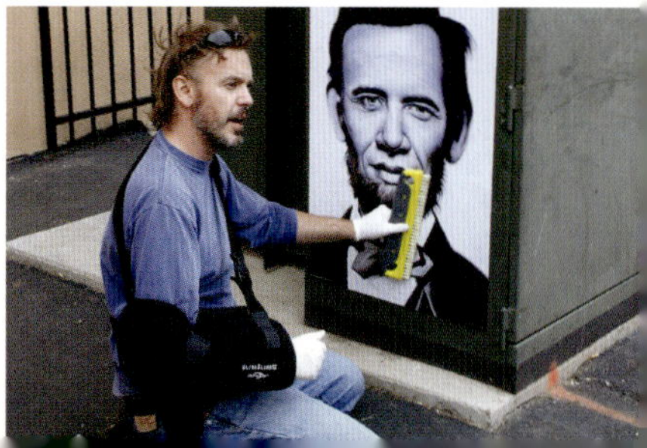

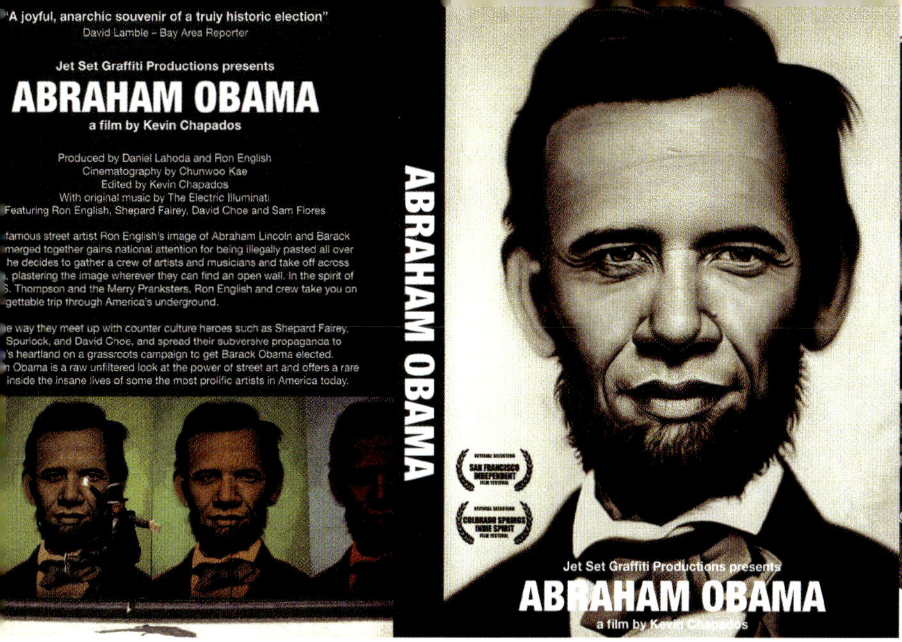
"A joyful, anarchic souvenir of a truly historic election"
David Lamble – Bay Area Reporter
Jet Set Graffiti Productions presents
ABRAHAM OBAMA
a film by Kevin Chapados
Produced by Daniel Lahoda and Ron English
Cinematography by Chunwoo Kae
Edited by Kevin Chapados
With original music by The Electric Illuminati
Featuring Ron English, Shepard Fairey, David Choe and Sam Flores
famous street artist Ron English's image of Abraham Lincoln and Barack
merged together gains national attention for being illegally pasted all over
he decides to gather a crew of artists and musicians and take off across
plastering the image wherever they can find an open wall. In the spirit of
S. Thompson and the Merry Pranksters, Ron English and crew take you on
gettable trip through America's underground.
e way they meet up with counter culture heroes such as Shepard Fairey,
Spurlock, and David Choe, and spread their subversive propaganda to
's heartland on a grassroots campaign to get Barack Obama elected.
n Obama is a raw unfiltered look at the power of street art and offers a rare
inside the insane lives of some the most prolific artists in America today.
ABRAHAM OBAMA
Jet Set Graffiti Productions presents
ABRAHAM OBAMA
a film by Kevin Chapados
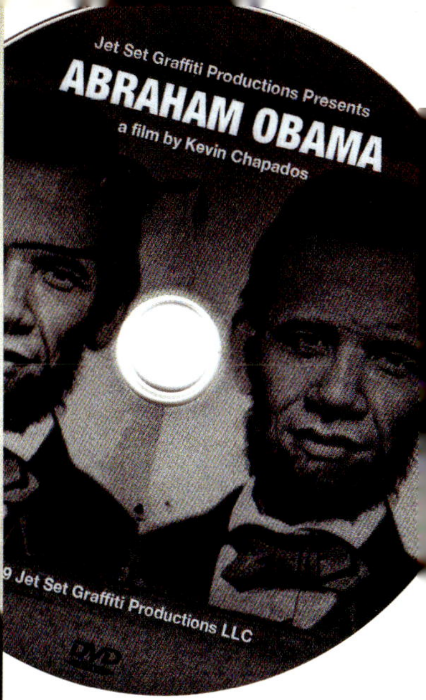
Jet Set Graffiti Productions Presents
ABRAHAM OBAMA
a film by Kevin Chapados
9 Jet Set Graffiti Productions LLC
DVD
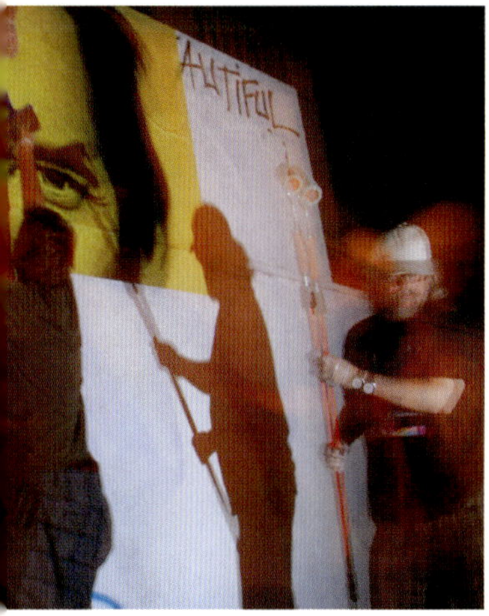
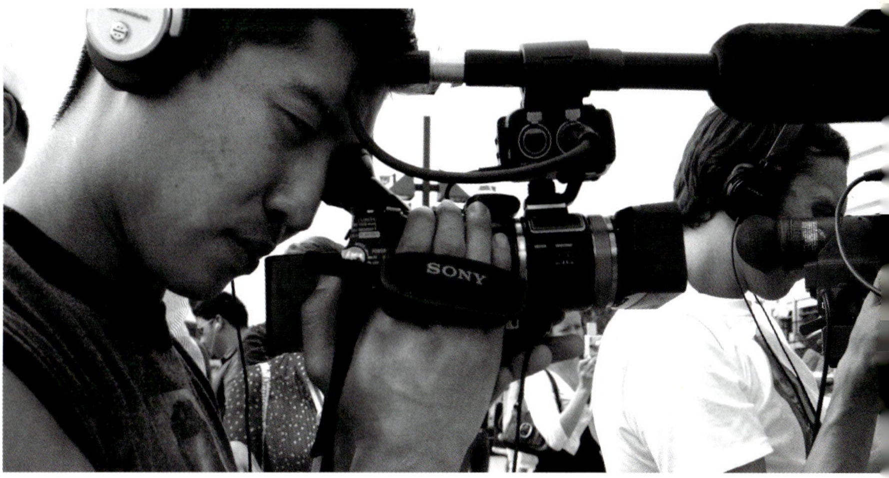
SONY
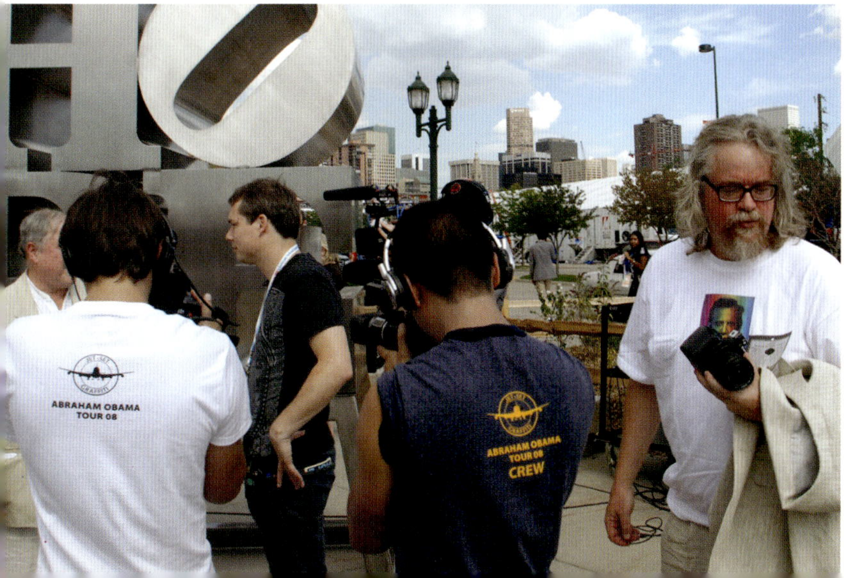
ABRAHAM OBAMA
TOUR 08
ABRAHAM OBAMA
TOUR 08
CREW
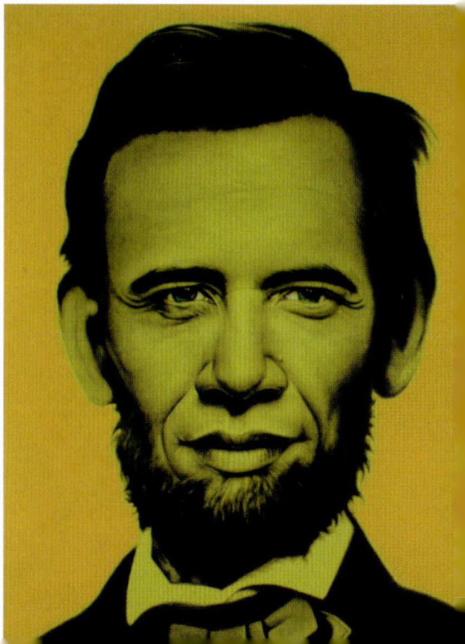

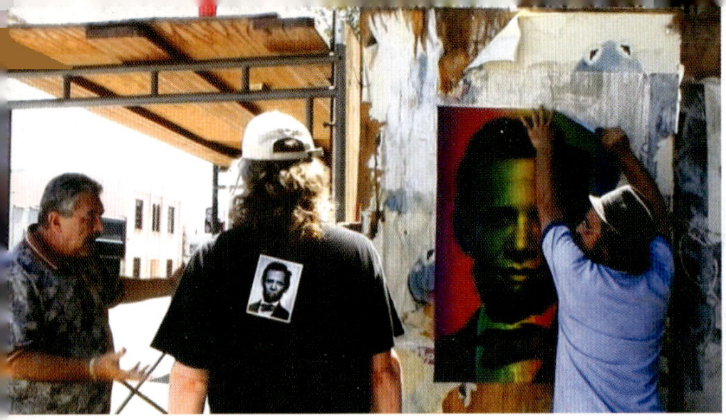

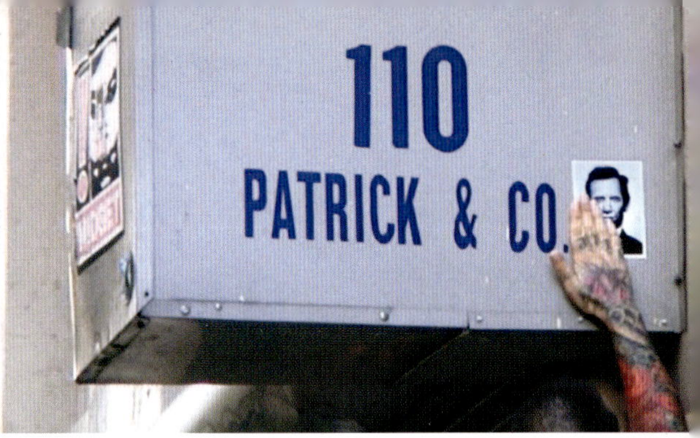
110
PATRICK & CO.

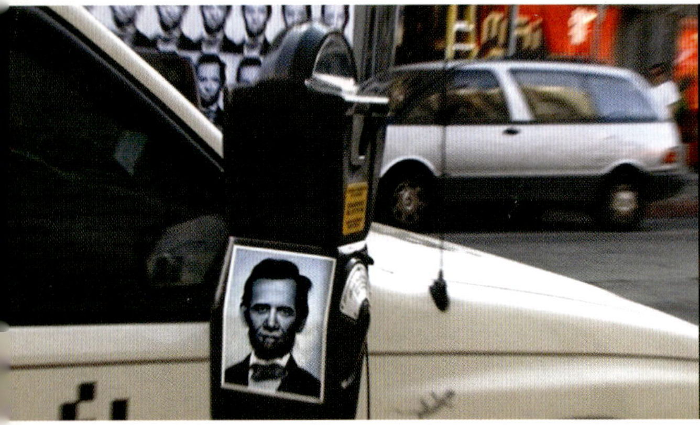

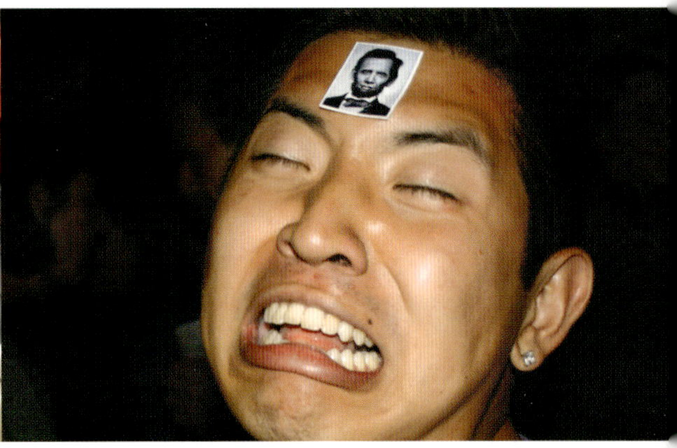

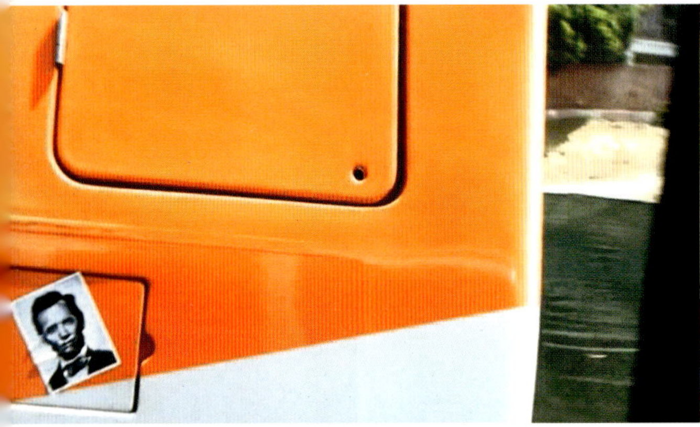

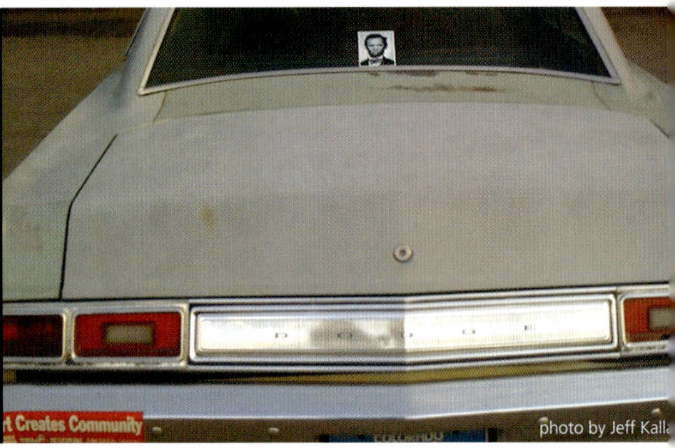
rt Creates Community
photo by Jeff Kall

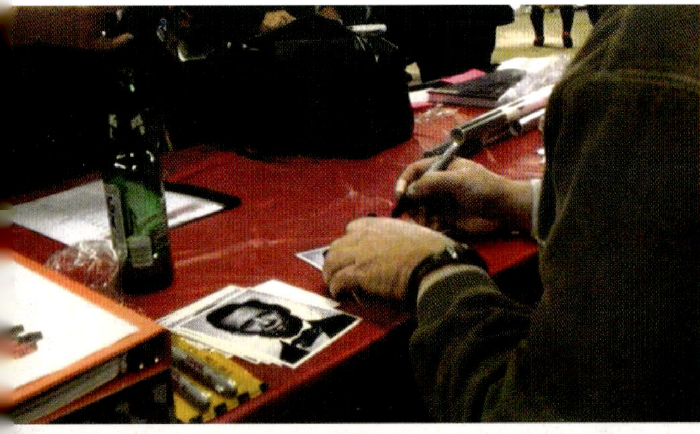

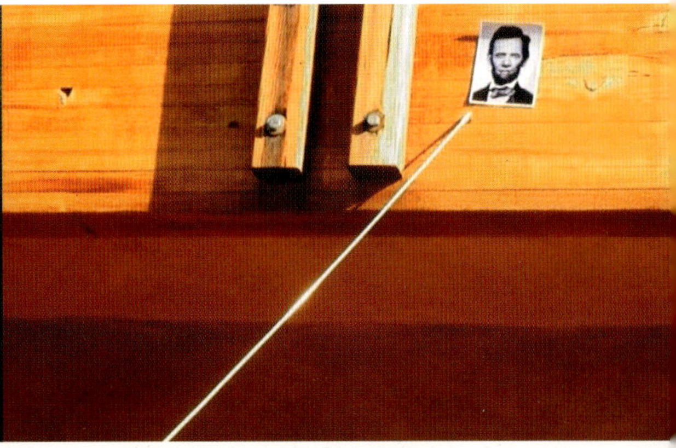